FINDING
HOME

ALSO BY PATTI DOTY

Runaway

FINDING HOME

PATTI DOTY

Lucky Bat Books

A Lucky Bat Book
Finding Home
Copyright ©2017 by Patti Doty

ISBN-10: 1-943588-43-0
ISBN-13: 978-1-943588-43-5

Cover Artist: Nuno Moreira
Published by Lucky Bat Books
10 9 8 7 6 5 4 3 2 1
Discover more from this author at pattidoty.com

Finding Home is a work of fiction. The story, characters, places, and incidents are imaginary creations of the author or are used fictitiously. Any resemblance between these fictional characters and actual persons, living or dead, or events or locales, is purely coincidental.

For Quinn and Cecily,
who inspire my life.

CHAPTER 1

UINN DeMELLO JERKED UPRIGHT WHEN THE landing
gear clunked into place and the cabin lights flickered into
a dim half-life. She wiped drool from the corners of her mouth
and scrubbed sleep from her eyes while her mind struggled
with the remnants of a nightmare, sticky as a cobweb in her
shadowy waking—buildings crashing, bodies careening to earth
like broken dolls, a hawk-nosed man glaring at her as though
she were something on the bottom of his shoe—visions more
real than her gray-green surroundings.

Around her, in a cabin rife with sweat and fear, the others—National Guardsmen, most young enough to call her
mom—roused from their own uneasy slumbers. In silence,
expressions grim, they gathered their gear: camouflage and
metal, uniforms and guns. Hard to believe just hours ago these
same men and women had been chuckling at her tales of horny
toads humping hikers' feet and squirrels whose bushy tails
served as umbrellas in Nevada's high desert.

Seen through the plane's meager windows, a thin line of lights
twinkled in a sea of primordial black. Unreal. She felt as though

she'd been dropped straight into the middle of an action movie—*Star Wars* maybe, or *Blade Runner*. Her smile at the thought of her favorite actor faded as memory brought her upright.

Memory: Four days earlier—September 11—terrorists had attacked her country. Like an old-fashioned newsreel, scenes scrolled in her mind: smoke obscuring a bright blue New York morning; one airplane and then another penetrating deep into two buildings—the Twin Towers, built to grace the skyline forever; people jumping, tiny bodies falling, screams unheard; then the buildings themselves falling; and dust like volcanic ash softly covering the horror. She blinked and the pictures changed, and, as bewildered news anchors stumbled for explanations, a plane crashed in a Pennsylvania field; the president, airborne, sought safety in a world suddenly unrecognizable; and, almost a pièce de résistance, the nose of an American Airlines 747 burrowed deep into the side of a sturdy and unfamiliar building.

Quinn sucked in a deep breath and forced herself back to the present. That building, she now knew, was the headquarters of the United States Department of Defense: the Pentagon, *her destination*. Mouth dry, sick with the memories, Quinn scrambled to gather her wits and her belongings as her plane touched down somewhere in Virginia.

"DeMello! Quinn DeMello, front and center!"

She heard her name before the cabin door fully opened. As it swung away from the plane, hairy hands reached in and grabbed her duffel bag and her wrist.

"Dammit! Come on! You're late," the man roared, sentences truncated, emphatic, needing more than one exclamation point. "You're late!"

She stumbled after him down the ramp and onto the tarmac just as the runway lights vanished. She could hear the others exiting the plane behind her, but reality centered on her left arm, where the man's fingers dug into the wrinkles of her funeral blazer. It hurt.

"Ow, watch it."

"Sorry." He loosened his grip but didn't let go as he half led, half dragged her toward the sound of an idling motor. Quinn didn't have time for fear before a thin beam from his flashlight illuminated an official-looking Jeep Cherokee with its lights off, rumbling patiently at the edge of the runway.

"Hurry up." A vigorous yank accompanied the words.

In the interest of her shoulder joint, Quinn struggled to comply. As they reached the vehicle, the man released her and opened the passenger door. Without waiting for another order, she scrambled inside.

In the pale light of the overhead bulb, Quinn sensed the man's assessment of her—tousled shoulder-length hair, wrinkled black garments, a narrow brown case clutched under her right arm—a disheveled mess, she knew. She imagined his thoughts: *I ask for a mental health volunteer, and I get a waif with bad hair and a fashion purse.* But he just tossed her duffel into the back as though it were weightless, said, "Buckle up, we've got to get back," and slammed the door behind her. Before her seat belt clicked, they were moving forward.

The vehicle raced along roads deserted and silent. In the intermittent glow of street lights rapidly passed, Quinn studied the man who had commandeered her: uncombed mat of sandy hair matching untrimmed beard, head bent slightly forward as though he didn't quite fit the confines of his seat. Grizzly. She suppressed a shiver.

As though aware of her thoughts, the man glanced her way, his beard twitching. "Sorry," he repeated an apology, apropos of nothing. "I'm in a hurry and your ride was late." He didn't sound sorry as he offered his hand across the littered front seat.

Quinn stared at the hairy paw. *What in God's green earth am I doing here?*

The flight from Nevada had been uneventful, boring even, after she had been vetted and finally accepted into the National Guard transport, one of a few planes allowed to traverse the dangerous sky. Now the previous days' trauma—terrorist attacks, her mother's death, friends lost, and love abandoned—all blocked by force of will and later by sleep, engulfed her. She sucked in the deep breath of one going under for the third time. Trained and certified as a disaster mental health provider, she still had no idea what to expect. This was the first time she'd been called; no previous disaster had met the magnitude of the one toward which they drove.

She took another deep breath before she stuck out her hand. It was immediately surrounded by warmth from a hand the size of a dinner plate, so she held on and tried for normalcy. "Hello. I'm Quinn DeMello, but you already know that. Who the hell are you?"

A rumble that seemed to be a laugh filled the space between them. "Sorry again," the man offered automatically. "I'm Chris McLean, and I'm your new boss." He kept her hand captive. "Let's get you up to speed."

Chris McLean talked. The radio whispered America's "A Horse with No Name," segued into "Bridge Over Troubled Water" and then some other oldie that Quinn remembered but couldn't name, before her attention was riveted on the man's voice. She heard pain and fatigue as he described the past four days, and she resisted the urge to pull away. Neil Diamond was singing "Sweet Caroline" when the man released her hand, flipped on the turn signal, and screeched off the highway.

"Almost there," he said. "Most of the volunteers are in town working the phones, organizing community resources, answering questions, but I need you on site. Somebody needs to help the helpers."

Brusque, his words produced more questions than answers, but those questions died, unspoken, when the sky ahead blazed like full day.

His voice dropped to a barely audible rasp. "They contained the fire initially, but new ones keep erupting. Pentagon employees got people out in a hurry before the upper floors collapsed, but they're still searching, wishing for survivors, mostly finding body parts."

She winced. Before her, in the firelight, the wounded home of America's military loomed, its pentagonal shape not appreciated from the ground.

Dumbstruck, Quinn stared. Chaos.

"They hit her on her birthday, the bastards." His voice cracked.

Tears, she thought, reaching toward him in sympathy before his rigid posture repelled the gesture, and she returned her hand to her lap.

In silence, her new boss maneuvered his vehicle around fire trucks and rescue rigs. Just when she thought he was finished talking, he cleared his throat and spoke again. "They broke ground for the building exactly sixty years ago. On Roosevelt's watch, during The Big One. For years it was the only nonsegregated building in Virginia."

A non sequitur? But his voice sounded so normal that Quinn faulted her overactive imagination for the tears assessment. She looked up just in time to dig her boots into the floorboard as the Jeep raced straight for a massive wall of white and came to a bone-jarring stop before the largest tent she'd ever seen.

"Your home away from home," he said. "Dante's version of hell."

White teeth flashed from the camouflage of his beard in what she interpreted as a grin. Before she could get her door open and retrieve her belongings, he was out of the vehicle and striding away. She grabbed her duffel and her flute case and followed his wide khaki back into the tent's maw.

As she came up beside him, McLean gestured toward a row of cots partially visible behind a makeshift canvas curtain. "Yours for the night. They call it Cot Central. Better quarters ..." he shrugged, "sometime. Stow your gear and let's get you acclimated."

Quinn peeked inside. Two cots seemed occupied, though the blanket-covered lumps didn't move. The cot nearest the opening stood empty but for a dark blanket and a white towel. Trying not to think about her last good night's sleep—the Wildflower Inn, the cozy down comforter, Owen's warm and wonderful body spooned with hers a lifetime away—Quinn tossed her things on the empty cot and tiptoed out.

Gently now, his hand on her elbow, McLean shepherded her around the tent. She staggered as a wave of heat struck and was grateful when his hand tightened in support. Television had not prepared her for the sight, breathtaking in its destruction. In the dark of night, spotlights and fire illuminated a scene that was, as he had put it, truly out of Dante's *Inferno*: scaffolding, scurrying forms vaguely human, yellow cranes hovering like their namesakes. Center stage, in full glory, the tail of an airplane protruded from the wreckage. They stood in silence, McLean's hand now protectively on Quinn's upper arm as she took in the immensity of the insult.

"Royally fucked, wouldn't you say?"

"Royally fucked," was all the reply she could manage.

CHAPTER 2

"SHITE, I'M TOO OLD FOR THIS," Dr. Chris McLean muttered, his Irish heritage obvious in his favorite expletive as he stood outside the white tent, ran his hand through his sticky, sweaty hair, and wondered whether the world could ever right itself. An experienced rescue worker, he'd been on the job since Tuesday morning when two airplanes, minutes apart, had hit the Twin Towers. Even before terrorism had been considered, he'd known there was work to do. He'd gathered his gear and begun working his way north through the traffic gridlock of the nation's capital before 9:37, when a third plane had crashed into the west side of the Pentagon. Terrorist attack virtually certain, he had already reversed direction when he received the order sending him south. The details of that morning were etched in his brain.

Now, four days later, he looked out over the darkness that was Virginia and chuckled as he thought about his newest recruit: *I ask for mental health help and I get a waif with bad hair and a purse.* Through his fatigue he felt a familiar quiver.

"Royally fucked," she'd agreed, and for several minutes they'd stood in silence, the woman trembling like a tree in a hurricane, each shiver traveling up his arm—electric fingers seeking his heart. He'd released her and stepped back, ignoring the pain in her eyes. He was a sucker for blue eyes, but no way could he hurt for each newbie. "Come on," he'd said, his voice gruff. "I'll show you the rest."

No one had looked up from their tasks as he'd hurried her around the working end of the tent, the adjacent mess tent, and the facilities off to the side. Ending where they'd begun, he'd lifted the canvas cover and shoved her none too gently into the sleeping quarters. "Sleep. Morning in three hours."

Now, his back to the tent, he stretched and shrugged in a futile attempt to ease what felt like bags of cement affixed to his shoulders. He'd been camping out on the cot he'd just assigned to Quinn and had been looking forward to one night on a hotel mattress. Not at all happy, he accepted that three hours wasn't much of a night to look forward to. *Could have given her a better heads-up*, he chided himself before visions of the steamy shower he'd get if he was really lucky blotted out her reproachful expression.

Fuck it. He settled into the Jeep, revved the engine, and headed toward his own skimpy quarters in Arlington. *She'll figure it out.*

HANDS CLENCHED IN HER LAP, QUINN perched on the cot, staring at nothing. Her stomach growled, food a faded memory. Too tired to scrounge, she ignored the plaintive rumble and focused on McLean's retreating footsteps. A door opened and closed, and after what seemed like an eternity, a motor coughed to life. As the sound of the vehicle disappeared into the night and darkness settled around her, Quinn recognized the small noises of sleep and, in the distance, the whispers of man and fire. She thought about her new boss, bearish and brusque, and wished he had stayed, had told her what she was supposed to do, had protected her from the loneliness that now tightened her throat. It had never been like this before, not even in the days when dealing with things had meant running away … that and sex and tequila. An impatient fist forced back the threatening tears—no sex, no tequila, never again. Tonight her coping toolbox gaped empty.

She sighed and pulled off her red cowboy boots. She sighed again as she removed the black jacket and slacks purchased for her mother's funeral, never to be worn again. A single tear escaped as she climbed under the rough army blanket. She'd never dreamed she would long for the imaginary and critical voices which she had deemed her "sister chorus," her own personal Jiminy Cricket, but right now even they would have been welcome.

Oh well, she thought as sleep took her, *I'll figure it out tomorrow.*

CHAPTER 3

"'SCUSE ME, MA'AM."

Quinn sat cross-legged on the floor of the circus tent into which she'd been deposited barely three hours earlier. Outdoor noise was faded, distant, like the scant light penetrating the interior. Eyes closed, mind fuzzy with fear and fatigue, she had just begun her daily routine when she heard a man's voice and looked up to see a soldier looming over her. She sucked in a startled breath and started to rise.

He pulled the helmet from his head to reveal the traditional buzz cut of a new recruit and a face not long familiar with shaving, then dropped to one knee beside her. "I'm sorry to be a bother, ma'am, surely I am, but my C.O., he says I have to come here before I can go back to duty."

Quinn huffed and looked around, but the few people remaining seemed uninterested, apparently inured to the vagaries of place, time, strangers. No one glanced their way.

Damn McLean. What do I do?

No desk, no chair, no office, and certainly no confidentiality. And she really had to pee. She shoved boots and duffel under the cot and patted the floor at her side. "Come on down, soldier."

He remained on one knee, and she wasn't surprised. *I surely don't inspire confidence*, she thought, acutely aware of her uncombed hair, her wrinkled tank top, the musty scent of woman in need of soap.

"No offense, ma'am, but I really don't need to be here. An' I got nothin' I need to talk about."

Up close she could see the fatigue scored into a face that should still be smiling at his mother across a bowl of Captain Crunch. Fatigue and something deeper. He didn't want to talk and she wasn't ready to listen, but here they both were—she looked around the tent but the remaining souls had departed— and she needed to do something.

Resisting the urge to take him in her arms and rock him like a baby, she patted the floor again. "Gotcha. No offense taken. You don't need to talk, and it's too early for me to be listening, so just plant it here while I finish my chores, and then we'll get you back to duty."

"DeMello," Chris McLean bellowed, "front and cen—"

His words dwindled as the open flap revealed his newest recruit sitting cross-legged beside her cot, eyes closed, oval face serene. Beside her, awkwardly cross-legged in his fatigues and combat boots, the equipage of a soldier dangling from his belt like charms from a bracelet, sat a dark-haired man, a kid really, his eyes shut, tears coursing down his smooth cheeks. Barely audible words issued unsteadily from the boy's lips in time with the chant from hers.

"*Om mani padme hum . . .*"

"I'm so angry, angry . . ."

"*Om mani padme hum* . . ."

"I'm so scared . . ."

"*Om* . . ."

"I shouldn't be scared, I'm not supposed to be scared, it's so awful . . ."

Then, as Chris stood transfixed, the soldier's voice found the woman's like a responsorial chant from the Catholic church of his own youth. Her hand clasped the boy's as the words became the soothing shush of a mother to her babe, and the usually stolid physician ducked his head and backed away.

Minutes later, a rattle of gear announced the young man's departure.

Chris stepped back into the space. "Finally up, are we?"

Her glance let him know she'd been aware of his earlier entry, but she just said, "Morning, boss. What happens next?" as she rose gracefully from the floor.

Tall, he thought, unused to a woman he didn't have to look down on, surprised he hadn't noticed the night before.

"I'm not used to looking up when I talk," she said, a smile playing across her lips as though she'd read his thoughts and found them amusing. "Do I get directions or do I just wing it? Oh, and where's the ladies'?"

Eyes on her butt as she strode toward the facilities, Chris savored the familiar tingling as it ratcheted up a notch. *Thank God for disasters.*

CHAPTER 4

AFTER SHE PEED, QUINN SPLASHED WATER on her face, brushed her teeth, and scrubbed ineffectively at her pits and privates. She jumped when the bathroom door rattled and McLean barked, "Snap it up, haven't got all day." She shot him a face mean enough, in her grandma's words, to curdle cream. She wanted to think about the boy and the chant. Something special had happened in that dark tent; maybe it could happen again?

The man obviously couldn't see her scowl. When his second impatient knock rocked the tiny space, she accepted the inevitable. With a huff, she straightened her clothes, stuck the toothbrush in her back pocket, and stepped into the dawn of this waking nightmare.

McLean shoved a mug of steaming coffee at her. "Here, you need this."

Before she could say thanks, he stalked away, and the coffee slopped onto her hand as she hustled after him. They reentered the white tent, which in another life could have housed elephants and clowns and a high-wire act or two. At its far end, accessed through a second door, the tent also housed a large empty space and a row of cubicles.

"Offices," McLean identified, as though the word could make it true. "Here's yours." He pushed her toward an empty cubby. Before he could say more, a shout from outside claimed his attention. He pulled something from his vest pocket, tossed it in her direction, and was gone.

Quinn stared at the granola bar settling at her feet. What now?

A head rose above the four-foot illusion of privacy. The woman it belonged to had curly brown hair, darker brown eyes with a mischievous glint, and a pleasant smile. "Hi, my name's Mandy, Amanda Blackstone, PhD, New York." She stuck her hand over the partition. "Drink and eat. You'll be lucky if you get another chance."

"Quinn. Quinn DeMello, marriage and family, Nevada." Quinn reached out to shake hands.

The woman's grip was firm, her gaze direct, and her grin morphed into wicked as she nodded toward McLean's retreating figure. "You'd better watch out for that one."

Quinn watched the broad back disappear and considered a response. Curiosity conquered her normal reticence. "Why?"

"Campus Lothario," Dr. Amanda Blackstone answered, mirth in her voice. "I've gotta admit, I wouldn't mind if I crossed his notorious path. For an old guy, he's pretty hot."

Quite sure the crusty man who called himself her boss, ordered her around, and gave her no instructions wouldn't appreciate the "old guy" epithet, Quinn dead-ended that conversation. But maybe this promising new source could tell her what she was supposed to be doing.

"What happens next? Surely we don't just sit here?"

Both women considered Quinn's cubicle—a four-by-six space, bare but for two folding chairs that had seen better days, an upended crate that held a digital clock, and a utilitarian lamp.

Mandy released an exaggerated sigh. "Makes home look like heaven, don't it? And to think I whined that my office chair was too hard." Her shoulders moved in a good-natured, what-are-you-gonna-do shrug. "But lamenting will get us nowhere and, to answer your question, yes, if we sit here, they will come. Then we do what we do best: We listen."

Quinn struggled to maintain a neutral expression as her heart rate skyrocketed. Surely there must be more order than this.

Apparently reading Quinn's dismay, Amanda chuckled. "Your first disaster, isn't it?"

It was more statement than question. Quinn nodded, uncomfortable and convinced there must be a scarlet *N* for "newbie" tattooed on her forehead.

"Well, you'll get used to it fast enough. *Too* used to it, probably." Mandy handed Quinn a cardboard sign that read "Back in 5."

"Here. Hang this on your pretend door when you need a potty break or when you just can't take anymore."

The appearance of two uniformed women, the smaller supporting her tearful companion, interrupted whatever else Amanda Blackstone might say. "See what I mean?" She flipped a wave and ducked into her own cubicle where the trio settled into confessional murmurs, leaving Quinn to digest the fact that someone else might hear too many stories.

She stepped into her own cubby and, in the lull, her abandoned lover filled her thoughts—Owen Johnson, her steady, reliable Indiana Jones lookalike, whose mouth . . .

A timid tap rescued her.

The odor of unwashed human and old smoke preceded the man into the cubby. Slender, attired in what had once been a suit and now was a wrinkled, smelly mess, he sank into a chair as though his legs would no longer support him. Sweat and soot streaked his immobile face.

Oh!

"Civilian employee. Andrew Lane," he said as though she had asked. "I was inside when it happened."

What to say? Quinn had known emergency mental health would be different from the usual counseling scene, where tidy clients settled into comfortable chairs and told and retold the stories that kept them stuck. She hadn't thought whatever she might say would make a difference then, and she wasn't sure it would now.

She pulled her chair next to his. "Wanna tell me?"

In one brief paragraph of nouns and adjectives, his expressionless voice painted a picture so vivid Quinn felt the heat and smelled the fear, heard the anguish in his scream as his fallen coworker was left behind.

"What now?" she asked when he fell silent.

"They want me to go home, get cleaned up, talk to somebody."

Silence again. Quinn waited.

Finally, voice flat, hands worrying a pink cardigan he held like a baby's comfort object, the man continued. "This was hers. I'm afraid if I put it down, she'll be gone."

Pain stabbed Quinn as her memory painted its own picture, and she saw her younger hand place a fuzzy pink bunny beside her sleeping daughter. They'd wanted her to talk, too, when Samantha had died, but she, too, had been afraid. If she'd let it out, her child would be forever gone. She'd been wrong, but she hadn't known it then.

She focused all her attention on the man by her side. "What is her name?" she asked.

"Karen."

"Well, Andrew Lane, why don't you tell me about Karen, and then we'll know what to do next." She held out her hand.

After a searching glance, he took the proffered hand and held on tight as he told Quinn about the friend he couldn't save, and, as he spoke, tears fell.

A few minutes later, Andrew squeezed Quinn's hand and released it. In a tear-thickened voice, he said, "Not my fault," as though the fact surprised him. After another moment, he smoothed Karen's sweater and handed it to Quinn. "Please give this to her family."

Quinn accepted the sweater and stood when Andrew stood, watching as his shoulders straightened.

"I need to go get cleaned up," he said. "My family will be worrying."

Before she could speak, he gathered her in an awkward hug, whispered, "Thank you," and left the cubby.

Blinking away her own tears, Quinn sat back into the uncomfortable metal chair. She glanced at the clock and saw that only seventeen minutes had elapsed. She wanted to think about what had just happened, but a murmur outside her cubby let her know thinking would have to wait.

IN THE HOURS THAT FOLLOWED, QUINN worked with more people than she had ever thought possible and came to know more than she wanted to know: that no one was left alive; that everyone was afraid there would be another attack; that fear had shut down rescue attempts that might have saved more people; that the G-D terrorists had all perished (this told with a quick sign of the cross, as though the speaker felt guilty for his glee). As Mandy had put it, she listened.

Finally alone, she mulled over her situation. Months ago, anxiety, a panic attack, and her own inner demons had driven her from her profession. Today, back to work, she was just tired. *Exhausted, sad, but not anxious,* she realized, *and I don't need to puke. Maybe I'm finally getting normal.*

She raised her arms above her head to stretch tight shoulders. *Normal. Now that's a hoot.*

A hearty thump rattled the cubicle and disrupted her reverie. She'd been so focused she hadn't noticed that outside her lamp's tiny circle of light, the world had grown dark. Now she was acutely aware of her need to pee, but before she could act on the thought, Chris McLean filled her space. "You do get a break, you know."

"Gotta go. Be right back." She scooted past him and out the door. He was still in the tent when she returned. The memory of Mandy's words tempered her rush of gratitude.

"Let's go to dinner," he said. "The mess tent is too loud, and I hate to eat alone."

She eyed him with suspicion, noted the unshaven cheeks, the straggling beard hairs that went off on journeys of their own, the circles under his eyes so dark they seemed painted on, and decided he was more grandfatherly than lecherous. She stifled a chuckle. He probably wouldn't appreciate that description either. She usually preferred her own company, but right now sinking into her own dark thoughts just seemed stupid.

"Okay, sounds good," she said and hoped she didn't sound too eager.

CHAPTER 5

MAKING NO ATTEMPT AT CONVERSATION, CHRIS McLean drove through empty streets, the only sign of life an occasional individual whose hurried steps and head-down posture seemed an apology for normal activity. Already wishing she'd said no, Quinn hardly noticed. She snapped out of her litany— *dumb move, dumb idea, how dumb can I be?*—when he pulled in beside a deserted-appearing storefront.

"Here?"

Without answer, he switched off the engine and climbed out of the vehicle.

Quinn opened her own door and stepped onto the sidewalk as McLean rounded the front of the Jeep. For a moment, they stood shoulder to shoulder and looked at the building, the evening air a cool whisper on heated cheeks. Faint light from inside illuminated the name La Trattoria in black letters stenciled on a water-spotted window. A neon sign above was dark. McLean, eyebrow raised and head tipped at a quizzical angle, gave Quinn a look before he stepped forward and reached for the door handle.

Not too tired for a bit of fun—*old cranky guy, indecisive blonde, a date or not a date?*—she grinned, let him do the gentlemanly thing, and preceded him into a low-ceilinged room redolent of garlic and Mozart's *Figaro*. The heels of her red boots clicked on the worn linoleum.

La Trattoria was obviously a mom-and-pop operation that had probably fed Pentagon employees for decades. *More*, Quinn thought, taking in the fly-specked ceiling and the Chianti bottles heavily encrusted with wax that decorated the tables—but tonight the dinner crowd was thin. A plump girl, her pleasant face marred by fatigue or grief or fear, leaned against a counter as though it were the only thing keeping her on her feet. In just one day, Quinn had come to know this look. The girl attempted a smile as she handed McLean plastic-clad menus and waved them toward the empty tables. "Take any seat you like, folks. Not much business these days."

Will we ever smile again? Hollow inside, humor forgotten, Quinn followed her new boss to a booth whose window looked out into darkness.

"This okay?"

She nodded, situated herself on the rump-sprung vinyl seat, and accepted the menu. McLean seemed to overflow the space as he took the seat across and adjusted himself. His knees didn't quite touch hers, but she felt their heat. She sagged, wishing for the amnesia of sleep, and stared through glazed eyes at the menu, aware of McLean's close attention but too tired to comment.

"Jet lag," he said. "It'll get better. You'll get used to all this. You need food. I'll order."

His voice pulled her out of her stupor and she nodded, grateful that she didn't have to think, not sure she could eat.

"Uh-hum."

As one, they turned to see a slight man in a stained white apron standing beside their table. He looked as though he'd rather be someplace else.

"Sorry to interrupt, folks, but I thought you might like drinks." The old voice fluttered around the words, then steadied. "Sorry, what can I get you?"

"No problem," McLean said and reached out his hand. "We just appreciate the opportunity to be here."

The man straightened, his morose, basset-hound jowls rearranging themselves into a smile. He stuck his pencil stub behind his ear and wiped his palm on the apron before he grasped the proffered hand. "Nathaniel Specchio, owner and proprietor of this little place. Nate to my friends. Not enough nighttime business to pay the help, even if they weren't too skittish to come out, so me and my granddaughter are manning the store." He shook his head as though trying to absorb this new world. "So what can I get you folks?"

"Good to meet you, Mr. Specchio." McLean clasped the other man's hand as though infusing strength. "Chris McLean, and this lovely lady," he nodded toward Quinn, "is DeMello, one of our valued volunteers. We can't tell you how much it means to us, that you stay open, give us this place away from—" he paused with a vague gesture in the direction of the despoiled Pentagon, "from the troubles. Thank you." His booming voice had softened and taken on a comforting Irish lilt.

"No, no, it is I who thank you for coming, for helping . . ." The owner-cum-waiter went on in this vein for so long that Quinn was sure he would not only buy them dinner but offer them his firstborn child. He finally interrupted himself, "But enough of this," withdrew from the safety of McLean's handshake, and retrieved his pencil. "Now, what shall I bring to such wonderful new friends?"

McLean's eyebrow raised as Quinn ordered her own meal, and he shot her a questioning glance but made no comment when she requested a Diet Pepsi with lemon. Ignoring the nonverbal questions, Quinn waited until he had placed his own order and Nate Specchio had withdrawn, then whispered, "I thought he'd give us his first born." She grinned, pleased with herself, as McLean rumbled, a sound now positively identified as laughter.

After a time, almost as though he were talking to himself, McLean said, "It's always like this at the beginning, then slowly it changes when life reboots and our presence reminds them that normal has changed." An unhappy sound more like wind than sigh punctuated his words. "Then we leave."

She waited, but he offered no more, just sipped the wine he poured from the bottle the granddaughter had placed on the table. "A good year for California zin," he said and rumbled again. "What the hell, they're all good years." The sound faded, and he gazed out into the night.

Curiosity again conquered reticence. "You've done this before?"

With a start, he returned his attention to her. "Sorry. Often. Almost forty years, in fact. But this is the baddest of all. Usually it's just the weather or Mother Nature that's the perp. Perpetrator," he added in an explanatory tone. "But this is evil-driven, and no one knows what to do or what to expect next."

Having heard variations on this theme all day, Quinn's mind filled with the now-familiar images and her own fear, twined with sadness and loss, so she just nodded, sipped her Pepsi, and wished for a tequila shooter, or at least a swallow of his dark red wine. When it again seemed he was done, she prompted, "So what others?" wanting his words to barricade her thoughts.

"Florida, California, the big 'Frisco quake, not the 1906 one." They both laughed and Quinn's malaise lifted.

Nate Specchio brought their food, McLean's steak running red, Quinn's Caesar salad, Greek style with plump shrimp and Kalamata olives lurking under chunks of romaine. The old man seemed relieved to hear laughter in his establishment.

McLean refilled his glass from the bottle at his elbow, then offered it in her direction. Quinn shook her head.

"You sure?"

"Sure."

He didn't press her. They turned their attention to eating. Quinn sucked at an olive pit. *A good addition, I'll have to tell Vivian*, she thought, and homesickness swept through her: for Vivian and Victoria, the twins who believed in her; for Owen, their brother: for the B&B and the retreats and Nevada's mountains ... everything she'd left behind.

She felt McLean's perceptive glance and looked up, and a shock ran through her as their eyes met. She dropped her gaze but not quickly enough, hating the ease with which he was reading her. Always fearful of self-disclosure and its consequences, she asked, "And where else?" in an attempt to divert the inevitable probing questions that would merit lies and half truths and send her searching for the ladies'. She was surprised when he just answered her question.

"Iran once, for an earthquake, too. That was a bad one. Russian River flood. You?" he asked, although he already knew the answer.

"My first." Mirroring his earlier gesture, she indicated the Pentagon. *My first, this newest attack on America's soil, here where terrorist blood now mingles with our own.* She thought of Vivian's son, Scott, lost in the debris of the second tower.

Chris McLean felt Quinn retreat, her voice closed and distant, her eyes on the table. She was transparent tonight, though he sensed that would not always be so. He'd had his share of first-timers, recognized tired and sad and probably homesick, but this DeMello person touched him. Nobody made him laugh much these days, but she had, and she had legs up to here and a great butt. A relentless fist tightened in his chest, and he wanted to taste her secrets.

Instead, he offered reassurance. "The first is worst, no matter what, and even this will get easier."

Quinn's hand moved as though seeking the wine glass, then fluttered to stillness on the table between them. Without thinking, he covered it with his own, felt the recoil though her hand didn't really move. Irritated, he resisted the urge to jerk his own back, patted her perfunctorily, and then grabbed his wine. "I remember *my* first," he said and drained the glass.

She glanced up. The question, "Which first?" was as clear in her eyes as if she had spoken it, and he almost snorted wine out his nose.

Her laugh turned heads, and smile lines sprang into existence at the corners of her eyes.

His own choking laughter took longer to subside, each glance at her innocent expression producing another paroxysm. By the time he could draw a reasonable breath, wipe his eyes, and accept the tissue she handed him, it seemed everyone in the place was watching.

He finished blowing his nose and was about to speak when she asked, "So you mean your first *disaster?*" Strong willpower wasn't enough; laughter erupted anew.

Looking smug, she sipped her Pepsi while he struggled to get himself back in control. He couldn't remember the last time he'd laughed until he'd cried.

When he could speak, he said, "Yes, my first *disaster,*" and ignored her expression. "It was that big earthquake in Mexico City." He sucked in air, the memory still strong. "I was a first-timer like you, didn't know what to expect, and it was god-awful. Hospitals, homes, everything went down, but we pulled kids out alive after all hope was gone. That sold me, and now I feel guilty when I don't go." He didn't mention that he'd been volunteered by a judge, that rescue work had kept him out of jail and cleared his record of the DUI that might have nixed medical school.

A comfortable silence settled over them. He finished his steak, mopped up the juice with the last chunk of bread, and chased the crumbs with the last drops from his bottle.

"Dessert?"

Eyelids drooping, Quinn shook her head.

He knew the feeling. "Then let's go."

They shook hands with the owner and thanked him for the gift of their meal. Without comment, Quinn stepped through the door he held open. She didn't mention the twenties McLean had left on the table and neither did he. Outside, he tossed her the keys, said, "You drive, DeMello," and climbed into the passenger seat. Quinn blinked but didn't protest as she got behind the wheel.

She negotiated the unfamiliar streets. Chris dozed, coming awake just as she nosed the Jeep into its slot and turned off the engine. He sat still for a moment, then released his seat belt and climbed carefully from the vehicle. She hesitated.

"Good night, DeMello. Thanks for the company." He waved her away and ambled into the night.

DR. AMANDA BLACKSTONE WAS READING WHEN Quinn entered Cot Central. She marked her place in the Nora Roberts romance and directed the beam of her head lamp toward her newest roommate. "So?"

"So what?"

"Well, did he . . . you know . . . make a move on you, I mean? We were all wondering, but I told them you weren't interested."

In the dark tent, all seemed quiet, but Quinn sensed other ears straining to hear. When she didn't answer, Mandy wheedled, "Come on, tell. What happened? Did he—"

Quinn held up her hand. Mandy stopped midsentence. "God, Mandy, even my mother doesn't (*didn't*, she corrected mentally) ask me questions like that. Whatever happened to privacy?"

"Privacy, smivacy," Mandy said, "that's for clients. As you'll find out soon enough, this is just one big dysfunctional family, and you're its newest member."

CHAPTER 6

Dawn rose too soon over her second morning in hell. A hard cot, unremitting noise and unfamiliar bodies nearby kept sleep shallow. The night full of ghosts, dream fragments that wafted through her sleep like Disney's Haunted Mansion holographs, left her sweaty and jumbled inside. Right now the camp was almost quiet, too early for the full crew of workers and scaffolds and metal-cutting tools, and her tentmates still snored. Hoping to find a private spot, Quinn threw on yesterday's clothes and walked out of the tent into a crowd.

She stepped back, startled. "What the . . ."

"I hope it's okay," the young man, hardly recognizable as yesterday's tearful soldier, stammered, "but some of my buddies wanted to sit with you, and I didn't know how else to find you."

Flanking him were six, no, seven, soldiers—if one could really call human beings who looked like children playing dress-up *soldiers*—garbed in camouflage with their charms on their belts. A pretty girl who should have been cheerleading stepped forward in a formal stance.

Oh, God, what if they salute?

At attention, sans salute, the young woman spoke, the liquid honey of some southern state dripping from her voice. "Please, ma'am. We'll be real quiet and no bother. Benjie," she flashed a smile at Quinn's soldier as she shared his secret, "said you made him feel better, and we'd all like to sit with you while you do … whatever you do." She pulled herself straighter, taller, as she asked formally, "That is, if it's all right with you, ma'am." Her request completed, she stepped back into the ranks.

Quinn took a deep breath. *This is what I'm here for,* she reminded herself, taking in the tired young faces, *and if it helps, why would I say no?*

Decision made, she nodded. "Follow me," she said and started off toward the small copse of trees she'd glimpsed the day before, the group splitting and then re-forming behind her.

The morning's chant was loud enough to reach Buddha's ears.

THE SUN WAS STILL LOW IN the east when Quinn entered the mess tent alone, her soldiers having melted away as the last *Om* shimmied in the muggy air. She poured coffee and ladled up oatmeal before settling at an empty camp-style table. The morning air promised a repeat of poor ventilation, discomfort, and the pungent aroma of fear and despair. She was scraping the last bits of oatmeal and raisins from the bottom of her bowl when Amanda Blackstone scooted in beside her on the bench.

Mandy set her steaming mug and her breakfast plate down and turned to Quinn. "So tell me all about you," she said without preface, flashing a cheeky grin and ignoring coworkers seated nearby, "and I'll tell you about *him.*"

Quinn's spoon paused, midair. She didn't need a map to know who *him* was, but she certainly wasn't going to tell this stranger about her family—the four sisters with C names, the alcoholic brother running the family business, the handsome Portuguese father dead too young, and the mother who hated her. And no way was she mentioning the dry-mouthed yearning for a tequila shooter or her propensity to end up in bed with the wrong guy (at least, until Owen). *Not talking about Owen, no thank you.*

Dr. Blackstone tucked a loose curl behind one ear, sipped her coffee, and waited. After all, waiting was her thing.

Relentless, Quinn thought, knowing she often came off as rude or unfriendly, but fear of judgment kept her silent. She chewed and swallowed slowly as though considering the offer, then shook her head from side to side.

"No?" The woman grinned as though she expected no other answer and turned her attention to her food.

Huh. Maybe I'll get off easy.

Nope, not so. Mandy followed a forkful of scrambled eggs with a swig of coffee, pushed her curls back from her face, and sent Quinn a wide, innocent smile. "Okay, I'll go first. Dr. Heartbreak, he's called, or Heartbreak Harry. Harrison Christian McLean, MD, cardiac surgeon—kids mostly, I hear—and volunteer director extraordinaire. Seems something happened and he had to do some volunteer time—DUI is my bet, but who knows—and he just keeps doing it."

Quinn drank her cold coffee and pretended disinterest as she soaked up information the man himself had neglected to mention.

Mandy continued. "Anyway, after a while, he got to be part-time surgeon and part-time director of all this. Does a pretty good job, it seems. This is lots better organized than my last volunteer stint, and rumor has it that he always leaves some lucky gal very happy."

Habit kept Quinn silent—habit and fear and precious little experience with friendly, gossipy women—but her own curiosity hummed. *McLean a womanizer? Who would have guessed?*

After a moment, Amanda issued an exaggerated sigh and picked up her fork.

Amused and glad for the respite, however brief, Quinn gathered her dishes and, with a brief, "See ya," adjourned to her cubby, leaving Amanda Blackstone to whatever conclusions she might draw.

It was dusk before Quinn escaped to the bathroom, battered flute case and toothbrush in hand. The day's moist heat lingered. *I stink*, she thought, aware of damp underarms and sweat-soaked hair. Her stomach roiled with the stories she'd heard all day as hot and dispirited soldiers and civilian rescuers made their way in and out of her equally hot and dispirited cubicle. She yearned for Nevada's evening air—cool, dry, refreshing. Finally, she pushed it all into a numb corner of her brain, brushed her teeth, washed her face, and stepped out into the night. She needed a place to practice.

Even away from the tents and Mandy's cheerful gossip, quiet and privacy were in short supply. Work on the tortured building progressed around the clock, and human suffering received no break either. In the twilight, Quinn looked toward the Pentagon and saw a slender woman, a service dog on leash at her side, climbing the steps. Transfixed, she watched a uniformed figure approach, kneel beside the two, and bury his face in the dog's neck. After a few seconds, the soldier wiped away tears, saluted, and hurried away. The woman and the dog walked on and were lost from view.

More than one way to offer comfort.

Uncomfortable with emotion so close to the surface, Quinn swiped at her own tears and strode toward the stand of trees where she'd held the makeshift morning meditation. For years, her flute had been her constant companion. *The flute and the sister chorus,* she thought, *and now the chorus is gone.* Some days she was sure only the rigidity of practice—flute, yoga, meditation—kept her from shattering.

The trees, leaves hinting at their upcoming autumnal fashion show, provided another illusion of privacy. Quinn hunkered down and opened the case. Safe in their blue velvet enclosures, the pieces gleamed in the uneven light. As she soaked in the sight of normal, more tears dribbled onto her cheeks. She scrubbed them away and reached into her pocket for the silent mobile phone.

She flipped it open, thumbed it on. No service.

"Shit."

No message.

"Shit, shit, shit."

She punched in numbers anyway, the desire to hear Owen Johnson's voice overcoming what little good sense remained, but the words on the tiny screen still read "No Service."

The flute waited. Ignoring as best she could the catch in her heart, Quinn tenderly lifted the shiny pieces from their velvet beds and slid them together—the body first, with its keyrings and rod axels, joined at the right by the foot joint, then completed as she aligned the head joint just so into the left end, the depth of penetration adjusted expertly—her routine so practiced she could assemble the instrument with her eyes closed. With the cool cylinder in her hands, she bit her lip, stifling a cry as memory punched her: their first retreat.

Early in her tenure at the Wildflower Inn B&B, before they had known how wildly successful the retreats for professional women would be, she had been playing during afternoon tea.

The colors of sunset painted the room, and their guests—Thalia, Carol, Nancy, and Angie—were sipping hot tea and contemplating digestive biscuits, quietly respectful of Quinn's ban against talking in the common areas, although they had no way of knowing that the silence was for Quinn's benefit rather than their own, when Owen Johnson slid onto the piano bench and his hands found the flute's melody. The rolled-up sleeves of his blue chambray shirt showed off muscles, which rippled as his skillful fingers moved over the yellowed ivory keys. His shock of damp hair, black as a raven's wing, bounced against the scar that puckered his eyebrow as his body moved with the music.

Skin humming with the memory, Quinn could almost feel those same skillful hands playing over her body, and her fingers wrapped around the puffy silver heart that hung on its silver chain between her breasts. The room, the guests, everything but the man and their music had dropped away, and when his eyes had met hers, she had been sure he could see into her soul.

And the rest is history, she thought now, releasing the heart and rubbing her arms to dispel the electricity memory had produced. *Too much thinking, too much remembering, too much, and I brought it all on myself.* This new place, even in the midst of its unspeakable anguish, was to be her first step toward wellness, the place where she could leave guilt and self-recrimination and rotten decisions behind. *Ha.*

She closed her eyes, directed a breath across the flute's embouchure, and brought forth the first notes. Blowing gently, adjusting angle and velocity until a perfect tone rose into the air, she let her fingers have their way, moving easily through scales and arpeggios and into the haunting melody of Pachelbel's *Canon in D Major*.

The notes blended with the sounds of destruction. When her tears fell, she didn't know whether they were for herself or for the world.

In the gathering darkness, a silent audience assembled, and when the last notes faded and Quinn bowed her head, her listeners slipped away.

CHAPTER 7

N THE BUENA VISTA VALLEY of central Nevada, miles away from the attack on America and home to the ghost town known as Unionville, Owen Johnson sat at the trestle table of his sisters' Wildflower Inn Bed and Breakfast, playing with the eggs benedict that Vivian had placed temptingly before him. Nothing tasted good; after three bites, he pushed the plate away.

Born and raised in nearby Winnemucca, Owen was an accountant whose common sense and good nature had served him well until the arrival of Quinn DeMello. Nine months ago, she'd landed in the ditch beside the B&B with nothing to do and no place to go. "Running away," his sisters had explained, and, against his better judgment and loud protests, they had taken her in, and the three of them had created women's retreats that had turned the fortunes of the little bed and breakfast. Quinn had become his lover. Now she was gone.

Think it through, he ordered himself. Logic, like numbers, couldn't fail. Hadn't logic carried him through the anguish of stillbirth and miscarriages, affairs and divorce? Even the psychiatrist his friends had forced on him had agreed that he was, in fact, "getting along with it" quite nicely. And the surprise revelation of his father's second family, of a brother and sister near him in age, had only momentarily pushed him off balance. *Think it through, man; you knew from day one she wouldn't stay.* Logic, yes; trust, no.

Hoping to dislodge the ache that centered there, he scrubbed at the bridge of his nose. *I know all that. Why does it hurt so damn much?*

VICTORIA JOHNSON, VIVIAN'S IDENTICAL TWIN, EYED her brother over the rim of her Welcome to the Bahamas mug with a frown on her round face and worry in her dark eyes. "Wen," she addressed her older brother with the nickname from their childhood, "you've got to get a grip. Quinn said she'll be back, so she'll be back. The phones are still crazy, and that's why you haven't heard from her." She looked to her sister for twin assistance.

"Vicky's right, Wennie darling. It took three days for Scottie to contact us—and he knew we'd think he was dead."

Vivian's almost-twenty-one-year-old son, Scott, had decamped from Nevada to *bond* with his newly discovered and ne'er-do-well father and learn the family business in his grandfather's office in the second tower. The young man had emerged from a fishing trip to discover himself delivered from tragedy by playing hooky.

"She'll call," Vivian said, wishing it true, "as soon as she can."

The women considered their brother—face buried in his hands, blue-striped shirt with sleeves rolled up over his elbows that looked like he'd slept in it—the picture of misery.

At their words, he raised his head. There was no heart in the smile he gave them. "I should have gone with her."

"You couldn't," they chimed.

At their feet, sensing the tension above, the corgis, Patience and Prudence, rustled and fussed until Vivian got up and put them out. She returned to her seat, her scowl suggesting she wished someone would put her out too.

"We've already discussed this," reminded Victoria, the practical one, "and you know you couldn't."

She got the coffee pot and refilled their cups. Outside, the quail made their funny little noises. The grass invited a last fall mowing, and the chickens clucked for their feed. Right now, chores would be a lot easier to deal with than this despondent man who sat slumped at the table staring into his steaming coffee as though it alone held answers.

She resumed her seat and tried again. "Owen, you couldn't go with her. Quinn's a volunteer, and she had work to do. Besides, the planes just aren't flying."

As though on cue, all three turned toward the picture window and the patch of blue sky, devoid of contrails. Vivian turned away and picked up her mug. "And can you even blame them?"

No one answered.

Vivian sighed. Her brother had always been the family rock. This new Owen upset her. Temper quivered in her voice as she stated what they'd all been thinking. "Quinn has issues that she's gotta work out. She told us and she told you. She has to work it out, and she's decided she has to do it by herself. You just don't want to believe it."

Owen stared into the black coffee depths. *I know!* he wanted to shout. *I know and it doesn't help!*

Quinn herself had told him, but knowing didn't mitigate the sense that he'd failed her. Her words shrieked in his memory: "Owen, it's this way: All my life I've taken a good fuck and a lot of wishful thinking and created a myth of salvation, and it doesn't work."

He winced as he remembered his reply. "Is that all this was to you? A good fuck?" He would be embarrassed for himself now if he didn't feel so pathetic. Hands on her hips, high-voltage tension snapping between them, Quinn had tried once more. When it was clear he didn't get it, she said in exasperation, "I can't stay here and fall in love and expect you to make my life okay." She walked away, and that was that.

What he knew in his heart was that he loved her, and, therefore, it was his job to make her life okay. He wondered, as he had before, why she thought so poorly of herself, but it really didn't matter. He wanted her. Whether she wanted him was another issue.

For three nights he'd slept in her bed, seeking the sweet scent of lavender and woman while the generic sheets mocked him. Clients' deadlines loomed. He needed to work, but instead he pawed through the antique basket that decorated the soot-darkened hearth in the elderly room she loved. He found a heart-shaped rock, a poem from an old throw-away newspaper, a broken arrowhead, a dried bunch of sage tied in pink satin, thank-you notes, and more. Vivian told him the guests had left Quinn tokens of appreciation, but he hadn't understood until now.

He ran his fingers over the heart-shaped rock, seeking her, but she was gone, and for only the second time in his life, Owen Johnson didn't know what to do. Resolutely, he'd slipped the stone into his pocket and gone in search of his sisters.

Now he looked at them through tear-filled eyes. "What do I do?"

Guilt tightened his throat when he saw Vivian's own tears spill, felt her struggle for an answer he might accept. Her words came slowly. "I don't know, Wen, but here's what I think. I think Quinn's got a bunch of stuff to deal with—her mother, guilt about her daughter's death, the new relationship with her sisters, us, you, and now this crisis and her work—"

"That she's been avoiding," said Victoria in the finish-each-other's-sentences manner that was their norm. "She's scared. Everything's too new for her—for all of us—and for being a therapist, she isn't the most effective coper in the world, now, is she?"

They grew quiet, each remembering their last meal with the long-legged blonde who had enriched their lives. Mary DeMello, Quinn's narcissistic and cancer-ridden mother, had died that morning. Silent and brittle, Quinn had dealt with hospice, ambulance, family, then retreated to her room. In the early evening, she joined them at this very table, pushed her food around her plate in silence until finally, disinhibited by red wine, she'd shouted, "She hated me! What's wrong with a daughter that her own mother would hate her?" Owen and Vivian and Victoria gaped like fishes as she railed at them. "You can't answer that, can you? *Your* mother loves you."

They'd had no balm for her pain.

Owen flushed, remembering that and more—Quinn's drunken, self-induced climax; her rape of his much-too-willing body; his tears and her remorse. "I'm so afraid of how I feel," she'd said, "that I use alcohol and I use sex, and I used you, and that's not okay."

"I want her back," he told his sisters. "Tell me what to do."

CHAPTER 8

UNDER THE PALE MORNING SKY, MORE soldiers awaited Quinn in the woody glen. *Word of mouth,* she thought. *Guess yesterday's chanting made them feel better.* Surprised and more than a little pleased to see them, she nodded, sank into her sitting pose, and stifled a grin as they settled amid a clatter of equipment. *So young,* she thought, her own forty-three years not technically old, but there were days—

Assuming naiveté about meditation from her audience, Quinn offered a simple explanation. "Meditation can bring clarity of mind and a sense of inner peace," she said. "We don't say anything, we just sit tall and let our thoughts go, and somehow or other we feel better." She looked out at the eager faces and opened her arms. "The chanting helps me focus, so that's what I do. Please close your eyes and join me."

Quinn closed her eyes and quieted her thoughts. This certainly wasn't traditional therapy, with its rules and regulations, but they were here and so she began, "*Om,*" her voice strong and true and inviting. Other voices hesitantly joined the solitary tone, and the chant grew fuller. Ten minutes later, with nods and shy smiles, the group dispersed, leaving Quinn alone with her thoughts. Her own unpleasant odor aroused her. *Wash first, think later,* she decided and headed for clean clothes and a shower.

After a quick shower under tepid waters, she dried off and wiggled into her last clean jeans and a black tank top, then donned Owen's blue chambray shirt, borrowed and never returned. The familiar scent of Jaipur and man wafted over her and she froze, willing it to stay, but seconds later only the memory remained.

Stop it, she ordered herself as she shook disappointment away. *He's gone, you're here, and you've got questions begging for answers.* Moments later, she entered the mess tent and scanned the crowd for Amanda.

Apparently oblivious to the noisy activity that filled the tent, the woman sat alone with her back to the door, attention focused on the paperback in front of her.

I'm going to regret this.

Saying good morning to the people she recognized, Quinn moved through the tent, poured herself a cup of coffee, and ladled up a bowl of oatmeal before she nonchalantly plopped down across from her quarry.

"He's a surgeon?" She picked up the conversation where Mandy had left it the morning before.

Amanda Blackstone raised her gaze from the printed page and smirked. "And good morning to you, too, Quinn DeMello."

I'm in for it now. Quinn knew she should walk away. Curiosity kept her seated. Whatever happened next, she'd brought on herself.

Methodically, the other woman slipped a bookmark into place, closed the book, and tucked it into the backpack at her feet, clearly relishing the situation and drawing out the suspense. "I never travel without a book," she said.

Quinn fidgeted.

Mandy laughed. "Okay, yes, he's a surgeon. Supposedly one of the best. He has a place in Washington, DC, works and teaches at George Washington University, originally from someplace in Connecticut. His wife lives there. Into horses, somebody said."

"He's married?"

"Of course. Aren't they all? Separated for years, I think." She flashed a knowing smile in Quinn's direction. "But as I told you yesterday, he ..."

Her words drifted off as Chris McLean approached. "Ladies, good morning," a hint of Irish present in his greeting. "May I join you?"

Without waiting for an answer, he set his loaded plate on the table. "Busy enough for the both of you?" he asked as he lowered himself to the bench beside Quinn.

Like a malevolent fog, supercharged air descended with him and stole her breath. *Oh!* A delicious and unexpected warmth coursed her body and became a throbbing ball of fire just below her belly button, behind the thin white stretch marks on her lower abdomen. *Oh!*

She stiffened as the big man's arm brushed hers and the throbbing intensified: exciting, familiar, unwanted. With an insight not habitual, Quinn recognized this punch, inevitable and inexorable, that led her to believe a man could save her—a knight on a white horse, a prince with a sword, a piano-playing accountant who looked like Indiana Jones. It didn't work. When she'd left Owen, she'd sworn never to believe again, but now ... This man oozed temptation.

Not happening, Quinn told herself as she gritted her teeth. *Oh please, not happening.*

McLean acted unaware of the conversation he'd disrupted and ignorant of the turmoil he'd churned up as he picked up his fork and attacked the scrambled eggs piled high on his plate.

The throbbing deepened, intensified. Tendrils of desire flicked.

Undaunted by the midgossip termination, Mandy launched into a monologue about a woman and a dog wandering the Pentagon steps and how she wondered why the hell they hadn't all been issued therapy dogs.

Get it together, Quinn ordered herself, but she couldn't catch her breath and her limbs squiggled like Jell-o as McLean's hairy arm again brushed hers. Trapped, she spooned oatmeal into her mouth, hoping that she might choke and be done with it.

A little voice at her shoulder said, "More coffee?"

As suddenly as it had appeared, the fog retreated, the heat diminished, and only a tiny ache remained. Quinn gasped. No one else seemed to notice.

"More coffee?" Dwarfed by the enamel pitcher steaming in her hands, the ponytailed girl cleared her throat and repeated her question. Her T-shirt sported a school logo and her jeans were cropped and tight. She propped the pitcher on the edge of the table and waited.

All three looked at the girl and nodded yes.

The girl poured coffee that was black and thick and looked almost as vile as the brew Quinn had shared with Old Joseph, her Basque friend and mentor back home. The ancient sheepherder had taught her to drink boiled coffee from a can, to take care of a mare erroneously christened George, and to find solace in the mountains of Nevada.

Tears threatened. Disgusted with herself—*I'm supposed to be taking control of my life, not having a repeat performance*—she blinked them back and turned her attention to the coffee pourer.

Holding her cup out for its refill, Quinn asked, "What school do you go to?"

"Washington-Lee High School in Arlington, ma'am." A surprised smile animated the young woman's face. "I'm a senior."

Quinn smiled back. "Not ma'am, just DeMello. No school today?"

"No, ma'am, I mean Ms. DeMello, we're released because of . . ." She gestured toward the destruction just beyond them.

Quinn's eyes encouraged her and she continued, "I'm accelerated sciences, pre-med and psych. We volunteer where we can." She paused as though something had just occurred to her, braced the pitcher against the table, and asked, "Are you the lady who chants?"

Quinn raised a questioning brow. "That'd be me."

The girl burst into a jumbled explanation that included a National Guard brother named Benjie, an interest in meditation, and a budding hero-worship for the woman she was addressing.

When coffee slopped on the table, Quinn intervened, discovered the girl's name was Molly, and invited her to join them when her school schedule allowed.

"I'll come, Ms. DeMello," Molly bubbled. "Benjie'll tell me when." With a wave that threatened the pitcher, she danced away to finish her task, the glance back over her shoulder filled with awe.

McLean stood, eyes following the young volunteer. "Nicely done," he said and rested a hand on Quinn's shoulder.

Her upward glance caught a gleam in his eye. Unsure of its cause, Quinn shivered and was sure that he noticed, but he just said, "Dinner tonight? Nate'll miss us if we stay away too long. You too, Amanda Blackstone. Food's good. You'll like it." He took a step away from the table, then turned back. "By the way, DeMello, emergency phone's available in the office tent if you want to use it."

He strode away, the assumption of her *yes* in his carriage.

They kept coming, the ones who needed to talk and the ones who just needed to sit in silence. In the cubby she couldn't quite call "my office," Quinn sat alone for several minutes before she heard Chris McLean bellow her name and realized another day was done. The man hadn't been in her thoughts for hours, but the ache deep inside rose so quickly she knew it had just been waiting for his appearance. *Not happening*, she told herself a little desperately and stood in time to see several heads pop up from their cubicles like turtles from their shells.

She flushed at the unwanted attention. "What's up, boss?"

He seemed oblivious to their audience. "Did you make that phone call?"

He growled like a bear with a thorn in its paw when she shook her head, grabbed her roughly printed "Done" sign, and draped it on the door. "Let's go do that, then, and we'll be off. Amanda Blackstone!" he shouted as though he knew she was listening. "Don't hide. La Trattoria, seven-thirty. Be there." He gripped Quinn's arm and propelled her out in the direction of a smaller tent.

His touch stirred her blood. Ignoring his huff, she shook away his hand. Distance was surely safer. In the western sky, barely visible between tall buildings, reds and pinks colored the end of another day. "What time is it, anyway?"

"Six-thirty. That'll make it about three-thirty your time. Here we are." He didn't touch her again but preceded her into a tent illuminated only by a busy computer screen. "Out, Clancy, DeMello needs the phone."

Clancy, a twenty-ish woman in jeans and the now-familiar volunteer vest, her short purple hair spiked above a smooth, round face, rolled her eyes at Quinn and exited the tent without comment.

Heat traveled up Quinn's neck and colored her cheeks. *DeMello, entertainment for the troops. Where's that invisibility cloak when I need it?* Hands on hips, lips pursed, she turned on McLean. "That was rude."

"What?" He pushed her down at the table and indicated the phone set-up. "There. This line will get you anywhere. I'll wait in the Jeep."

Annoyance vanished. Quinn flashed a grateful smile, slid into Clancy's seat, and picked up the receiver, her stomach suddenly an unruly creature twisting and kinking and threatening to take over. She pushed the anxiety down. *I want to hear his voice, whether he wants to hear from me or not. Leaving didn't cancel out loving.* She waited until her body's protest subsided, then punched in Owen Johnson's numbers and held her breath.

Eight rings later, an unwelcome mechanical voice insulted her ear: "Owen Johnson. Leave a message."

She released her breath with a sob as she visualized Owen's wounded face, the anger that struggled to hide his pain, and remembered his words, "Is that all this was? A good fuck?" She cringed.

"Success?" McLean's voice penetrated the memory. He wasn't waiting at the Jeep after all.

"No one home." Her heart ached and her hand shook as she replaced the receiver in its cradle. If the man had been watching, he withheld comment.

"All right then, let's be off. You can try again later." He stood aside to let her exit. Eyes on the ground, Clancy slid back into the tent.

"Mandy?" Quinn asked him, sure that the other woman had been discouraged from joining them.

"She'll be meeting us there. She's got her own car, and she's picking up a couple of others." His words trailed behind him as he strode off toward the Jeep.

Relieved, Quinn followed. *Just gossip*, she concluded, yet the smoldering glance he threw over his shoulder had her wondering.

As if he knew her thoughts, McLean added, "Safety in numbers, you know." His beard twitched, and she was pretty sure he was laughing.

"Well, all-righty then." Running shaky fingers through her hair, she shoved misgivings aside and scrambled into the Jeep. *Sometimes a dinner is just a dinner.*

CHAPTER 9

B<small>Y HABIT</small>, V<small>IVIAN AND</small> V<small>ICTORIA</small> J<small>OHNSON</small> spent the last hour of most days in their tiny upstairs sitting area. Identical twins, thirty-eight years old, and each single by choice, they had used a small inheritance from a maiden aunt to purchase the run-down house and several ghost-town acres from family friends, turned it into the Wildflower Inn Bed and Breakfast, and planned to live in it forever. They loved the solitude of this home where they had raised Vivian's son and where they entertained the few guests who braved Nevada's wilderness, but love and entertainment didn't pay the bills. Then Quinn DeMello had arrived like Santa in a snowstorm, bringing ideas and enthusiasm and possibility. Together they had created women's retreats with meditation, yoga, scrumptious food, work, and silence, and they had prospered. Now Quinn was gone. Their brother was miserable. They were scared.

There wasn't much pacing space in a room filled with antiques, but Victoria was doing her best. More than a century old, the white frame building creaked with her every step. Vivian helped herself to sherry from a cut-glass decanter, topped off her sister's scotch, and watched in silence. Finally, she couldn't stand it. "Vicky, stop it. You're making me—"

"Crazy. Yeah, I know, but I feel like if I stop moving, things will just fly away." Victoria dropped into a chair beside her sister and gulped her drink. "My god, Viv, what are we going to do?"

Their anxious eyes met. End-of-day shadows and the flickering glow from the wood-burning stove exuded otherworldliness. Neither had seen the hellfire of the Pentagon, but it was on their minds just the same, that and their fears for the inn and for the brother who was clearly deranged.

Vivian threw back her sherry. It wasn't her job to answer questions; she was the intuitive one, the creative one, the one who kept an organic garden and soothed her family with homemade bread and chicken in the pot. When Scott had emerged unscathed from the nation's tragedy, it had seemed that the world had righted itself, but it really hadn't.

"He's fretting himself into a nervous breakdown, isn't he?" She never said anything negative about her sensible older brother, but truth was truth. "I can't quite figure it out. He's always been ... well, you know, just a regular guy."

"I know," Victoria said after some thought. "Quinn said she'd be back, and she's only been gone a few days. He's got some kind of hair up his butt that we don't know about."

"Vic, language."

Victoria laughed. "Sorry, Vivvy, but it's true."

She rose, offered a sherry refill, and raised her eyebrows when Vivian nodded. *Unusual times, unusual measures,* she thought as she filled her sister's glass to the rim, topped up her own drink, and walked to the window to stare into the now complete dark. "We can't fix things for Owen. We don't even know what needs to be fixed. But Vivvy, what are we going to do about *us*?" She turned, knew the worry in her sister's eyes mirrored her own. "The retreat's almost here. All those people are coming and I'm scared. Quinn came up with such good ideas. What if ours tank and they hate us? What are we going to do?"

Vivian had put their fear into words. "How can we do it without Quinn? She's the one with magic."

Steeped in their fear, both sisters were ignoring a simple fact: Quinn may have been the innovator, but they were the hosts, and the retreats had been successful.

Victoria pulled the heavy curtains closed, shutting out the late September draft and the night sky. "We need to get a grip, Vivian. Owen always said we gave Quinn too much credit. Quinn says we can do it; maybe they're both right. No matter—she left us with ideas and a plan. We'll just follow the plan." The smile she directed at her sister was not as bracing as she imagined.

The change of subject had, however, diverted their attention from their troubled brother—at least for the moment.

CHAPTER 10

A t La Trattoria, Mandy introduced the others—two women in their early forties from Arlington and a young man with a ponytail and a full-sleeve tattoo from Auburn, California—and by the time they'd explored each other's reasons for volunteering, their meals arrived and they tucked into food a little tastier than that served in the mess tent.

Face flushed, Quinn parried the good-natured comments about her early-morning entourage. By the time she swallowed the last morsel of tiramisu, her mood had improved.

While the others laughed and talked and got acquainted, McLean worked his way through another rare steak, half a loaf of garlic bread, and a bottle of zinfandel, then wiped his mouth and shoved his chair away from the table. "Catch a ride back with Mandy," he said to Quinn, nodded at the rest, and walked out the door. His Jeep was still parked out front when they left.

"I think he walks to the hotel," Mandy said in response to Quinn's questioning glance.

An hour later, Quinn settled under the familiar trees, nodded at her gathering audience, and assembled her flute.

Dinner's lighthearted camaraderie had brightened her mood, but now, even as her fingers found their places and she worked through the music, troubling questions brewed. Drawing from lifelong discipline, she completed her routine then wiped down the flute and returned the shiny pieces to their blue velvet beds. Her listeners dispersed. The familiar tasks failed to soothe; she wanted a drink.

Denying herself that oblivion, Quinn hurried to Cot Central and threw herself fully clothed onto her bed. *Sleep,* she ordered. *I'll figure it out tomorrow.*

Questions more disturbing than her usual nightmares kept her awake. *Owen doesn't answer his phone. Who can blame him? I'm the one who left. Does he love me? Who knows? McLean dumped me on Mandy—what was that about? And what's wrong with me, throbbing here in the dark for one man and in love with another?*

She didn't want to think about her conflicting emotions: guilt, fear, love, lust. She didn't want to think about the mother who'd died with condemnation on her lips. She didn't want to think about her own bad decisions, a list too long to count. She'd been certain that accepting this volunteer work was the right thing to do—to take charge of her life, expecting nothing, depending on no one—but now, aware of the ache in her belly, she was consumed with doubt. Was this just another runaway event, albeit with a better cover story?

Hours passed before sleep rescued her.

SHE WOKE BEFORE DAWN AND BANNED both Owen Johnson and Chris McLean from her thoughts while she prepared for the day. She dressed then lifted an ornate silver frame from her duffel and considered her daughter's image: Samantha, only three months old when death had stolen her, her legacy a permanent ache in her mother's heart. *Ache and guilt*, Quinn thought, hunching her shoulders as if her mother's stinging words, "She killed her own daughter, you know," still resounded.

A tentmate walked by and looked back. "Quinn, you okay?"

"Yeah, fine." The obligatory lie slipped out easily. With an effort, Quinn straightened her shoulders and stood. Issues for another day, she knew, shaking off the dark memory. She forced a smile and planted a kiss on Samantha's baby face, then replaced the time-worn picture and headed toward the trees.

Each morning brought more—soldiers, volunteers, and, today, the girl named Molly—and Quinn smiled as she led the chant. When it was over and the group had dispersed, Molly remained, peppering Quinn with questions about chanting and meditation until her brother returned and dragged her off. "Thank you, thank you, thank you," billowed in her wake.

Bemused by her elevation to heroine, Quinn cleaned up and scooted into her cubby, thinking about Molly and wishing she'd had better answers. *Next time*, she promised herself, sure that the girl would return.

The day assumed its usual routine as she sat with bruised and fearful hearts, held hands in need of comfort, wiped away tears, and said words that maybe helped. Thoughts of McLean fluttered. Owen remained an ache in her heart. She wondered how long it would last.

"DeMello, front and center." McLean's bellow from outside the tent interrupted the hum of therapeutic conversations.

In her tiny cubicle, Quinn was focusing her whole attention on a very large, very young man in uniform as he stuttered out the words that named his feelings, that painted a picture of scenes too horrible to say aloud, a man who mumbled as though he was embarrassed to need her. When she heard, "DeMello, front and center," her head jerked up. The man beside her went silent. *Damn McLean.* Counseling was about listening, providing safe space for memories, feelings, experiences to be released. It had taken almost an hour to get this kid talking, and now this.

"In ten minutes, Dr. McLean," she said through gritted teeth, hoping she sounded polite but firm.

"Talk. Now!"

Heads popped up, like turtles again.

"Excuse me." She touched the man's arm briefly. "I'm sorry. He wasn't raised well."

That generated a watery smile, and he nodded.

"DeMello." McLean grabbed her arm as she emerged from her cubicle.

Quinn allowed herself to be pulled outside. As the tent door closed behind them, she twisted out of his grasp and turned to face him, hands on her hips and turquoise eyes blazing.

Her words seethed through the humid air. "Do . . . not . . . ever . . . do that again. Especially when I'm with someone. You . . . have . . . to . . . wait." She spaced her words as if speaking to one of poor understanding, and his face reddened.

"But I—"

"But nothing. I'll be out when I'm done and I'll find you then." She opened the door and, aware of the audience, tempered her tone. "Please tell me where I can find you."

"Office. Thirty minutes." He turned and lumbered out of sight.

Huh, that went well. Several minutes passed before her hands stopped shaking and she could return to her client.

Thirty-two minutes later, Quinn still fumed as she stalked toward McLean's office, fanning her anger with a list of his transgressions. He might be the boss, but no fizzling out now. In the past, she would have walked away—*run* away, more precisely—but not this time. *Turning over a new leaf, a new leaf, a new leaf*—she was trembling as she stepped through the door.

CHAPTER 11

Chris McLean looked up.

Half an hour earlier, he had marched back into his office in high dudgeon. A brilliant idea had occurred to him as he'd watched the young ones come away from the trees with smiles previously absent. Whatever she was doing was good stuff. His staff told him people were always trying to find her. Why not kill two birds with one stone and put her on the schedule? An unorthodox idea, it needed her blessing. Pleased with himself, he'd sought her out and had met with his biggest rebuff since day one of his internship. He didn't like it any more now than he had then.

Who the hell does she think she is, anyway?

He had fanned his anger into flame before Quinn stood silhouetted in the midday sun, golden hair just brushing her shoulders, an angel in his doorway—an angel with steel in her voice. "What was *that* about?"

If he'd expected an apology for her earlier flagrant disregard, it didn't seem to be coming. Intrigued and amused, he tamped down his own pique. "What happened to, 'Sorry, I was busy?'"

"I'm not sorry," Quinn snapped, "and you knew I was busy. You may be the big cheese around here, but I don't jump just because you say jump. Send me home if you want to, but while I'm here, if I'm with somebody, I'm with them for as long as it takes." She crossed her arms, shot her hip, and glared at him. "And you'll just have to wait."

Silence and something else shimmered between them. He could see an explanation about therapy hovering on her lips, but she compressed them, tightening her arms instead. He hesitated—nobody challenged him anymore. The glare directed his way interfered with clear thinking.

"Sorry," he said, startled to find himself the one apologizing, "won't happen again." He motioned her into the tent. "Please come in, if you can spare the time." He didn't try to smooth the sarcastic edge. She ignored it. Inside, her hair was just stringy blond, and he wondered where his angel had gone.

"Sure," she agreed, voice and expression suddenly amiable, rapid breathing the only sign of her recent distress.

More than a handful, he thought, distracted by the rapid rise and fall of her breasts and the stirring below his belt. With an effort, he forced his eyes away. "Truce, DeMello?" he offered, hoping she hadn't noticed and trying for the high road.

If she had, she ignored that, too. "Truce, McLean, if you promise no more bellowing."

"Bellow? I don't—"

"Yes, you do, so just promise you won't."

Then she smiled, and the Irish in him couldn't resist. "I surrender." He held up both hands. "No more bellowing." Then he accepted her handshake.

"Good." He noticed her eyes linger on their joined hands for a long moment before she tugged herself free and perched on the edge of the folding chair, lips pursed, hands loose in her lap, just like the prim young teacher he'd loved with all his third-grade heart. "So what did you want to see me about?"

I don't get this woman, he thought, nonplussed at her abrupt change, *but I want to kiss her.* Reminding himself that he didn't like thin-lipped women, remembering his father's long-ago injunction about their stingy dispositions, didn't help. Nothing stingy about this woman—just lips waiting to soften under his own. She leaned forward, her breasts straining at the tank top visible under a man's blue shirt, and his father's warnings disappeared. He clenched his fists to keep himself in place as he returned his gaze to her face.

QUINN WATCHED EMOTIONS RIPPLE THROUGH HIS beard—indignation, annoyance, something she couldn't recognize—none of the usual signs of sexual interest. *Just a cranky old man who's working too hard and not getting his way.* She ignored the stirring in her belly, softened to him even as his eyes riveted on her face.

"Dr. McLean," she repeated, "what *did* you want me for?"

He took a big breath and then another before he settled back in his chair and told her.

"They tell me you've got quite a following."

In three days? I don't think so. She wanted to correct him, but, mindful of his status and her recent win, she remained silent.

"I'd like you to continue your morning thing."

"Meditation," she offered.

"Meditation, whatever, but let me post it on the board." He held up his hand, and she stifled an automatic protest. "The staff's hard-pressed to answer questions when they don't know anything. And," he concluded, "a lot of folks are lookin' to join you."

What could she say? He was her boss after all. And they *were* coming. "Yeah, I guess it's okay, but it's just a little chant."

"Whatever." He waved her silent. "They seem to get something out of it, so we should just as well make use of it. What's a good time?"

She relented. "How about six?"

"Where?"

She hated to give up her solitude, not that she'd had much lately, but she already knew the only quiet location. "The trees?"

"The trees it is. They'll appreciate it, having a time and all, so they don't have to wonder." He rose, having gotten what he wanted. Or had he?

"Dinner tonight?"

She considered his motives and hers. The evening stretched long ahead, her last attempt to reach Owen a disaster she wanted to blot out. A little company wouldn't hurt. Ignoring the warning tingle, she was ready to say yes when she noticed the twitching beard. An old TV quote flashed in her mind: *"Danger, Will Robinson! Danger!"* She choked on a laugh. "I think I'll pass, McLean. But thanks."

He looked as though he might protest, then shrugged and stepped aside. She felt his eyes follow her as she walked out the door and resisted the urge to look back.

CHAPTER 12

Vivian Johnson, a pot of tea at her feet and a pink wool blanket draped over her shoulders to ward off the afternoon chill, was studying the final details for the upcoming retreat when her sister, chores complete, joined her on the inn's wide front porch. She smiled as Victoria chanted the words of their new mantra—"Quinn thinks we can; Quinn thinks we can"—and scraped goose poop off her boots before she poured herself a cup of lukewarm tea. Vivian had just scooted over to make room on the swing when Owen's silver Audi squealed to a halt.

Ignoring the corgis that had scurried over to investigate, Owen pushed open the gate and strode up the walk. Hands on his hips, he glared at his sisters. "Okay, girls, I've waited and it's not working. What next?"

Now, the women shared the pink blanket and the porch swing and watched their brother pace. Hair rumpled, eyes red from lack of sleep, he was hardly the self-contained man they were used to.

Worry crinkled Vivian's brow. "Nothing from Quinn yet?"

"One missed call. One in Reno, too. Both blocked numbers. And Karle said someone called while she was at my house this morning but hung up when she answered." He held out his hand to forestall comment. "I know, I know, she shouldn't have answered, but it was just reflex, she said—you know."

Vivian and Victoria exchanged a twin glance. They knew that Owen's landlady and former lover, Karle Moran, intended to have Owen's ring on her left hand. Her plan had been disrupted with the advent of Quinn DeMello, but neither sister believed it had disappeared.

"Karle was at your house, Owen?" With an effort, Vivian kept the screech out of her voice.

"Yes, Viv, Karle was at my house." Impatient voice. Impatient fingers raked his hair. "I know you two don't like her, but for God's sake, cut her some slack. She was only trying to help, and besides, she just got dumped, too, remember?"

When they said nothing, he continued. "She dropped off some stuff from the Reno office. My bad mood's no get-out-of-jail-free card for my clients."

His snarky tone didn't engender sympathy, but aware of the September-October deadlines every accountant faced, they did sympathize—a little. This current mood didn't bode well for clear thinking.

In a terse voice, Owen explained his business partner's plan to keep things moving. "Pat saw Karle yesterday at Rotary. When she offered to be our office mule, he couldn't say yes fast enough. I guess it was easier than FedEx or trying to get me back to Reno." His wry smile didn't reach his misery-darkened eyes. "Besides, why wouldn't she just leave me a message?"

Why not, indeed, the sisters' glance echoed.

Their silence apparently demanded further explanation.

"Anyway, Karle started to fix lunch while I went to the post off—" His thick brows drew together in a look of surprise as he broke off midsentence. "You don't think ...? No, there's nothing between me and Karle anymore."

Victoria said mildly, "Maybe *we* know that, brother dear, but does Quinn?"

CHAPTER 13

N THE MESS TENT, QUINN SAT as far from the noisy dinner crowd as possible, eyes down to discourage conversation.

Earlier in the day, before her toe-to-toe with her boss, she had slipped into the communication tent and for the third time dialed the familiar number. This time a tiny voice had answered. "Hello, Owen Johnson's residence."

Memory had produced an instant and unwelcome visual: Karle Moran, Owen's Reno landlady and love interest—*past? present?*—a red-headed beauty still in love with him. Why was she answering his home phone?

"Hello, hello?" Karle's well-modulated attorney voice had questioned Quinn's silence. "Is anyone there?"

Resisting the urge to throw it across the room, Quinn had set the receiver gently back in its cradle. "Answering machine. I'll try again later," she'd muttered to Clancy and ducked away from the curiosity in the young woman's eyes.

Work and the confrontation with McLean had distracted her. Now it flooded back, and she was filled with longing for the unlikely accountant who carried a gun and reminded her of her movie hero, Harrison Ford.

Head down, arms wrapped around herself in a tight hug, she cradled the ache, and her thoughts flew like caged birds:

What can you expect? You walked away from him, didn't you?

But he never said he loved me, never asked me to stay.

Right, but you didn't have to hand-deliver him.

And then there was McLean's attention and his odd plans, the physical attraction she couldn't ignore, her screaming need for the solace tequila offered. She wanted to put her hands over her ears and scream, *Shut up! Shut the fuck up!*

She dashed away the one tear daring to sneak down her cheek. *Enough already.* In the past, with the help of Jose Cuervo and a willing sexual partner, she had corralled unwanted thoughts, feelings, and memories into neat boxes in her mind. Tonight, no Jose, no man, no boxes. *"I'm at my wit's end," the twins would say,* Quinn thought and snorted at her own absurdity. Before more tears could flow, she rose from the table and bussed her untouched dinner tray. What to do?

A few people were milling around, as though reluctant to return to their duties, when she exited the tent and started toward the trees. She hoped no one could read misery in her body language, but an interruption of her thoughts would be nice. A few nods followed her, but no one spoke, and Quinn reached her destination alone.

With a huff, she dropped to the ground. Behind her, workmen's clamor provided a reminder of destruction, loss, and tragedy. She flipped open the flute case: *When all else fails, practice.* In the glare of the work lights, the shiny pieces winked sadly as though they knew her heart wasn't in it. With a whispered apology, she assembled them and readied herself. *Tomorrow I'll call home—at least Viv and Vic will be happy to hear from me. And I can find out about the retreat, reassure them. I just won't ask about Owen.*

Decision made, she emptied her mind. Her fingers caressed the flute, and she brought it to her mouth. As the clear, crisp tones emerged, bodies settled silently onto the grass around her, and, for the first time in days, she soared.

Minutes later, she felt a zing that tumbled her back to earth as Chris McLean stepped into view, his thick form backlit and unmistakable. Her fingers stuttered on the keys. *Damn, what's HE doing here?*

Under lowered lids, she watched the man prop himself against a tree, cross his arms, and go still. His face was in shadow, but she could feel his penetrating blue gaze. Heat rose inside, swept upward across her chest, her neck, her cheeks. She closed her eyes. *Make him go away,* she prayed, wishing she were playing anything but "Annie's Song."

The song ended. She paused. He didn't leave.

Another, she thought. *Maybe "Jaws"?* At that notion, an inner chuckle steadied her and she raised the flute. One breath then her rebellious fingers betrayed her, and her audience swayed gently with "Sweet Caroline."

Resigned, she focused her breathing and forced her thoughts to Owen: high, sharp cheekbones; nose slightly curved, finely drawn between eyes dark as a midnight pool; impatient mouth; demanding fingers. She shivered as her own fingers coaxed forth the melody. One piece flowed into another, Quinn and her listeners lost in music, memory . . . surcease, until the last notes hung in the air like twinkling dust motes then one by one blinked out.

Her audience departed, and Quinn hummed under her breath as she nestled the last silver piece in its velvet bed. When she heard footsteps, she stilled. Chris McLean crouched beside her.

"Nice," he said.

She thought he meant the music, bobbed her head in thanks, then glanced up and realized he meant her, too. Heat again flooded her breasts and rose up her chest and neck to color her cheeks. Aflame, she hated that he saw and started to pull back. He caught her arm.

"What?" She stared at his offending hand, her tone flat.

He released her. "Come out and have a drink with me."

"No, thank you, I don't drink."

"Coffee?"

The case clicked shut. Cross-legged on the grass, vulnerable, she folded her arms across her chest. "What do you want, McLean?"

"This." He slid his big hand beneath her hair, cupping the back of her head, and brought her toward him. "This," he breathed as his lips covered hers.

She didn't resist. Instead, her mouth opened to his, and she savored the full-body surge as her own wanting, held in check for days, engulfed her. She hadn't looked for this, but, now offered, it was impossible to refuse. She rose on her knees to meet him.

His mouth, gentle at first, plundered. His arm came around her, and she let him draw her closer, curve her to his roundness. Her arms twined around his neck, and she ground against him as desire spiked, stole thought and good intentions and left only heat and the pounding of her heart. His tongue tickled hers, then plunged—exploring, tasting, possessing—and the first delicious shiver took her.

Stunned and breathless, she dropped her arms and pulled back.

Breathing hard, McLean tightened the hand that now cupped her bottom and held her captive. She didn't try to escape, just leaned her forehead against his and gasped for air, then managed a quivery laugh. "'Heartbreak Harry.' You are good."

He sat back on his heels, leaving a cool space between their heaving bodies. "Heartbreak Harry?" His brow furrowed and his eyes darkened with realization. "Mandy?"

Quinn didn't blink. "Uh-huh. 'A girl in every disaster,'" she repeated Amanda's words, using air quotes for emphasis, "but not this girl." Blazing cheeks belied the words. Again, she hoped he didn't notice. Still on her knees, she straightened her back, glared, and wondered why she lingered.

His gaze didn't waver. "Boyfriend?"

She nodded yes.

"The one who's never home?"

Surprised, she cocked a questioning eyebrow.

"Mandy's not the only one who talks," McLean said.

PANTING AND WHEEZING AS THOUGH HE'D just gone ten rounds with Muhammad Ali, Chris McLean scowled when Quinn pulled away and called him Heartbreak Harry. He only sought out women who, like himself, just wanted a bit of fun. He hadn't meant to touch this one, lustful stirrings or no, but these impromptu concerts had been the main topic of camp conversation—"Who is she? What's it all about? Can I go?" Pretty sure the *she* in question was his newest recruit, he'd returned from a solitary dinner to check it out. When "Annie's Song" had risen in the air, he'd followed the love song.

The lights that facilitated the round-the-clock retrieval and repair cast the scene into flickering unreality. He shivered and the hairs on his arms stood like soldiers at attention: "Piloerection—the involuntary bristling of hairs in response to cold, shock, or other conditions"—the definition remembered from *Stedman's Medical Dictionary*, his dog-eared copy tucked away in his den, and a very distant past. He'd shaken away memory—life had been simpler then—contemplated those "other conditions" with a grin, and watched the skinny blonde as she caressed the flute, watched as a breath like a whisper drew out the melody, watched the deep inhalation that filled her lungs and strained the dark knit stretched across her breasts. The black jacket she'd worn like a uniform since her arrival had lain beside her on the grass. He'd noted the hollow at her collar-bone, the ribs stark in contrast to the generous breasts, the fine muscles that danced in her bare forearms as her fingers moved over the keys, and he'd imagined those fingers on his skin.

I don't like tall, thin, mouthy women, he'd reminded himself, the thought of his tall, thin, long-estranged wife in Connecticut briefly crossing his mind, but he didn't turn away. Instead, he'd crossed the now-empty space to say thanks. Softened by the music, he'd knelt in front of her, and she'd raised her eyes: *Damn those eyes, better men than me couldn't resist.*

At least that's what he told himself now as he ignored the quickening of danger and lust, settled against a tree, and patted the grass at his hip. "So tell me about him," he said.

"Not a prayer," Quinn said, the corners of her mouth curving upward. Still breathless, she knelt where he had released her.

He removed a silver flask from an inside pocket, waved it toward her, and, when she refused, unscrewed the lid and took a long swig. The familiar whisky bite steadied his breathing, quieted his heart.

"You drink too much, you know," she said.

"And you don't drink enough, smart-mouth woman," he retorted. When she just shook her head, he drank again, wiped his mouth on the back of his hand, and returned the flask to his pocket. "Why not?"

She turned her face away and didn't answer.

He couldn't see her eyes, but in this instant he knew what was there—he'd seen it in his own eyes the times when he'd quit, the times he'd longed for oblivion and denied himself. Finally, he'd stopped trying. Now, he was a drinker with rules—a little bit every day, none in surgery weeks, an occasional runner carefully scheduled to affect no one but himself. He knew there were names for old drunks like him—the most recent he'd heard being *functional alcoholic*—but the only danger he courted was his own.

"Ah, me darlin'," he crooned in the Irish he'd heard at his mother's knee and put on for special occasions, "if ye won't talk about him and ye won't drink wi' me, then just come over here and tell me a wee story instead." He patted the ground again, heartened that she hadn't picked up and left when he'd released her from the embrace that had overwhelmed them both.

They faced each other. He considered another swig of whisky before she sent him a cheeky grin.

"No more grab ass?"

Challenge. His eyes met hers, still smoldering from their kiss, and all of a sudden in this mangy little glen, with its backdrop of blazing lights and construction racket and tragedy, all things seemed possible. A flicker of something barely remembered held him silent.

"No more grab ass?" She was laughing at him now.

Spell broken, his own laugh rumbled. "Not tonight. I promise." He wriggled his eyebrows, Groucho-style, and leered.

She chuckled. "A wee story," she mimicked. "Just remember, *you* asked." She released a sigh so soft he almost missed it and settled in against him. "I was born in a blizzard in a little town in Nevada, to a father who loved me and a mother who did not." As she spoke, her head nestled into the soft notch of his shoulder, and he held her close.

CHAPTER 14

ALL TREES WITH LEAVES JUST BEGINNING to turn lined the old Reno streets. In the dusk, house lights flicked on and illuminated homey scenes. An orange tabby scooted across the street and disappeared under a porch. Gripping the wheel of his Audi, Owen Johnson wound through the darkening neighborhood without appreciation for the autumnal beauty or the views of family life and not at all concerned about the cat's safety. Instead, his sisters' parting words—"*We* know you're not with Karle, but does Quinn?"—circled like vultures and suggested the impossible: that Karle wanted him back, that Karle would sabotage his relationship with Quinn, that Quinn would be dumb enough to fall for it, that he could be as dumb as he apparently was. Jaw clenched, emotions in overdrive, he stoked his anger.

Years ago, as a fledgling accountant, he'd worked for her father. Karle had been around, vivacious and pretty and wrapped up in her college football quarterback. He'd been earnest, ambitious, and starry-eyed in love with his schoolteacher fiancée. Twelve years later, emerging from the dregs of divorce, he'd let mutual friends and a Fourth of July party at Tahoe reintroduce them. The very pretty woman and a bottle or two of very good wine had gone a long way toward soothing his wounded soul.

When Karle suggested he take over her newly renovated basement apartment as a favor to them both, he couldn't move in fast enough. His home and his family were in Winnemucca, but more than half of his clients were in Reno, and this home away from home had been heaven sent. When she'd slid into his bed, warm and willing, his heart—broken by stillbirths and infidelity and loss—had rejoiced.

Two years later, it was over.

"I can't love," he'd told her, unwilling to explore the reasons that his lust had not blossomed into love.

"We can still be friends," she'd replied.

Like the Godfather's deals, Owen thought now, *strings attached.*

Light shone through the uncovered windows, and he knew Karle was home. He parked at the curb, strode up the walk, and opened the door without knocking.

A cheerful blaze crackled in the river rock fireplace he'd helped build. Karle sat opposite, curled up on her plush green sofa, legs tucked beneath her, when Owen stomped into the house. The door slammed. She looked up, her hair cascading like a fiery waterfall, and her mouth formed a perfect O of surprise. "Owen, I didn't expect you."

He stood in her living room, striving for composure. "So it was her?" A senseless question. He couldn't find the right words for his anger.

Long dark lashes shielded Karle's green eyes. She patted the seat beside her. "Owen, honey, I didn't know it was her. Still don't. I just picked up your phone without even thinking. No one answered."

"You shouldn't have…" *You shouldn't have been in my house,* he thought as his voice trailed off. In her amused presence, he felt foolish, an unfamiliar sensation he didn't like. Berating her had seemed reasonable. Now, in this beautifully appointed room he knew as well as his own, he wasn't so sure.

"Wen," she used his sisters' baby name lightly, affectionately, and he was suddenly grateful for her presence. "Wennie, I'm so sorry. I just didn't—"

"Think. I know." His voice softened, and he sank onto the sofa at her feet. "But you shouldn't have—"

"Answered." As she completed his sentence, her foot kneaded his thigh. "You're right. I'm so sorry. I won't ever do it again."

Silence. Idly, his hand played with the little foot now ensconced in his lap, his anger ebbing away as the room's warmth worked its magic. An ember popped in the dying fire and Karle gasped. Owen looked up to see her hands flutter to her mouth.

"Oh, Wen, do you think she thought that I…that we…?" Her eyes went wide.

"Maybe." He considered the question, hers and his sisters' before her. "Maybe."

"Oh no!" Her voice quavered and tears threatened.

Owen reached for her hand. "Not your fault, Karle. It's all my fault." He groaned. "My fault. I never told her I love her."

He appreciated the gleam of sympathy in the redhead's eyes.

CHAPTER 15

I n Winnemucca the following evening, Victoria Johnson wandered into the living room of Harold Anderson's small duplex. The windows stood open, and the scent of fall surrounded her. She had just finished one of the best meals of her life—prime rib, pink and juicy; baked potatoes, flaky and full of butter; sliced tomatoes that still tasted of outdoors—all perfectly prepared by her sister's beanpole of a boyfriend. In his kitchen, Harold and Vivian laughed as they put away leftovers and cleared the table.

The day before, her brother had gone off to confront Karle. This morning, Quinn had called. *All good,* Victoria thought, *so what's twisting my guts?*

She plopped into a faux leather recliner and immediately recognized her mistake as the chair, designed for a much larger person, engulfed her. She was struggling to escape when Harold walked into the room carrying a Drambuie bottle and three glasses.

He stifled a laugh. "Trapped? Sorry, I should have warned you—it's a woman eater."

He set the bottle and glasses on the coffee table and offered his hand. She allowed herself to be extricated and resettled into a more practical chair. Vivian snuggled into the corner of the threadbare plaid couch.

As Harold filled the small, flower-painted glasses, Victoria eyed her twin. Vivian was supposed to be the intuitive one, but she didn't seem fazed by their brother's craziness or Quinn's call earlier that day. "Please tell me again what Quinn said." She'd already heard every word, but maybe repetition would help. "None of this makes sense."

Harold raised a questioning eyebrow as he handed Victoria her drink. He didn't seemed surprised when Victoria murmured thanks but kept her attention on her twin.

Vivian took her time, accepted her own glass, and sipped while Harold arranged his six-foot-plus frame beside her on the couch. When he was situated, she said to him, "I told Vicky about Quinn's call and she doesn't like it."

Victoria snorted but didn't contradict her, and Harold's other eyebrow rose.

Vivian took another sip of her drink before she went on. "Quinn was relieved that Scott was alive, of course, since we all still thought he was dead when she left, but now she's mad at him for not calling sooner." Irritation colored her words. "Harold, you don't know her so well, but she's kind of—"

He opened his mouth to reply.

"Sassy," Victoria interrupted, completing her sister's sentence in their usual twin way.

Vivian threw a questioning glance at the man beside her and laid her hand over his on the sofa. A smile playing on his lips, Harold linked their fingers and seemed content to let Victoria speak.

Victoria glanced at the clasped hands and imagined Harold's thoughts: *If you're determined to marry a twin, there are things you just put up with.* It was disconcerting to see the sister who hadn't looked at a man since her son was born hand in hand with this tall, scrawny man who looked like he wanted to eat her sister up. She ignored the ripple of discomfort. "So she wasn't happy with our boy?"

"Nope. Said, 'About time. If he was where he was supposed to be, it wouldn't have happened.'"

"Did she ask about—"

"Owen? Not a word. I was surprised, but we just talked a few minutes. She says there's only one line they can use and she can't hog it."

"Good excuse. Did you tell her about Karle?"

Harold looked up from his contemplation of Vivian's fingers. "Karle?"

The women stared, so used to their running dialogue that they'd forgotten he was listening. Vivian laughed and squeezed his hand. "Sorry, thought I'd told you about her. Karle Moran, Owen's Reno landlady. Teeny tiny, gorgeous, masses of red hair, a real manipulative—"

"Bitch." Victoria's tone left no doubt as to her feelings. "We thought they were going to get married and then it was all off. Oh, happy day! Owen thinks we're too hard on her, even gave us a lecture the other day, but there's no excuse for acting like she's better than us poor mortals."

She waited for Vivian's nod of agreement before continuing. "Not that we don't worry about him and Quinn, but Karle would be disaster with a capital D." Having taken her bad mood out on the absent Karle, Victoria savored a generous swallow of her Drambuie and turned her attention back to Vivian. "But answer my question; did you tell Quinn?"

"Tell Quinn what?" Howard asked.

Vivian explained the Karle phone-answering debacle before she answered Victoria's question. "No, I didn't tell her about Karle. She asked about the retreat." Heaving a discouraged sigh, Vivian interrupted herself. "Harold, Quinn knows we're afraid we can't do a retreat without her."

Harold squeezed her hand and made encouraging noises.

She flashed a smile. "Thanks, you're right. We can, of course, but it just won't be the same, and that's what I told her. Then I asked how she was, and she said it was rewarding to be able to help." She turned again to Harold. "You don't know her very well, but she's always doing something nice, and she never gives herself any credit."

"Uh-huh, it's like she has low self-esteem embedded in her genes...or her psyche...or someplace." Victoria made a face. "Who wouldn't, with a mother like Mary?"

Vivian nodded vigorously. The twins had been Mary DeMello's hospice caregivers. "Vicky's right. The mom was nice as pie to us, but the way she treated Quinn...you'd never believe a mother could act like that." She shuddered.

In unison, Victoria and Harold said, "What else?"

Vivian grinned, not averse to being the center of attention. "Not much more—weather's hot and muggy, bed's hard, food's okay—but then she described the circus tent they were sleeping in and made me laugh, and before I could ask any questions, she hung up. You know—"

"How she is. I do. Queen of secrets."

"Are you going to tell?"

"Already did."

"What'd he say?"

"It was odd, Vicky," Vivian said. "I'm not sure what I expected. He was quiet so long I thought we'd been disconnected—you know how cell phones can be—and then he just said thanks and hung up. He did mention he'd talked to Karle and that everything was okay." She looked at her sister, then at Harold. "You're a man, Harold, what do you make of that?"

CHAPTER 16

OWEN JOHNSON SAT BEHIND HIS DESK, the afternoon sun bright on the Reno skyline behind him. His fingers drummed on the desk's polished surface. The phone was jammed against his ear as though getting closer would ensure the right answer. It wasn't working.

Georgia Pryor, his favorite travel agent, came back on the line. "You're not going to like this, Owen, but what you've got is the best I can do. Late afternoon departure, several stops along the way. Get into Washington the next day. Nothing earlier."

Voice tight to keep from shouting, Owen asked, "Are you sure?"

She repeated the familiar story: no regular flights yet, anything flying already full, nothing more to do.

He sagged in his chair. "Thanks, Georgia, I know you tried. You've got my number. You'll call if anything opens up? Thanks again." He ended the call and barely resisted the urge to hurl his new mobile phone against the wall. "Damn." He wanted to leave right now, but he was stuck with the reservations he already had. He would fly to Washington, DC, on September twenty-second. He could only hope that was soon enough.

Like most Americans, he'd spent hour after hour in front of the television, frustrated with the replays of the crumbling towers and the lack of information about the Pentagon. He wanted to see where Quinn was, know what she was doing. The new president oozed reassurance and Owen felt pride, even if he hadn't voted for the man. Now, if he could just get a few more planes in the air.

I'll get there, he reassured himself. *I'll get there and it'll all be good.* Closing his eyes, Owen pushed back in his chair and envisioned the scene: himself striding toward Quinn, purpose in his gait, maybe the Washington Monument in the background, her marvelous eyes lighting up when she saw him, then . . .

Then what? He slumped. He had no idea. *I just want to hold her. No, I just want to bring her home.*

Relief had flooded him when Vivian told him she'd called—relief and a pain in his heart at not hearing her voice himself. No more hang-ups on his phone—he was afraid to analyze that. Too bad Karle had answered; it was too easy to misunderstand.

"Karle was so contrite, she wouldn't do it again," he'd told his sister. He knew he'd screwed up and didn't need her implied and unfamiliar criticism. He hadn't mentioned how welcome Karle's warmth and understanding had been. She had really been sorry, snuggled against him as though she'd known he needed comfort, and then served him macaroni and cheese like his mother had when his world had gone wrong. They'd sat up talking until very late, finished the bottle of wine she'd been keeping just in case, and they'd parted at his bedroom door with only a long hug and a comforting kiss. It had felt wonderful to let some of the tension drop away, and he'd slept well for the first time since Quinn's departure. Best of all, Karle's input had helped him figure things out.

Now he stood looking over the rooftops. There were no remnants of Quinn here and it was easier to think about her—the chuckle that always drew his smile, the eyes that met his fearlessly, the body fiercely willing under his own—here where she had never been, and he wondered why he'd kept her out. *I love her and I didn't let her into my life.* His gut clenched at the thought. Resolutely, he turned back to the pile of work on his desk. Lots to do but, thanks to Karle, he had a plan. He'd go get Quinn, and he'd bring her home where she belonged.

CHAPTER 17

AWN JUST PINKED THE EASTERN SKY as McLean, from his vantage point in the trees, watched Quinn lead the young ones through a series of chants that soothed even him—soothed, but didn't slake the yearning. A more introspective man might have wondered about the yearning, but McLean just reveled in the lusty rise. Filled with impatience, he waited for the others to gather their things and leave. He'd waited a whole five days.

The evening in the trees had shaken him. Propped against a trunk, the taste of her mouth still fresh on his lips, he had wrapped Quinn in his arms and listened as the night had grown old and his butt numb and she had woven her *wee story* for his entertainment. He'd known he was meant to laugh at her tales of a jack-of-all-trades father and a cold and beautiful mother and sisters whose names all began with the letter C, but it didn't require a psychiatrist to diagnose the mother's narcissism, and only a brute could miss the pain in Quinn's voice.

He wasn't a brute, and he couldn't fathom parents who so neglected their children. His own mother had been large of heart and form, comforting her children against an ample bosom and thumping them on the head with her ever-present thimble when discipline was in order. His father was small of stature, towered over by his three sons; he was a man who quoted poetry at the dinner table and governed his family with praise and laughter and an occasional trip to the woodshed.

So when Quinn had teared up, he'd wiped her eyes with his own handkerchief and imagined strangling her parents. Then he'd walked her back to the tent and vowed to stay far, far away.

That resolution had lasted five days.

He'd kept himself very busy elsewhere, but now he was eager to approach. *She'll like this*, he thought, almost rubbing his hands in glee and refusing to examine why it mattered. As he stepped toward her, laughter threatened at the wary look in her eyes. *This will be an offer she can't refuse.*

Quinn rose from her now-accustomed spot in the secluded copse and watched McLean approach. Her acolytes were gone. They were alone. Neglect and anger and other feelings she didn't want to examine jostled for pride of place as he closed the gap between them.

Five days—not that I'm counting.

At breakfast yesterday, Quinn, pleased by the burgeoning friendship with Mandy, had been talking and laughing when Mandy had said, "Haven't seen McLean lately. What's up?"

Her defenses down, Quinn had said, "He kissed me and then I cried all over his shoulder, and I guess he's on to new pastures," then covered the O of her mouth with both hands, aghast at her own disclosure. Amanda, almost as surprised as Quinn, had giggled, and they'd changed the subject.

I guess I was counting, Quinn thought now as her busy hands folded and smoothed the sitting blanket and her cheeks flamed in remembrance. *Where has he been? What was he doing? Why was he avoiding me?* Eyes on the ground, blanket now clutched like a shield, she waited.

McLean stopped an arm's length away and nodded at the red cowboy boots standing empty beside her. "Time off, DeMello," he said as though they had parted just yesterday. "Let's see if those boots are good for something besides decoration."

"Riding? Horses?" Excitement vaulted over jumbled feelings.

"Yep, horses, and yes, they even come large enough for me." The rumble that passed for a laugh issued forth and she chuckled—so clearly had he anticipated her thought. Besides, like the Godfather, he'd made her an offer she couldn't refuse.

"Where?"

"There's a stable about twenty miles from here. Horses in need of exercise. The owner says nobody's leaving home these days. She'll be glad to see us."

Quinn believed him. Everyone seemed glad to see this bear of a man who made you feel like you were the only person in the world. Chagrined, she knew she'd fallen prey to his charisma the night he'd kissed her—why else would she have opened her life history to his scrutiny?—and she'd found comfort in the big arms that had wrapped her close as she'd cried.

Girly tears, for God's sake, she'd thought later, embarrassed and exposed and determined to rebuff any further intimacies. She'd had no chance; he wasn't around. Now she just grinned at him. He was back and all she could be was happy. "I'd like to ride," she said. "When?"

THE CHESTNUT GELDING HEAVED UNDER HER and responded to the tightening of her knees with greater speed. The trail they galloped wound through forests of orange and red and green, as wild as the back country of Nevada. The wind snarled her hair and cooled her neck, and, for the first time since she'd arrived in this strange new land, Quinn felt at home.

The stable's owner, Clarice Kennedy, a rangy woman with a tidy gray ponytail whose seventy-plus years showed attractively in her smiling face, had taken one look at Quinn's boots and, like a miracle worker, unearthed a western saddle. She was, as McLean had surmised, happy that the horses in her care would get real exercise.

McLean, mounted on the largest horse Quinn had ever seen, surged past her. "Race you," he called over his shoulder. Her horse didn't need encouragement. All four were sweating when they thundered into the stable yard.

"That was fun," she gasped as she dismounted, free for the moment of the images of Owen and Karle that had taken up residence in her imagination. Clarice's yard boy took the reins and led the sweaty horses away.

"Lunch and back to work." McLean held out his hand, and, without hesitation, she took it.

DAYS SEEMED MEASURED BY SUNRISE AND sunset, time in between unmarked by minutes and hours. Through the door, Quinn saw wisps of pink as she shook hands with her last client. *Must be quitting time.* Sore all over from the morning's ride, she stood and stretched, tingling a little as she considered what the night might offer.

"DeMello." The now-familiar shout interrupted her musings. "DeMello, front and center."

"Hold your horses, McLean, I'm coming." Grinning, she rubbed tired eyes and looked out toward the darkening sky.

Owen Johnson stood in the doorway.

Slack with surprise, Quinn stared and for a moment thought she might faint. "Owen?"

She looked at him, not believing her eyes, then at McLean, framed in the doorway behind him, then back at Owen, who had not disappeared in the second her eyes had strayed. "Owen?"

He took a step toward her, held out a tentative hand.

Quinn closed the space between them in a flying leap, and his arms closed around her. Over Owen's shoulder, she saw McLean's eyes darken just before he turned and strode away. Then only sensation, no room for thought, as her arms wrapped around her man and she fit her body to his. Through his leather jacket, she could feel his heart pounding against her own.

Owen held her so long without speaking that she squirmed. "Owen, I can't breathe." He loosened a fraction, and she looked him in the eye. "What are you doing here?"

He shrugged. "You're here. And I forgot something when you left."

"Forgot something? What?"

Owen held her gaze. "I forgot to tell you that I love you." Without waiting for a response, he claimed her lips.

CHAPTER 18

I love you. I love you.

Breathless, senseless, Owen possessed her mouth, taking the kiss deeper until she returned fire with fire, until she went soft in his arms. Only Quinn, only her mouth, her breath, her body.

Finally, flushed and panting, she yanked away, looked back at the tent. "Not here," she choked out and stalked off.

Lips suddenly bereft, Owen took a minute to reorient, then strode after her and grabbed her arm. *Rough, too rough,* but he was afraid—he'd seen something troubling in her backward glance. She stiffened. Instantly, he released her, using the offending hand to indicate a car parked next to a green Jeep and caught her mocking glance—a rental Audi, for God's sake?—before she climbed in and buckled up. He got behind the wheel, backed out, and maneuvered the car toward the freeway. Throbbing with want, need, fear, he said nothing. Neither did she, but when he reached for her hand, she didn't refuse, just squeezed his tight and held on, and he hoped.

His flight had touched down several times, dispersing and collecting passengers as he'd tried to sleep and failed. It had been late afternoon when he'd arrived at Reagan International, and he'd come straight from the airport, pausing only to leave his bags in the luxury hotel chosen simply for its proximity to the Pentagon. It had taken some ingenuity to bypass the security at the site, finally acquiring an escort from the rescue coordinator, a large man who introduced himself as Chris McLean and escorted him personally to the big tent, and to Quinn.

Now at the hotel, she waited, still silent, while he fumbled with the lock and opened the door. Barely inside the room, he fought her jeans to her knees; she jerked his zipper down. Arms and legs entangled, they slid to the floor. Lost, mindless, he took her hard, her voice urging him on as he poured himself into her. Sated, he slumped, and they sat forehead to forehead, panting and grinning until he scooped her up and dumped her onto the king-sized bed.

By the time they finished undressing, he was ready again. This time he loved her slowly, mouth and hands, lips and tongue holding her at the brink until she begged for release. Only then did he slide inside her, and only when he felt the rhythmic squeeze of her pleasure did he let himself go. After, neither moved for a very long time.

Just as he thought she'd drifted off, she poked his ribs. "Off, you're squishing me."

Her voice held humor, but other things, too. He knew she had questions; he wasn't sure he had answers she would accept. Regretfully, he peeled his body from hers, left safety behind.

Like a goddess, glistening with the sheen of sex, Quinn propped herself up against the mountain of pillows. He could see the heart he had given her nestling between her breasts as she turned on the bedside light and looked around: richly polished furniture in the colonial style surrounding the bed, Champagne bottle chilling in an ice bucket on a side table, smooth white sheets pooling at her feet—evidence of his intention to seduce everywhere. She reached down, pulled a sheet up over her body, and turned her gaze to him.

"What's this all about, Owen?" Her no-nonsense tone was at odds with the hand that riffled his hair. "Don't get me wrong, I'm not complaining, but what *are* you doing here?"

He raised himself on his elbows, thought about all he wanted to say, then settled on simplicity. "Ahh, Quinn, after I got over being mad, I missed you. And after I got over being dumb, I realized I'd never told you how I feel."

She stiffened and pulled the sheet tighter. The dark of night grew between them as she waved her hand at the rumpled bedding, evidence of their recent encounter. "This doesn't change anything, you know. I still have issues you can't rescue me from, even if you want to . . . and I don't want you to try."

Taking her hesitation as a good sign, Owen slid his hand under the sheet and claimed one ripe breast. He knew she was wrong. He could rescue her and he meant to, but right now wasn't the time to argue. With a gentle thumb, he circled her nipple until it responded, and he smiled when she moaned and arched toward his hand.

"Damn you, Owen, this doesn't solve a thing," she muttered, but her hands moved to find him, and for a moment he was safe again.

It was full dark when Quinn and Owen stepped from the building, the moon hidden behind clouds. The wind had risen and the promise of rain filled the air. Quinn shivered. "I've got to get back."

Owen wrapped his arm around her shoulders. "Your boss said you could have the night off."

She jerked away. "What? The two of you deciding my schedule now?"

"Easy," he soothed, hiding a smile at her pissed-off tone and tucking her back under his arm. "When he was escorting me through the Fort Knox-style security, he just said to tell you he'd post a notice that you had the night off, and you could take it if you wanted. Seems like an all right guy with a big job."

"McLean? Yeah, he's all right." She pushed her hair back and held her face up to the wind. "Feels like a storm coming in. Let's find food before we get blown away."

He noted her abrupt change of subject—wondered, but didn't comment. Arm in arm, they walked to the car.

In La Trattoria, Owen was surprised when Quinn hugged Nate, a little old fellow she introduced as the owner, and pointedly told him that McLean had given her a night off. He didn't like her introduction: "Owen Johnson, an old friend from Nevada." The encounter raised questions; he wasn't sure he wanted the answers.

They ordered their meals. Owen looked over the wine choices and selected a California zinfandel. He raised an eyebrow when the owner, unasked, slid a soft drink in front of Quinn. More questions.

"Tell me about everybody," she demanded as they sipped their drinks and giggled as she ticked off her list: "Viv and Vic, Scottie, George, the chickens and the geese, everybody."

Relieved by the lightness of her mood, he happily produced updates: the B&B, the retreat and his sisters' fears, Scottie's current plans to return home by Christmas, details of post-terrorist life in Nevada. He didn't mention Karle and Quinn didn't ask. To his delight, she laughed out loud as he described Girl

George's new trick—escaping the corral to nibble greenery with the deer—and, again to his surprise, repeated the story to the proprietor when the old guy brought out their food.

They talked and laughed and ate spaghetti and lasagna. Quinn grew serious when she described the Pentagon as she'd seen it the first night, and he realized he'd been so busy finding her that he hadn't even noticed the building. He started to ask a question, but she shook off her somber mood—"Sorry, no dark talk tonight"—and reached across the table to wipe sauce from his lips.

Better, Owen thought. Laughing, talking, lovemaking he could drown in. Maybe he was reading too much into things; maybe Karle was right.

But even in his besotted state, he noticed that for every bite of food she'd eaten, two had been pushed around and shoved to the edge of her plate. No wine, but she guzzled the Pepsi as though parched. And he hadn't missed the look she'd shot her boss as the man stood behind him at the tent door, nor the expression on the other man's face as he'd left them alone.

Quinn might not acknowledge her own desirability, but he knew it well, and, he was certain, so did Chris McLean. It hurt him that she hadn't responded to his declaration of love, that she hadn't said the words in return, but otherwise her welcome had been all he could have wanted. She was *his* Quinn, familiar, sexy, the woman who made his heart beat faster and his thoughts turn to mush, and yet...He decided to bide his time.

QUINN PUSHED HER LASAGNA AROUND HER plate. She'd overreacted when Owen had announced her night off. *Pissy. I sounded pissy, but I don't care, Owen and hot sex are not compensation for the flash of fear. I do love him, but I don't dare get lost again.*

Conversation flowed around her troubled thoughts. She told him about the Pentagon and a little about her work. He told stories about the people and places she'd come to love. *I forgot how much I like him, forgot that he gets me, forgot that he makes me laugh,* she thought, laughing until tears ran down her cheeks at the mental image of fat little Girl George grazing with the deer, laughing more as she related the story to Nate.

"So Scott's coming home," she said when her laughter was finally contained and Nate had moved on to another table. She berated the young man's behavior for a bit, then grew serious again. "The little ingrate—I just hope he has sense enough to get help for the drugs before he does something else stupid and hurtful."

Owen's eyebrows drew together in surprise. "Did Vivvy tell you?"

"About the pot? No, Owen, it's my job. I see people in trouble all the time. Just because I screw up my own life doesn't mean I can't recognize the signs in others. My brother's an alcoholic, for heaven's sake; I know what that looks like in a family."

Stunned by her own words and the ease with which they'd emerged, Quinn twirled a loose strand of hair and wondered what Owen would say. She rarely spoke of personal things, at least not when she was sober. The disclosures to McLean had apparently loosened her tongue.

Now she watched Owen from beneath lowered lids. The man didn't like change, and this was a big variation on their norm. *He loves the me he thinks he knows, but I'm trying to change. Will he love the Quinn evolution? Will I? Will there even be an evolution?* With an internal shrug, she released her hair and wrapped both hands around her sweating glass. *Oh well, fat's in the fire now.*

Owen's dark gaze settled on her. His eyebrow quirked up, but he said nothing.

Disappointed, Quinn changed the subject. "Are they ready for the retreat?" she asked, although Owen had already described the situation. "They really can do it, you know."

"I know, and they'll find out." Owen took a gulp of his wine, set the glass down, and followed her into personal territory. "They understand why you left, better than I do, I think."

Surprised, she gnawed at her lip. The conversation had veered in a new direction; now it was her turn to say nothing.

He went on. "I mean, I know why you're here, the need for your skills and all that. God knows we all need help right now. But the other, the stuff you talked about, I don't understand why you can't do that at home, why you can't let me help you."

He looked like he wanted to add something—or maybe take something back. He grabbed his glass and took another big gulp instead. She was grateful he hadn't said I love you again. She was afraid to say it back, even if it was true, afraid it would commit her to just the course she couldn't follow—even if she wanted to—not right now. She'd seen the hurt in his eyes, knew what he wanted, knew she wasn't yet ready.

"Owen, I—"

"Ms. DeMello," Nate interrupted, sliding his hand in front of her to remove her empty plate, "I am sorry to interrupt, but there's a phone call for you."

"Thank you," she said, happy for the interruption.

Used dishes in hand, the old proprietor hovered, and she was sorry she'd brought Owen here, but it was the only place she knew. The old guy had been cordial, but she could read the confusion in his eyes and, in spite of their earlier laughter, loyalty to McLean radiated from his stiff posture. "In the kitchen," he added as she rose.

She nodded and turned back to Owen, her movie star look-alike with the dark tousled hair, the eyes so deep and black you could drown in them, just now hooded and watchful. "Let's talk about this later," she said and walked away to take the phone call she knew was from McLean.

The call was short and sweet, and she wondered why she'd expected anything more.

"DeMello," he said in his gruff voice, "take tomorrow off," and hung up before she could say "Thanks" or "What if I don't want to?" and certainly before she could tell what he was feeling.

Irritated for even thinking about it, she glared at the phone and waited a minute for her emotions to settle before she returned to the table.

"What'd he say?" Owen asked as she slipped back into the booth, eyes down, and picked up the coffee mug Nate had delivered unordered.

"McLean? Just wondered if I wanted a whole day off," she said, the lie slipping easily off her tongue. "I told him I didn't know your plans but that I could use one." She looked up. "Fits your plan, I'm thinking?"

"Yep, fits perfectly."

She laughed at his lascivious grin and appreciated the enthusiasm in his voice, even as she wondered what he was thinking and what would happen next. Turns out he could still surprise her. He just said, "Let's go watch movies," and that's what they did.

CHAPTER 19

BEFORE THE FINAL CREDITS OF *A Star is Born* rolled, Owen and Quinn were asleep wrapped in each other's arms. In the morning, Owen hummed a slightly off-key version of "Evergreen" and flipped through television channels for news while Quinn showered. The local weather station filled the screen when the bathroom door opened. In the escaping steam, Quinn stalked into the bedroom wrapped in an oversized white hotel towel waving a pink undergarment like a flag.

"What's this?"

She had stepped out of the shower to find neatly folded clothes lying on the counter: Levi's with the tags still on, crisply pressed plaid shirt, blue tank top and, like frosting, pink panties atop the pile.

Attention fixed on the television, Owen didn't look up. "Tornado watch."

"I mean this." Quinn stamped her bare foot and dangled the frothy garment in front of his face. "Where did these come from?"

The patch of pink swung past his nose.

"Oh, care package from Camille," he answered, eyes riveted on the scenes of uprooted trees, broken branches, roofless houses, and dark, dark sky scrolling across the screen. "They say it's a tornado."

Panties momentarily forgotten, Quinn dropped onto the bed beside him and they stared at the destruction. What to do? There were no tornadoes in Nevada. She glanced at her hero, but Owen's eyebrows were drawn together in a bewildered frown as the weather man plotted the tornado's movement up the state of Virginia. *Clueless, like me,* she thought. *No point in seeking his advice.* Apparently you were just supposed to know what to do.

Quinn wasn't afraid, thought maybe she should be. But if you'd survived rattlesnakes and lightning in Nevada, what was there to fear? Restless, she stood and padded to the sliding glass door hidden behind heavy drapes with a red colonial print, which she yanked open to expose a tiny veranda and a storm-dark sky. Worrying about the Pentagon, the volunteers, and McLean, she stepped out into the hovering calm. The phone rang. Owen tossed her the handset as she stepped back inside.

"Hello."

"Stay put where you are," McLean ordered. "We're all hunkered down until the storm passes. No worries." He hung up.

Quinn frowned as she set the phone in its cradle. With an effort, she banished both annoyance and worry and plunked back down on the bed. "He says 'stay put' and I obey." Catching the absurdity, she giggled, snatched the remote from Owen's hand, and pressed the *off* button. "Kiss me quick and then tell me about these damn clothes."

MUCH LATER, STILL DAMP FROM A joint shower, Owen dumped the contents of a small black overnighter onto the freshly rumpled bed. "I called Camille," he explained, "and all your sisters wanted to help. I think they spent a whole day putting this together. Cecily couldn't be there, so she sent the list of stuff she was sure you needed."

Sounds fishy. Until their mother's illness and recent death, she'd been estranged from her family, four sisters and a brother, whom she was sure blamed her for all manner of ills. She'd expected their criticism, even magnified it and called it her sister chorus. *Deal with family* was on her issues list. She rifled through the contents—more jeans, black slacks, shirts, tank tops, and several tiny thongs—and thought, *Maybe I'm making this a bigger deal than it is.* In disbelief, she held up another delicate thong, this one fuchsia. "Camille sent these? She *bought* them?"

"Well," Owen hemmed, "I might have added a few things."

She jumped him again. He didn't protest.

Much later, Quinn emerged from yet another shower and donned her fresh clothes. She pulled up the Levi's, sucked in her flat stomach, and zipped. They fit as though they had been painted on. *God, they really know me*, she thought, marveling at the unfamiliar sense of well-being that filled her.

Hand in hand, they explored the hotel, shared a burger and fries, and returned to the room, where they propped themselves on pillows in front of the television and watched the tornado march toward them. Just after four, they stared in awe as wind snatched the Pentagon exit sign and flung it away.

The phone rang immediately.

"McLean," they shouted in unison. Quinn answered.

"Dodged a bullet. It's moving north. See you for your thing in the morning." McLean hung up.

She stared at the silent phone, willing it to tell her what was happening, how things were, how *he* was. She wanted to yell at him, but he was gone.

"What's up?" Owen frowned as he lifted the phone from her hand.

She shook away the disquieting moment. "All good. Just McLean being McLean. I have to work tomorrow."

He scowled, eyebrows meeting, a wrinkled scar butting through the right one, the tiny twitch of his set jaw, and she remembered how good he was at reading her. Forestalling questions, she snuggled against him and nuzzled his neck, breathing in the scents of Jaipur and man—*her* man. Their punch drove all else from her mind.

CHAPTER 20

I<small>N THE WEEK THAT FOLLOWED,</small> O<small>WEN</small> worked from the hotel's business center, thankful for fax and email and FedEx and a business partner who sometimes shouldered more than his share.

He was awed by the devastation and the anthill of activity that the Pentagon site had become, and even more awed by the way Quinn straightened her shoulders and returned to her cubicle each morning.

She wore her new clothes without comment and grinned when she reported that someone named Mandy was jealous. Knowing Quinn still thought of herself as an outsider, he hadn't been sure how she'd respond when he contacted her sisters. He'd been surprised when Camille, the eldest, had welcomed his interference, and, along with the suitcase full of clothes, he'd gained a new perspective on Quinn's conflict with her mother. *Someday we'll talk about it*, he promised himself. *Maybe if she understands, things will be easier.* Most nights she slept beside him and, as she twisted and turned, he knew the dreams—a kaleidoscope of blame and guilt and pain—still plagued her.

One night they joined her colleagues at La Trattoria for dinner. He'd enjoyed Mandy's friendly curiosity and, against his will, warmed to the man he'd identified as rival.

"What did you and McLean talk about?" Quinn asked on their way back to his room, her voice dripping with suspicion.

He swiped a hand over his mouth to hide his grin. "Oh, he wondered what you were like in the sack, and I was happy to share some of your finer—"

She scowled and punched his arm hard enough to send him against the wall.

He chuckled. *So damn good to tease, to laugh, to relax and not guard every word.* "Just kidding." He rubbed the offended arm. "We talked about the economy, the effect of all this on our country, how long it will last."

He didn't tell her the whole of their conversation. McLean had described Quinn's work, the way soldiers and civilian volunteers flocked to her morning meditations, the way they clustered in the evenings as her flute brought hope and promise. Owen recognized the admiration in the other man's voice, knew from his own experience the magic Quinn dispensed.

He dared a glance at her set jaw and his confidence shook, just a little. "Honest, just that. He did say that he was sending some of the volunteers home soon."

When she didn't respond, he let it drop, keyed open the hotel door, and stepped aside for her to precede him. Inside, he grabbed her and fell back on the bed with her in his arms. "But in case he asks, let's give him some juicy details." Before she could struggle, he reversed their positions. His tongue found its way into her mouth; his hands held her tight until she loosened beneath him.

By Saturday she'll be ready, he promised himself, *and I'll bring her home.*

CHAPTER 21

THE GUESTHOUSE OF THE WILDFLOWER INN Bed and Breakfast nestled beside a tree-lined stream about a hundred yards from the main house. Its mullioned windows sparkled like diamonds in the afternoon light, and a fire warmed the large common area and the adjacent kitchen. Inside, Vivian and Victoria Johnson refreshed the rooms—two upstairs called Yin and Yang; two more on the ground floor, Romeo and Juliet—full of wrought-iron bedsteads, old-fashioned duvets and lacy pillows, and antique dressers with watery mirrors. Quinn's tiny room in the very back remained as she had left it.

Retreat time: Four guests, forever friends from California, would arrive in two days.

Vivian silently fiddled with an already perfect arrangement of chrysanthemums. Victoria wielded the hand vac as though it could suck away the gloom that had crept in like fog. What else could they do? Quinn was gone. Owen's encouraging presence was missing. The retreat would fail.

Vivian stopped fiddling, cocked her head toward the door, and held up her hand. "Vicky, turn it off. I heard something."

"Huh?"

"Turn it off."

Her sister complied. "What's up?"

A timid knock answered her question. They looked toward the sound.

A petite blond woman stood in the doorway, hand raised to knock again. "Hi, sorry, but I knocked downstairs and nobody answered. I followed the vacuum and here I am." A weak smile left the unhappiness on her face undisturbed. "I'm Kristin Amundson, from summer, remember?" She pulled up her pant leg and revealed a prosthesis.

The twins shared a startled glance, then Vivian stepped forward, hand outstretched. "Of course we remember." She took the younger woman's cold hand in her own and drew her away from the door. "Let's go down. It's more comfortable and we can talk." Firmly in charge, Vivian proceeded down the stairs.

Victoria followed, her mind busy. Of course they remembered. How could they forget the pasty-white woman who had arrived with her sister and two friends for the Fourth of July retreat and startled them all with her artificial leg? The sister, a twin named Karol, had divulged Kristin's sad history, and Quinn's typical let's-just-see-what-happens approach had ended in a magnificent retreat but also a row with Owen that had never quite healed. What in God's green earth was the woman doing here now?

Thoughts a-jumble, Vivian sent her sister for drinks and escorted their unexpected guest into the great room, cozy in the late September sunshine. Looking like she wanted to cry, Kristin perched on the horsehair settee and plucked at the knees of her jeans. Vivian's commonplace questions—"How's your sister? Your friends? Don't you like this weather?"—met one-word answers and finally stumbled into silence. Curiosity could wait until Vic returned; they always coped better in twos.

Through the window behind her uninvited guest, Vivian could see the turkey vultures coming to rest in the poplar trees. Her count had reached eleven when her sister puffed into the room and, with a sigh of relief, Vivian reached for the tea pot.

Tea poured, cookies offered and refused, Vivian gathered herself, but Kristin spoke first. "You're probably wondering why I'm here. I don't suppose people usually just drop in unannounced. Well..." She paused and raised her eyes to the twin faces opposite. "Well, I got the impression that you took in strays, and"—her face crumpled—"and I'm...a stray."

Amid tears and protestations, the story emerged: Kristin had returned to her position at the bank after a year of illness and rehabilitation; within a week she had realized that numbers were no longer her passion. In fact, each day had been misery. She'd tried to put on a good face and get back into her life. "Karol hovered like a hawk," Kristin said with a watery laugh, "telling me it just took time, that it would get better. I felt smothered with all that love and determination, and I couldn't even protest 'cause she's done so much for me. Then *it* happened." She flung her arms about in wild gestures that somehow brought terror and death and destruction into the room. "It happened," she settled her hands primly in her lap, "and I knew I had to do something different."

Shadows filled the room. Kristin reached for a cookie, apparently relieved now that the story was told. The sisters eyed each other, both wishing Owen would get home fast.

Finally, Victoria said, "Kristin, I get it that you're having a hard time but...why are you here?"

CHAPTER 22

I*T'S TIME,* OWEN THOUGHT EARLY SATURDAY morning. *No more pussy-footing around.*

Eyes filmy with unshed tears, Quinn sat cross-legged on the bed as Owen buttoned his shirt sleeves and slid into his jacket. His suitcase stood near the door, packed and ready. In three hours his plane would take off for Reno and, by damn, Quinn would be sitting next to him in first class, celebratory flute of Champagne in her hand. The only problem remaining was how to get her from here to there. He wanted this woman more than he'd ever wanted anything in his life. He wiped suddenly sweaty palms on his jeans.

This morning, he had just risen from a dream when she had reached for him and wordlessly led him in a dance of such slow, sweet love that he still ached with it. She hadn't given him the words he wanted, but he knew she loved him. Karle had helped him prepare for this moment—no time for second thoughts. He shot his cuffs, patted the jacket pocket, and sat beside her.

"Quinn," his voice cracked. He cleared his throat and started over. "Quinn, I want you to come home with me now."

He pulled an airline ticket from his pocket and placed it in her hands. "Now," he repeated, his voice not as firm as he would have liked. "Here's your ticket; there's time for us to pick up your things and get to the airport. You're tired and you're sad, and I can't stand to see you suffering. You've done enough here and you need to come home."

He held his breath.

For almost a minute, Owen sat mesmerized as Quinn's slender fingers with their torn cuticles and ragged nails turned the ticket over and over. Just when he thought she hadn't understood, she spoke, voice flat, eyes fixed on the ticket.

"Owen, you just don't get it, do you? I thought you did, that you understood and could give me space, but you don't and you won't. You're just too fucking busy finding somebody to rescue. And that's not going to be me." She smoothed the ticket and laid it down gently, then unwound from the bed and, moving as though she were ill, started for the door.

He stood, hope shredded. If she would just yell, he might know what to do. His hands ached to grab and hold, his mouth to silence and ravage, his words to explain and convince and promise—if she could just see. His hands unclenched and reached toward her.

Quinn touched the handle, paused.

His heart lurched. *Maybe.*

Suddenly crackling with attitude, she turned, and in three steps they stood nose to nose, her flashing eyes challenging him to look away. "How dare you think you can know what's best for me. How dare you make plans . . . buy tickets . . . without my consent!" One fist gripped the heart he had given her as though she might rip it off and throw it at him.

Before he could defend himself, before he could explain, her face paled, then like a flame her whole body flared, and he retreated until the bed was against his knees.

"God," she whispered, disbelief coating the words. "You already cleared this with my boss. McLean thinks I'm leaving?"

The truth was in his eyes.

She stepped back. "You did, didn't you?"

Stricken, hands dangling helplessly at his sides, he could only stare.

She stood at the door, feet wide, hands on her hips, voice now devoid of emotion, and delivered the death blow. "Go home, Owen Johnson. You don't want me, you don't know me, and I ... don't ... want ... you."

The door closed behind her without a sound.

CHAPTER 23

POWERED BY ANGER AND GRIEF, QUINN made short work of the distance from hotel to Metro. By the time she ascended into the morning sunshine at the Pentagon, she had schooled her expression to a neutral one, but she crept into the tent just in case. There were twelve messages flapping on her cubicle wall and a curious Mandy was just taping the thirteenth.

"He's persistent, your man," she commented as Quinn stopped beside her. "Definitely wants you to call him."

"He's not mine, and don't bother with any more of these." Ignoring Mandy's questioning look, Quinn snatched the papers off the wall, balled them up, and tossed them at the wastebasket. "Don't bother with any more."

She ducked into her space, pretending not to see the startled looks directed her way. "Show's over. Let's get to work, shall we?"

All morning, people filled the waiting area, slumped on folding chairs or on the floor, backs against the tent walls, eyes fixed on nothing as they waited. Patience seemed to be a soldier's greatest skill. The others were a little less patient, but they too waited, and their stories were the same, even as the scene shifted and the threat of another attack diminished. They told of scouring the rubble for life, of finding pieces that had once been human beings, of walking through the crowd that gathered each morning still seeking loved ones. And they told their own stories of loss and fear and grief.

"I just want to go home, ma'am. My wife and kids need me."

"Ali, that's my girlfriend, wants me home. Our baby will be here any day and—"

"My aunt worked in the first tower. My mom and my uncle are in New York, and that's where I should be."

"Why does God let something like this happen?"

"Did you see the news, ma'am? They say there's going to be more. I just want to hurt them . . . real bad."

Numb, Quinn listened to the stories and mourned her own loss. *I thought he understood, that he got it. How could I have been so wrong?* Her heart quickened as she thought about the day he'd arrived, how glad she'd been to see him, how good it had been in his arms. Anger evaporated, and grief threatened to flatten her.

At midday, Mandy's cautious knock roused her.

"What?"

"It's Mandy, Quinn. May I come in?"

She ran her hand through jumbled hair. "Sure, come in." She noted her new friend's equally jumbled appearance. "What's up?"

"I'm going home, Quinn; they need me there. Our little town has so many victims from the towers that the mayor has requested we work at home. I wanted to say good-bye."

Instantly ashamed of her own self-absorption, Quinn stood and opened her arms. Mandy came briefly into her embrace. "Mandy, I'm so sorry. I didn't know."

"Didn't seem like dinner conversation." She swiped ineffectively at tears. "Anyway, I needed to give you this." She handed

Quinn an envelope bearing the Marriott Hotel logo. "I think it's from that hot boyfriend of yours. Dr. McLean asked me to bring it in."

Quinn accepted the letter with two fingers, holding it at arm's length as though it might explode. As Mandy backed out of the cubicle, she said, in a Mandy-like way, "Some people get all the luck." If Quinn had noticed, she would have chuckled. Instead, she stared at the sealed missive, her need to read his words vying with dread. *What will he say? What will I do?* She chewed off a corner, tore open the thin white envelope, and pulled out the stark white letterhead, words hastily scrawled:

Quinn,

I guess this is it. I can't seem to do anything right with you, and I'm tired of being jerked around. You're so busy thinking you're the only person in the world with problems that you wouldn't recognize a good thing if it bit you in the butt—which I did, by the way, if you remember—so I'm out of here. I won't bother you anymore. OJ

She crumpled the letter into a tight ball and hurled it toward the trash can. When it missed she grabbed it, hurled it again, and, when it bounced back to lie at her feet, stomped on it hard. When the paper crinkled and refused to stay flat, she picked it up, smoothed away the wrinkles, and slipped it between her breasts next to the silver heart. Feeling its warmth against her skin, she sank to the floor and cried.

The rest of the day passed in a blur. Afterward, she knew she'd worked as usual, and no one had mentioned her strange behavior, but she felt as if her shell were there and she were somewhere else, somewhere dark and painful from which there was no escape.

When the waiting room was empty and the cubicles still, Quinn emerged into the dusk. She circled the tent and gazed at the gaping wound in the Pentagon's side. *That's how I feel*, she thought. *How can you still stand?*

Turning her back, she checked her pocket for cash and headed toward the Metro station.

Chapter 24

Chris McLean was working late. Paperwork vied with action for his attention and usually lost. Tonight it couldn't be ignored. Alone, the space around him long since empty and dark as colleagues had gone on to food and drink and whatever else brought them a few moments' peace, he rubbed his eyes and squeezed them shut. When he opened them, the desk lamp with its forty-watt bulb still cast its reproachful glare on the mountain of paper in front of him. *I'll be glad when this is over. It's bad.*

Outside, the clamor of construction and deconstruction continued, a backdrop for his uneasy thoughts. Chris scrubbed his face with his hands, an unconscious attempt to rub away the unrelenting fatigue. Fifteen days. Fifteen heart-wrenching days since the world had changed. Hope of finding anyone else alive had been officially relinquished by the end of day one, and after that, efforts had been directed toward recovering bits and pieces. He could hardly wrap his mind around the enormity of it. One hundred eighty-nine souls were dead on the ground behind him: fifty-five military personnel and seventy civilians from inside the Pentagon, fifty-nine airplane passengers and crew, and five terrorists. All that and more than one hundred wounded.

Add in those who'd perished in New York and Pennsylvania. Grief and speculation dominated the news. What would the president do? How would people cope? Would we ever smile again? In spite of the volunteer hours and efforts, it was early days to speak of healing. The army would take care of its own. The helpers would soon be gone. The contractors would make their profit. He didn't like his dark thoughts, tried to put them aside. *Work's done, just want to pack up and go home.*

In this moment, Chris sensed all those souls still lingering in this broken landscape. He drew in a shaky breath. *Tired,* he thought, *just tired—time for a little R & R.* His imagination conjured up the fifth of Maker's Mark tucked into his duffel, and he grinned. *A drunk, yeah, but not a cheap drunk.*

And then what?

He'd had an idea about Quinn DeMello, something about writing up an additional mental health program that included yoga and meditation and music, but right now he was too tired to pursue it. No matter, the boyfriend was taking her home. That he didn't like the idea disturbed him. He cocked an eyebrow as he thought about his modus operandi for disasters: First came the work—long days filled with distress and misery—relieved by lust; then, crisis over, romance *fini*, and, no one the worse for wear, he moved on with nary an internal ripple.

Not this time.

He scowled and scratched the stubble on his chin. He'd grown used to being alone, unattached—preferred it really, but only once in a while. Uncomfortable with the direction of his thoughts, he squirmed in the pygmy-sized metal chair and considered the woman who'd turned him down. DeMello—funny, sexy, good with all these kids . . . and totally clueless. That was her charm, he decided, that and the fact that her laugh was infectious, that the fullness of her breasts straining against the ubiquitous tank tops made men want to touch her, and that her inner darkness made him want to save her. *Dear God, she'd laugh out loud at that.* He laughed at his own folly, readjusted himself, and reached for his glasses.

"McLean? McLean, you in here?" Quinn's voice, slurred, was loud in the tent's silence.

What the hell? He hadn't heard her enter, glanced at his watch—ten-thirty. "In here, DeMello."

She shambled in and slumped to the floor. His world electrified and he leaped to his feet, the chair crashing behind him. "What?"

"Sorry, just a little dizzy. This'll fix it." She saluted with a familiar bottle, then tipped it to her mouth for a healthy swig. Her free hand swiped at the yellow dribble on her chin.

Jose Cuervo, almost empty. He lowered his bulk to eye level. "What's up, DeMello?"

She treated him to a sloppy grin that didn't touch her eyes. "You wanted to share with me, so I thought I'd share with you." Hiccups punctuated her words as she waved the bottle. He jerked back just in time to avoid a blow to his chin. "Wanna drink, big guy?"

He stifled temptation, his mind busy. *What to do now?* Clearly, his work was finished for tonight, but he couldn't just leave her here. "No, thanks," he said, "but I need some food. Come with me?"

Her head jiggled assent so he turned off the light, left his glasses on the pile of untended forms, and pulled her to her feet. As he released her to right the overturned chair, she wobbled and peered at him through disheveled blond strands. "Must be an earthquake." Her laugh held more crazy than mirth.

He winced and grabbed her arm and resisted the urge to crush her against his chest. "Nope, just a tequila quake."

She giggled and repeated his words in a sing-song manner as he supported her to his vehicle. "Tequila quake, tequila quake," she warbled, while he threaded her in and buckled her seatbelt.

He stepped back. "Shut up, DeMello," he said and was almost undone by the sadness in the gaze she fixed on him.

Then she giggled again and the moment was gone. "Where we going, Harry the Heartbreaker?"

It was a good question, but, truth be told, he'd known where they would go the minute she'd landed at his feet like the answer to prayers he no longer believed in. He started the Jeep, backed away from the tent, and accelerated toward the freeway, foot heavy on the gas. His hotel was only minutes away; he'd feed her, tuck her in, and let her sleep it off—no harm, no foul.

A McDonald's drive-through provided burgers and fries, and in minutes they were back on the road, the aroma of fat and salt saturating the air. Quinn kept up an indecipherable monologue punctuated with swallows from the bottle she clutched. Along the way, she slipped out of her restraint and draped against him, her free hand sliding up and down his inner thigh.

Nothing good will come of this. His thrumming body disagreed. *I should tuck her in and walk away,* McLean thought, but, chagrined, he knew he would not.

At his hotel, he struggled to get the food, himself, and the staggering woman out of the vehicle and through the back door. The boyfriend had departed. He'd seen the devastation on the other man's face when he'd handed Chris the letter to deliver and turned down the offer to find Quinn. Chris recognized rebound. Right now, he just didn't care.

Two more steps and they were inside. Generic hotel, few amenities, dim light through an undraped window. Her stance broad-based and swaying, Quinn surveyed his room. Sounding almost sober, she said, "Not bad, McLean, for a home away from home." Without warning, she placed both hands on his chest and pushed. "Let's try out the bed."

Tequila splattered. Food hit the floor.

Caught unawares, Chris lost his balance and tumbled backward. Before he could recover, Quinn was on him.

Bad idea, bad idea, his brain tried one more time. *She's drunk, you idiot, you're not—bad idea.*

She brought her mouth down to cover his, and his mind went blank.

QUINN'S EYES POPPED OPEN, AND SHE was awake in a dark and unfamiliar place. Her stomach roiled. She lay still, partly to keep the cocktail of tequila and bile from overflowing, partly because she was secured at the waist by a hairy log.

McLean?

Heat rose in her cheeks: Tequila quake, the smell of French fries, an insatiable mouth, and demanding hands. His? Hers? The memory generated a spasm deep inside and dampness between her legs. Her muscles went loose. McLean!

As though sensing her surrender, the man pulled her tight, and Quinn felt him hard against her back. The heaviness of sleep still on her, she squirmed into position so he could enter. His hands found her breasts. His whisky-perfumed breath whispered at her ear as he thrust and she pushed to take him deeper. She cried out as he finished, almost over the edge herself, and then she remembered: Owen!

Bile filled her mouth, and she stumbled from the bed.

Hanging over the toilet, she heaved until there was nothing left, then crumpled to the cold white tile and whimpered.

The bathroom door crashed open. McLean stepped over her, entered the little room, and turned on the light. "DeMello, you okay?"

She blinked up through strands of sweaty hair, swallowed hard, and nodded, hoping her head wouldn't fall off.

"Hair of the dog," he said, wrapping her fingers around a tumbler half-filled with yellow liquid. "Drink this, you'll feel better." When she just stared, he sighed, sat on the tub's edge, and steadied the liquor toward her mouth. She turned away. He slid a hand behind her head, pushed the glass against her lips. "Down the hatch, woman."

The liquid stung her lips, then slid down her throat in one long swallow. Eyes streaming, she gagged and coughed and pushed him away.

With a chuckle, he stepped back over her and left, closing the door behind him. She huddled against the commode, forearm soothed by its cold surface. Her stomach churned. The liquor burned, searing her with forgetfulness. She waited to make sure it would stay, then climbed into the tub and turned the tap to hot.

CHAPTER 25

HE WATER STARTED, STEAM WHISPERED UNDER the bathroom door, and McLean grinned an evil grin—he'd had plenty of days like this himself. He'd waited to hear the flush, then, glass of tequila in hand, he maneuvered his way into the tiny bathroom. Quinn was sprawled on the cold white tile like a broken doll, head supported against the toilet, lank blond strands partially obscuring pale cheeks. Straight-faced, he sat on the edge of the tub, elbows on hairy knees and the porcelain icy on his bare butt, and delivered his remedy. She gagged and retched and pushed him away. He closed the door behind him when he left.

Now, relishing the scent of sex and lavender that clung to his body, he sat on the bed and called room service—the only perk the hotel offered—delivered warm from the coffee shop next door. He ordered juice and coffee, to be followed in an hour by a full breakfast for two. That done, he dressed and straightened the bed and waited. He was doctoring his second cup of quite good coffee when Quinn, encased in steam and a large white towel, stepped into the room.

A goddess rising from the mist, he thought, a long-lost snatch of poetry quoted at the breakfast table coming to mind. His heart rate accelerated. He started to stand.

"What am I doing here, McLean?"

She sounded more peeved than confused. He smothered a chuckle and settled back on the bed. "Good question, DeMello. I could ask you the same. But you first. You showed up in my office slightly . . . under the weather, as they say, and, having nowhere else to take you and being a rescuer by nature, I brought you here." Amused, he kept his voice light. *She's a big girl.*

"And what you were doing there," she indicated the bed they'd just shared, "is all part of the service?"

Memories flashed: the push that had toppled him, laughing, under her; the rapacious hands that had torn at his clothes; the teeth that had bitten his skin; the body ripe for his. His mild response covered a sudden and surprising hurt. "I don't remember a protest."

She flushed. "Sorry."

"Just saying, not complaining."

His nether parts were not complaining now, and he was glad he was dressed as he rose from the bed, poured a cup of coffee, and carried it to her. "Here."

She reached for the cup, and the towel slipped. He wanted to touch her again, felt like a schoolboy with his first woman. Instead, he repositioned the towel and tucked the edges to hold themselves, his fingers tingling with the warmth of her skin. Not his normal morning after; the discomfort didn't sit easily. He backed away and settled onto the edge of the bed.

Quinn perched on the desk chair. "So we . . .?"

She doesn't remember, he thought, surprised again as pain, heart-attack strong, pierced his chest. "Like rabbits," he said.

"Heartbreak Harry," she murmured, eyes fixed on the steam rising from the cup in her hand. "I wasn't going to be your girl in this disaster, but..."

When she didn't go on, he prompted, "The boyfriend?"

"Toast," she spat out, a turquoise flash daring him to contradict, but he saw her hand creep protectively around the silver heart dangling between her breasts. "Toast."

Emotions played over her face before she turned her attention back to the steaming coffee. Neither spoke for a moment, then she set the mug aside and dropped the towel.

Chris McLean held his breath as she stalked toward him.

"Toast," she repeated firmly. "And since you've already provided disaster assistance, maybe it's my turn." She grinned then, mischief disguising the pain in her eyes. "After all, I am a disaster volunteer."

She dropped to her knees between his legs and reached for his zipper.

CHAPTER 26

PALE MORNING LIGHT PEEPED THROUGH THE curtains of the Wildflower Inn when a clatter startled Victoria Johnson out of her deep sleep. Usually an early riser, she'd turned off her alarm and prayed for a good lie-in. The retreat would begin tomorrow, and she could at least be rested. Discombobulated, she jumped out of bed, grabbed her robe, and rushed for the stairs where she nearly collided with her towel-clad sister, still wet from her bath. Together, they clambered down the stairs and into the kitchen.

"I'm sorry, I'm sorry, I'm sorry," wailed Kristin.

The twins stared at the oatmeal congealing on the old pine planks. Their shared thought: *What have we gotten ourselves into now?*

The night was long gone before Kristin finished answering Victoria's questions.

"I know Quinn's gone," she'd said. "I'm volunteering to take her place." A self-deprecating smile had fluttered and disappeared. "Not with the meditation or the flute or anything like that, but you must need an extra hand with food or cleanup." She'd produced another smile, barely perceptible, then straightened her shoulders and strengthened her voice. "But I can take them on hikes and I can help with trail rides and—"

Ah-ha! Victoria had thrown her sister an I-told-you-so look and said, "Would this have anything to do with Adam Singer?"

Adam Singer, scion of an old Buena Vista family, laconic trail guide, hunting scout, and cowboy poet, was the trail boss for adventures into the canyons beyond the B&B. Only his closest friends knew he also had a PhD in English literature and wrote novels under a closely guarded pen name.

Color had rushed onto Kristin's pale face. "I liked him."

And he had liked her, the twins remembered, thinking of the tall, forty-something man who'd taken up a post at Kristin's side during the July retreat.

"He's the one who encouraged me to show you all the leg." There had been some defensiveness in her voice. "But it's not just him. I wanted to come here because I feel normal here."

Another twin look. What could they have said? Quinn's earlier decision, "Let's wait and see what happens," made after Kristin's sister had disclosed the disability, had been brilliant, and Kristin had gone home tanned and smiling. But now she'd returned, pale and tearful—who could blame her for wanting to return? They had shrugged and fed her dinner and invited her to stay the night. Over coffee and peach pie fresh from the oven, the three had decided that Kristin could try out as Vivian's kitchen helper.

Now they stared at the glutinous mass and wondered. Their brother would have words to say about this, too, and usually his advice was solid. They did hope he was in a better mood tonight when he returned than he'd been when he left. They hoped he would bring Quinn home, too, but in their hearts each knew it was too soon.

And, ready or not, their guests would arrive tomorrow.

A BUMPY APPROACH AND A HARD landing did nothing to improve Owen Johnson's state of mind as the American Airlines 747 arrived in Reno at exactly 11:59 on Saturday night.

The three drinks he'd gulped in quick succession early in the flight had plunged him into an uneasy sleep from which he'd emerged exhausted, angry, and still heart-wrecked, but he retained enough sense to know he wasn't safe for the two-hour drive home. He knew his sisters wanted him at the retreat—at least they wanted the sense of security he provided—but he just wanted to sleep it all away, so he gathered his belongings, found his Audi in long-term parking, and then almost nodded off as he sped through deserted streets. Sleep would block the constant replay of Quinn's words.

Lights showed through Karle's upstairs shutters as he let himself into his basement apartment, ignoring the scent of rosemary that rose from the big bush near the stairs. In the dark, fully clothed, he threw himself onto the bed.

Minutes later, he roused to a knock on his door. When he stumbled to his feet and opened it, Karle stood there, a bottle of wine in one hand and a plate of meatloaf and mashed potatoes in the other. He straightened under her assessing gaze, hoped he didn't look as bad as he felt.

"You look like shit, Owen."

She stepped into the room and turned on the light. "Go wash your face and then come eat. You'll feel better."

He didn't want to eat. He didn't want to talk. But Karle looked like a succoring angel—green silk robe slithery around her, wine in one hand and a plate of steaming food already arousing his salivary glands in the other—and he knew she wouldn't leave anyway, so he followed her instructions.

He did feel better when he stepped out of his compact bathroom, face and hands washed, teeth brushed, and hair straightened. Karle, one smooth leg crossed over the other, satin mule jiggling from one tiny foot, waited at his dinette table, a glass of deep red wine in her hand.

A big smile crossed her face. "Good job," she murmured. "Feel better?"

He nodded and accepted his own brimming glass.

She tapped his glass with her own and nodded in approval as he took a big drink. "Eat," she said, "and then tell me what happened."

He did. As they shared the wine, he ate and poured out his anger and frustration. Sympathy didn't fix his heart, but it sure smoothed the jagged edges.

CHAPTER 27

OR QUINN, SUNDAY BLURRED IN AN orgy of sex and booze and emotion too intense for words. Entangled in sweaty sheets and McLean's body, she let lust buffer her thoughts. McLean's big hands and surgeon's fingers took her to new heights. When his mouth claimed her, she could only beg for more, and when he lay back, sated, she gave him the oblivion he offered her. Finally, exhausted, they slept.

The alarm woke her. The digital numbers read 5:45. Morning? A faint rim of light was visible at the window. Monday? She recalled a song called "Monday Monday" and hummed it under her breath. Surprisingly clearheaded despite the little men with jackhammers behind her eyes, Quinn considered: *Morning. Time for the real world.* Her overused body protested as she wriggled to escape McLean's somnolent bulk. She dug an elbow into his belly and squirmed away from the arm that would pull her in.

"Rise and shine, McLean, we need to talk."

An hour later, showered, combed, and shaved, Quinn and Chris stared at each other across a scarred Formica table in the twenty-four-hour café beside his hotel and waited for their coffee. Still tingling with postcoital exultation and exhaustion, Quinn fought her inner battle. Knowing the effects of the man's sleepy eyes and hungry mouth, she delayed until she was armed with coffee and presentability ... and a table between them.

He eyed her warily. She was certain she wore the same look.

The host, a man of about twenty who'd put aside his *Complete Shakespeare* text when he'd hurried to seat them, returned with their coffee. "Ruth will be right with you," he said, accepted their murmured thanks, and returned to his studies.

Quinn wrapped her hands around the heavy mug and considered how to begin. Owen didn't understand; there was no reason to expect anything different from Chris McLean.

"So talk," McLean invited, breaking the silence that stretched between them. "You said we needed to talk."

She recognized the look on his face. He knew when a woman said, "We need to talk," he wouldn't like the conversation. His knuckles whitened as his hands clutched the mug, and, in a flash of amusement, Quinn thought he'd rather have them around her throat. Distracted by the image, she twisted a strand of still-damp hair around one finger and stared into her coffee as though she might find words there. *He's gotta think I'm nuts.*

"So talk," he repeated, impatience in his voice.

Yep, she thought, *angry, annoyed, probably wondering why he bothered—at least I won't be hurting this one.* Still, it was hard to start. When she finally spoke, her voice felt raw and rusty.

"I know this is a game for you, McLean, and don't get me wrong, it's been great."

He looked up from doctoring his coffee. For a moment, as their eyes met, she imagined a spark of protest. Did she want him to say, "No game, not this time"? Before she could decide, he turned his attention back to his coffee, and, not sure whether she was relieved or disappointed, she continued. "I guess I'm officially another notch in your belt, but I can't keep it up. I've got some pretty big issues that I need to deal with, and since I seem to make the mistake of falling in love with anyone who's a good fuck, I can't afford you right now."

"That was a compliment, right?"

For a moment the air felt lighter. "You bet it was." He heaved a big sigh and seriousness returned. "I wasn't quite truthful about him." The softening of her voice made it clear which *him* she meant.

A middle-aged woman in jeans and a yellow T-shirt with a brown coffee mug on the front and a badge that read "Ruth from Indiana" interrupted. "Take your orders?"

Sure she couldn't swallow a bite, Quinn said, "Just coffee, thanks, Ruth."

McLean shook his head. "Orange juice and pancakes and scrambled eggs for two."

Ruth scribbled the order and walked away as Quinn glared. "I can order for myself."

"Well, you didn't order enough." He cocked his head toward her and raised an eyebrow. "We used up a lot of calories yesterday."

She couldn't help but smile—the set of his jaw indicated a battle she couldn't win. Smile faltering, she returned to her subject. "I wasn't truthful. Much as I hate to admit it, Owen's gone, but, surprise, I'm not over him. I have a habit of using people to make me feel better, and I think that's what I did this weekend." She made herself meet his eyes.

Their pale blue turned stormy, but his voice remained light. "Always happy to oblige. Plenty more where that came from."

A hoot of laughter escaped her. The man was more than just good in bed. She got herself under control, sipped the orange juice, and wished it was mixed with tequila.

Silence stretched almost to breaking before she spoke again. "That was funny, McLean, but get serious. Plenty more is just my point. I can't keep doing this. It hurts me and it hurts other people. I've got to get myself figured out."

His brow furrowed. "I am serious, DeMello. Everybody has issues. You of all people know that. What makes yours so special that you can't let someone help you?"

They were an echo of Owen's last words, but she knew what made hers different—different, not special. In her head, her mother's words thundered, so loud she feared he might hear: *Quinn killed her baby, you know.*

He couldn't hear, of course, just as he couldn't know, and the pain of being different gripped her. What she wouldn't give to be like everybody else. She shrugged. "Just doesn't work that way for me, I guess."

Mouth dry as dust, she turned her attention to the breakfast the waitress set in front of her.

FRUSTRATED, CHRIS MCLEAN WATCHED QUINN PUSH scrambled eggs around her plate. He wasn't about to let her go, not yet, not before he figured out the feelings storm that swept him, not while the taste of her still tantalized his mouth.

"My turn to talk?" he asked when it seemed she was done.

"Sure. Do your worst."

He planned to convince her that no one would get hurt if they enjoyed the few days left. Then he'd sell her his idea—that she should stay here, help set up a new mental health module that incorporated her unique approach, convince her she owed it to herself and the country, bring in motherhood and apple pie if he needed to, anything to keep her close.

He surprised himself when he said, "You're an alcoholic, you know?"

Her head jerked as though he'd slapped her, and her face went slack.

Fascinated, he watched denial, defense, and disbelief scroll across her unguarded features, words considered, only to die unspoken. Slowly she raised her eyes.

"You think?"

"I know."

His eyes held hers. In them he saw recognition bloom and a new raw look that struck him like a knee to the groin.

Eat your words, McLean.

Too late—free, they hovered and refused to back down.

"I know because I am too."

A low moan escaped her lips. "Does he know?"

"Probably not. People that love us are usually the last to know." He watched as she assessed the statement for truth, accepted it, and settled a little. "There are ways to deal with this."

"Like you do?"

He shrugged away the insult. "I do what I have to, follow my own rules ... So far it's worked for me." He ignored his lie. "Most people quit, deal with their other issues, and then find out whether they can drink moderately, like normal people, or not." He shrugged again. "I didn't quit, but I did learn something in treatment."

Quinn sat in silence, still transparent to his knowing eyes, digesting his words, considering the truth—*not me, it can't be me, I just drink when I can't stand it anymore*—knowing it would all be better with just one tequila shooter.

Desperately clutching denial like a shield, she shoved her plate away. "Let's go to work. I can't do this right now." She stood and bolted for the door.

Not sure where this was leading and wishing he'd kept his mouth shut, Dr. Chris McLean looked with regret at the pancakes and eggs still on his plate, then extricated himself from the booth, tossed twenties on the table, and followed Quinn into the morning.

CHAPTER 28

OUNDED SOULS STILL WAITED. QUINN SAT, tailor-style, on the thin blanket that protected her from the uneven ground and let her voice ease into the chant. Her flight from McLean's diagnosis to the trees' respite a desperate blur, her meditation was all that would protect her from the crushing exposure. Through her fog, she heard the others join in, raggedly, until the air ripened with the words, "*Om mani padme hum...*" As she chanted and fought to clear her mind, her own thoughts battered her:

He must be wrong. You're not a drunk. You just drink too much sometimes.

What if he's right? No wonder my mother hated me. No wonder I couldn't save Samantha.

That's stupid. You know it wasn't your fault. Just don't think about it anymore.

I have to think about it. Otherwise it will never change.

Before her mother died, Quinn's mind had been full of her sisters' voices—the sister chorus, she'd labeled them—critical, mocking, blaming. But she had come to know they were her own ugly words, and today they were louder than her chant. Today, scoured raw by McLean's pronouncement, she was filled with the memories, clawing their way out, fighting to define her.

The last *hum* blended into the morning birdsong. Leaving a little of their troubles behind, the soldiers and workers faded back to their duties and Quinn sat alone, her distress unresolved. Drunk or not, what was she to do? She had no answers.

She stood. If meditation didn't help, maybe work would. As she shook out her blanket, she heard a jingle, saw a flash of gold as an object disappeared into the grass. Her fingers searched, closed over a tiny golden bell, and something moved in her chest. Without questioning her action, she threaded the delicate charm next to the puffy silver heart and released them to nestle together between her breasts. She folded the blanket and headed toward the tent. *No running, no drinking, no fucking. What am I going to do?*

Her cubicle door was bare. No Owen Johnson missives fluttering from scotch tape restraints. Running shaky hands through blond snarls, she waited for work to relieve her.

END OF DAY FINALLY ARRIVED. ACUTELY aware of the ravished building behind her, Quinn hurried toward Cot Central. The word had just come out that the camp was closing, its work complete.

Steeped in her own misery, she still wondered how that could be, then forced her thoughts to her own short-range plan: *Find a place to stay, transfer money from grandpa's trust fund, figure out how to live the rest of my life.*

She didn't think about suicide anymore, not since the night on the mountain when she'd held Owen's gun to her temple and hadn't pulled the trigger. Without the thin comfort that death offered, life loomed long and hard. Suicide? Nope. Knight on a white charger? Sent him away. Tequila shooters? Living without tequila's soothing magic might be harder than dying. In the tent's dim light, she gathered up her meager belongings. *Maybe just as well most of my new things got left with Owen*, she thought. *Just a matter of time before I'll be moving on.*

"DeMello, front and center."

In spite of the drama she'd created, a smile brightened her face. "Hold your horses."

She stuffed her clothes into the duffel, tucked in a wayward edge of fuchsia silk, and forced the zipper to cooperate. Was she supposed to bring her stuff or leave it here? She shrugged and grabbed it all—thin brown flute case, duffel, red boots—and stepped into the early evening.

McLean's back was to the door, impatience clear in his shifting stance. He'd been her boss, but now he was somebody different, somebody more...confusing. She looked at him with new eyes. He wore his hair short, not quite spiked, although it took on a spiky look after he'd run his hands over it, as he often did. (She wondered what he did with his tension when his head was covered with the surgical cap, his hands sterile in their gloves.) His brow was broad with deep creases. A straight nose, a little small for the face and the wide-spaced blue eyes, its lack of length compensated by the full-lipped mouth. He was a big man with a gruff voice and magic hands. A man with purpose.

She wondered about her own purpose as she stepped out of the tent. "What do you want, McLean?"

He jerked at the sound of her voice, no sign of the lover about him now. "Dinner at Nate's. Things to discuss."

"No grab ass?"

She heard the familiar rumble. She'd said that once before, and both remembered how that had worked out. "Not right now," he said.

She doubted his word and laughed with him anyway.

His eyes traveled her up and down as though he liked what he saw, and she flushed. How had she ever thought him grandfatherly?

When he noted the cases, he nodded. "Good, you packed. We'll find you a spot in town." With that, he grabbed the duffel, seized her arm in a non-lover-like grip and pulled her toward the Jeep.

Music, dinner conversation, and a loud crash from the kitchen competed in a cacophony that almost stopped them as they stepped into La Trattoria.

"Loud," McLean said, raising his voice to compete with the din.

"'The Triumphal March' from *Aida*," Quinn said as she looked around the small café. Totally different from her first visit, more than half the tables were occupied; candles sparkled, and the pungent odor of garlic roused her taste buds. She grinned as Nate Specchio bounded to greet them, his lugubrious air lightened by the twinkle in his eye.

"Busy tonight," McLean said as they followed the little proprietor toward the back of the room.

Looking happier than Quinn had ever seen him, Nate smiled and bobbed his head. "But you'll be leaving soon, I hear?" His soft voice gave the statement a question mark ending. "Then what do we do?"

Disturbed by the question that so mirrored her own, Quinn slid into the booth and waited for McLean's answer. The big man leaned against the banquette, his shoulder to Quinn, a thoughtful look on his face.

"I know there's still work to be done, Nate, just as you do," he said, "but your community is ready to do it now. We just come in to fill the gap, like a pressure dressing or a tourniquet or a crutch, but it's only until you get your breath back, until the bleeding is staunched, and then you—your community, your people, your friends—you can take on the work yourselves and do a better job than we ever could." His words seemed practiced, oft repeated. "You know the way, my friend, better than I." He gave Nate's shoulder an encouraging squeeze, then slid into the booth beside Quinn.

His body against hers loosed shivers—pleasure, anticipation, desire—and she started to inch away, but a big hand on her thigh stopped her. *Shit.* She saw his shoulders shake as she trembled and glared, but the men just continued their conversation.

"A big job, my friend," the old man was saying with a frown. "I hope we have the courage."

"I hope we all have the courage, Nate. We're going to need it." McLean refused Chianti and ordered two coffees, then finally removed his hand from Quinn's leg and picked up the menu. He chuckled out loud as she scooted into the corner, but he made no comment, just flipped open the menu and said, "Now, what's good tonight?"

Between worry and desire, and once again sure she couldn't swallow a bite, Quinn chose the spaghetti, thinking one or two noodles might slither down. McLean ordered his usual bloody steak. Nate took their orders, and when he left, Quinn expected McLean to continue the conversation, but the big man said nothing, apparently lost in the careful preparation of his coffee, strong and sweet and laced almost by half with cream.

Nothing more about leaving, nothing about where she was to go or what she should do, and, most surprising, no mention of their weekend activities or the morning's gut-wrenching conversation. Quinn sipped her own black coffee and wondered why, and silence stretched between them, minutes filling themselves with questions unasked.

After a time that seemed forever, McLean, his eyes on the spoon clinking lazily against the side of the mug, said, "They completed the search for remains today, and the site has been officially turned back to Pentagon officials."

He seemed miles away, his expression closed.

Quinn tensed, waiting for him to elaborate. More minutes passed, but he said nothing further. Impatient now—*the man holds my life in his hands, for God's sake*—she faked an attention-getting cough and said, "So we're really done?"

"Uh-huh." He kept stirring.

"Really?" Impatience gave way to anger, and she glared at him. "That's all you can say?"

He looked up in surprise, but before he could respond, Nate was back at their table with steaming plates, then more bread, then coffee refills, and the moment was lost.

Stifling her impatience, Quinn twirled spaghetti noodles with fork and spoon and coaxed them into her mouth as McLean concentrated on cutting his meat into precise bites. The steak knife looked small in his hand. Each time the big arm brushed hers, desire closed her throat, and after a few hard-won bites she conceded defeat, pushed her plate away, and drank her coffee.

Finally, McLean broke the silence and, between bites, provided the details of moving on, a standardized procedure that allowed the community to close behind them. "Most of the volunteers are already gone, and I'm scheduled to be out of here Thursday, Friday at the latest." He mopped up the meat juices with the last chunk of garlic bread. Nothing, it seemed, dimmed his appetite.

She waited for him to explain her own departure. She had no money, no ticket home, no place to stay after tonight. And through no fault of her own, she clearly was not in the "most of the volunteers" category. She made a face as he carefully placed his knife and fork diagonally across his empty plate and pushed it away.

"I'll have to come back some," he went on, seemingly unaware that her feelings were about to overflow. "That's expected, but we're really done here. The bigger task now is at home."

As Mandy had said, they were needed at home—hate crimes increasing, war pending, relatives grieving. Guilt tempered irritation as the specter of Ground Zero, the media name for the rubble that had been the World Trade Center, rose in her mind. *It's not just about me,* Quinn thought, *but still—*

"So when do I get *my* marching orders?"

"God, DeMello," he said as though she should have known all along, "that's what we're talking about."

"What, I'm supposed to be a mind reader?"

She cocked her head, and his beard split in a big-mouthed grin that drew her own reluctant laugh.

"Sorry," he said, "sometimes I forget." He rumbled again and patted her hand.

A tingle raced up her arm. "McLean."

"Okay." He caressed her fingers before he let her go. "So here's the deal. What happens next with you?"

She scowled and reached for her coffee mug. *What does happen next?* She didn't have an answer, but she was pretty sure she knew why he'd asked.

"Wait," he butted in as though reading her mind, "before you say anything, let me talk. Sorry, I'm screwing this up, but I've got a deal for you. Got the green light from the higher-ups, so here it is."

He raised his hand as Quinn spluttered. "I had the idea before this weekend, DeMello, so just shut up and listen."

CHRIS MCLEAN SCHOOLED HIMSELF TO BE patient as Quinn scowled and muttered and finally made herself small in the corner of the red vinyl booth and stuck out her lower lip. Clear as day, her expression read, *Okay, tell me, but I'm not going to like it.*

With difficulty, he stifled his grin. *I'm fucking this up big time, but she's still making me laugh.*

All day he'd stalked the camp—overseeing the withdrawal of the volunteer staff, meeting with community resource people to ensure a smooth transition from his services to theirs, paving the way for a new normal—knowing there was still work to do, knowing that they couldn't stay any longer. Already there were rumblings about military action in Afghanistan, and he knew what the aftermath of that would be.

All day, feelings for his blond mystery woman had hummed like electric current just below the surface.

All day he'd wondered, *What am I going to do?*

Now, buoyed by his own laughter, he knew. He looked at the pouting woman at his side and grinned. "That's better," he said. "Now here's the deal."

The idea had germinated the day he'd seen her on the floor with the young National Guardsman. He'd called it, "that chanting thing you do," although by now he'd researched it, knew about meditation and mindfulness and their healing properties. He described a training module that would augment the standard mental health instruction they all received with mindfulness and music.

"I watched them cluster around you," he told Quinn, "and I watched them walk away a little taller, a little less green around the gills. I want to incorporate your work into what we already do. As I said earlier, I got an okay for you to develop the program." He waited a beat, noting that her pout had disappeared. "What do you think?"

He felt like Santa delivering a pony.

Quinn opened her mouth, but no words emerged.

His voice slipped into a persuading Irish lilt as he added, "There might be a wee bit of money in it . . . and it's for a good purpose." He held his breath for what seemed like forever and waited for her response.

"But . . .," she finally said, "but . . . that's just what I do. It's not therapy, it's just . . . what I do."

CHAPTER 29

O F ALL THE THINGS SHE'D EXPECTED him to propose, this wasn't it. When she'd said, "It's just what I do," she'd really meant it. She chanted or played her flute when she had no clue what else to do; it was the only thing that kept her from shattering. Now she tortured a strand of hair and wondered if the idea might have merit, even if it was hers. The word *purpose* tickled her brain.

"Not much of a protest, DeMello." Amusement tinged his voice. "I expected better."

When she just stared at him, he went on. "Okay—shock. You'll hit me with the rest of it later, I guess." He downed his coffee and raised his hand for a refill, and the old proprietor hurried to the table, coffee pot in hand. McLean said something she couldn't make out—about her, she suspected. Both men laughed, and she glowered pro forma, but really her heart was racing.

Could she do it? Did she want to? If not, what else would she do? Fear and hope and disbelief jumbled together as she struggled to organize her thoughts. Nate refilled their mugs and cleared the dishes. McLean gave his attention to stirring sugar into his coffee as though her answer were unimportant, but tension rippled off him in waves. She knew this mattered. She wasn't sure why.

She didn't trust either of them.

"Get real, McLean," she finally said. "It's a crock. I don't have any experience writing modules or programs or whatever you said. There must be at least a dozen people on staff who can do a better job than me." Suspicion swam in her eyes. "What's the catch?"

He beamed. "I thought you'd never ask. I get to keep you around a little longer."

Ah, there it is. She shook her head.

He waved off any protest. "Kidding. Really, in spite of your modesty, I think you *are* the one to take this forward. The DC office has a good staff writer. The trainers like the idea. Our resources are always stretched too thin, and what you do would allow us to serve a larger population more quickly." He waved his hand in the direction of the Pentagon. "You can't deny it helped here. I know it doesn't replace the standard face-to-face stuff, but it adds a valuable piece. Seems to me, anyhow." His gaze didn't waver as she considered. "You don't have to say right now. When we get there, you can talk with the people who'll be helping you and also see what money's in it."

"There?"

"Sure, Washington, the capital, my chapter. What did you think?"

She thought about the Washington Monument, visible from the freeway, and all the other monuments and museums: the heart of her country, so close and yet ...

"I've never been there," she said.

A sly smile peeked through his beard. "I know, and I've got thoughts about that, too."

Crazy, she thought as Chris McLean outlined the rest of his plan. He offered her a place to stay, something worthwhile to do, and no strings attached—at least that's what he said. In a way, it felt like another wild proposal, one that had delivered friendship and love and heartbreak. Her stomach churned, and she excused herself to find the restroom.

Business complete, she washed her hands and splashed water on her flushed face, then leaned on the counter and stared at her mirror image. A confused expression matched the confusion within. That she didn't feel she'd earned the offer or was good enough to do it apparently was beside the point. That a wife lurked in his background appeared to be irrelevant. That she was tempting fate seemed obvious. She shrugged and threw her image a grimace. *It is what it is.*

On her return, she slid into the booth across from McLean, planted her elbows on the table, and looked him straight in the eye.

"Okay, McLean, let me make sure I've got it right. You want me to create a training program so that mental health volunteers can do meditation and play the flute. You want me to contract with the Red Cross to do this, getting paid probably enough to cover one month's rent and maybe buy cat food for dinner. And you want me to do it in a city I don't know, living with a man I also don't know, in a situation that will probably leave me penniless and heartbroken. Have I got it right?"

"Sounds about right." His eyes gleamed.

She stared at him until he squirmed, clearly more than emergency work on his mind. *Or maybe I'm emergency work—who knows?* Maybe, just maybe, this would be a path out of the past that held her captive. Giddy with possibility, she suppressed a smile and affected a nonchalant shrug. "Sounds okay with me. When do we start?"

A handshake sealed the deal.

"Good," McLean said, holding her hand a little too long. "Now, let's find a bed for you." He tucked a twenty under his empty coffee mug and extricated himself from the booth. The candles were guttering, and Quinn felt a pang of nostalgia as they left LaTrattoria for what she knew would be the last time.

A short, silent ride later, they pulled up at McLean's hotel. He set the brake. "Come on."

Suspicious, she didn't move. "You promised."

McLean threw her a look she couldn't interpret, slung her bag over his shoulder, and headed toward the outside stairway. His room was on the ground floor.

Not sure whether she was glad or sad, Quinn swallowed temptation and remorse and followed him. He stopped at A-213, fumbled with the key, and opened the door, and Quinn stepped into a room. The size and smell produced instant memories of her high school gym locker. Turning up her nose, she flicked on the light. "Where's everybody?"

"Gone home." He dumped her cases on the narrow bed.

Her mood plummeted as she looked around the dingy space. *I want my mother*, she thought, recognized the absurdity, but didn't want to be alone. "Stay a minute," she said.

He grinned.

She could almost hear his heart rate accelerate. She pointed at the desk chair. "Sit."

The beard closed around the grin.

She surprised them both by reaching for her phone. "Don't leave. I'm calling Camille."

Eyebrow raised, McLean paused, then flipped the indicated chair around and sat, his arms folded on its back.

Hardly understanding herself, Quinn tried to explain as she punched in her sister's number. "Camille's the oldest, the smartest of us all, I just thought I should—"

Should what—ask for her blessing? I haven't asked for her advice since I was twelve. She started to hang up when Camille answered. Nothing for it now but to tell her.

WHEN THEIR CONVERSATION WAS OVER, QUINN turned to McLean, now thumbing through the tourist guide from the desk. "Camille thinks it's a good idea," she lied. "Want some coffee?"

He nodded. His look said, *I know a lie when I hear one.*

She fixed two cups of in-room coffee and considered her sister's words. "Are you sure," Camille had asked, "that you're not just…just doing the same thing again?" That was the problem, of course; she wasn't sure. She handed McLean a cup, leaned back against the headboard, and looked at the man whose offer would lead her down yet another unexplored path.

The grin he'd thrown her when she'd invited him to stay still hovered. So did the gleam in his eyes, but fatigue etched his countenance, and his big shoulders sagged as he played with his heavily doctored coffee, wishing, she surmised, that it was heavily doctored with something more potent than pasty-white cream substitute and seven packets of sugar.

Earlier, as they'd closed down LaTrattoria, he'd been all business, agreeing with her conditions, assuring her that whatever relationship they might have had nothing to do with the job at hand. Quinn hadn't believed him then. She didn't believe him now.

"Whatever." She waved at the phone, dismissing Camille's concerns and her own lie. "I just want to make sure we understand one another. We need to back off," she said, "not because you're not great at what you do, but because you are. I lied when I called Owen *toast.* He's out of my life, that's for sure, but not . . ." she wondered how honest she could be, decided to tell the whole truth for a change, and, as her father used to say, let the devil take the hindmost, "not out of my heart."

McLean snorted.

She shot him a hard glare. "Enough from you. You said alcoholics had to deal with their issues. Well, big guy, this is one of mine. I've been *easing my pain*"—her voice took on the dulcet tones of an old-fashioned southern belle—"like Scarlett, with good liquor and mind-blowing sex and a lot of tomorrow-be-ing-another-day, and it just gets me nightmares and depression and, if you're right, a rotten liver. So no more booze and no more sex until I get this figured out."

He grimaced. "So it's my own fault I'm cut off?"

"You got it." She suppressed a giggle and fixed him with a wide-eyed stare. *Next stop, Washington, DC, and a new home, a new job, and a new man. Not much of a change; wonder why I said yes.*

"Agreed?" she asked.

He glanced at the bed, and she could read his mind: *booze and sex and the delicious meeting of their insatiable bodies. Who wants to give that up?* She was surprised when he nodded. "Agreed," he said, and again she wondered.

CHAPTER 30

A WEEK AFTER HIS ABORTED QUINN RESCUE, Owen Johnson forced himself to face his sisters. Vivian fixed his favorite coq au vin, and he choked it down while the twins took turns providing a minute-by-minute rendition of the Quinn-less retreat—wildly successful, in large part due to a woman named Kristin, whom he was supposed to remember and didn't.

After dinner, silent and scowling, gut churning with guilt and anger and misery, he stalked the kitchen floorboards while Vivian washed the dishes, Victoria dried and put them away, and both threw him dirty looks. His apology for missing their first retreat had been dismissed with a summary wave, sincerity doubtful. He wished he were somewhere, anywhere, else. He dropped back into his chair and reached for the wine.

He'd just uncorked the second bottle of merlot when Vivian wiped her hands, laid aside the dish towel, and resumed her seat at the table. "Okay, Wen, it's all good, and we're over being mad. Now, tell us about your trip."

Victoria shoved the last plate into the cupboard and plopped down beside her.

Owen filled his glass, threw back half of its contents, and told them. Minutes into his rant, he was on his feet again, pacing, wine sloshing in its glass.

His sisters watched, silent, until he finished. Then Victoria said, "I don't understand, Owen. She was glad to see you and you spent time together and then she sent you packing? Something's fishy—"

"In Denmark," finished Vivian. "Why would she?"

"That's what I mean, Vivvy," Owen interrupted. "Karle said I should just bring her home, so I gave her a ticket, first class even, and all hell broke loose." With the memory, his chest tightened and breath caught in his throat. He drained his glass and poured another.

The sisters exchanged glances.

"A ticket?"

"Karle said?"

"Uh-huh. I told Quinn she'd been there long enough, and that it was time to come home." He shrugged and drank. It *was* time, especially with that doctor boss of hers sniffing around, but he wasn't about to share that tidbit, and he hadn't meant to bring Karle into the conversation, so he left that question untouched, too.

The tick-tock of the kitchen clock filled the room. Clearly, his sisters weren't getting this. It was so simple. He wasn't bossy. He just loved Quinn and wanted her home. He stuffed his fear down. Easier to be angry. If she wasn't so stubborn, so bullheaded, so . . .

"I mean," he continued, "a lot of the volunteers were leaving, and she had time to spend with her boss and all, and she was still having nightmares and . . . What?"

Both sisters were glaring at him now.

"What? She's too thin and she drinks too much and she doesn't know what she's doing, and she acts like a bitch jerking me around, and I'm fucking tired of it." His voice rose. The cat scurried out the door. The corgis cowered under the table. "I'm just—"

"Shut up, Owen, just shut up," his sisters shouted in unison. Shocked, he obeyed.

Victoria said, "You are *so* out of line," and Vivian said, "You need to get over yourself, you stupid man," and the argument was on, all three yelling as they hadn't since the last time their mother had taken a switch to their bottoms and ordered them to play nice.

In a sudden lull, Owen dropped into a chair, covered his face with both hands, and sobbed.

The fight was over. Without another word, his sisters tucked him into bed in the spare room under the stairs, kissed his cheeks, and left him alone.

SHAKEN, THE WOMEN SOUGHT REFUGE IN their little sitting room.

Vivian stared at her twin. "God, that was awful. I can't believe—"

"That we yelled at him when his heart is breaking?"

"Yeah, that too, but really he has his head up his—"

"Vivian Johnson!"

"Well, you know what I mean. She told him she has to figure things out, and we told him, and then he goes and tells Quinn what's best for her like he knows. These aren't *Father Knows Best* times anymore, you know."

"I know. And what about the boss he mentioned earlier. Do you think—"

"He's jealous? Hmm, could be, and it would serve him right for being so pushy."

"So man-like?" They both laughed, and the mood in the little room lightened.

"I don't think there's anything we can do but watch him self-destruct. Except maybe we can get him to help with the next retreat and keep him nearby. Bet that Karle's rubbing her hands in glee—that must be where he's been hiding out the last few days."

"And taking her advice, it sounds like." Victoria shook her head. "Like Quinn said last year about Scott—he's of age and he's been raised right. Maybe he'll get it together before it's too late. And maybe we can protect him from himself."

"And maybe we'll hear from the Queen of Secrets herself one of these days." Like girls, they saluted themselves with crossed fingers.

CHAPTER 31

WHAT THE FUCK WAS I THINKING? Chris McLean chewed at himself as he gathered his belongings. The dispirited hotel room held no trace of the electricity he and Quinn had produced just days earlier. He would be picking her up in less than an hour and, in effect, taking her home as a roommate. He threw clean underwear on top of dirty in the ragtag case that he'd carried for forty years. *My idea. I convinced her. I must be crazy.*

His mind filled with visions of Quinn as he'd seen her every day for the past three weeks—Quinn cross-legged and chanting, her eager acolytes filling the space around her; Quinn with the silver flute, her tunes drawing wounded souls like the Pied Piper; Quinn devastated by the poor devil who'd been her lover, tearfully seeking oblivion; Quinn naked and shiny, sharing his bed. In those three short weeks, she'd taken over his thoughts; now she would invade his space at his own invitation. *What the fuck am I doing?*

He zipped the case, cast one look around for forgotten items, and left the room and his doubts behind.

An hour later, Quinn sat pasted against the Jeep's passenger door as Chris drove across the Potomac River into the District of Columbia. Lighter traffic than usual, he noted, understanding that people were still staying close to home, but the cars that were out flew American flags from little plastic holders, and the gigantic flags waving from truck beds made him smile. Quinn said nothing, her look of rapt attention not disguising her apprehension. He filled the awkward silence with a guided-tour monologue but grew quiet as he negotiated the tricky off-ramp into the city and turned north toward his home. The closer they got, the more fiercely his heart beat, and his hands grew slippery on the steering wheel.

He resumed his narrative as he turned down a neighborhood street. "Foggy Bottom, where my place is, is an area of the District named for the smoke of its previous inhabitants—wharves, breweries, lime kilns, and glassworks—combined with the low-lying swampy air into a permanent fog along the waterfront. Not so much fog now, just university students and government employees and such."

The tour ended as he brought the Jeep to rest in the driveway of a three-story brick townhouse. Without waiting for invitation, Quinn climbed out and looked it over—brick facade, steps up to a red door with windows on both sides like parentheses, down to the basement apartment, pots of varying sizes overflowing with bushes and vines. He eased himself out of the vehicle, slammed the door, and stood beside her, wondering what she was thinking as she surveyed the residence of H. Christian McLean, MD.

"Wow." Hands on her hips, she looked up at him. "Pretty grand."

"Home," he said simply and nudged her up the steps.

She balked, something on her mind. "Your wife?"

"Huh?"

"Wife. Mrs. H. Christian McLean. I know it's a little late to ask, but what's she gonna say when I come waltzing into your house?"

His laugh sent a bird scooting out of the overhanging tree. "Oh, DeMello," he said when he could speak, "you continue to amaze me." He reached around her, unlocked the door, and pushed it open. "In—it's safe, I promise. Let's get settled and I'll tell you."

Quinn hesitated, wiped her hands on her jeans, and, urged on by a less-than-gentle shove, stepped into a wide, wood-paneled entry that opened into a large room whose floor-to-ceiling windows provided a tree-filled view. McLean touched her elbow and nodded to the left. An open door revealed a quaint, old-fashioned bedroom.

"Yours if you like it." He gestured her in.

She took two steps into the room, dumped her duffel, her flute case, and the red boots on the floor, and turned back toward him.

"No unpacking?"

She shrugged. "I don't imagine I'll be here long."

He harrumphed in exasperation.

The corners of her mouth tipped up. "Sorry, didn't mean to sound ungrateful, but this whole thing seems like pie in the sky."

Just as he remembered the story of the twin sisters and their clichés, her smile flickered and died, and he knew she was thinking of the other man.

He wanted to shake her. *He's not here. I'm here.* Instead he forced his shoulders to relax. *One day at a time.*

"Pie in the sky or not," he said, "you're here, so let's go out and get you acquainted with the neighborhood. Gotta get something out of my investment before you bolt."

STATELY OAKS AND ELMS, MAPLES AND sycamores, their leaves just taking on their autumn colors, lined the street, shading homes similar in age and design that marched along the sidewalk. Like old friends, these trees had watched his daily journey from home to hospital, knew his joys and sorrows, welcomed him home. Now he was sharing them.

"I like to walk, helps clear my head," he told the woman at his side as they moved along his familiar route, ignoring a twinge of unease at the self-disclosure.

"Most of the Bottom has been taken over by GW, George Washington University," he continued, nodding at a stately old home, Greek letters like a tattoo above its door. "Fraternities, sororities, offices, even some graduate programs are housed in antique splendor. I like that. Lots better than tearing them down and replacing them with uglies."

Farther along, as he identified other places of interest, he realized he was showing off. Flustered and a little embarrassed, he was glad when the rumble of Quinn's stomach interrupted.

"Sorry, here's me going on like a ten-cent tour guide and you're starving." He checked his watch. "Guess we missed lunch." He tipped his head toward a restaurant across from the Foggy Bottom Metro Station. "I like this place. How about an early dinner?"

They sat on Circa's patio as day faded and ordered food and drinks. The early evening crowd flowed around them. The air pulsed with anticipation.

Toying with his wine glass, Chris lapsed into silence. Quinn squeezed lemon into her Diet Pepsi. "The wife," she prompted finally.

He grimaced. "Spoils the mood."

She glared. "I need to know."

"If you say so." He drained his glass, motioned the server for another. He didn't like to talk about his failures. When his wine arrived and Quinn's intensity hadn't wavered, he sucked in air, released it slowly. "Okay. Gen and I married while I was in med school. We had two girls. Then we decided we were better friends than married people and we separated. I live here and I'm happy as a clam. She lives in Connecticut and raises horses, much better off without me. Sometimes we celebrate grandchildren's birthdays together." He emptied his second glass. "That's it in a nutshell. Satisfied?"

She cocked her head at him. Satisfied? Maybe, maybe not. But when their food arrived, she let it drop.

Relieved, he sliced into his steak but kept a wary eye on Quinn as she worked her way through the soft-shell crabs.

"What?" Quinn laid her utensils across her plate, folded her napkin on the table, and addressed his scrutiny. "Spinach in my teeth?"

Shaking his head, Chris laughed and signaled for the check. Her energy was palpable. Excited, wired, worried—not at all ready to call it a day. He levered himself to his feet, which *were* ready to call it a day, and held out his hand. "Ready for more?"

At her nod, he pulled her up, and they followed Twenty-Third Street toward the National Mall.

Blocks later, Quinn's steps faltered, and her mouth dropped into an O of perfect awe. Before them, illuminated brighter than day, the Lincoln Memorial stood in regal majesty.

McLean smiled. *Good old Abe always gets the newbies.* He ached to wrap his arms around her, draw her against his chest, and share her amazement. He took a step back to avert temptation.

Quinn glanced up, cocked an eyebrow at him, and grinned back.

Devil woman, reads my mind. Like a little kid caught stealing cookies from the jar, he shoved his hands in his pockets. *Better safe than sorry*, he thought, and tried to be content with watching as she soaked up the magnificent sight.

"Wow," she said after a bit and reached back for his hand. When she didn't find it, she turned toward him with a questioning look.

Before his brain could vote no, McLean pulled his hand from his pocket and clasped hers. *Safety's overrated.* His thick fingers linked with her long slender ones before she could change her mind.

Hand in hand, they strolled to the base of the memorial. Even in the October twilight, crowds swarmed up and down the steps. More than once, McLean had rested on these steps and savored the sweep from Lincoln's feet to the Washington Monument in the distance. Sometimes he brought troubled thoughts here and left feeling more peaceful. Tonight, he lowered himself to a step, relieved that this vista, at least, was unchanged by the nation's tragedy.

Quinn scampered up to stand at Lincoln's feet, and he was happy to release troubled thoughts and let his eyes follow her— tight jeans, firm butt, black jacket hiding the treasure of breasts that overflowed his own large hands. His stomach clenched and he shuddered. *Crazy. I'm crazed, bewitched, befuddled, and I need to get over it.* He forced his gaze toward the reflecting pool and resolved to let her go.

He started as Quinn settled in beside him, two steps down, and rested her head against his knee. His heart beat faster, his recalcitrant hand tangled into her hair, and, when he felt her sigh, his resolutions crumbled.

They sat in silence for a long time, the monuments to history spread around them in their personal tableau. At her whispered request, he named them—Vietnam, Korea, World War II, and Washington, surrounded by wind-whipped American flags. Then, arm in arm, they journeyed home.

BACK AT THE TOWNHOUSE, MCLEAN SLID the key into the lock, opened the door, and stepped aside for Quinn to enter. As he closed the door behind them and switched on the light, Quinn felt her smile wobble. He stepped toward her, and electricity flickered as his arm brushed hers.

"Here." He placed the key in her palm. "Yours."

Time crept as they stood eye to eye. In his, Quinn saw desire as thick and sweet as her own. Caught in their icy blue depths, mouth suddenly dry, heart racing, she felt her resolve melt. She couldn't move. If he took her here on the fancy rug in this beautiful hallway, there would be no protest. Breathless, she waited.

But as she watched, everything changed: His eyes grew opaque. He gave himself a quick shake as though escaping quicksand, and he stepped back.

No! She blinked at the unwelcome space between them and lowered her eyes. Tension released, her shoulders dropped, and she wanted to cry.

"We start tomorrow at eight," he said as though nothing untoward had occurred. "Help yourself to whatever's in the kitchen." He dropped a kiss on the top of her head, turned right into his bedroom, and closed the door, hard.

Alone in the hall, emotions buzzing like the creatures they resembled, Quinn stood for a long time. The touch of his lips lingered. Her mouth yearned. The key held the warmth of his hand. She closed her fingers around it, turned off the light, and entered the bedroom that was now her own.

At first glance, she had judged the room quaint, old fashioned. Now, in the puddle of light from the bedside lamp, she could see it was more: walls softly off-white; drapery damask and a few shades darker; duvet and pillows rosy, plump, inviting. The colors wrapped around her, drew her in. She ran her fingers over the dresser's surface—birds-eye maple, smooth, simple, functional. Its clean lines brought Owen's woodwork into her mind and, with it, his hands—sanding, polishing, caressing the wood, her body. On a pulse of pain, she sank to the carpet, huddled in her own embrace.

She must have dozed, and when she woke, the pain was gone. Distressed by her own weakness and determined to banish both Owen Johnson and Chris McLean from her thoughts, Quinn got to her feet and looked around. The room was still soft, inviting, and she sighed in relief and surprise. *This is okay, feels homey, whatever that is.*

Her thoughts drifted and a smile took over her face. *Lincoln. Wow.* She'd seen pictures of it all, but the reality ... *double wow.* As patriotic as most Americans, she saluted the flag and voted and knew the words to the "Star-Spangled Banner," but the recent tragedy had shaken her, shaken them all. She'd been sorry when McLean had stepped away. He'd almost broadcast his desire, and she craved the safety of his arms—that and a shared love of country. Huh!

Love and safety? And the old dog had kept his word, at least for tonight.

She wasn't entirely sure how she felt about that, so she brushed her teeth, pulled her sleep shirt over her head, and slipped between the cool white sheets.

CHAPTER 32

HEAD POUNDING, OWEN CAME OUT OF sleep in a dark and alien room. His stomach lurched as the walls spun around him for an unbearably long time before settling back into their recognizable places. For a moment he couldn't think how he had come to be in his sisters' spare bedroom. Fearful that his head might fall off, he gingerly assumed a seated position and remained still as memory returned, pain and embarrassment its unwelcome attendants. Drawing a shuddering breath, he fought to orient himself.

No light peeked through the curtains. No early morning noises emanated from the adjacent kitchen. He located his watch, tucked by a sisterly hand into the breast pocket of his shirt—five-fifteen. He slid off the bed. Feet bare and cold on the wood floor, he stood still until the need to vomit passed. Thinking *I can't face the girls right now*, he donned yesterday's clothes and tiptoed from the house. To the east, the sky lightened as he fumbled for the car keys.

Home, gotta get home. I'll just rest a few days and then figure things out. Like an escaping teen, he let the Audi roll half a mile down the hill before he started the engine.

As the car wove its way down the gravel road, Technicolor images exploded in his mind. Roiling and streaming scenes—tangled in her hair, drowning in her eyes, finding home as her body opened like a flower to take him in, and then thrust out like that goddamned angel from paradise. He didn't want to think; he didn't want to dream. Chest tight, mouth rank as a sewer, heart thudding as though it had no motivation, Owen felt old as dirt and grievously used. Anger churned his empty stomach, and he pulled off the road to puke.

Banning images from his mind, he negotiated the twenty-two miles to Winnemucca with the care of the still-inebriated, stopping only at Walmart for two bottles of Maker's Mark.

Chapter 33

QUINN WOKE, STRETCHED, AND REALIZED SHE hadn't dreamed at all. The bedside clock blinked 7:10, then 7:11, then 7:12. Light trickled around the edges of the drapery, but no sounds emanated from the house. Reluctant to leave her cozy nest, she wondered where McLean was, what she was expected to do. Once again, he'd left her without an instruction manual. With a mental shrug—*at least I won't be running into a wife*—she clambered down and straightened the bed clothes, then hurried through her morning ablution.

Clean, she rummaged in her duffel and retrieved her clothes. Dismayed, she considered the black jacket and the black slacks—wrinkles and dirt and a faintly unpleasant odor. No help for it now. She shook them hard, put them on over the last of her clean undies, and hoped no one would stand too near. She needed a washer and dryer, she needed new clothes, she needed to get some money, but first she needed to find her host. Squaring her shoulders, she stepped into the hall.

To her left, a wall of bare windows revealed a rooftop view of trees and city and the pale light of a fall morning.

She headed in that direction. Finding the room empty, she looked around. In sharp contrast to the girlie nature of her room, this one was all male: overflowing bookshelves, a brick fireplace awaiting the touch of a match to send flames skyward, a brown leather chair that boasted the obvious contours of its owner facing the fireplace as though ignoring the buttery leather sofa. Two other chairs and an ottoman completed the seating choices. Reading lights and side tables stood ready, and she could picture him there, cut-glass tumbler of whisky in hand—Waterford probably, nothing else was tough enough— in front of a fire crackling just for him. "Happy as a clam," he'd called himself. She envisioned herself snuggled into the buttery sofa, happy and—

"Quinn, good morning."

She whirled at the sound of his voice.

HEART THUNDERING, CHRIS MCLEAN HAD WATCHED Quinn check out the home he had crafted for himself, the home that until now had never had a female in residence. He wondered what she would make of it. As he worried and hated that same worry, Quinn examined the books, considered the photos in their assorted frames, admired the fireplace, and, with a dreamy expression, stroked the sofa. Instant imagination overdrive.

Get it together, he ordered himself and greeted his guest. "Quinn, good morning."

She jumped, whirled around. "McLean, I didn't hear you. Sorry, I was just—"

"Acquainting yourself with your new home, I expect. I hope it's to your liking. But come now, let's explore the kitchen and see what treats Connie has for us."

"Connie?" She sucked in a breath and her eyes darkened.

He guessed her thoughts and suppressed a smile. "Connie's my minder, I guess you'd call her, or maybe my keeper. Connie Marvel. I hired her one day not long after I'd moved in here, twenty years give or take, because it was crystal clear I'd not be cleaning up well after meself, living here alone and all as I do. Now she cleans and puts food in the fridge and tells me weekly how she'd have been for retiring except that I'd never make it on my own." He didn't notice that he'd slipped into his mother's Irish.

Quinn's mouth quirked upward, but she said nothing more. *Laughing at me?*

Interrupting the awkwardness that had taken him, he said, "So let's see what treats Mrs. Marvel has in store for us," and led the way into the kitchen. Walls the color of rich cream and polished cherry-wood cabinets showcased the black and stainless appliances and the brightly colored dishes arranged on open shelves. Here, too, tall windows faced trees and city roofs.

Every morning, Chris drank his coffee here with the light pouring in and the view as familiar as his own hand. Alone in this cheerful room, he prepared for whatever his day might bring: a difficult surgery, frightened parents, a tragedy miles or continents away. They were habits developed over the years, habits he knew and understood. Now this woman stood beside him.

What in God's green earth was I thinking?

A man of action, he eyed her, considering—he *would* feel much better if he kissed her senseless. He stepped forward. She stepped back. *Devil woman.* He huffed and gestured toward a stool at the counter, already set for two. "Sit. This morning only I'll do the fixin'."

With the counter safely between them, he poured coffee and handed Quinn a steaming yellow mug, then set about breakfast.

The shiny refrigerator disgorged platters of sliced meats and cheeses, rolls and biscuits and a bowl of fruit salad, all double-wrapped in plastic. Once again, he blessed his house-keeper as he set out the food and a pitcher of orange juice and topped off their coffee. Impulsive behavior tamped down for the moment, he settled himself beside Quinn at the counter. "Eat. It's all good."

He tucked into his breakfast, hopeful for the days ahead.

CHAPTER 34

ARLY ON A MID-OCTOBER MORNING, JOHN Perry and Mike Sakelaris stood on the doorstep of Owen's Winnemucca home avoiding each other's eyes and hoping no one in the neighborhood was up. Best friends since childhood, John, Mike, and Owen had played football and basketball together, graduated kindergarten and high school together, stood up at each other's weddings, and become Uncle John, Uncle Mike, and Uncle Owen.

"Are you sure we should be doing this?"

John's life view involved letting people do their own thing. The idea of an intervention was so far from his reality that he hadn't even understood the word when Victoria and Vivian Johnson had cornered him two days earlier in the hunting supplies aisle at Walmart.

"You know he's a mess," Mike replied, echoing the word Owen's sisters had used. "I mean, we all drink, but nobody holes up for two weeks with a bottle." They were hard-drinking men for sure, but only on Friday nights. On Saturday, it was back to business.

A chill ran down his back, and John fiddled with the zipper on his windbreaker, unsure whether his discomfort stemmed from the frosty October air or the task at hand. "This is just weird, man. We're supposed to play basketball, not be therapists."

"It's a puzzlement, for sure," Mike answered obliquely. He and John were still married to their original wives, and this business with Owen and *that woman* confused them both. But they'd met her, and they'd liked her, and both had seen their old friend come back to life in her company. Mike took a deep breath and grinned down at John. "Besides, if we don't do this, the twins will skin us alive. And it's Owen, for God's sake."

"Okay." John shuffled his feet and bent to retrieve the hidden key. "Somebody's got to do something, and I guess that somebody's us." He paused, key in hand. "Should we knock?"

"Hell, no. In fast, no chance for escape. Let's get his head out of his ass so we can get back to work."

John turned the key, Mike pushed open the door, and they stepped in to confront their best friend.

OWEN LOOKED UP AT THE SOUND of his front door opening. *Shit*, he thought, *should've seen this coming.*

Flushing, he knew what they would see—mail and papers unattended on the floor; empty glasses sticky with whatever booze he'd found in his kitchen after the two bottles of Maker's Mark had gone dry; food wrappers from Pizza Hut and the café on Main Street that delivered and the remnants of last night's frozen pot pie; himself in rank, sleep-worn sweats with bloodshot eyes and a ten-day beard and the world's worst bedhead. And to top things off, his beautiful living room smelled like a sewer.

He hadn't meant for things to get so out of hand.

At first, it had been about avoiding the dream images of Quinn that had come as soon as he closed his eyes, but it quickly morphed into avoiding his own thoughts and memories and the feelings he'd long shoved inside and labeled *Done*. Without the viscous coating of alcohol, they had all clamored for his attention: Mimi, whom he'd loved with a young man's passion, the woman who had married him and borne children who died and then left him to love another; Karle, who wanted him, whom he'd tried to love and couldn't; his sisters, who no longer needed him; Quinn, who bewitched him against his will, who needed him but had just left him—for another, he was sure, remembering the look in the big man's eyes. He had trusted them all. Now he was alone. Thoughts of his father's second family—his father's lies—had been buried deep. Grief, anger, fear—these feelings had coursed through him, and he'd poured another drink.

Many other drinks, he thought now. With a grimace, he ran his hands through his tangled hair and stood to face his friends.

"Owen," said John, also grimacing.

Behind his shorter friend, Mike nodded and wrinkled his nose.

"Guys," Owen said, eyes on the floor and wishing himself invisible or, better yet, dead. "Sorry you got dragged into this. The girls?"

Both men nodded, unsure what their next move was supposed to be.

Feeling ill-used and cranky, Owen continued. "An intervention, is it? I thought that only came after years of heavy drinking. I'm apparently only allowed a week?"

"Two," his friends responded in unison.

Owen raised his eyes from the floor and didn't like what he saw: John's eyes riveted on his own shoes, Mike's hand clutching the door handle, and both men looking as though they would bolt at any minute. In that moment, he was very tired of himself and his homegrown drama and very sorry for these good friends.

"Ten days," he shot back, feeling ridiculous and suddenly awash with the stupidity of it all. "Just ten days." When they looked up at him, he grinned and stuck out his hand. "Come on in, but leave the door open, let in some fresh air. I'll put coffee on and you can say what you've come to say."

Chapter 35

"So what's next?" Quinn asked as she rewrapped the depleted breakfast trays and slid them back into the refrigerator. "And just so you know, I need a washer and dryer, a bank, and a Macy's."

McLean outlined his plan for the day, which included introductions at the Red Cross office and dinner at some place she didn't know.

"Clothes, money," she prompted.

"Laundry in the basement, Macy's downtown, but what do you need money for?"

Quinn's temper flared—another man to take care of her? Furious, she turned on him. "I pay my own way or I leave."

"I invited you," he shot back. "I don't need your money."

The fight was on. She shouted. He growled.

In the midst of her own rant, she really looked at him—jaw set, expression mulish, eyes full of worry—a prideful man who took care of things and only wanted to take care of her. *God,* she thought, *another one.* For whatever reason, humor surfaced and she started to laugh.

"Jazus, woman," he began.

She crossed the kitchen to him and put her hand over his mouth. "McLean, shush up and listen."

He did.

"This is important to me, and I can afford it," she said and told him about her trust fund. "Gramps was an engineer. He invented some stuff and made a boatload of money and set up a trust for me."

She didn't mention the rest of the story—that she'd been flabbergasted by the lawyer's disclosure, ten days after her maternal grandfather's sudden death; that her mother had been furious that his money had not come her way; that she considered it sacred, drew on it only for emergencies and felt both grateful and guilty whenever she did.

"I have to do this," she said now.

McLean tipped his head in a considering way and stared at her for a long moment before he nodded.

After that, things went smoothly. By the end of day one, she'd accomplished her goals: She'd met the Red Cross staff and signed an agreement; she'd transferred money to a new bank account; and she'd shopped at Macy's, where she'd splurged on new jeans, new black slacks, and two sweaters, one blue and the other green.

Not bad for one day's work, she thought as she put away her new clothes, set the washing machine to work on the old ones, and went off to dinner at the Capital Grille.

WITH SURPRISING EASE, THEY FELL INTO a routine. Mornings, Quinn's yoga and meditation, McLean's coffee and newspaper, and then off to work. Evenings were the same in reverse: drinks on the deck or in front of the fire as winter approached, McLean with his heavily doctored coffee or, as she had suspected, whisky in a cut-glass tumbler, and Quinn with Diet Pepsi iced and lemoned and sipped with resignation; meals in local restaurants or Connie's specialties at the kitchen counter; heated debates about the proposed Patriot Act, the invasion of Afghanistan, the search for Bin Laden, the traffic and the weather. There was never a mention of things more intimate.

She wanted Owen, but he was gone. McLean was tantalizingly here, and she yearned but didn't dare. She wanted tequila and endured Pepsi. She wondered what McLean wanted—surely not just her less-than-stellar company. Alone in the darkness of her own room, thoughts and memories tormented her, and she woke from half-remembered dreams that left streaks of tears on her cheeks.

Daytimes, it was easier to put away sadness. She'd felt a bubble of excitement as she signed the agreement. *Not much money,* she thought, *but a little, and a ticket home as promised.* Whatever else, these people thought she offered something of value, just like the twins. *One day I'll tell McLean about the Wildflower Inn,* she thought and giggled, surprised and amused at the idea of the man in her future. Then Owen's sad-eyed face swam into view and the bubble burst. With apprehension, she settled in to do her job. Creating a program was as hard as it sounded.

Jenny Chang, one of the local staff, volunteered to co-create the new module. "Let me sit with you," she'd requested, "so I can get the feel of it. You show me, and I'll do the writing." Relieved, Quinn agreed, and soon anyone lucky enough to be present gathered with them in the limited space of the training room.

NEAR THE END OF OCTOBER, two weeks into the task, Quinn arrived at the office early, "bright-eyed and bushy-tailed," she'd reassured McLean after a weekend of nonstop sleep. She'd skipped her daily yoga, left him to eat alone, and only when he threatened to drag her off to a doctor had she roused enough to choke down a bowl of chicken noodle soup.

Ensconced on her mat, Quinn tried to ignore her queasy stomach, focusing instead on the earnest young woman who sat beside her. Face round and smooth, at present devoid of expression, Jenny was all business. She mirrored Quinn's pose, made copious notes, and exuded self-esteem. Quinn wanted some of that. But she had seen the sparkle in the younger woman's mysterious dark eyes, the way the corners of her mouth had turned up whenever Chris McLean entered their space, and then the clouding as he left, seemingly unaware of her regard, and she didn't like the direction of her thoughts.

"Jenny, how old are you?"

Chang considered the abrupt question and apparently decided it wasn't inappropriate. "Twenty-three. Why?"

"Just wondered." Quinn shrugged, annoyed at herself for letting personal matters intrude. "Anyway . . . this is what I do."

At the end of the day, McLean found her in the parking garage, curled up in his Jeep. "Christ, DeMello, I thought you were lost. What the hell are you doing here?"

She struggled into a sitting position and hastily wiped her tear-streaked face. "I just needed some space, okay? You don't have to play chauffeur, you know. I can go public like everybody else." She wasn't about to tell him that she'd been so tired she'd almost crawled to the Jeep and had fallen asleep the moment her head hit the seat.

"Easy . . . God, you're prickly these days." Scowling, he climbed in, buckled his seat belt, and started the engine. "I just didn't know where you were, and I was worried."

She scowled back. She felt great now—nothing to worry about.

"So sue me," he said. "If you need your space, I'll get you the fucking bus schedule."

Invigorated by her afternoon nap, mood improving as his deteriorated, Quinn straightened. "Nope, it's taxis or nothing for this working girl."

His beard twitched, but he didn't comment on her self-descriptor.

"Seriously, McLean." She ignored the twitch and suppressed her own grin as he eased them out of the garage. "Seriously, this is harder than I thought it would be. I know what I do but I don't have a clue how it's helpful to anybody else." A raised hand warded off his words. "I know it is . . . otherwise they wouldn't leave me presents."

CHRIS HAD SEEN THE COLLECTION OF tokens arranged on her dresser, feathers and shells and stones and tightly folded notes in front of an antique silver frame, the only things she had unpacked from the battered duffel she carried. The tiny gold bell he'd tucked into the folds of her blanket dangled on a chain next to the puffy silver heart. She fingered them when she was thinking, clutched them in one fist when her eyes clouded. He wondered if she knew it had come from him.

Veering away from dangerous thoughts, he maneuvered through rush hour traffic. Beside him, Quinn still fussed. "But I don't get it, and I can't expect that little girl . . ."

"Chang?"

"Yeah. Jenny Chang. Say, McLean did you ever—"

He jerked the wheel, earning an angry honk from the car beside them. "Christ, DeMello, she's young enough to be my granddaughter."

The corners of her mouth turned up. "Just wondered."

Snorting, he finessed the roundabouts. "Used to be busier," he muttered, changing the subject. "Wonder if this place will ever be the same."

"Toughen up, McLean, it'll all get back to normal someday."

He grinned, happy that *she* sounded back to normal. He'd been ready to pack her off to the urgent care. He pulled into his driveway and turned off the engine. With an abrupt change of mood that had him reeling, she threw open her door and tumbled from the car. "Come on, McLean, last one to the corner buys ice cream."

Chapter 36

On Trigger, John Perry's big blond stallion, Owen cantered down the lane toward the barn and the Wildflower Inn Bed and Breakfast. The sun had just broken the horizon, and he was hungry—hungry and sober and sane. *Maybe the twins will be happier with me*, he thought. *Maybe they'll give me breakfast. And maybe a chance to make up.*

The message from his friends had been straight: They would not let him drink himself into oblivion, no matter how bad he felt. They had Trigger trailered and parked in front of his house, saddle bags bulging with food and water. He was to go up into the hills and not come down until, in John's words, "your head is out of your ass."

He knew they were right.

They drank his coffee. He showered and dressed. Mike fixed the eggs and bacon they had brought on this excursion into Intervention Land. Then his best friends watched as he drove toward the hills and his rendezvous with sobriety.

Now, tired and sore from sleeping rough, ready for a hot shower and a razor, he felt better than he had in weeks. *It's about trust,* he thought, *and about knowing what's mine to fix and what isn't. About not being mad all the time. And about believing that what I want is possible. God, how do I do all that?*

He unsaddled the horse, wiped him down, and filled the water trough. When he looked up from the chores, his sisters were standing on their veranda watching him. Neither said a word. Neither brought him coffee.

A deep breath for courage. *I deserve this,* he reminded himself, all too aware of the worry he'd caused not only his friends but these two as well. He vaulted over the corral fence and strode toward the house.

They watched.

"Girls," he said as he drew closer, "I'm sorry."

That was all it took.

Later, around the remnants of breakfast, the siblings sat in silence, coffee mugs in hand, elephant still in the room.

Owen cleared his throat. "I know I've been acting like a loony toon," he began, "between feeling sorry for myself and blaming Quinn and then hiding out in," another throat-clearing, "in the bottle. Just so you know, I won't be doing that again. It took three days before my head stopped pounding."

Vivian and Victoria exchanged glances that held no sympathy.

"Yeah, penance sucks." He hoped he looked as contrite as he felt—it had been a really bad three days.

Victoria chuckled, having paid such penance herself on occasion. "So, what now? How will it be different?"

Throwing her sister an appreciative glance, Vivian addressed her brother. "Yes, Wen, what's going to be different?"

He took a big gulp of coffee. "Not sure exactly," he said, "except no hiding out. Bottom line, I can't help how I feel about Quinn, and I can't make her love me." He rubbed his hands over his face in a cleansing motion. "I'll just have to deal with that. And believe it or not, I've got as many skeletons as she does … 'issues,' I mean." He made air quotes around the word as they'd seen Quinn do often enough, and then scrubbed at the bridge of his nose. "I guess I need to deal with them, too. But I thought, if you'd let me, that I'd help with the next couple of retreats while I get it figured out."

Expecting an ecstatic response, Owen was stunned by their silence. "What? You don't want me?"

Vivian answered for them both. "It's not that, Owen. Are you sure that's what *you* want to do?"

"Of course. It'll be grand." He flashed a smile.

They accepted his offer.

He couldn't interpret the look in their eyes.

FOR THE NEXT FEW DAYS, PREPARATION for the upcoming retreat claimed everyone's attention. The weather was holding, cold but no snow, and this one would be different—three mother-and-son pairs, the children preteens, all friends from Gymboree days, a perfect group for hiking and riding.

In the kitchen, the sisters pored over their meal plans.

"Enough's enough. This will be fine. The kids can do cleanup, the moms prep—sharp knives and all—and what kid doesn't like mac and cheese?" Victoria tossed her pencil on the table and stood, hands massaging her perpetually sore back. "Want a beer?" She went to the refrigerator and selected a Corona.

Giving the menu one last look, Vivian shook her head. "Not yet, but I think we'd better talk while we have a minute to ourselves."

"Kristin?" Victoria asked.

"Dusting, hopefully not breaking anything else." Housework was clearly not in Kristin's skill set. The last piece to fall had been the ornamental shepherd girl with her ruffles.

"Owen?" Earlier, they had watched Owen rake leaves in a hyperactive frenzy.

"I know," her sister groaned, "it's like having toddlers in the house. Or wounded—"

"Warriors," Victoria finished. "Yep. At least Wen worked at his real job this week. Kristin seems glued in place. What're we gonna do?"

In unison, they chanted, "Where's Quinn when we need her?" Laughter followed. Vivian got her own beer and clinked the bottle neck against her sister's. "They're adults. They're safe. We'll just have to watch while they figure things out."

CHAPTER 37

HE EAST COAST WEATHER GREW BRISK as November approached. Cold damp air insinuated itself up her pant legs and swirled around her neck as Quinn pulled her green sweater tighter and hurried toward McLean's—*home*, she corrected, ignoring the discombobulating sensations that agitated her gut—and the fireplace always ready to take away the chill. Her demand for taxis notwithstanding, she had mastered the Metro system and enjoyed her time on the trains. Some days, the walk from the station seemed longer than others. Today was one of those days—long blocks and gloomy skies. Her hair whipped across her face. Perpetually cold, she longed for crisp, dry Nevada air. Along the way, orange candles twinkled in windows and carved pumpkin faces leered at her from front steps.

Oh my God. It's Halloween. Nevada Day. How could I forget?

Thinking about home and Nevada's October 31 birthday celebration—a parade, street vendors, costumes from the 1800s, and plenty of booze—she climbed the stairs and let herself into the house, flicked on all the lights, and touched a match to the kindling in the fireplace. Only the crackling of the new blaze broke the silence, but she called out anyway. "McLean, you home?"

Her voice echoed. No one answered. McLean had resumed his hospital practice. Many mornings, he was gone before she woke and returned long after she'd fallen asleep. She missed him. She knew most of the volunteers by now and was included in their after-work plans, drinks and movies, and even Saturday excursions, but she usually demurred and spent the evenings curled in McLean's big chair reading or watching old movies. She was used to being alone, but not to being lonely.

Now she was lonely. And it *was* Nevada Day.

On a whim, she picked up the phone. Harry Reid, Nevada's senior senator, seemed like a person too busy to call about parties. John Ensign, Nevada's junior senator, was a better bet. She'd never met him, but at home that didn't matter: Everybody knew everybody in Nevada. She got the number from information and punched it in.

"Senator Ensign's office, Aaron Kinne here."

"Aaron?" Surprise colored her voice. "Aaron Kinne from Carson City?"

"I am. And who might you … Oh my God, I recognize your voice. It's Quinn, Quinn DeMello, right?"

They talked, excited strangers in a strange land. Aaron had graduated from Carson High the year before Quinn. His wife, Leslie, a high school girlfriend who'd stuck, remained in Nevada with their four children, so Aaron had a bachelor pad in DC and went home when he could. By the time she hung up, Quinn had an invitation to his annual home-away-from-home Nevada Day party.

IN THE GATHERING DUSK, CHRIS MCLEAN trudged up his front steps and let himself in. The little heart he'd held in his hand yesterday morning had been too tired to keep beating, and he had spent today with unsurprised but grieving parents. He'd lost patients before—not often, but still too many—and there was no avoiding the anguish of it. He wanted a drink, more than one if he could, and he wanted a woman, just one it seemed, and he knew he would have neither.

Quinn's voice rang out before the door closed. "Hey, McLean, we're going to a party."

She danced down the hall and wrapped him in a big hug, then danced away caroling, "They say there's a party," like a four-year-old on her birthday. He wanted to smile as he hung up his jacket and followed Quinn's chatter, but he couldn't quite manage it.

"A Nevada Day party. Nevada's birthday, anniversary of statehood." Her words sang over her shoulder, and her feet jigged to an imaginary tune as she filled a mug with freshly brewed coffee and the requisite cream and sugar. "And here, well, Nevadans are Nevadans—and we're invited."

He'd seen her giddy with drink and sex, but never like this. He straightened his shoulders, screwed a smile on his face, and tried to disguise his grief.

"Nevada Day, party ti…"

As she turned to hand him the coffee, her words trailed away, and he knew he hadn't done a very good job.

"My God, McLean, what's wrong?" She reached her free hand to his cheek. "What's wrong?"

His habitual stoicism faltered as she led him into the living room, pushed him down into his chair, and secured the mug in his hand. It had been years since he'd poured out a patient story—there had been no one to listen, and he never thought he needed it anyway—but now, as she perched before him on the footstool, one comforting hand resting on his thigh, he told her and felt the better for it.

Partway through the telling, she climbed into his lap, snuggled against him, and murmured soothing noises, and in the silence, when the story was done, they held each other. Finally, she pulled away and wiped his tears and then her own.

She dabbed at his shirt front. "Got you wet, big guy."

"Thank you," he said as he caught her hand and brought it to his lips. "Thank you."

LATER, AFTER A BRIEF BUT HEATED skirmish over whether to go to the party or not, Chris McLean and Quinn DeMello stepped out the door to be met by a small Darth Vader and a slightly smaller Princess Leia.

"Trick or treat," they chorused, the boy's voice carrying his sister's whisper.

As Quinn laughed out a jumbled story about celebrating Halloween on the thirtieth to protect Carson City's children from real-life ghouls and goblins, assorted minions scurried closer and held their pillowcases open. His heart lighter, Chris dug in his wallet for dollar bills in lieu of candy. No one complained.

Loot collected, the huddle of children and their hovering parents surged toward the next festooned doorway. As a sudden breeze fluttered costumes and swirled the leaves around their ankles, Quinn shivered and linked her arm with his.

"You need a coat." Chris snuggled her close to his own always-warm body.

"Nah, I'm never cold." She didn't pull away.

He said nothing more as they traversed the six blocks to the party.

The revelers greeted Quinn like a long-lost friend, these men and women she didn't know, and they included Chris in her Nevada credentials. The door had barely shut behind them when she disappeared into the crowded room.

As Chris shrugged off his jacket, a tall, slender man of uncertain age greeted him. "Aaron Kinne," he introduced himself and pressed a small glass of something dark and vile-looking into Chris's hand. "Here, this'll catch you right up."

"Chris McLean." The men shook hands. Chris made a face at the drink. "Thanks, I think."

His host laughed. "Picon punch," he said. "It's a Nevada thing."

It tasted vile, and then it didn't. Knowing his hospital calendar was clear, McLean became a willing convert to the "Nevada thing." *One won't hurt*, he told himself and snorted at his own folly. With the second drink, the lingering grief slid away. After that, he easily slipped into conversation—politics, war, speculation about the future—and was swept into the current of hope that filled the crowded room. *Maybe we will smile again*, he thought, accepting his third Picon. He was laughing at a Nevada story that didn't seem to have either a punch line or an ending when Quinn sidled up to him, a silly grin on her face. "Almost time to go home, big guy?"

He felt a pull in his belly—was that invitation in her voice? He raised his brow at the glass in her hand.

"Oh, it's just a Picon, no big deal." She giggled and threw back the remains. "I was practically raised on 'em."

She turned, stumbled, and righted herself. "Whoops. Gotta say good night, and I'll meet you at the door."

He felt a little unsteady himself as he finished his drink, thanked Aaron Kinne, and hunted down his coat. Apparently, Picon punch—"ice, small bit of grenadine, shot Picon, splash soda stirred and finished with a brandy float, *in that order*," he'd been advised several times—held a bigger punch than expected. He watched Quinn circle the room, strutting in her butt-hugging jeans, green sweater stretched tight, red boots flashing. A hug, a light kiss, a laugh—it was hard to reconcile this joyous creature with his sad-eyed Quinn. He shook away this conundrum as she returned to his side, black jacket in hand.

"Ready then?"

She flashed her dynamite smile. "Ready when you are, H. Christian McLean."

His heart rate shot skyward.

They navigated the now dark and empty streets, steadying each other as their feet crunched in the thick bed of leaves. Here and there, a pumpkin grin still glimmered. Chris held her tight against his side. "Those Picons are potent," he commented as she stumbled.

"*Three* Picons anyway," she giggled, "over my limit. Over anybody's limit."

Laughing, they fought the wind down the streets and up the stairs and fell into the house.

CHAPTER 38

Chris McLean only meant to smooth her windblown hair, thank her for a fun night, and escape alone to his room. What he *really* wanted, that was a different matter. He wanted to take her over and over and over until he could understand this thing that bound him, again and again until he could be done with her and let her go.

His fingers tangled in her hair.

She froze.

His hand stilled, waiting, as need pulsed in the winter air.

She stepped closer and raised her eyes. In them he saw the sad, the need.

She laid her palm on his cheek. "I want you," she whispered. "God help us both, but I want you."

His heart leapt even as he knew this was not about him. No more grab ass, she'd made him promise. Holding himself in check, he cupped her face with his hands. "Darlin' girl, is this wise? We're both a bit the worse for the drink, you know."

She cocked her head as though considering, then whispered

so low he had to lean in to hear. "In vino veritas, don't they say? Please."

His control broke. With a moan—half prayer, half protest—he scooped her into his arms and headed for the bedroom.

The moon cast shadows, and a king-sized sleigh bed held dominion over this room that had never before known passion. Warm, inviting, tempting, like the woman in his arms.

Toss her down, tear off her clothes, take her now. He ground his teeth against the surging need. His body thundered, *Do it, do it now.* His heart, usually silent, whispered, *No.* Gently, he placed his pliant burden on the bedside chair.

She sat motionless as he removed the burgundy bedspread and smoothed the crisp white sheets, but when he turned back to her, she stood and held out her arms. In her moonlit eyes, he saw desire and something else he couldn't name, and again he listened to his heart. His hands encircled her arms and gently urged her down. She melted back onto the chair, and her breathing was as unsteady as his own when he knelt at her side.

She trembled as he pulled off one red boot, then the other, and when his hand took her bare foot, she stiffened and moaned. *So far so good*, he thought with a smile, but his hands were shaking as he slid the black jacket off her unresisting arms and pulled her green sweater up over her head.

She shimmered in the moonlight. He drank her in—the trip-hammer pulse at her neck, the cool creamy skin warming to his touch, the arch of her body as his fingers trailed over breasts straining in their lacy cups—a vision that frayed his ragged control. She didn't move, helpless it seemed as his thumbs trailed over her nipples and released her bra. He heard her breath catch, felt her nipples rise, felt his own arousal.

Every cell of his body strained for release, but his heart still cautioned patience. *One breath, let it out slowly, another.* When self-control returned, he stood and slid his arms around her. Cradling her against his chest, he lifted her to the bed.

Then, because he couldn't help himself, he leaned in and kissed her.

She came alive, mouth demanding, arms and legs encircling, pulling him close. He swallowed a laugh—this was the Quinn he knew—and it took all his determination to draw back. Tonight was for cherishing, not ravishing.

Her eyes questioned.

His fingers found her zipper.

She writhed.

It's hard to seduce a woman in jeans, he grumbled to himself as he struggled to free her legs of the garment that had looked so good just an hour earlier. Finally, she lay naked under his gaze. Again she reached for him. "Wait, just wait," he whispered, and she quivered beneath his restraining hand as his mouth, no longer gentle, again found hers.

Kissing, licking, nipping ... lips, tongue, and teeth made their slow journey over her body. Kisses outlined her collarbone, trailed over smooth shoulders and around her breasts until his mouth took her nipple. Mindless, full of her, he suckled. She moaned and strained upward to give him more. Pleasure, hers and his, filled him.

He bit. She whimpered. He chuckled, then stroked and petted, his hand traveling inexorably downward. Wet and warm, she opened to him and with one thrust he drove her up. Inside and out she pulsed as his fingers teased. Uttering undecipherable sounds, she arched against his hand, taut for a moment, then boneless. She was his, her pleasure was his.

Nothing could be greater than this. His body strained to hers as his damp fingers traced her inner thigh.

Quinn reached for his zipper. It stuck. *Damn.* He stepped back.

"No, no, no," she moaned as cool air separated overheated bodies.

Frantic for her, he kicked off his shoes, tore off his own clothes, and settled onto the bed at her side. She rose to her knees and struggled to mount him.

"Now, inside me now." Not an order but a plea.

He captured her hands, eased her back. "My way," he said. "My way this time."

One hand held hers above her head, the other stroked and petted, until, as though stunned into submission, she stilled. He released her. She trembled. Thrilling to the agony of pleasure radiating from every inch of her warm, damp skin, he trailed kisses lower and lower until his mouth found her center.

Feelings swarmed as he gloried in her scent, her taste. No longer still, she writhed, panted, begged. "Now, please, now." Up and down he took her, denying her flight, until her voice grew hoarse with her pleas, and he pushed her up and over. Mad for her, overwhelmed by the pleasure he brought her, by the love he offered her, he wanted more than anything to let go and follow her.

Finally, unable to bear any more, he rose up over her, slid into her warmth, and felt her tighten around him. His mouth took hers.

Her body stiffened.

He froze. "What is it, dear heart? Am I hurting you?"

With a desperate wail, she wrapped her arms around him, spread herself wide for him, melted around him. Her hands raced over his body, and her mouth devoured his as though giving him life. No longer able to think, he plunged—again and again—*only her, only this, only now.* He poured himself into her. Together they crested and fell.

CHAPTER 39

QUINN WOKE IN AN ENVELOPE OF warmth and well-being. A hairy arm enclosed her and a heart beat steadily against her back. The bedside clock glowed 5:11. She drifted back toward sleep, then, *Oh my God, I've done it again,* and disgust engulfed her. The November sun had not yet risen as she gathered her scattered clothing and left Chris McLean snoring in his bed.

No grab ass, she'd made him promise. *I've got issues,* she'd told him. *No more booze or sex,* she'd told herself. And here she was, buck naked, hungover and remorseful in the pitch-black hallway, mind racing. *I used him. Can't face him. Gotta fix it.* She struggled into yesterday's clothes and pulled the big front door shut behind her without a sound.

Frigid air surrounded her as she fled the house and its unsuspecting occupant, and she was shivering as she entered the coffee shop around the corner. Small, just a long counter and a few booths, the place burgeoned with activity and the unwelcome aroma of freshly brewed coffee, doughnuts, and bacon. In the fog of her own thoughts, Quinn slid into the booth farthest from the door and fought to control her nausea.

"Hey, girl, how goes it?" Iris, the café's early morning server, greeted her. "Coffee?"

Without waiting for an answer—Quinn was a regular—Iris poured the steaming brew, then stepped back and took a good look as Quinn pushed the mug away. "No coffee?"

"Maybe hot tea this morning, Iris," Quinn said, trying for a smile. She could only imagine how she looked—shabby white girl sans makeup with disheveled hair and despairing eyes. Pathetic.

"That good, is it?" Iris said, sympathy in her chuckle as she retrieved the unwanted mug. "Who's the unlucky guy?" Before she could say more, a thin man in overalls sitting at the counter motioned for her attention. "Keep that thought, honey; I'll get your tea."

Quinn rested her head in her hands, thankful for Iris's friendly smile. This hole-in-the wall café was nestled close to McLean's, convenient when she wanted alone time or when she'd had too much. Iris always worked the early shift, always had a kind word and a story or two about her five-year-old son's aspirations to be the new Denzel. One morning, for reasons she still didn't understand, Quinn had told her about Samantha. A pretty colossal ice-breaker, she'd thought later, but since that day, a rapport had flourished, and this morning she wanted a friend, even if she no longer deserved one.

Iris returned, set the tea and a plate of rye toast on the table, and plumped herself down, bumping Quinn over with one soft round hip. Her chocolate brown hand covered Quinn's and squeezed. "Wanna talk?"

Quinn shook her head, "Nah, just having a bad morning. What's the newest on Marcus?"

Needing no urging, Iris provided a detailed update on her son's newest adventure. By the time she had finished and moved on to deal with other customers, the pain behind Quinn's eye and the matching one in her heart had subsided to a dull ache. She nibbled on the toast and sipped the tea, wishing she did have someone to talk to.

She'd never had a real girlfriend, the kind you told anything and everything. *But if I did*, she thought now, I'd say, "It was like in *Gone with the Wind*. My own personal Rhett Butler scooped me up like I was a southern belle and carried me into his bedroom."

Through the haze of liquor and desire, she had known she was making a mistake, and when he'd placed her on a chair and turned away to prepare the bed, she'd gotten to her feet, meaning to apologize and stumble away while she still could. Instead, he'd put his hands on her and nothing else had mattered.

Her tea grew cold as she remembered. *It was like his hands turned me to water and I couldn't move, didn't want to. He undressed me one boot at a time, one button at a time. When his hand took my bare foot, I almost lost it. He huffed a little into his beard. Jesus, whoever heard of a foot orgasm?*

"Want a warm-up?" Iris interrupted her thoughts.

Quinn looked up. "Huh?"

Iris poured steaming water into the metal teapot and added a fresh tea bag. "You let yours get cold." She cleared away the cold tea and handed Quinn a clean cup. "No wonder, you looked like you were a mile away and in a really good place." With a little laugh, she moved on to the next table.

It was a good place, Quinn acknowledged, *and I shouldn't have been there*. Her head ached, her heart ached, and her stomach threatened rebellion. Determined to put the memories aside, she bit off another morsel of toast, took tiny sips of the scalding tea, and tried to think sensibly, but the big man filled her mind. He'd had his own agenda, that was for sure. She could almost feel his hands on her body now as heat built, and she shrugged out of her jacket. She'd expected him to throw her on the bed and take her as he had before, or that she'd do the same, but he'd been so gentle, so slow and tender, as though she were something precious. *Damn.* She flushed as she remembered her own demands, her body straining for him, screaming "Now!"

McLean had released her mouth to whisper, "Wait, just wait," and returned to her lips. Just when she'd thought she could bear no more, his mouth and tongue and teeth had moved down over her neck and shoulders and boobs. Her breath had caught when his mouth found her nipple.

I begged.

The coffee shop slipped away and, as though she'd stepped backward in time, Quinn was in the dark room with a man who worked magic: *The devil ignored me, sucking and nipping and licking, and lightning struck, surged, again and again. I thought I'd die. Never before—oh God, never before.*

In the café booth, a minor earthquake shook her. Like Meg Ryan in *When Harry Met Sally,* Quinn covered her mouth to stifle her own "Yes," and was a little surprised when no one said, "I'll have what she's having."

She kept her eyes on the table until her body's aftershocks subsided. It *had* been magical. He had taken her high, played her body like an instrument of pleasure until there was nothing but his hands, his mouth, him. It was like a different McLean, the McLean whose hands healed tiny hearts, the McLean who rescued souls from rubble, the McLean who loved Quinn. Oh God, *that* was the problem.

She'd realized it, paused in shock, and then, not knowing what else to do, wrapped her arms around him, spread her legs for him, melted into him, and felt his surrender. His body had melded to hers and she'd met kiss for kiss, touch for touch, taste for taste, until, just as she knew she'd go mad, he'd slid inside and they'd moved together, crested together, fallen together.

Shaken, Quinn sat in a back booth in the tiny café, orgasmic with memory, and dropped her head into her hands. *Oh God, what have I done?*

She crumbled her toast, guzzled more tea, and considered. Jenny Chang expected her at noon. Five hours to remake her life. *That should be enough,* she decided wryly. *Forty-three years hasn't done it.* She paid her bill, hugged Iris, and started to walk.

She followed the route they'd taken the day McLean introduced her to his city and his life. She climbed to Lincoln's feet, wishing she could lay her dilemma there and receive wise counsel. Damn it all, she wished she had a mother from whom she could receive wise counsel. A little voice inside whimpered, "I want my mommy," and her burst of laughter almost choked her. Quickly, she looked around to see if anybody had noticed the crazy lady mumbling and laughing to herself. Her mother would have been no help at all.

A cold breeze from the Potomac promised an early snow, its chill finding its way up her pant legs and through the thin material of her jacket. Arms wrapped around herself for warmth, Quinn wandered away from the National Mall, jostled by pedestrians with someplace to go, tormented by her dark thoughts. It didn't matter, really, whether McLean loved her or Owen loved her—they were now part of the long list of men she had used to make herself feel better. And it did make her feel better, she thought with a flush of shame, better for a little while. So did running away when things got too tough. She fumbled in her purse—yep, driver's license and airline voucher were there. *Tempting. Leave it all, clothes and job and man. Taxi to Dulles, get on a plane, start over.* Her heart raced as she picked up her pace. *I can always buy a new flute.*

She stumbled, her feet suddenly not obeying her commands.

"Watch it, lady," a man beside her grumbled, but his hand came to her elbow to steady her and his eyes were kind. "You okay?"

She attempted a smile. "I'm okay. Just wool-gathering, I guess. Thanks."

"Be careful," he said and moved on.

She wasn't okay. She remembered Owen's face bleak as she'd left him and McLean's full of love as he gave himself to her, then a scroll of all the people and places and jobs and things that she'd left behind—for what? She squeezed her eyes tight to stop the tears, but, like her memories, they flowed anyway.

She ducked into an open door.

Once she'd gotten herself under control and thanked God for Starbucks' bathrooms, she splashed her face with cold water and considered her reflection in the mirror—splotchy skin, stringy hair, eyes puffy and red. Hard to believe anyone could find her lovable. She shook that thought away. *No matter. My life's a mess, and what I'm doing isn't working too well.*

She jumped when the door handle rattled, reminding her that she didn't own the space. Pretty soon someone would be rapping at the door, asking if she was okay. And suddenly she was.

"Sorry, out in minute." She finger-combed her hair, straightened her clothes, and abandoned her hideout. If McLean was right and she *was* an alcoholic—and he probably knew what he was talking about—then what she'd been doing, the model for her entire adult life, had been crazy. She knew AA's definition of insanity: doing the same thing over and over and expecting a different outcome. She just hadn't applied it to her own escapist behavior.

Leaves danced on the pavement as she pushed her way through the early lunch crowd and hailed a cab. *Work first,* she thought, *and avoid McLean until I can figure things out. No repeat performances. Never again.*

Jenny Chang waved as she paid the cabbie, and the two women entered the office together.

CHAPTER 40

DIRTY, TIRED, HEARTSICK FROM FOUR DAYS of distraction and despair, Chris McLean rested his forehead on the smooth wood of his front door as though he didn't have enough strength to open it and walk in. Four days ago, dingy light had filled his room and his bed had been empty when the phone woke him. No time to revel in remembered delight or think about the future. No time to find her, tell her—tell her what? Churning inside, he'd thrown on his clothes, loaded his disaster kit into the car, and gone to work. There was always rescue work, this time a fire in a skilled nursing home in New York, and then, since he was in the neighborhood, a memorial for more victims of the Towers. His heart broke for the families, for the men and women whose lives had been taken, for the world. Worse still, if there could be worse, he was unsure of his reception in his own home. She'd been willing, for sure, but she'd also been drunk, and he'd broken his promise.

Squaring his shoulders, he opened the door and stepped inside. The high, sweet tones of the flute greeted him, and his heart lifted. He dropped his battered case and, carrying a colorful gift bag and internal trepidations, followed the music.

The city shone around them as he found Quinn on the deck sharing "Autumn Leaves" with any in the neighborhood who cared to listen. Melancholy dripped from every note, and he saw dejection in the set of her shoulders. His heart plummeted. The amazing night they had shared had changed nothing. Downcast, he stepped onto the deck. She must have heard him because she didn't jump when he said, "Here, it's cold," and draped the chenille throw from the couch around her shoulders. His hands lingered. He couldn't help it, and when she lowered the flute and leaned back into him, his arms went around her.

"Easy, big guy," she said, but closed her hands over his and let him hold her.

Lights twinkled through bare branches. Far away traffic murmured, punctuated by the beep-beep-beep of an impatient horn. Everything distant as though a dream, his only reality the scent of lavender wafting from her skin, the firmness of her back against his chest, the tickle of her hair as it moved in the brisk evening air. As he breathed her in, fatigue and discouragement drifted away, and he was filled with a wonder so new it had no name. With a shuddering sigh, he released the breath and, giving in to temptation, buried his face in her golden hair. *Ahhh.* Then he knew it—contentment.

As his body molded to hers, the bag still hanging on his arm rustled. She stiffened and his arms tightened. "Happy Birthday, darlin' girl," he whispered in her ear before he released her.

She turned, surprise lighting her face. One look at his face changed things.

"God, McLean, you look beat."

Ignoring the bag he tried to hand her, she pulled him inside, aimed him toward his chair, and bustled toward the fireplace. She touched a match to the kindling standing ready on the hearth and lingered until it crackled into life, its flames lifting the gloom. *Something's different*, he thought, but he couldn't quite catch the *what* as she stood backlit by the flickering firelight.

Then she turned and saw him still standing. "Sit." She pointed down and waited until he sank into his chair, the yellow and green Happy Birthday bag perched on his knees, before she left him. Bemused, he stared into the flames. Contentment, like a mirage, had vanished.

Minutes passed before she returned carrying a tall glass of whisky, neat. She thrust it into his hand and turned away.

Her back to him, she poked at the fire. He watched the ripple of muscle under her ubiquitous green sweater while silence stretched between them. Just when the tension itself seemed combustible, she faced him, and he waited for her to ask what was wrong. If he told her, she'd know him for a fool . . . worse, an old fool.

Instead, she perched on the footstool by his chair. Her clear blue eyes searched his face as though looking for clues. Apparently satisfied that questions could wait, she reached for the bag, forgotten in his lap. "Now, what's this about a birthday?"

Without waiting for an answer, Quinn tore into her gift like a child, scattering tissue around the room in puffs of green and yellow. That done, she plunged her hands into the bag and a look of wonder crossed her face. With care, she lifted a coat from its festive wrappings, shook it out, and buried her face in its rich cashmere folds. The room stood still for a moment before she raised her eyes and graced him with a beatific smile. Her words were less saint-like. "Shit, McLean, this is gorgeous."

Chris let out the breath he'd been holding, her obvious delight reward enough for the miserable hours he'd spent looking for just the right thing.

As he congratulated himself, Quinn shoved her arms into the sleeves and pulled the hood over her shiny hair. The fabric framed her face and swirled around her ankles. She pulled it close, then twirled, and the coat circled out and fell back as though it were part of her. She flounced and strutted and whirled around the room, and the whisky sloshed in his glass as she ended her runway walk by flopping into his lap.

Before his arms could wrap around her, she leaped to her feet. "Sorry, sorry." Face aflame, she stepped back, pulling the coat tightly around her.

Armored, he thought. *Against me? Herself?*

Cursing, he set his drink aside and started to rise. Her expression softened and she moved closer, pushed him back down, and leaned in to smack him on the lips. "I've never had a better birthday," she said, "thank you," but she didn't return to his lap.

She did let him serve her a bowl of Chunky Monkey, laughed at his attempt to sing "Happy Birthday," and blew out the candle he'd planted in the ice cream.

As far as he knew, there had been no other birthday remembrances. His own birthday came and went, usually without notice; he wondered if she cared that hers, too, was ignored.

He refreshed his drink and sank back into his chair as silence, holding all things unsaid, settled around them. The fire crackled and popped and threw shadows that danced on the walls like the figures in Plato's cave.

She said nothing about their night together, and he was afraid to. He didn't want to hear her apologize for what had been the most magnificent night of his life—unplanned, marvelous—and only when they had lain spent in each other's arms had he realized that it had been love he'd given.

I'm in love with her; how crazy is that?

Her face was hidden in shadow, and he wondered if he'd ever really know her. The work she'd come to do was nearing completion, and he'd preened like a proud papa at the compliments he had received on her behalf. Now he wished his own plan to change her mind, *one day at a time*, was doing as well. He stared into the rich depths of his drink, tormenting himself with memory, while he waited to see what she might say.

"McLean." Her voice drew him back to the room. "Earth to McLean."

She had set the empty bowl aside and now faced him, her back to the coals, and the red of them reflected in her hair, turning it to strands of gold. He felt a tug in the vicinity of his heart, a warmth in his groin, and willed himself to remain seated.

"Sorry to interrupt all that deep thinking." A grin flashed and disappeared. "Or wool-gathering?"

So much he wanted to say. He clenched his teeth to keep the words inside.

"Whatever." She shrugged, studied her fingernails. "Anyway, do you have Dr. Blackstone's phone number?"

"Amanda?" Whatever he'd expected, it wasn't this.

"Uh-huh."

Intrigued, he started to speak, but the steely glance she shot him extinguished his questions. "Sure. You want it now?"

"Please." She looked relieved that he hadn't asked why. He was sorry he hadn't, but that moment was history, so he hoisted himself out of the leather chair to get the psychologist's number.

Full of her own woes, Quinn had forgotten her own birthday, and McLean's gift had taken her by surprise. No one celebrated her birthday, and she had long since convinced herself that it didn't matter. Still wrapped in the glorious coat, she took Dr. Amanda Blackstone's phone number and retreated to her room.

Earlier on the deck, as his arms had encircled her, the familiar punch in her gut stole her breath. Worries, doubts, self-hatred could dissolve in those arms. Shuddering with the need that threatened her resolve, she put aside her flute, covered his hands with her own, and let herself relax into him. *Just a little won't hurt. Just this.*

The rustle of paper brought her back. *I promised I wouldn't use him anymore.* She turned to speak and saw his face.

One look and her own misery fled. She didn't know what had etched him with such despair, thought it might be her own foolish self, and set about bringing him right. *Time for talk must come, but not tonight.* So she plied him with liquor and danced and played until he rumbled with laughter, and then she let him tend her with ice cream and birthday silliness. In the silence that followed, while neither spoke of what lay between them, she made a decision.

"Earth to McLean," she'd said. "Do you have Dr. Blackstone's phone number?"

Now alone in her room, she ran her hands along the smoothness of her new coat and then set it aside, undressed, and, tingling with unfulfilled desire, climbed between the sheets. *I need help*, she thought. *Time to ask for it.*

CHAPTER 41

ANOTHER TRUCE ESTABLISHED WITHOUT WORDS, LIFE resumed a peaceful rhythm, and Quinn was loath to disturb it. In the evening when they were together, she'd think, *We have to talk*, but the words stalled unspoken. She didn't know what to say. Her work was almost complete. From the twins, she knew the retreats were doing fine without her, Kristin Amundson a helpful surprise. Owen's silence proved he was done with her. She was still a drunk without a real job. Her daughter was still gone. And her mother, though dead, still hated her.

Quinn, being Quinn, clung to the things she knew—her flute, her yoga practice, her meditation—but she scheduled the appointment with Amanda Blackstone, PhD. In two weeks she would ask for help. In the meantime, she assumed a new gentleness toward McLean and introduced him to the old movies that had sustained her.

Scarlett O'Hara's parting words, "Tomorrow is another day," hung in the darkness. Chris McLean lounged in his big chair, feet propped on the footstool, staring at the scrolling credits. On the couch opposite him with her legs tucked under her, Quinn swiped at tears that had been flowing since Bonnie Blue died, and said, "I had a baby, you know."

Blinking his own tear-filled eyes, McLean turned away from the screen. "I wondered."

"Her name was Samantha. She died."

He handed her a tissue and settled onto the couch facing her. "Do you want to tell me?"

She did.

She told him about the daughter, born to an eighteen-year-old mother alone and afraid and a college jock father who never saw his child and divorced the mother right after the birth. She told him about Samantha, who had lived only three months.

"It was SIDS—sudden infant death syndrome," she explained as though he wouldn't know. "I thought it was my fault, something I'd done, gotten drunk before she was born, whatever, and my mother told everyone who would listen that I'd killed my baby."

His big hands captured hers.

She went on. "Viv and Vicky, and Owen," she added honestly, "convinced me that it wasn't my fault, but it's hard to stop feeling guilty."

She slid her hands from his grasp, scrubbed at her eyes, and blew her nose. "You'd think I'd run out of snot," she said with a watery chuckle.

He didn't laugh, handed her more tissues. "Your mother was wrong, you know."

She nodded. "My head knows, but it's still hard to convince my heart. It was my job to keep her safe, you see. They told me I'd have more babies, as though that would mitigate the loss, but I knew they were wrong. And the doctor said I shouldn't, that I'd die. None of it mattered. I just wanted my sunshine girl, and she was gone."

Later, as she lay waiting for sleep, Quinn wondered why she'd told him, blamed it on the movie, but for some reason felt better that he knew.

AFTER SHE'D GONE OFF TO BED, story told and nose wiped, Chris McLean sat in the darkness of his living room, nursed another whisky, and thought about this woman that he loved and the dilemma he faced.

Despite heartache and worry and horniness, he'd kept himself plenty busy. There were always patients to round on, interns and residents to mentor, guest lectures to give anytime he was willing. If he considered it a method of denial, he didn't admit it, even to himself. Quinn's project neared completion. They hadn't discussed what came next, another path he wasn't ready to go down. Besides the sex, which he now craved like the addict he was, he liked the time they spent together. She was smart and funny, and she listened with her whole being. He'd known she'd had a child, had kissed each tiny stretch mark that made interesting the perfection of her belly, just as he'd kissed the rose tattoo she'd attributed to an inebriated weekend with a man memorable only for his stamina and his insistence on matching tattoos, but he'd been surprised tonight that she'd told him, almost shattered as he understood the pain and guilt she still carried. He thought about his own daughters, tall and sturdy and married with children of their own, and felt the familiar twinge of regret that he'd spent so little time with them, that he was now just an adjunct, someone they loved but didn't much need.

Quinn spoke to her sisters occasionally, the youngest usually, he thought, as he eavesdropped on the brief conversations. *How else was a man to know anything?* And she didn't act like she cared. Once in a while, she would mention something that had been said, but now, going on three months since he'd dragged her off the plane and into his life, he still knew little about the family that seemed in such turmoil since the death of the mother, Mary, the day before the Towers fell.

More entertaining, if just as brief, were the conversations with Vivian and Victoria. Quinn had described their first meeting: Tweedledee and Tweedledum, she'd thought them, identical twins as wide as they were tall, who finished each other's sentences and spoke in clichés. These were the boyfriend's younger sisters, but from them she asked nothing, just gathered stories about the B&B and the retreats they had established, and told them little in return. As far as he knew, there had been no contact with the boyfriend. Chris had never known a person quite so self-contained, so . . . alone. And yet, he wanted her and he loved her.

What am I to do?

CHAPTER 42

Puffed up with pride, Owen Johnson leaned against the corral fence, one boot propped on the lower rail, and observed the action. He'd done it. Since returning from the mountains, he had forsworn alcohol, caught up on his clients' needs, and thrown himself into his sisters' retreats. Today he decided he was earning his keep. A sense of well-being crept in and settled comfortably with the eggs and sausage and slightly soggy pancakes prepared by the Inn's newest guests. *Content*, he thought. *This is what contentment feels like.*

Through a friend of a friend, the Johnson sisters had attracted a new clientele—boys and their mothers—and the last retreat had been a rousing success. The mothers embraced the atmosphere, particularly the "No TV" and "No talking" rules. The boys, three preteens who were best friends, much as Owen and John and Mike had been, participated in the activities with energy enough for a battalion. He'd enjoyed riding herd on them, listening to their chatter, dealing with questions about everything. *Well*, he reminded himself now, *everything but the "Where do babies come from?" question that followed the barn kittens' birth.* Lucky for him, one of the moms had intervened.

Three weeks later, this new group promised success as well. *Content,* he thought again as he watched.

In the lane between the main house and the barn, horses sidled and stomped as four boys and their city-bred mothers prepared for a trail ride. Chimerical, a long-legged woman strode through the melee, snapping his self-satisfaction like a twig. Owen straightened, heart pounding, but when he blinked, the blue-eyed blonde was gone. Shivering as a blast of November wind whistled down the canyon, he zipped up his jacket and banished Quinn from his thoughts.

"Morning, Johnson."

The trail boss, Adam Singer, interrupted Owen's morose imaginings as he situated himself against the rails at Owen's side, eyes on the small woman working her way through the mass of horses and helpers and guests: Kristin Amundson.

"Singer." Owen nodded, and the men settled back to watch.

Kristin had proven herself irreplaceable during the last retreat—she could handle small boys, hovering parents, and restless horses as though born to the job. This morning she moved easily around beasts and riders, adjusting stirrups, patting rumps, encouraging nervous mothers. The four boys, cousins on a birthday high, needed no encouragement. One of the younger horses danced away from the others, and Owen started forward. The older man touched his arm then shook his head.

"She needs help," Owen said.

"She'll ask if she does."

The men watched Kristin work the now-remorseful horse back into the line.

"But—"

"No buts. It's her job. We're the hired help."

Owen shut up. Adam swung onto his own horse and moved to the head of the line. As the animals followed obediently up the lane, Kristin took her place in the rear. Shaking his head, Owen mounted Girl George and followed.

The going was slow as the cavalcade moved into the narrow canyon. Hooves crunched along the creek bed; breaths hung like miniature clouds. A boy's voice, unbroken yet by age, echoed ahead. Owen loved this canyon carved by time and the movement of the earth—the sheer cliffs, the craggy rock walls sparkling as bits of quartz caught the sun, the eagles and their nest visible only as reward for braving a precarious trail, the slice of sky vivid azure in summer sunlight, shot with pinks and blues on a spring evening, gray and foreboding on a winter day. But now, as Girl George made her careful way over slippery pebbles, he slouched into the warmth of his coat and saw only Quinn. More than enough time to ponder Adam Singer's words.

Was the man right? Was it disrespect he had offered her? No wonder she'd turned away.

Like writings on a wall, memory images overlaid the ravine and dimmed the flat, heavy sky. He'd brought Quinn to this place twice, ostensibly to see the eagles—*to show off*, he thought now—and both trips had been shadowed in conflict as she'd rescued him from a careless slide off a precipitous edge and, later, run from his school-boyish declaration, "I want you, you know."

By the time the group had worked its way up the canyon to its rim, snowflakes floated in the air. Ravenous boys dropping from their mounts like fleas off a dog roused Owen from his self-flagellation. He slid from Girl George's back, ready to assist as the moms, eager to vacate their saddles, dismounted in a more decorous fashion.

Martin Edwards, a Winnemucca boy still saving money for his trip to the next Olympics, had a bonfire blazing and food ready, and for several minutes only munching noises broke the plateau's silence. When the mountain of sandwiches had been reduced to crumbs, Adam and Owen settled against a nearby boulder warmed by the blaze while Kristin orchestrated campfire songs and the construction of s'mores.

Adam's eyes followed the woman's every move. Sensitized, Owen recognized love when he saw it, love and worry. He felt the man tense as Kristin stumbled on a loose rock, then relax as she righted herself and reached to rescue a flaming marshmallow.

"She's amazing."

Owen meant what he said. When she'd first come to the Wildflower Inn less than a year ago, Kristin had been just out of rehab following blood clots and amputations and life-threatening infections, protected by a twin sister who felt guilty for being well. He'd lacerated Quinn for letting Kristin ride and hike, in fact for treating her like a normal person. The memory of that day when he'd stood in the barnyard and accused Quinn of putting his own sisters in jeopardy, when she'd faced him down, hands on hips and eyes blazing, then cut him out of her life, put a frown on his face and a pain in his gut. Turns out she was right. Now, although unable to walk through a room without breaking something, Kristin handled the outdoors like she owned it.

But, Owen thought now as he heard her laugh, *she still has that damn fake leg.* He couldn't help it; when he was near her, his protective instincts went on high alert.

"She is," Singer agreed, eyes never leaving the scrawny blonde, "amazing."

"You worry about her?" A daring question, more intimate than their relationship allowed, but Owen wanted to understand.

"Of course. I'd have to be dead not to." Adam chewed on his toothpick for a while, then surprised Owen by continuing, "I'm going to marry her, you know, as soon as she agrees."

"Congratulations. Easier to take care of her if you're married."

The man harrumphed. "Not likely. She's not one to be taken care of, missing leg or no. More likely she'll be taking care of me."

"But," Owen began, thinking of Quinn and his need to take care of her.

"But nothing. If I take over, it just tells her that I think she can't do it. I can't love her and send that message."

Kristin signaled, and Adam strolled to her side in time to avert a marshmallow catastrophe.

Conversation over, Owen once again had a lot to think about.

CHAPTER 43

NPREDICTED, THE STORM HAD SWOOPED DOWN with freezing intensity. Chris McLean, irritated, as though November's change of weather was directed at him personally, grumbled while he brushed off the snow that clung to his coat and let himself in the front door. Two long days in New York— Ground Zero, where the dust was still thick enough to turn his tears to mud and clog his throat. The posters remained, tatters fluttering in the winter winds, and it hurt his heart to see the faces of loved ones still missing. A news pundit had recently noted that the only smiles in New York City were on those posters. More than most, Chris knew that bad things happened, but still, he hoped . . . for the world, and for himself.

Now he was home, not as early as he'd wanted, but home. As usual, Quinn occupied his thoughts. He'd planned to suggest dinner out and a movie, maybe something newer than the oldies she'd been renting. Maybe it wasn't too late. He had a yen to see something that would make them both laugh and thought *Bridget Jones's Diary* would do the trick. And after that, finish it off with a stop at the ice cream parlor for her new drug of choice.

It's been a very long time since I've made such a fool of myself over a woman, he thought with a wry smile, *but what the hell. At least she'll like my plan.* Mood improving with each step, he moved into the dark hall and flicked on the light.

"DeMello, you home? DeMello?"

Echoes. No answer. Fear, now as much a part of him as his blood and bones, stretched and stirred. His heart rate accelerated. His smile disappeared. She'd said she was done running. She wouldn't just leave.

As though normal acts could normalize him, Chris bent down to retrieve the mail. He picked through it, then tossed it on the entry table with his keys. Quinn's arrangement of wintergreens and autumn leaves rattled a complaint. *Where the hell is she?*

"DeMello," he bellowed again. "DeMello, where—"

A sound like a kitten's protest caught his attention.

He whirled toward Quinn's bedroom door and, without compunction, yanked it open. No one. Across the room, the bathroom door stood ajar. He hesitated. "DeMello?" No answer. The door banged against the wall with his shove.

Quinn sprawled on the tile floor like a rag doll, ill-used and thrown away, jeans still down around her ankles and sweater hiked up as though she'd slipped from the commode and hadn't noticed. A strip of something was in her hand, and similar strips littered the tile around her. She raised her head as he stormed into the room and dropped to his knees beside her.

"DeMello, for God's sake, what's wrong?"

He wasn't sure whether the look she gave him held hope or despair. The words were pure DeMello.

"Joke's on me, Heartbreak Harry. I'm pregnant."

Pregnant? The word hung in the air. His outstretched hand paused. "Are you sure?" As though the mountain of little sticks weren't evidence enough.

"Unless it's a really bad year for pregnancy tests."

Unbidden, his burst of laughter filled the room, then died unanswered. He shook his head. "Mine?"

She shrugged and met his gaze, her own guarded and unreadable, and he didn't ask again.

In the living room, minutes later, he coaxed stubborn logs into flame, happy for the work that kept his back to her, gave him time to organize his mind, feelings firmly boxed. The sight of Quinn sprawled on the sterile bathroom floor etched in his brain, he fought the clenched hand in his chest. He'd thought she was dead.

Not dead—pregnant. Wrapped in the green chenille throw, she sat curled in his leather chair with her feet tucked under her, sipping the hot tea he'd forced on her, and he wondered what to do next.

She saved him the trouble. "In case you're wondering, my last period was late August. They're never regular, and I'm getting old and was blessing early menopause, so I thought missing a couple months was no big deal." The smile she attempted was more a grimace. "Apparently I was wrong."

He left the fire, and the ottoman sank toward the floor as it accepted his bulk.

She threw off the blanket, got to her feet, and sidled around him, facing the flames and avoiding his eyes. "You asked if it was yours, McLean, and you've got a right to an answer, but the truth is," she swallowed hard, "I really don't know."

He envisioned the other man, his eyes desolate. "Johnson?"

She turned on him. "Of course, you fool, what do you think I am, a loose woman?"

The words stopped them both, but before he could respond, a twinkle shone in her eyes and a hiccupping chuckle blossomed into a belly laugh that dropped her to the hearth. "Christ, McLean, that's just what I am. Just what my mother predicted." She laughed until the tears took over.

He crouched next to her, rescued the teacup, and gathered her in. She let herself melt against him, tears flowing into the flannel of his shirt, and he heard himself say, "Marry me, Quinn. Marry me."

Her tears stopped as abruptly as they'd begun. "Marry you? You've got a wife, McLean, why would I marry you?"

"Because I love you," he said, surprising them both.

So much for one day at a time.

HOURS LATER, QUINN SAT IN THE middle of her bed, alone, clad in Owen's shirt, its faint tease of Jaipur lingering over the pungent odor of her own body, her monkey mind busy. *I shouldn't have told him; I should have just left.* But McLean had looked so solid and safe kneeling in her pile of little blue sticks that she hadn't thought, just blurted the words out before her tongue could be guarded, reality too mysterious to contain. Even now, emotions swirled like the fog in old horror movies.

After his surprising announcement, he'd kept her in his arms as though afraid she'd disappear (*or run*, she imagined), situated them both on the leather sofa that flanked the fire, and opened his heart to her.

"I want you, but I meant to wait until you'd had time to get over him before I said anything. That is, after you forced 'no grab ass' on me. I figured if you were here long enough, you wouldn't be able to resist my Irish charm."

Their Nevada Day relapse was ignored.

"You've got a wife, McLean," she'd repeated, sidestepping the topic of love. "I've still got issues. And people don't get married just because they're pregnant anymore."

And isn't that lucky, she thought now, remembering the farce of her own brief marriage.

"I know." His eyes had darkened. "I know somebody—"

He hadn't said *abortion,* but she'd known what he'd meant. His arm had tightened around her, and she couldn't be sure how he felt about the offer he'd just extended.

Reluctant to be alone, wanting relief from the heartache that threatened to overwhelm her, she'd lingered in his arms, hungrily returned his kisses—*what difference does it make now?*—and finally, in front of the guttering fire, had taken his body into her own.

But that's not the answer, she reminded herself now as she burrowed into the well-worn shirt. *That's not the answer at all.* The clock in the hall chimed midnight before she dialed the phone and listened to it ring a continent away.

CHAPTER 44

AMANDA BLACKSTONE, PhD, USHERED QUINN INTO her office. If she'd been surprised when her partner in rescue had called and requested an appointment, she didn't show it now. In a gray pinstriped suit, its severity relieved by a lacy pink shell that peeked out at the neckline, Blackstone exuded competence, and Quinn had almost not recognized her, so different was she from the brash and gossipy woman in jeans and T-shirts who'd worked beside her in the hot and dusty Pentagon horror.

Quinn extended her hand. "Dr. Blackstone."

Amanda took the offered hand between her two smaller ones. "It's still Mandy, DeMello. Come on in."

She waved her new client into an upholstered chair the color of thick cream, smiled as Quinn fought to stay perched on its edge, then succumbed to the inviting cushions. "A little different from the tent, yes?" The psychologist sank into a matching chair and waited.

In the ensuing quiet, Quinn looked around the office—anywhere but at the put-together woman who regarded her with quiet interest. The shelves held books familiar from her own abandoned practice and others she hadn't seen before. Water cascaded over pebbles in a small dish and filled the room with its soothing sound. Inviting, comfortable, successful. Unease swept over Quinn like a wave.

Mandy allowed silence for a few minutes, then cleared her throat and said, "Let's cut to the chase, Quinn. What are you here for? I don't know whether to serve you tea or read you the suicide cautions."

At the no-nonsense approach, Quinn grinned and raised her eyes from her tattered fingernails, grateful that Mandy wasn't one of those counselors willing to outwait her client. "Christ, Mandy, I feel stupid. I should be able to deal with this myself. It's not that I don't know the stuff, but I can't seem to get a handle on how to change things and I thought—"

She struggled for words. This time Mandy did wait. The clock ticked. The water burbled. Who knew asking for help could be so hard? Finally, Quinn muttered, "I thought you might be able to help me, but I guess it was a dumb idea." She tried to rise; the chair held her captive.

Amanda Blackstone watched Quinn flounder. "It's hard to escape, isn't it?"

The chair a metaphor for life? Quinn wasn't sure.

"Why don't we just talk a bit, and then we can decide if I can help you or not," Mandy said. "I'll make us some tea, and we can pretend it's just a visit."

Quinn recognized the other woman's struggle to contain her mirth. "Okay. I can't get out of your damn chair anyway."

With a ladylike snicker, Mandy turned to the tray at her right. As she prepared the tea, she chatted lightly about her work, how people seemed to be dealing with the recent tragedy better than one might expect. "We humans have such resilience, don't we?" she said as she poured the tea into bone china cups with tiny painted flowers, handed one to Quinn, took her own, and settled back into her chair.

Resilience. Quinn accepted the fragile cup, unexpectedly encouraged by the twinkle in Amanda's eyes and the compassion in her voice. *Is that what I need?*

"I used to have a cup almost like this," she said, remembering how afraid she'd been each time she'd held it, afraid she'd break it and suffer the sting of her mother's pretty hand. She shook away the thought but knew that Amanda had seen it. "It had little shamrocks on it."

"Belleek," Mandy identified. "My mother had one of those, too, but when I went to Ireland, I didn't get to the factory, so I got these instead." She sank back into the creamy cushions and sipped the fragrant tea as though she had all the time in the world. "Do you want to tell me about your mother?"

In his office at the university hospital, Chris McLean stared at the telephone on his desk. Finally, he reached out and picked it up, looked at it as though he didn't even recognize the everyday object, and then, taking a deep breath, punched in a familiar number.

Three rings later, a woman answered. "Highland Hills Stables, Genevieve McLean speaking."

He took a deep breath. It was past time for this conversation. "Gen, it's me, Chris. May I come home, dear heart? We need to talk."

Miles away, Owen Johnson stood at his office window and stared at the snow just beginning to coat the streets of Reno. The weather matched his mood—gray and glacial. He spent most of his working hours in Reno now, the retreat season over until New Year's Eve. He forced a smile at his window image. His sisters were excited about their upcoming Winter Wonderland extravaganza: sleigh rides, sledding, a special excursion to the local hot spring. He'd agreed to be there and wished he hadn't. His heart wasn't in Unionville.

The girls were right. I have been hiding out.

He'd worked long, hard hours until their property was as manicured as the old place could be. He'd done whatever was needed for the fall retreats. His body grew stronger; the autumn sun darkened his skin; his hair, shot now with silver, touched his shoulders; his heart still hurt. There were no answers in a ghost town.

Four days ago, in desperation, he'd walked the block from his Winnemucca home to St. Paul's Catholic Church. The winter air stung his cheeks and the snowy remnants of an earlier storm crunched beneath his boots. Though it wasn't yet Thanksgiving, several homes along the street shone with lights twinkling red and green in the dusk. Illuminated by spotlights, the spires of St. Paul's reached toward heaven.

Spirit heavy, Owen trudged past the church.

Next door, the rectory, separated from the sidewalk by a wrought-iron fence, looked less imposing than its spiritual neighbor, but its windows glowed. He hesitated, then let himself through the gate, stepped onto the porch, and knocked on the door. At the sound of footsteps, he wanted to bolt. *Crazy idea. What am I doing here?* Before his own feet could take him away, the door opened and a slight man in black smiled a welcome.

"Owen Johnson, good evening."

Father Chuck, longtime priest and confessor to the Catholic community of Winnemucca, reached out his hand. "Come in out of the weather, man." As though used to reluctant guests, he maintained their handshake until the younger man was safely inside.

Owen glanced around the steamy room, unchanged from his youth—worn leather and polished wood furniture in the Mission style, widemouthed fireplace that never drew quite right, desk, two chairs off to one side—and felt again that touch of panic.

The priest looked worn, older than Owen had remembered, his last business with the man having been in a hospital chapel as the good Father had traced the sign of the cross on the smooth forehead, the closed eyes, the blue lips of his stillborn son. Blinking away the memory, Owen noticed the napkin in the man's free hand. "Sorry, Father, I've interrupted your dinner. I should go." He backed toward the door.

With no apparent concern for his meal cooling in the kitchen, Father Chuck, Charles O'Brien from Boston in another lifetime, tossed his napkin aside and chuckled. "Irish stew warms up nicely, son. Come in and take a load off."

A lifetime of religious obedience prevailed, and Owen slumped into a chair by the roaring fire. Father Chuck went to a side table and poured whisky into two squat glasses, then returned to the fire and handed one to his guest. "Here. Always good for what ails us, and for what doesn't."

He sat, sipped his own drink, and appraised his brooding guest. When Owen showed no inclination to speak, Father Chuck cleared his throat and began. "As you might imagine, Owen Johnson, this is a bit of a surprise. Before you tell me why you've come, I need to know if this is a social visit or a professional one."

Startled, Owen looked up.

The priest indicated his bare throat. "You see, if it's professional, I'll need to put on my collar."

Both men laughed, and Owen's silence withdrew. By the time he'd told his story, the glasses were empty and only embers glowed on the hearth.

AND HE NEVER PUT ON THE *collar*, Owen thought now, unable to recall what exactly he'd said or how the priest had responded, but he'd stepped out into the evening dark with a glimmer of hope in his heart.

The office intercom buzzed. Mrs. Blake, the receptionist, said, "Mrs. Mason's here, Mr. Johnson. Shall I send her in?"

An automatic "yes" on his lips, Owen paused. It would be so easy to do nothing, to nurture his hurt and bury himself in work.

"Forgiveness," he remembered suddenly. Father Chuck had said, "Forgiveness and trust, love and action." He'd laughed and added, "We're not all lilies of the field, now, are we?"

It *would* be easy to do nothing, Owen realized, wondering how he could ever manage forgiveness, let alone all the other. *Easier, but not what I want.* He shook his head. *This is crazy; I've got to make this right.*

"No, Mrs. Blake," he answered, a catch in his voice, "please tell Mrs. Mason I'll be just a few more minutes. I've got a phone call to make."

CHAPTER 45

MELODIC TONE INDICATED THE END OF the hour, and Quinn stopped midsentence. *An hour ... I talked a whole hour. Oh my God, what did I say?*

"Sorry, Mandy, I didn't mean to blather on."

"Hush, that's what you're supposed to do." The psychologist's murmur was so gentle, Quinn knew she'd told her everything.

"Pretty hopeless, aren't I?" She tried for lightness as she levered herself from the chair.

"Pretty hopeless," Amanda agreed.

Startled, Quinn looked up and saw kindness and the amusement that she herself often felt for her own clients when she knew they were more capable than they felt themselves to be.

Amanda stood when Quinn stood and tipped her head up so she could meet Quinn's eyes. "Not hopeless at all, and you know it."

Now, watching the murky winter scenery pass by the train window as she headed home, Quinn considered Amanda's words. "When we experience suffering, we believe we can't bear it, so we stuff the feelings and the memories."

In little boxes in my brain, Quinn had thought but not said.

She'd been shocked when Amanda had added: "Sometimes, DeMello, we have to stop avoiding. Maybe even your chanting helps you hide."

The psychologist hadn't waited for Quinn to agree or disagree. "Pema Chödrön—you've read her books, haven't you?—says we have to lean into our fears, our feelings, and as we do, things change. Perhaps you can allow a feeling or two into your chant and see what happens."

She'd suggested a few simple changes, then said, "Why don't you think about it for a bit? Call me if you want to talk again." At the door she'd offered her hand, warm and reassuring in Quinn's cool grasp, and with a smile disappeared into her office.

As the rhythm of the train lulled her toward sleep, Quinn folded her hands over the small lump that was her baby and considered the possibility. *Feel the feelings. Lean into the fear. Maybe ... maybe it's time to try.* Her mouth curved into a rueful half-smile. *What I'm doing isn't working too well.*

She arrived late to a dark and empty house. Two Post-Its covered with McLean's scrawl revealed nothing—"I'm away for two days, no more than three. Call my cell if you need me"—and ended with a Bogartesque, "Keep your chin up, kid," that raised a wobbly smile. They'd watched *Casablanca* on Friday.

Exhausted from the journey and her self-disclosures, Quinn gave little thought to McLean's whereabouts. He was often gone; he owed her no explanations. Still in her coat, she went to the kitchen and poured milk, then chugged it as she leaned against the counter and looked out at the city lights. Inside-outside. Another metaphor: the city bright and full of light, herself sad and dark and cold? With a sigh, fighting the self-pity that threatened to engulf her, she rinsed the glass and turned out the lights.

In her bedroom, she dropped coat and clothes to the floor and crawled naked under the covers. *I'm on my own*, she thought before sleep claimed her, *and I need a plan*.

AT FIVE-THIRTY, SHE EXTRICATED HERSELF FROM the tangle of sheets and dreams and, praying that morning sickness would not become a permanent condition, rushed to the bathroom. When her stomach was finally empty, her mouth rinsed, and her teeth brushed, she rummaged in her duffel and unearthed a yellow legal pad, then slouched into the kitchen. Still no McLean. Morning dark, city lights still twinkling, snow piled on the deck—not a very auspicious day. Shrugging, she poured a cup of steaming decaf. Thanking God that coffee no longer made her puke and thanking the universe for automatic coffee makers, she sipped the fragrant brew. Half a cup and deep breaths to focus—ready. She couldn't afford to wait for an auspicious day. Picking up a pen, she began to write.

When she was done, her hands had stopped shaking. A weak winter sun peeked through the clouds, and three yellow pages covered in what appeared to be hieroglyphs lay on the counter—a list of simple steps. *Simple?* She shuddered. *More like impossible*. She straightened her shoulders and ran her hands over the pages. "My Lean-In Plan," she'd titled it, thinking Amanda would be pleased. *"My Big Fat Impossible Plan" is more like it*.

She took another deep breath and smiled. *Lean-In Plan Number One: Protect my baby*. Everything else was Number Two.

No cheerier than her mood, the winter light filtering through the windows was just bright enough to illuminate the tiny entries in the *Physicians and Surgeons* section of the phone book.

CHAPTER 46

N THE DAYS THAT FOLLOWED, THE District of Columbia segued into the holiday season, and Quinn activated her list. After consulting the phone book and the Board of Medical Examiners, Quinn selected an obstetrician and snarled at the poor scheduler until she had secured the top spot on the doctor's cancellation list. Who knew most people planned their OB needs in advance?

Home from wherever he'd been with no explanation for his absence, McLean provided the numbers of two physicians who performed legal abortions. He offered no opinions, and she asked for none. *Playing it by ear*, she told herself, not trusting her fragile plan to anyone else's scrutiny.

But, her conscience nagged, *McLean has a right to know.* Guilt weighed heaviest when his big, gentle hands held her hair out of the toilet bowl as morning sickness wracked her. She resolutely blocked thoughts of Owen, so he intruded into dreams from which she woke glowing with orgasmic delight or drenched in tears. Between dreaming and fantasizing and vomiting, she finished the training module and handed it off to Jenny Chang.

She was letting go; it was someone else's project now. She hoped that the work she'd done would benefit someone.

Banning booze was both harder and easier now. It was hard to imagine a life without Jose Cuervo, but it was easy to abstain when the thought of alcohol sent her rushing to the nearest bathroom. *Alcohol and unborn babies don't mix* became her mantra as she attended daily AA meetings. Her favorite was the noon meeting on Mondays in the basement of Iris's church. She wasn't brave enough to stand and introduce herself—"Hello, I'm Quinn, and I'm an alcoholic"—but she went and she listened. *Leaning in sucks*, she thought, but she joined hands at the end of each meeting and chanted, "Keep coming back, it works," with the rest.

After the early morning sessions with the commode, Quinn settled onto her mat in the light-filled kitchen and allowed memories to emerge from the padlocked corners of her mind. With them came forbidden feelings, and on most days tears clogged her throat before the first *Om* emerged. Meta, or loving kindness, Amanda had reminded her, was a powerful meditation that heals with the development of goodwill toward others. Since she'd always chanted, she did so now, letting words of goodwill flow in her thoughts and from her lips. "May I be peaceful, safe, free," then, "May *you* be . . ," and finally, "May *they* be . . ."—her daughter, her mother, Owen, McLean, maybe even herself. She wasn't sure that anything could free her from guilt and longing, but it was what she could do.

More often than not, McLean sat at the counter with his syrupy coffee and a newspaper or a journal. Strange at first, as though she were invading his space, his presence became comforting, and more than once she'd heard a faint rumble as though he were chanting with her. She didn't mention it, but once when she peeked, she saw his eyes were closed, too.

Midday, December eleventh, the doctor's office called. "Come tomorrow at ten," the scheduler said. "He had a cancellation."

Unable to sit still, excitement dancing over her skin and quickening her heart, Quinn was pacing the kitchen when the front door opened, letting in a blast of frigid air and McLean's "DeMello, front and center."

She wiped sweaty hands on her jeans, sucked in a quieting breath, and turned in time to catch the coat he tossed at her. "You're early. What's up?"

"Get your coat on, woman. You've been inside too long. We're off to see a tree."

Ignoring both protests and questions, he coaxed her into her coat, pulled the hood up, and marched her out the door. At the Foggy Bottom Metro station, the escalators teemed with couples in matching hats, smiling parents hanging onto kids, singles chatting with everybody, and clots of giggling teens jamming the holiday-infused trains—infectious joy. By the time they disembarked at Capitol Station, Quinn was humming "Jingle Bells" with the rest of the crowd.

They stepped into the crisp evening, and McLean tucked her gloved hand into the crook of his arm. "It's the beginning of Christmas, my girl, and we don't want to miss it. They do it every year, started in 1964, officially that is. The trees are donated and decorated by different states—this year a white spruce from Michigan—and then some politician lights it up."

Quinn couldn't help but smile, swept along as she was by folks who seemed to know where they were going even if she didn't. As they neared their destination and their steps slowed, she peeked around the edge of her hood and, in McLean's shining face, glimpsed the little boy he'd been. Her chest tightened with sadness at all she couldn't give him. *By damn*, she decided, *he deserves more than this, but at least I can give him an amazing Christmas.*

His voice grew pensive, and she clutched his arm as they approached the West Front Lawn of the United States Capitol, where a tall tree—seventy-two feet, she'd learn later—stood waiting. "It's usually just the Capitol Christmas Tree," he said, "but this year they're calling it 'The Tree of Hope.' Seems about right, doesn't it?"

"Seems just right." She raised her gloved hand to his cheek. In the air, frost glistened. *Fairy dust,* she thought, and willed it down on them all as thousands of hopeful citizens quivered in anticipation.

His arms wrapped around her, drawing her back against him. With a sigh, she relaxed into his warmth, and a smile curved her lips. *In this moment,* she thought, *it does all seem about right,* and she held his hands tightly as they watched the blue, amber, and clear lights of the Tree of Hope wink on.

CHAPTER 47

N THE WILDFLOWER INN PARLOR, RESPLENDENT with Santas and snow men and flickering candles, Victoria Johnson perched on the highest rung and reached for the top of the tree. Vivian steadied the ladder, fingers crossed that the angel would assume her rightful place without a disaster. She did, and Vivian heaved a sigh of relief when her sister's feet touched the floor.

Victoria laughed. "Next year we'll make Scottie do it."

Vivian smiled at the mention of her son, soon to be back in the nest. Scott hadn't been in the Towers on that awful day. He'd been fishing at a little lake in the mountains with his father and his grandfather, so they had all survived, physically at least. Emotionally was a different story. Scott had remained in New York City to support his grandfather in his grief, and now, three months later, he was coming home. They didn't know what to expect.

She stood back to assess the tree. "He sounds older, I think."

"No wonder, Vivvy, with all that's gone on. Maybe it's a good thing."

Vivian nodded. They had raised Scott together after her unexpected pregnancy had almost ended in disaster, and she knew her sister worried, too. "Maybe. And maybe we can just worry about him and not our brother."

These days thoughts of Owen automatically raised thoughts of Quinn. "Quinn called earlier, didn't she?"

"She did. Let's have a little nightcap and enjoy the tree, and I'll fill you in."

An hour later, cozy in the new flannel pajamas they had given each other, the sisters snuggled in front of the tree with egg nog in hand, and Vivian recapped Quinn's conversation. "She says she's fine, finished now with that rescue project. She wished us merry Christmas, mentioned a new friend called Iris, and said she's teaching a yoga class at Iris's church. She had a story or two about that, and I got laughing so hard I forgot to ask her any questions so—no, I don't know when she's coming home; no, she didn't ask about Owen; no, I don't really know how she is or anything at all about that man she's living with." She hung her head in playful remorse. "I failed, didn't I?"

Victoria laughed. "The Queen of Secrets still. What can you do?"

"And speaking of secrets, what's this that Owen needs to tell us? He's back to spending most of his time in Reno, but he called a family meeting after Christmas dinner."

"Dunno, Vivvy. Bet Karle's making hay with him around so much, but he did seem better at the last retreat, spent a lot of time talking with Adam Singer, I thought. He did laugh once in a while—"

"And didn't look like he'd lost his best friend. And Karle's not invited to Christmas dinner, thank heavens. I hope that intervention we forced on him did some good. He never said a word about it, and when I ran into John Perry in the store, he kind of glazed over and muttered and practically ran out without buying a thing."

With no more discussion, they finished their drinks, settled the house for the night, and climbed the stairs. At the top, Vicky hugged her sister. "Let it go, Viv, let it go. It's only a few days 'til Christmas, and besides, we've done all we can do."

Vivian looked like she wanted to argue, then gave Victoria a wry grin and returned the hug. "You're right, of course," she said, "and as I always say, tomorrow is another day."

CHAPTER 48

HE NEXT DAY, IN THE BRUTAL cold of DC in December, Quinn shivered her way downtown to keep her ten o'clock appointment with Dusty Oakes, MD, Fellow, American College of Obstetricians and Gynecologists. Pulling her coat tighter didn't help; the shivers emanated from inside. Anxiety had replaced excitement. *This would be easier if I had a drink—or two,* she thought, wishing the sidewalk would open up and swallow her *and* her Big Fat Impossible Plan. Her heart thumped harder and faster as she entered the building and walked down the hall.

"Dusty Oakes, MD" read a tasteful sign on a dark-wood door. *Walnut,* she thought, hoped the man was as solid as his door, and squared her shoulders. *I like his name. It makes him seem approachable. I've got to trust someone, might just as well be him.*

A puff of warm air and a cacophony of voices greeted her. A middle-aged woman with straight, brownish-blond hair done in a stylish manner looked up when the door opened.

"Good morning. You must be Quinn DeMello. I'm Evelyn Lloyd."

The placard on the counter identified her as the office manager. She shook Quinn's hand and handed her a clipboard. "If you don't mind, please fill out these papers. Dr. Oakes will be with you shortly."

Quinn glanced around. The waiting room pulsed with protruding bellies, attentive fathers-to-be, and multitudes of children scurrying from their mothers' knees to the play tables and back. Evelyn noticed her gaze and laughed. "Yes, they're here, too, but they're to see our young associate, Dr. Michaels. He hasn't learned yet to be prompt, but he's trying." She indicated a door to her left. "Let's put you in here where it's calmer."

The smaller area resembled an old-fashioned sitting room— patterned curtains, wing-backed chairs, polished-wood tables, and the sticky humid heat that Quinn associated with the Wildflower Inn's parlor and its potbellied stove. Awash with longing for that overheated room, she slumped into the nearest chair and started filling out forms.

Dusty Oakes was a slender man a few years older than Quinn, fifty-one or −two, she surmised from the dates on diplomas modestly occupying the back wall. She was pleasantly surprised that the interview was held in his office rather than in the chill of an examination room, where the only thing between her and naked would be a flimsy paper grown.

He went over her history carefully, noted the six DeMello siblings—a good sign of successful pregnancy, Quinn figured— and then his eyes met hers, the first time since he'd shaken her hand and escorted her here. "You are a little older than many of our first-time mothers, Ms. DeMello?" His inflection suggested not a statement but a question.

She cleared her throat and sat up straighter. "I apologize, Dr. Oakes. I was not quite forthcoming in the paperwork. I was pregnant many years ago, when I was eighteen, and delivered a daughter who died three months later of SIDS."

"I see."

She glanced up and saw that he didn't, so she cleared her throat again and started over. "At that time, I was told never to have another child, that something—the pregnancy or the delivery, I'm not sure what—was amiss and that I could and probably would die in the attempt. In the past, it's never been an issue. Now I guess it is."

Without comment, he asked additional questions, and she almost choked on the need to apologize for her many "I don't know" responses. Finally, he leaned back in his chair, steepled his fingers in front of his mouth, and sat quietly for so long she thought she might need to prompt him.

When he spoke, he leaned forward and his voice was gentle. "Ms. DeMello, I can't quite figure this out. As you know, medicine, especially obstetrics, has changed considerably since your first pregnancy. You're apparently a healthy woman. Let's do your examination and get some initial blood work and try to get your old records. Then I'll be better able to advise you." He kept his eyes even with hers. "That is, if you plan to continue this pregnancy."

The moment of truth. It would be so easy to stop now, to terminate before she felt that flutter she remembered as vividly as though Samantha had resided in her womb just yesterday. *My life is so friggin' messy,* she thought, not for the first time. *All I need is a baby.* She sucked in a deep breath. *Lean-In Plan Number One, protect my baby.* She held the doctor's troubled gaze. "Dr. Oakes." She enunciated her words clearly to give them all the power she could muster. "I intend to have this child."

Ten days later, Quinn hurried along city streets dressed in Christmas reds and greens that she barely noticed. She'd had the tests, signed the records releases, and waited. Following her plan, she'd found a gym that needed a yoga instructor and agreed to teach four classes a week. She went to daily AA meetings. She let tears fall when she chanted. This morning, she'd gotten the call. Dr. Oakes's medical assistant, Joy, a young woman whose name described her well, had instructed her to come in at the end of the day.

End of day—can't be good news. Heart racing, Quinn sidestepped a Salvation Army bell-ringer and plunged into the office building, almost giddy with relief at the sight of the solid wood door.

Now, as she waited for the doctor, the birthday coat that enveloped her like a baby blanket didn't protect against the insidious cold. By the time Dr. Oakes stepped out to greet her, she was shaking visibly, and he kept her hand in his as he led her into his office, where they sank into the matching chairs in front of his desk.

"Ms. DeMello...Quinn," Dusty Oakes began.

Her breath stalled in the suddenly oppressive air. Her muscles contracted like a runner's at the starting block, and every instinct urged her to jump up and race from the room. She forced herself to remain seated and raised her eyes. The man beside her looked as though he wanted to pat her hand and tell her everything would be all right, which surely meant it would not.

He cleared his throat and said, "I have most of the information we need. Your old hospital records were available, and the physician notes were not, but I think I can piece it together for you."

Quinn saw compassion in his eyes—again, not a good sign. Now she wanted to reach out and pat *his* hand. She refrained.

"I'm afraid the news isn't as good as I had hoped."

She sank back into the chair and willed courage to appear. "Tell me," she whispered.

The physician stood and moved to his desk, where he sat and opened the single file that lay there. He shuffled the contents, tapped the edges even, shuffled and tapped, shuffled and tapped before he replaced them on the desk and stared as though they might explode.

Stalling, she thought, her own skin crawling with nerves. "Tell me," she repeated, hoping she sounded braver than she felt.

Without meeting her eyes, Oakes began. "As you might imagine, pregnancy imposes dramatic physiologic changes on the cardiovascular system. Increased resting—"

Quinn interrupted. "Cut to the chase, Dr. Oakes, and in plain English please."

He flushed, and she almost apologized. He clearly wasn't liking this day any more than she was.

"Sorry, sorry." Oakes left his desk and reseated himself in the chair beside Quinn's, kept his eyes level with hers, and outlined the situation.

She heard "VS defect" and "stiff valve" and "preeclampsia" and more as her doctor outlined the problems with her heart, then explained how the pregnancy would strain it, depriving both baby and mother of the nutrients and oxygen both needed for life. Plainspoken now, he explained when medical jargon became incomprehensible. Finally, looking like a man who hated his job, Dusty Oakes stopped talking and leaned back in his chair.

Quinn sat silent, numb. She wasn't surprised, and yet she was. For a moment, the only real thing in the room was the vision of Samantha in her pink flowered jammies lying cold and still in the dresser drawer that had been her bassinet. *No more dead babies. I can't bear another dead baby.*

From a great distance, she heard Oakes ask, "Any questions?"
She shook her head.

The doctor scooted forward, placed one hand over hers as
she clutched the arm of her chair, and waited until she raised
her eyes to his. In a voice deadly serious and profoundly sad, he
said, "Ms. DeMello, given the situation, I would strongly advise
that you terminate this pregnancy as quickly as possible."

Quinn saw him wince just before the words struck—a
boxer's punch, full in the face, just before her eyes rolled and
the world slid away. Then he was at her side, one hand pushing
her head between her knees, the other searching for her pulse.
Her head felt light, as though emptied of all thought; her heart
knew something was terribly, terribly wrong.

She shuddered, and Oakes lifted his hand. She took a deep
breath and remembered: This baby would die, too.

A little moan escaped into the silence. Surprised, she realized it was her own. Head down, she took two deep breaths and
then pushed herself upright.

"Slowly," he said. "Take a minute."

Erect, Quinn waited as the room spun and lights sparkled
behind her eyelids. "Huh," she muttered when she could finally
string words together. "Thought that only happened in the
movies."

"Happens all the time," he said. "Why don't you lie—"

Interrupting his suggestion with an impatient shake of her
head, Quinn gripped the arms of her chair and resumed their
interrupted conversation. "Terminate," she said, wrinkling her
nose as if she smelled something foul. "And if I don't?"

A surprised look crossed his face, and he answered bluntly,
"If you don't, you could, probably will, die."

"What about the baby? Will the baby die, too?" She
straightened her shoulders.

"I take it you're not going to follow my advice?"

"That's right," Quinn said, swallowing her fear. "This baby is going to get a chance at life, and it's my job to make that happen. I picked your name out of the Yellow Pages because you sounded like a Texas brawler, but if you don't want to help me get through this, maybe you can suggest someone who will."

CHAPTER 49

"MERRY CHRISTMAS, MOTHER," VIVIAN AND VICTORIA caroled as they stomped their snowy way into their brother's Winnemucca home. Crisp winter air wafted around them and jingled the bells on the tree Owen had placed near the front door. Traditional greens with silver ornaments and red velvet bows carried Christmas throughout the cottage he'd renovated, and the scent of pine and cedar, turkey and pumpkin pie swirled like the finest perfume. Because their mother was so frail, the siblings had decided to celebrate in town so she could be with them, and Gertrude Johnson now held court in Owen's leather chair before a blazing fire. She smiled and held out her hands to the daughters she didn't always remember.

"Girls, merry Christmas." Wiping his hands on a red and green dish towel, Owen stepped from his kitchen. He kissed Vivian's cheek, then Victoria's, and let himself be enveloped in a twin hug. Over Vivian's shoulder, he saw his mother smile. *Maybe a good day*, he thought and smiled back.

Drinks in hand, the siblings fell into their usual kitchen routine, interrupted only by Harold's arrival and their mother's demand that she be moved to her piano bench. They stood close as she touched the yellowed keys and, after a prayer-like moment, let her fingers ripple up and down the keyboard. Soon familiar Christmas carols filled Owen's home.

Just as they were sitting down for dinner, Scott burst through the door, a late arrival that had eyes rolling and set the meal back an hour. No one complained. Food reheated, they took their places at the table, and Vivian recited their traditional blessing. "Thank you, God, for home and food. Thank you, God, for all things good." The *amens* were loud and heartfelt.

A very good day, Owen decided. *Just needs Quinn to be perfect, but that's for another day.*

Full and happier than he'd felt in months, Owen left the others to clean up while he returned their mother to her room in Happy Acres, the assisted living facility that was now her home. He helped her inside, arranged her Christmas gifts on her dresser where she could see them, and kissed her goodnight. Back in his car, he teared up. She had recognized all three of her children, at least for a few minutes, and his heart had almost stopped when she'd raised her withered hand to his cheek and whispered, "It will all come right, dear boy. You must make it so."

He didn't know how, but even in her diminished state, she knew his heart. "You're right, Mom," he whispered now into the evening dark as he sat alone in his car in his driveway. "I will do my best to make it so."

Then he made a face at his own drama and readied his defense—his sisters would not approve of his action plan.

THE DAY AFTER CHRISTMAS, THOSE SISTERS sat in their own kitchen drinking coffee and discussing their brother's bombshell.

"'An Action Plan,' he called it, with capital letters." Vivian rolled her eyes.

"An intern to do his work?"

"He says it's not unusual to hire an assistant, and all the new graduates need hours. Besides, Pat will be there for supervision, and it's not like it's April fifteenth already." Vivian's tone was less positive than her words.

Victoria rolled her own eyes. "I heard him. Just seems—"

"A little strange that he's going off somewhere but he won't say where, and he's not sure when he'll be back either. It's not very—"

"Owen-like?" Victoria rose and replenished their coffee, her expression troubled. "No, it's not. But you know, he seemed lighter, happier than he's been—"

"In months." Vivian moved to the window and looked out on the lane Owen had plowed on Christmas Eve. Even after he returned from the hills, she'd feared for her brother, his smile a pale imitation and his laughter a memory. She turned back toward her sister. "You're right, Vicky. The other day he even threw snowballs at the goats. And last night, he and Scottie were laughing about some dumb thing just like they used to. I just wish we knew what was going on."

Victoria stood and linked her arm through her sister's. "Thank God Scottie's back, and none the worse for wear. And Owen's not leaving until after the New Year's retreat. Maybe we can get some more out of him before he goes. This King of Secrets routine is making me—"

"Nutty," they finished in unison.

CHAPTER 50

RECUMBENT, QUINN BENT HER KNEES SLIGHTLY to ease the strain in her back as the ultrasound probe in Dusty Oakes's steady hand roamed her belly, the gel cool and smooth and soothing as a mother's touch. After Oakes had explained about her heart condition and her nonexistent chances, they'd worked out a survival plan that included medications, rest, frequent checkups, and a consult with a cardiologist whose specialty was cardiac disease in pregnancy. In the process, she and Dusty had become friends, so, when she'd felt the flutter, her baby's first hello, she'd come straight to his office, wanting to share her excitement with someone besides the pigeons in the park.

Now her thoughts drifted as she lay on an exam table wrapped in a warm blanket while her doctor got first peek at this tiny life she was cooking. Christmas had come and gone. In spite of the nausea, in spite of the fear and doubt that often threatened to undo her, she sizzled with health and energy. She smiled remembering McLean's surprise when he'd come home to a house Christmassy enough for the cover of *House Beautiful*.

The traditional dinner, prepared with Vivian's long-distance help, was a bonus.

Basking in the glow, she thought. *Playing house.*

Denied the sexual fog within which she usually conducted her relationships with men, she was filled with feelings long buried. Buried with Samantha, she vaguely understood, or maybe even before that as she endured her mother's neglect. Now she was awed by the power of tenderness and love. Who knew tenderness could be so big it hurt, and love—the kind that makes you want to wrap the person up and keep him from harm—that hurt, too.

Not just a person, she chided herself, *McLean.* McLean, the maybe-father of her child, the kind and gentle man whom she loved and whose heart she might break. Tonight was New Year's Eve. They'd talk tomorrow.

The doctor's words scattered her thoughts.

"Where the hell did that come from?"

The steady hand jerked. The image on the screen stuttered and went dark, but not before Quinn saw the second tiny pulsing blip and knew without a doubt whose babies she carried.

CHAPTER 51

OMFORTABLE IN HIS LEATHER ARMCHAIR, CHRIS McLean swirled the rich brown liquid in his snifter and listened to his own private concert as Quinn worked through her evening practice and they waited to greet the new year.

Med school, residency, fellowship, building a practice and an expertise—these had edged out everything, including music. Now he allowed himself the luxury of Quinn's performances and the mini-lectures that followed. Tonight, she glowed.

"You'd think they'd get all used up," he said. Concert over, he watched as she nestled the shiny instrument into its case. "The notes, I mean. There are only so many, right?"

She nodded.

"And probably only so many possible combinations?"

She nodded again.

"So how can they keep coming up with new things, especially things that sound as beautiful as what you just played?"

The corners of Quinn's mouth turned upward, and she looked pleased as she answered. "Just trust, McLean. I guess we just trust that it happens."

The clock on the mantle chimed midnight.

"Happy new year," Quinn whispered as she brushed her lips against his. Before he could return the kiss, she picked up the instrument case and left the room.

Trust. Alone now and thoughtful, the kiss a tingling memory, Chris stared into the coals and then tipped his glass for the last few drops.

Earlier in the day, he'd spoken with Jenny Chang and the rest of the development team. Quinn's project was a go. Lots of consultants—it was amazing how many people wanted to volunteer in these post-9/11 days—and both yoga and meditation practitioners had happily conferred, but it was the simplicity of Quinn's approach that provided form for the project.

"We're almost done here, Dr. McLean," Jenny had told him. "We'll implement on an experimental scale, get a few people trained locally, and monitor how it goes." She'd smiled up at him, batted her dark eyelashes, and he'd grimaced, remembering Quinn's earlier question. *She is a pretty little thing*, he acknowledged as he thanked her. *Not too long ago I might have—*

Letting the thought expire, he rose to stand at the window. Winter wrapped his city in its grip, bits of snow clinging tenaciously and icicles patiently inching their way toward the ground. *Almost four months*, he thought as he watched the lights of the cars gliding beneath him. *Almost four months since the Towers fell, since Quinn DeMello disrupted my life.* He'd seen and felt so much: the nation's heart, broken by the tragedy but beating still; people mourning and rebuilding, trusting in themselves, in their country, in the future. Pressure rose behind his eyes, tears threatening the way they always did when the fireworks exploded over the Washington Monument on the Fourth of July. *Corny, but I'm proud to be an American.* He snorted. *Corny sentimental old guy in love with an ethereal, aloof woman who doesn't love him. Shit, sounds like a bad movie for television.*

Impatient with himself, he pulled the heavy drapes closed, shutting out the draft and the city lights and the world, and his bare feet left footprints in the dense carpet as he paced. *I make decisions and I act on them. What's wrong with me now?*

Near the fireplace, the lights on the Christmas tree twinkled, catching red and green from the simple decorations and bringing life to his home—Quinn's work. She'd cooked a turkey, too, with stuffing and mashed potatoes and gravy that didn't come out of a can. "Vivian's recipes," she'd told him. "They're safe." It was the best Christmas he'd had since med school. Memory flashed: his daughters, little bitty things dressed in new Christmas pajamas with the sleeves and pant legs rolled up ("growing room," their mother had called it); a glittering New England Christmas tree sheltering a mountain of gifts; himself and Gen, doting parents still thinking they could beat the odds; and the ending, with its sadness and grief, hovering just outside their awareness.

The vision with its lingering sorrow faded, and his thoughts returned to Quinn. They hadn't talked, he and Quinn, really talked, since the night she'd confirmed her pregnancy and allowed his body to comfort her.

He worked up fury and steam as he traversed the room. *I want her to tell me what's really going on,* he thought, *with her pregnancy and with her heart. I want to know what she's planning. Shit, I want to know if the kid's mine.*

He paced.

Goddammit, why don't I just ask? he snarled at himself, flushed with shame as he remembered what he *had* done. Days ago, Quinn had left the house earlier than he, and, frustrated with his own impotence (even as he'd mocked himself for his word choice), he'd let himself into her bathroom. Pill bottles lined the counter. Appalled at his own behavior, he had checked the labels: prenatal vitamins prescribed by Dusty Oakes, an obstetrician he knew, good; Metoprolol, a beta blocker, prescribed by Mason Orr, a well-respected cardiologist in the District, not so good; Lasix, a loop diuretic also bearing Orr's name, not good at all. Shocked, dismayed, and afraid, he'd carefully put each bottle back in its place and almost tiptoed from the room.

Now he banked his anger; Quinn was pregnant and she was sick. He had no business being angry.

She *had* been more accessible lately, spending time with him instead of retreating to her room or, worse still, into the silence of herself, and the songs that she played weren't so dismal. She still looked pale, but her hair was shiny and her slender frame had assumed the contours of early pregnancy. He liked the roundness of her cheek, the new shape of her belly. He liked the time they spent together. He did not like her silence.

Brooding, he tossed a small log on the fire, poked at it until sparks flew. "Damn," he yelped, as one sizzled on his forearm and he jerked away, almost happy for the pain that snapped him back. *I make decisions and I act on them, and that's what I'm going to do.* Quinn was a gift that he didn't intend to squander. He dropped the poker and strode toward her closed door.

"DeMello, front and center. We need to talk."

MINUTES EARLIER, QUINN HAD BRUSHED A kiss on McLean's warm mouth, wished him a happy new year, and scurried off to bed before she forgot her resolutions. She'd played "Tambouren," a fast and difficult flute solo that she'd practiced for weeks, and was pleased at McLean's praise, and her body still tingled from the desire she'd seen in his eyes. Tomorrow was soon enough for the conversation she knew they must have.

In a daze after the amazing ultrasound, she had meandered home, each step wondrous and new, through a world no longer populated with question marks. If there were twins, then Owen must be their father. She'd told Dusty about Owen's twin sisters, and he had carefully explained that this fact did not guarantee paternity. But inside she was sure. Now, warm from the fire, simmering with her news, Quinn pulled off her clothes, perched naked on the bed, and reached for her phone. Risky. So many things she couldn't yet say. The twins had dubbed her "Queen of Secrets," and they were right, but tonight of all nights she wanted them. She punched in the familiar numbers. *It's not midnight in Nevada yet. I'll just wish them a happy new year and hear friendly voices and then get off before they ask too many questions.* Justifications, she knew, and she almost burst into tears when Vivian Johnson said, "Hello."

Time flew. When her news threatened to overflow, Quinn stuffed everything inside, said, "Gotta go, Viv. Happy New Year to all of you," and hung up just as "DeMello, front and center" thundered through her door. She laughed out loud when an unrestrained fist pounded the wood and displaced the rest of his words. A skirmish with McLean was just what she needed.

"What'd'ya want, McLean? I'm sleeping."

"No you're not. You were talking to those women." He slammed her door open. His gaze swept her battle-ready grin, her pregnancy-enhanced breasts, and the rise of her belly before she belatedly pulled her sleep shirt over her head. As though he'd never seen her naked, his face flushed and confusion suffused his usually confident features.

"I want to talk to you, if you have time, that is."

Surprised and disturbed by his conciliatory tone, Quinn felt a twinge of regret for the battle ended before it began. "Okay, just give me a minute."

Eyes on the floor, McLean nodded and backed out. The door closed behind him without a sound.

The exhilaration of the day disappeared as though banished by the snap of an evil witch's fingers. Fatigue, heavy as a mudslide, took its place. Sighing, Quinn ran her fingers through hair grown long, then pulled the GWU sweatshirt that served as her robe over her head, leaving Owen's shirt, like chain mail, against her rounding belly. Stick-thin legs, untouched by the pregnancy above, stretched bare to the fuzzy socks that had arrived the day after Christmas, a gift from Vivian, whose tag, with her loopy handwriting, had read, "Warm feet, warm heart."

Guess we'll be having that conversation tonight. With another sigh, Quinn left her room.

Chris McLean sat in his usual chair, staring at the coals, a snifter of brandy motionless in his hand. She knew its taste and didn't long for it, but a little tequila might make this easier. With a sigh, she got a bottle of water from the fridge and assumed her usual spot on the sofa, wondering what he wanted and not really sure she wanted to know. Her part of his project completed, he was probably ready for her to move on. *Rightfully so. I haven't really risen to his expectations.* Her mental picture—Heartbreak Harry stuck with a wildly hormonal pregnant woman who wouldn't even share his bed—set her lips twitching. *It is time to move on, but I can't go home quite yet.*

Thoughts swirling, she settled onto the sofa, back straight, feet side by side on the carpet, hands gripping the water bottle. "Okay, McLean, what do you want now?"

His answer rendered her speechless.

"I'm getting a divorce, DeMello, and I want to marry you."

CHAPTER 52

A CAB PULLED TO THE CURB JUST as Quinn waved back at McLean and pulled the heavy door shut behind her. *There is a God*, she rejoiced. In this second week of 2002, she had a lot to do, and a crazy taxi ride seemed preferable to facing icy streets and a cranky transit system.

Pregnancy weeks passed quickly, she had discovered, and her days were full: yoga classes, AA meetings, volunteer work with the local SIDS organization. *The only fly in the ointment*, she thought as she waggled her hand at the cab, *is McLean*.

New Year's Day, barely past midnight, before she'd even gone to sleep, McLean had summoned her from her room, and as she'd settled into her accustomed place on the sofa, he'd announced, "I'm getting a divorce and I want to marry you." She'd almost fainted at his feet until she'd realized he must be kidding and giggled in relief. Not a surprise that he thought he loved her, but marriage?

His scowl shoved the giggle down her throat. "I'm serious, damn it. I've gotten used to having you around. You seemed to think that having a wife got in the way, so Gen and I signed papers. I already said I love you."

As she stared, his expression softened, his eyes filled with hope, and her heart broke. She couldn't say the words he wanted to hear.

"McLean," she whispered, "I can't—"

Tears stood in his eyes as he interrupted. "I know you've got problems, but I can help—"

Her own eyes filled. *Damn, I should have told him. Things should never have gotten this far.* She left the sofa and went to him, sat on the footstool in front of his chair, and took both his hands in hers. "Oh, my darling McLean," she said, "I am so, so sorry."

They talked that night and into the next day.

"I have a heart condition," she said, "and I might die."

His hands squeezed hers. "I saw your pills," he said. "Tell me."

"Mitral stenosis," she said, not bothering to ask why he'd been in her bathroom. "Even if I don't remember being sick, having rheumatic fever. I just remember my older sisters hauling me around in our little red wagon. That must have been the prescribed 'rest time' that Dr. Oakes has mentioned. I just thought they were being nice."

He was squeezing her hands so hard it hurt—an effort, she realized, to remain calm, to maintain a professional distance. This was, after all, his field. She didn't pull away.

"They must have heard a murmur," he said. "That's probably why you were told not to get pregnant again. But today, even pregnant people don't die from mitral stenosis. That's no reason not to marry me."

She tried for a smile. "There's more."

After that second visit, when she had fainted in his office, Dusty Oakes had referred her to a physician who specialized in cardiac disease in pregnancy. She'd liked Dr. Orr, had listened carefully as he'd explained what she couldn't hear from Dusty: VS defect, a tiny hole between the ventricles in her heart previously undiscovered; the mitral stenosis, a stiffness of the valve that impeded effective blood flow; and the presumptive cardiomyopathy from her undiagnosed preeclampsia. She had no symptoms initially, but if the pregnancy continued, she would have. Orr had advised an immediate abortion. She had declined. Now both doctors monitored her progress.

McLean paled, anticipating.

She outlined what she knew. He didn't need an explanation to understand the ramifications. The pregnancy would tax a heart that already had problems.

"Abortion?"

"No!"

He pulled her into his lap, wrapped his arms around her as though he needed her warmth. "Still no reason not to marry me," he whispered against her hair.

"Ah, McLean," she whispered back, knowing the other things she needed to say, knowing those words would be even more hurtful, "if only it were that simple."

"I love you," he said.

"And I love you," she replied, "but not the way you want me to."

She heard him swallow hard, a sob maybe, and then he stood with her in his arms.

"I don't care," he said as he deposited her back on the sofa, his hands sliding down her arms in a gentle caress. "I have enough for both of us."

She felt his words; they stopped her heart. His eyes held hers for a very long time before he looked down and she could breathe again.

She sobbed out the rest: In love with Owen, not sure that he wanted her; twins, Owen must be the father; already decided to go home, babies needed a family; afraid—that she'd die, that the babies would die, that Owen would talk her into an abortion she would always regret. Finally, she hiccupped into silence. McLean already knew the rest of her stuff.

He held her for a very long time, his arms so tight she could hardly breathe, until finally when both their tears had dried, he said he understood and let her go.

Now, remembering, she felt her throat grow tight. He'd said he understood, that she needed to follow her heart, but when he offered his home for as long as she wanted to stay, his hope that she would change her mind was obvious.

Every time I look at him I feel like a jerk, she thought ruefully. *It's not his fault that I'm in love with somebody who doesn't love me. Guess we're kinda in the same boat.*

She shook away the miasma of sorrow and guilt and flailed at the cabby again, ignoring the man stepping from the back seat. Her time in the big city had at least taught her how to hail a cab. Tiny snowflakes swirled, and she kept her face down as she rushed toward the heaven-sent vehicle.

Immobile, the man blocked its door.

"Excuse me?"

He didn't move.

"What's your problem?"

It was cold and she was in a hurry. Waiting for a dawdling tourist wasn't on her Monday agenda.

"Quinn?"

She looked up, her gloved fingers pushing away long blond strands already wet from the swirling snow, and her heart stuttered. "Owen?"

Knees suddenly like jelly, she grabbed at the yellow door to keep herself upright. The man's hand reached out to steady her, stopped as she gestured him away.

"Lady, you okay? He bothering you?" The taxi driver's voice penetrated the buzz of surprise filling her head.

"Thanks, I'm fine."

She stepped back, both hands now clutching the camel coat protectively closed. "Owen, what are you doing here?"

Impatient now, the driver leaned across his seat and demanded, "So you want a cab or not?" as he held out his hand for the fee his passenger had not yet paid. "It's twenty-five bucks, buddy."

"Sorry, sorry." Owen reached for his wallet and pulled out a handful of bills. "Keep the change."

The driver's scowl morphed into a grin. Owen pushed the door closed, stepped onto the sidewalk, and, before Quinn could protest, wrapped her in his arms.

THROUGH THE HEAVY COAT, OWEN JOHNSON sensed a change.

Quinn's hands clutched the lapels close, keeping their bodies apart, but something was different. Feeling high-school gawky, he stepped back, his own body quivering as he fought the need to kiss her. "Sorry."

"Owen, what are you doing here?" Quinn repeated, her eyes focused on a spot just above his scarred eyebrow.

He'd prepared for this moment, but now, arms at his sides, breath coming hard, he stood in front of a woman who didn't meet his gaze, in front of a brick townhouse in a strange city and wondered, *What the hell am I doing here?*

One step backward created a Maginot Line. Now he could think, string words together in a coherent manner. "Seems pretty obvious to me. I need to talk to you, and I wasn't sure if you'd see me if I called first." His voice sounded harsh in his ears.

He willed her eyes to meet his own. In them, he knew she would see all that he could not speak. When she looked down, his heart quaked.

She said nothing.

He softened his voice. "So here I am. Will you talk with me?"

She stood silent, attention fixed on the sidewalk, and his senses went on alert, but he pressed on, not allowing her a chance to refuse. "There's a coffee shop on the corner. Please come and talk with me." He grasped her elbow, gently but firmly, and took it as a good sign when she didn't pull away.

Quinn stared at the hand that held her, then looked up. Snowflakes clung to her lashes as her eyes met his, those turquoise eyes that tormented his every dream, sometimes heavy with need, sometimes sated, more often flashing with the anger he'd seen as she'd sent him away. He held her gaze, afraid if he even blinked she would disappear. The snow swirled between them, and he sensed something change, as though she'd come to some conclusion not yet clear to him, but when she shrugged carelessly and answered, "Why not," he wasn't sure.

Turning away, she shook off his hand, pulled up the hood of her coat, and strode left in the direction of the sign he'd seen from the cab window, leaving him to catch up.

The café was surely the model for every movie coffee shop he'd ever seen: backless stools at the long counter, bench seats wearing scarred red vinyl in every booth, and, overall, the nauseating odor of burnt coffee and bacon that permeated the warm and humid confines. *Nausea and nerves don't mix well*, Owen thought, forcing himself not to gag as he followed Quinn inside.

In a much warmer tone than he'd yet heard today, Quinn greeted the server. "Morning, Iris."

As though dressed for her part, the woman wore a white uniform and a ruffle in her tight curls. "Hey, girlfriend," she welcomed Quinn and donned a smile the size of Texas when Quinn asked, "How was the play?"

"Oh my goodness, it was wonderful." The woman's voice rippled with excitement. "It was the most wonderful thing you've ever seen." She picked up a coffee pot and followed the couple to a booth at the window. "Decaf?" she asked as Owen slid into the seat, but her attention was on Quinn and, not waiting for his answer, she filled the mugs already on the table. "They were all adorable, but Marcus, my Marcus was perfect. I'm so glad you encouraged us. You'll see, when you come. He's just perfect."

Interest, pleasure, happiness colored Quinn's voice as she and the woman conversed. *She's made a life here*, Owen realized, *without me*. He ground his teeth, stared into his black coffee, and wished the woman in perdition.

Finally, Iris moved on, leaving menus that Quinn pushed aside. "First starring role. He's six," she answered the question he wasn't interested in asking. "Has ambitions to be the next Denzel."

As Owen watched, her smile faded. One hand reached out for her coffee, the other pulled the coat closer before it joined the first around the thick mug's warmth. Eyes fixed on the coffee's mesmerizing steam, she said, "What *are* you doing here, Owen Johnson? What do you want from me?"

Not harshly, as he'd feared, just a whisper of curiosity that almost undid him. *Christ, she's all I want. Why is this so damn hard?* His heart thudded as he tried to read her expression. Color outlined the sharp cheekbones, emphasized the fullness of the lower lip that he wanted to kiss, but her eyes were hidden by bruised lids, denying him access to her thoughts. She was here, but not—an ocean raged between them—and his stomach clenched.

"Quinn." He cleared his throat as the single word stuck, croaked out, "Quinn, I love you, and I want to be with you."

He'd said this before. What was different now? A gulp of coffee didn't rinse down the taste of bile and fear. *What if she doesn't want me? What if it's really over?*

The silence lengthened.

Gaze still on her coffee, Quinn twisted a strand of damp blond hair around her index finger, a movement Owen associated with hard thinking, and, taking it as a good sign, he plunged on. "I've said that before, I know. And I know I've tried to run things. That's just what I do. I wanted to take care of you, make your life easier. I don't know what's wrong with that, but I realize now that's not what you want."

When her eyes lifted from the mug to his face, hope surged. "Yeah, even I can figure things out eventually." The turquoise went from flat to gleaming, and he ventured a tentative smile. "Quinn, I want to make a life with you, on our terms, not just mine, and I'm ready to do whatever it takes to help you believe me."

Iris slid into view. "More coffee?"

His smile died. *Drat.*

Chest as tight as though he'd just completed the Boston Marathon, Owen could only wait while Iris topped off their mugs and laid several pieces of paper that looked like homemade tickets on the table. "Maybe you'll come tonight, Quinn. He would be so happy if you came to see him."

She beamed. Quinn beamed back. Owen fumed as they praised each other for getting the little boy on the stage. Finally, Iris cut a glance his way. "You can come, too, if she wants you."

When he just glared, she seemed to notice the tension. "Oh, sorry. I'll leave you two alone." She shot a grin at Quinn, patted her hand, and started to leave, then turned back. "But do come. He's the prince, you know."

Quinn's eyes twinkled as she watched her friend ply the coffee pot at the next table, went flat as she turned back to Owen. Her left hand crept under the heavy folds of her coat, and emotion Owen couldn't decipher flitted across her oval face.

Secrets. I hate secrets. He gritted his teeth.

He wanted to still her restless hands, gather her up, and take her away. Instead he sat, rueful, remembering his abortive attempts to do just that. With as much patience as he could muster, he waited for Quinn's response. *There's something I still don't know.* Fear rose and he concentrated on choking it down. Trust. *Say something!* his insides screamed.

"Be with me," he finally whispered.

Her lips twitched, turned upward as her eyes lifted. He saw a glimmer of the humor that so defined her; he didn't know its source but was sure it would be at his expense. Right then he didn't even care. *Whatever, whatever, as long as she doesn't send me away.*

"Well, shit, Owen."

His heart stuttered as she reached across the table for his hand and almost stopped as the folds of her coat fell apart to reveal an unmistakable mound on the rail-thin body he knew as well as his own.

QUINN FELT THE JOLT—LIGHTNING STRUCK—AS OWEN saw, recognized, processed. She hadn't meant him to know, at least not this way. Her hand, abandoned on the table between them, quivered with the need to cover herself. She forced her gaze steady as his dark eyes met hers.

Unmasked, the eyes revealed the man.

Shock, disbelief. She looked away, unwilling to witness the rise of anger.

She ached. *I meant to spare him.* Her hands slid under her coat. The two tiny hearts beating in rhythm with her own demanded honesty. *No, this was a test. I just didn't plan it.*

Ashamed, she took a deep breath—*whatever he says, I deserve*—and brought her attention to his face. There she saw what she'd never expected: joy.

It washed over her like cleansing rain.

"Wow," he murmured, "a package deal."

A weight lifted. She blinked back tears and beamed. "Well, then, Owen Johnson, you *do* know just the right thing to say."

CHAPTER 53

"So, THEN WHAT HAPPENED?"

Curled into the sofa corner like a cat, Quinn regarded Dusty Oakes as the physician, feet propped on his desk, considered the story she'd just told him. He always seemed a little amused by her, at least when he didn't seem horrified, and since she could tell him anything, she usually did. She recognized the unusual nature of their relationship. He'd become a friend when she'd needed one most. She wasn't sure what this cost him in terms of conscience—medical ethics and morals and all—but she was grateful. With a twinkle in her eye, she continued her story. "Then I went to work and he went back to . . . well . . . back to wherever he'd come from."

"Quinn!"

"Okay. I went to my AA meeting, and he went back to his hotel. He's at the Four Seasons in Georgetown. And we're getting together for dinner at seven."

Questions chased across his face, and she laughed as he selected the one most pertinent. "Did you tell him?"

She knew what he meant. "Nope."

"Why?"

The room seemed to hold its breath.

She pondered—not the answer, but whether she would give it. The need to be heard won. "It's too early. If I can believe the look I saw this morning—and it was a surprise, let me tell you—he's happy about the pregnancy. If he knows there are two, he'll be convinced they're his and probably want them even more." She held up her hand to forestall Dusty's comment. "I know, you said it's not a sure thing. No matter, he'll think it anyway. If he knows about my heart thing, it'll break *his* heart, but he'd still want me to abort. I won't do it. You know that, but I also don't want it to feel like his decision. I don't want it on his conscience, whatever happens."

Dusty Oakes nodded, less, Quinn thought, in agreement than understanding, as he probed for the rest of the story. "So you still think he's the father?"

"I told you, his sisters are twins."

"Ahhh, yes." Oakes shrugged. "You could be right. What about McLean?"

Quinn sighed. She probably shouldn't have said anything, but she had, so Dusty knew about McLean's part in the story as well. "He proposed on New Year's Eve."

"Jesus, Quinn, what are you . . . a collector?"

Tears filled her eyes and spilled silently down her cheeks. Oakes dropped his feet to the floor and started toward her.

She raised her hand to ward him off. "Sorry, Dusty, hormones du jour."

He didn't look convinced but sat back in his chair.

"I didn't mean for this to happen. Harry the Heartbreaker, I called him. I thought I was just another in his long list of short-term lovers. You know him." Her look appealed to Dusty's understanding. He did, after all, know the man's reputation. She saw the knowledge in his eyes and continued her story. "I was wrong. He and his wife talked. That's where he was the time he was gone. Remember, when I was throwing up so much I thought he'd just escaped the stink? Anyway, he asked her for the divorce they'd been putting off for years, and she agreed. The papers were filed on the thirty-first, and since he's a man of the moment, he popped the question that night."

"Timing is all," Dusty murmured. "And what did you say?"

"How can you ask that? I love McLean, but I'm *in* love with Owen, even though I thought he was gone forever. I'm trying to get my life together, although you'd never know it to look at me." The complacent hand on her belly belied the words. "And I don't want to get saved by any man. I've already tried that; it doesn't work." She laughed, a bitter sound. "My mother said I wasn't very lovable."

"Your mother didn't love you, so no one else can?"

"What? You're my shrink now?"

Anger snapped through his words. "No, I'm not your shrink, but goddammit it, Quinn, you need one. Somebody's got to get it through your thick skull that she was a sick, narcissistic woman and that you need to get over it. What she thought of you has nothing to do with who you are, and it's time you figured that out."

Surprised by his outbreak, Quinn felt her own anger retreat. "I know, Dusty . . . at least, my head knows now, and that's an improvement. Before she died, I couldn't even see *that* much. But sometimes . . . God, what if she was right?"

He came to her then and held her against his chest as he would hold his two-year-old when she cried, patting her back until the sobs ebbed and the nose-blowing began, then retreating behind his desk where the picture of his wife smiled at him with great compassion.

Quinn sniffled and wiped her eyes. "Sorry, doctor mine, I

didn't mean to be such a watering pot."

"'S okay. Are you going back to see Dr. Blackstone?"

"And deprive you of your chance to play psychiatrist? Not on your life." Her laugh was still watery but a laugh nonetheless, and it won his smile. "Seriously, no. I know what I need to do. I need to trust myself and get on with things."

The odd pair sat quietly for a while, thinking their own separate thoughts. Dr. Oakes finally broke the silence. "So what happens next?"

She rummaged in her shoulder bag, pulled out a dog-eared ticket, and passed it to him.

He read it, frowned, and handed it back. "Departure date February ten. Purchased...December thirty-first? You bought two weeks ago?"

She nodded. "Right after the ultrasound. Suddenly it was as clear as rainwater, Dusty. I just knew."

"Knew?"

She shifted on the couch. "I knew that I need to go home." A sheepish expression played across her face. "I can't stay here and use McLean, even if he's willing." Once again, her hand spread over her belly. "And these guys need a family."

Their eyes met in understanding; the children might survive even if she did not. Finally, Dusty produced an encouraging nod and she continued.

"If I can believe you and Amanda, I don't have to be all by myself to figure things out. In fact," she chuckled "being alone seems rather dangerous for me." She waited for her physician to comment. When he didn't, she went on. "So I figured when February got here and an abortion would be off the table, I would go home and see if I could mend fences with Owen. Then McLean suddenly proposes, and Owen suddenly appears, and, voilà, here I am."

Voilà. There really was nothing more to say. All those days ago, she'd called him a brawler, and Dusty Oakes had taken her challenge and done all that he could to help her. Now Quinn watched her friend consider what she'd told him, then take a deep breath and cloak himself in doctor persona before he returned to his desk to begin the transfer of her care. Trusting his decisions, Quinn quietly left the office and went home to tell McLean.

CHAPTER 54

HE TAXI DREW UP IN FRONT of The Capital Grille at ten past seven. The slush on Pennsylvania Avenue had slowed traffic, and she was late. *I hope he waited,* Quinn thought as she handed bills to the driver and stepped to the sidewalk in front of the District's most famous place to see and be seen. She wasn't really worried. Owen had come this far; of course he'd wait. The uniformed doorman did his job, and a whoosh of warm air and lively conversation welcomed her inside.

A multitude of well-dressed people resigned to their one- to two-hour wait for a table packed the anteroom. She spied Owen among them, his black brows drawn together as he consulted his watch. She slipped out of her coat and made her way to his side.

"Owen."

He whipped around. Relief erased the frown, but he still grabbed her hand and held on as though afraid she would disappear.

She brushed a kiss on his cheek before she slid her hand from his grip. "Hi. Sorry I'm late, traffic."

He nodded, his gaze scanning the red boots and the fuzzy sweater stretched tight over last summer's slinky purple dress. Suddenly aware of the elegance of his dark gray suit, the swish of surrounding satin and silk, she flushed, but when his eyes came to rest on her face, she knew none of it mattered. For a moment, they just looked at one another while the bustle of the Grille fell away.

Movie moment, she thought just before the maître d' touched Owen's arm. "Sir, your table's ready. Shall I take the lady's wrap?"

Owen dragged his attention from Quinn and nodded. "Yes, thank you."

"Very good." Like the butler in an English period piece, this maître d' wore sharply pressed black and immaculate white and with a flourish took Quinn's coat and laid it across his arm. "This way."

They followed as the man crossed the crowded room to a table tucked into a corner filled with soft lights and shadows. An invisible string quartet whispered Vivaldi's "Four Seasons."

Pitch perfect, Quinn thought, *for this seminal scene.*

Few words passed between them as they sat and ordered drinks. Owen perused the menu, and in the play of candlelight, Quinn studied him, this man who had come to claim her: hair long, almost to his collar, straight and black as a raven's wing but streaked now with silver; face narrower, darker, wrinkles carved more deeply—her fantasy pirate come to life. Remembering, she averted her eyes to keep from leaping over the table and into his lap.

Down girl, this is his show.

In a rigidly enforced pretense of calm, she sipped her Perrier and waited. They ordered their meals. Owen played with the stem of his glass. Salads came and went, barely touched.

Okay then, me first. She commented on his expertise in finding such a nice place, spoke lightly of the task that had brought her to the District and her pleasure in its success. She asked about the twins and the retreats and Girl George and Scottie's progress toward home and couldn't decide whether she was angry or amused at his truculence. This *was* his idea, after all.

Their entrées arrived with a flourish.

Quinn's Steak Diane steamed in its mushrooms and veal sauce. She sliced into the filet and savored the first succulent bite, all the while watching Owen handle his knife and fork as though he'd never seen utensils before. Sense of humor engaged, she thought. *If I were writing a book, I'd say, "The tension was so thick they could cut it with a knife."* With an internal chuckle she decided enough was enough, reached her knife across the table, and tapped his glass.

The burgundy liquid swayed, sparkled. Owen looked up, his flush apparent even in the dim light.

"Your turn, Owen. You said you wanted to talk." She hoped he didn't remember how many times she'd sullenly and silently pushed food around her own plate.

"Sorry, sorry. Just thinking." He cleared his throat. "Do you still practice your flute?" The non sequitur was so abrupt that Quinn brought her napkin to her mouth to muffle a giggle.

Laughter stayed near the surface as Owen arranged and rearranged his Chef's Special into a gelatinous mass guaranteed to stop any chef's heart. "And do you still do those salute things every morning?"

The real questions hovered unspoken, imbedded in every syllable, floating like cartoon balloons above his head—*Do you remember my touch? Do you love me? Is it my baby?*

Quinn chewed and swallowed another large chunk of steak and washed it down with milk served ice cold in a generous stemmed glass. Ravenous in spite of the situation, she wasn't going to waste a bite, but at last she took pity, dabbed the corners of her mouth, and responded as though only the spoken words were relevant. "Yes, I do my yoga every day." She patted her midsection. "Some of the positions are getting a little dicey."

His face went still. She ignored the stony demeanor.

"And, yes, I still practice."

Memory of the duet they'd played and the look they'd shared generated the familiar tingling in her core. Skin humming with her own arousal, she mopped up the dregs of her excellent meal and considered what might be next on the Owen Johnson menu.

The waiter intervened, offering dessert and accepting beverage orders. Table cleared, they sat with their after-dinner drinks, hers a virgin Mexican coffee, his a brandy warmed over a candle and now clutched in both hands like a lifeline. She was afraid he'd shatter the glass.

He looked up to catch the quiver of her lips. "What?"

She shook her head as if to say "nothing." *It won't hurt him to squirm a little. This mess isn't all my fault.*

"You think this is funny?"

"Kind of." She allowed the smile to surface, knew he could see the twinkle that danced in her eyes.

"We need to talk," Owen said.

"I thought that's what we were doing."

Annoyance flashed across the hawkish mien, darkened his eyes, and she didn't want to talk anymore. She just wanted him to quench the fire suddenly raging. She stared him down, not caring now if he saw her need.

When he spoke, voice thick with emotion, she knew his desire matched her own.

"Ah, Quinn, you know what I mean. I want you, and I don't know how to make that happen." He tossed back the brandy as though it were water and reached for her hand. "Please tell me what to do."

His grip was firm, almost rough, but she didn't pull away. She'd tell him what she wanted since, for a change, she knew her mind, and then she'd see how it went. The puppy dog devotion he wore now wouldn't last, she knew, nor did she want it to, but it was kind of fun for the moment—Owen Johnson, her own Indiana Jones, a slave for love.

"Will there be anything else?" The black-clad server placed the wallet containing their bill at Owen's elbow and stepped back. Quinn had no difficulty interpreting his actions: *He wants to get us out of here before we jump each other's bones. Smart fellow.*

"His professional duty," Owen whispered as though he could read her thoughts, then thanked the blushing young man and let him escape.

Chuckling, Quinn excused herself to the ladies' room while Owen settled their outrageous bill. Several times she'd sensed numbers flitting through his accountant's brain, knew he was comparing costs and discovering those in the nation's capital pretty pricey.

She returned to find him near the door, her coat held ready. "Nice coat," he commented as he wrapped it around her—an excuse, she thought, to touch her.

"Birthday present."

"From him?"

Ah, the bite of jealousy.

She nodded yes and slid away from his touch before it erased what sensibility she retained. In silence, they waited for his rental car, and she hoped he couldn't see her grin.

A shiny black Cadillac DeVille slid to the curb, its V8 engine purring, and the valet reluctantly handed Owen the keys. "Nice ride, Mister," he said as he pocketed Owen's twenty-dollar tip then opened the passenger door. Quinn slipped into the toasty vehicle.

"Nice," she murmured as Owen settled behind the wheel. The car moved soundlessly into the stream of traffic heading west on Pennsylvania Avenue. Absently, she stroked her rounded abdomen as she turned toward him.

With laughter in her voice, she asked, "Are you abducting me, Owen Johnson?"

CHAPTER 55

OULD THAT I WERE, HE THOUGHT as he watched her fondle the rising belly. Questions pounded through him, the same ones that had tormented him since they had left the coffee shop, the ones that had persisted through a punishing run, a cold shower, and a magnificent and expensive dinner no more flavorful than cardboard in his mouth. He wanted her, he wanted answers, and, most of all, he wanted to know what to do next.

"I thought we'd go to my hotel," he answered, holding up a hand to forestall the expected protest. "I have a suite. We can have a private, civilized conversation, without interruptions. I didn't think you'd want to go …" he paused, unable to utter the word *home* for the other man's house, "to your place." He realized he sounded lame and half expected her burble of laughter.

"You're probably right, Owen. McLean's wouldn't lend itself to our little talk, now, would it?" Amusement dripped over her words, stoked the hot spot he'd buried deep inside along with the image of his woman with another man.

"Damn it, Quinn, this isn't funny."

"But it is, Owen, just a little." She reached across the seat to give his arm a kindly pat.

He captured her hand, soft now from city living, and drew it to his lips. Suddenly he didn't care if she laughed, as long as her hand stayed in his.

Heavy traffic slowed their progress, and forty minutes of silence ensued before the Four Seasons Hotel came into view, then another twenty before the valet whisked the sedan away and the elevator deposited them on the twelfth floor.

Owen opened the door and gestured her into a spacious suite, modern in décor, with a lush bouquet on the entry table and tall windows with silk drapes open to the night. Quinn could see a kitchenette to the left, a mirrored bar to the right, and straight ahead an inviting sofa with flanking chairs arranged before a dark fireplace.

Owen picked up a remote, and his touch brought the gas log to flame and warmth to the impersonal room. Another touch, this one trailing along the edges of her belly as he took her coat, shattered Quinn's thin veneer of amused calm. Heat flared, and she fled into the corner of the sofa. *Talk*, she thought, *talk first, and then we'll see what happens.*

His back to her, Owen busied himself at the bar. Utensils rattled as his impatient hand searched the drawer. Moments later, a wine cork reluctantly released its hold with a loud pop.

Lust and nerves warred inside until Quinn thought she would vomit. *What am I doing here? I want him—it would be so easy to leave it at that, but this time sex isn't enough.* She was in the middle of her third calming breath when Owen set her drink on the coffee table at her knee.

"Diet Pepsi, right?"

She nodded and grabbed the drink.

Owen sat on the high-backed chair beside the sofa and crossed his knee. The wine he swirled reflected the firelight. Through the undraped windows, city lights twinkled.

Like actors in a play, Quinn thought: man, dark eyes playing over her as though he could discover her thoughts, her secrets; woman, toying with her drink, suddenly shy; both needing a script. *Where's Spielberg when you need him?*

Her mouth dry, she realized that knowing what she wanted didn't help. A gulp of Pepsi didn't help, either. Things hadn't changed since she'd tried before—well, maybe a little, with babies and wanting a home and her heart thing. *How do I say I want you and I want me, too?* She captured an ice cube, pulverized it with her teeth, fought her doubts.

Having gotten her here, Owen Johnson once again seemed content with silence.

Quinn cleared her throat. "Owen."

"Quinn." His eyes, soft with longing, met hers.

Pedantic matters fled before that look. "Owen Johnson, I love you so much."

Whatever else she would say was lost as he moved to her side and crushed her against him, sought out her mouth, and silenced it with his own. Raw need surged as they grappled, tongues twisting, mouths grinding as though each could take the other in. His hand found her breast, froze, and he pulled back, his mouth easing and the pressure of his body on hers giving way to unwelcome space.

What? Of course. I'm pregnant. What man wants to touch a . . .

"Oh my God, Quinn, can I look at you?"

Without waiting for permission, he pushed her sweater aside, let his hands roam across breasts taut and full, nipples like cherries visible through the fabric of her dress. His hands trembled against self-imposed restraint.

She could tell he wanted to rip away the dress, and she leaned back against the sofa to give him room.

His hands left her breasts, cupped the mound of her pregnancy, circled his thumb gently over the protrusion of her belly button. "It's an outie," he murmured before he laid his cheek against her.

The gentleness of his touch was too much. "Jesus, Owen, I won't break."

Panting, she struggled out of his reach long enough to strip off the sweater and pull the dress over her head. The first orgasm shook her as he devoured her with his eyes. Then he covered her, and they were lost.

MUCH LATER, EYES NARROWED, QUINN CONSIDERED the man beside her, his hand drawing lazy circles around the outie. Both naked, they lay in a tangle of white sheets.

"Geez, Owen, I think you just took advantage of a pregnant woman."

His hand continued its exploration as he steadily returned her gaze.

Looks like a well-fed lion king, she thought, pretty satisfied herself.

"Which time, Quinn DeMello?" he asked. "On the floor? On the couch? Or maybe it was on this large and well-used bed? Which time, my love?" His voice held a trace of mockery, but the tiny twitch of his jaw gave him away.

Wet and sore, nipples throbbing from their recent contact with his teeth, she wanted Owen Johnson back inside her. *Who's the love slave now*, she wondered and, in an unexpected burst of energy, she pushed against him, neatly turning him onto his back. "Not sure, lover," she purred, "maybe once more will help me figure it out."

He pulled her close. "Happy to oblige." His hands, rough and sure, claimed her breasts, then brought one ripe nipple to his mouth, and she arched and groaned as tongue and teeth pushed her up.

"Omigod, omigod, omigod." Her voice filled the room and then became, "Owen, Owen, Owen." With his name on her lips, she gave herself, and, with a triumphant cry, he took her. As one, they crested and fell.

CHAPTER 56

"RISE AND SHINE, LAZYBONES."

Morning light filled the room. Owen tossed the plush hotel robe over Quinn's head and laughed as she struggled to uncover her face without moving from the bed he'd just vacated. The doorbell chimed, and, with an effort, he squelched the impulse to ignore it and climb back in beside her. He slipped on his own robe and left the room, laughing as a shoe bounced off the wall near his head.

So far, so good, he thought. *Sex isn't the whole answer, but it does grease the skids.* Puffed up at his success so far, Owen answered the door.

"Your breakfast, sir."

Without waiting for his reply, a young woman dressed in conventional server attire pushed a heavily laden cart through the door. As he dug in his wallet, the girl glanced around at the empty room, then scanned Owen's dishabille, raised one carefully shaped eyebrow, and handed him the tab. "Lots of food for one?"

With a grin and no comment, Owen handed her a twenty and closed the door behind her just as Quinn scurried from the bedroom to hover over the room-service cart.

"I think you planned this." She sniffed at the enticing odors emanating from the silver domes. "Admit it!"

Fuck. Well-being vanished. He didn't know what answer she wanted; he was never sure when a word from him would signal loss of control and she would rear up and bite him. Out of the safety of her arms, he was back on eggshells.

"Yes and no," he said, pulling off one cover to tempt her with fragrant bacon. "Yes and no."

She reached for a crisp bacon strip. He moved the plate just out of her reach.

"Give it to me, you seducer," she demanded, laughter in her voice.

Relief flooded and annoyed him. *Pussy-whipped, the guys would say.* He moved the plate back within her reach. They'd be right—but for today it didn't matter. "Your wish is my command."

"Yeah, right," she mumbled as she stuffed one whole strip into her mouth and groaned with pleasure, greedy eyes scanning the cart.

He returned the serving dish to its place and pulled out a chair for Quinn. When she was settled at the table, he pushed the cart closer and then joined her. "I wasn't sure what you could eat, so I ordered a little of everything." He watched while she ladled eggs onto her plate and grabbed two pieces of sourdough toast. "Guess I didn't need to worry."

He sat down, helped himself, and toyed with his food. *She's with me now. No matter what, she's mine. Isn't she?* His stomach clutched, and he pushed his plate away.

He had plenty of time for hope and doubt before Quinn finally poked under a silver cover, snagged the last sausage, and dropped it on her plate after only one bite. "Done," she gasped. "I can't eat another bite."

He laughed and refilled their coffee cups. "That's good 'cause there's nothing left."

"Oh, did I eat it all?" She surveyed the ravaged table. "I guess I did. I can't tell you how good it feels to be hungry. That's the first breakfast I've enjoyed since—" She gestured toward her middle. "Usually I force myself to eat and then puke it back up. For a while, even McLean couldn't ..."

Her voice trailed off. His smile died, and he felt color drain from his face.

She must have noticed. "We do have to talk, don't we?"

When he said nothing, she covered his hand with her own greasy one. "Owen?"

The heavy chair struck the floor with a thump as he pushed himself away from the table and strode to the windows, unseeing gaze on the city below. Frozen, thoughts and feelings too painful to entertain, he clenched his fists and held himself still.

Behind him, Quinn spoke, anger now sharpening her voice. "Well, shit, Owen, you know what the deal is. You blew it with me, and I got drunk and found McLean. That's what I do. That's what I do, and you of all people should know that. I'm trying to learn a better way, but ..." She shrugged. "Anyway, you're the one who brought me here."

He stood, misery or rage—he wasn't sure which—clogging his throat. "You're right, Quinn, and maybe it was the biggest mistake of my life."

She moved to stand beside him at the window.

He was surprised. Running was more her thing. But he stepped away when she slid her arm around him. "Not now.

Don't touch me right now." Before she could speak, he escaped into the gleaming white bathroom.

In the king-sized shower he'd hoped to share with Quinn, Owen let the scalding spray punish his body. His fists clenched and unclenched as he wished for something, someone, to use them on. He couldn't turn the images off—McLean holding her, McLean's big body on hers, McLean thrusting himself inside her, McLean tending her as she suffered the ravages of her pregnancy. His stomach roiled, and he forced himself not to retch.

I should have been here. It should have been me taking care of her. Thoughts emerged, then swerved. *She shouldn't have left me. She shouldn't have sent me away.* The thoughts swerved again. *That bastard, taking advantage of her.*

But the thought of any man taking advantage of Quinn was so funny it completely disrupted his mental tirade. His laughter boomed and echoed against the white tile. Ashamed, he turned off the shower and reached for his towel, hoping that Quinn hadn't given up and left. It was damned hard work tracking her down.

EVEN OVER THE SHOWER'S ROAR, QUINN could hear him laugh. *Tantrum's over.* She smiled and realized she'd been holding her breath.

When the bathroom door had slammed behind Owen's rigid back, she'd remained at the window, berating herself for not anticipating his reaction. Then, still clad only in the plush white robe, she'd forced herself to sit and wait him out, afraid if she dressed the temptation to run would overcome her. She knew what she wanted, had said it out loud to make it true; now she replayed that conversation for courage. She didn't know what would happen next, but damned if she'd run away again.

Yesterday—*was it just yesterday?* she marveled. *It seems like forever*—Dusty Oakes had soothed away her tears and then asked what she was going to do.

"I want to love somebody," she'd told him, "love somebody so much it hurts. And care more about him than I do about myself." She looked up to see if her ramble was making sense. He nodded. Satisfied, she continued. "And I want to commit to somebody so completely that when we get mad and argue nobody runs." Deep breath. "And I want to fight with my kids about brushing their teeth and making their beds and read them bedtime stories and feel little arms around my neck." She blew her nose, backhanded her tears. "That's about it, and Owen's the unlucky man."

Remembering the concern in Dusty's voice brought clouds into the opulent hotel room. She patted the babies inside her gently. *I have to see this through, and if it means I can't tell the truth for a little while longer, then so be it. The poor guy's stuck with me now.*

Determined, Quinn abandoned the robe and pulled her clothes on. *Armoring up,* she thought as she buttoned the sweater to cover the ill-fitting dress and twisted her hair into an untidy knot on the top of her head.

Owen would be compliant now, his wanting her shading everything, but spots don't change, and soon she'd have to battle not only his need to take care of her but her own propensity to look for salvation. Fear coursed through her as she remembered the men she'd buried herself in, the drunken nights that had hidden her from herself, the flights from job to job and place to place, seeking—what? Now she knew. For however long she had, she wanted a home. She wanted a home that she helped create.

The bathroom door opened.

Quinn stood tall, squared her shoulders, and turned, the morning light from the windows behind casting a golden glow. *Ready when you are, lover.*

They stared at each other for what seemed an eternity. Then Owen whispered, "God, Quinn, you are so beautiful."

His softness staggered her. Boneless, she sank to the sofa, eyes only for him. "Owen."

"No, let me talk first." He dropped to one knee beside her, caught her hands in his, and brought her fingers to his lips. "I am so sorry. I was totally out of line and I'm sorry. Can you forgive—"

She freed her hands to cup his face—prominent nose, cheekbones high and sharp, and eyes deep and dark that promised forever—and marveled. In this face, she saw her children. Awestruck, heart overflowing, she covered his mouth with her own.

His response was all she could ever want. When his arms encircled her and drew her close, she slid into his lap.

Finally, breathless, she pulled back and looked into his eyes. "There's nothing to forgive, Owen, not for either of us. We just need to trust and love and move on."

CHAPTER 57

"I WANT TO CREATE A HOME WITH you. I want to create a home with you."

As American Airlines flight 1355 traversed the continent, Quinn's words played and replayed in Owen's mind, distracting his attention from the in-flight movie he'd thought he wanted to watch.

I got what I wanted. She's coming home. What's wrong with me now, and why the fuck didn't I ask if the baby is mine?

The adjacent seat mocked him with silence. Its prior occupant, her charms rebuffed, had scooted across the aisle to a more receptive audience. *No fit company for man nor beast,* Owen mouthed another of his sisters' clichés as he glanced at the attractive woman who might at a different time have engaged his attention.

Restless, he stared at the screen, but two minutes later he was back in his own head. Thoughts ricocheted: *Create a home? Whose baby? Does it matter? Will she run? Can I do this?*

Aggravated, he motioned to the flight attendant and ordered a drink. At least in first class there was an unending supply of temporary surcease. *Something's wrong, something she's not telling me, and there's not one damn thing I can do about it.* Heart pounding, chest tight, Owen Johnson downed the tawny liquid and signaled for another.

Hours later, sobriety but not peace of mind regained, he braced for the usual bumpy landing into Reno-Tahoe International. *What next?* Pondering the questions that neither whisky nor sleep had answered, he left the plane, collected his bag, and headed toward the taxi stand. *Dear God, tell me what to do.*

Steeped in his own confusion, he jerked in surprise when they fell in beside him—two round, soft women who each tucked a hand into the crook of an arm and sandwiched him in their familiar comfort.

"Girls, what are you doing here?"

Bemused, he shortened his stride as his sisters nudged him toward short-term parking.

Vivian squeezed the arm she held. "Thought you might need—"

"A ride home," finished Victoria. "Besides, we couldn't wait to hear—"

"The rest of the story."

With no further ado, the women shepherded him into their old truck, and within minutes they sat under the fluorescent lights of the Denny's on Plumb Lane and watched him toy with rapidly congealing french fries. The hamburger he'd ordered sat untouched on his plate.

Finally, Vicky spoke. "Well, Owen, are you going to tell us what happened?"

He wanted to tell them. He wanted to talk to somebody, but the questions swirled inside, mixed as they were with the lavender of her memory, the touch of her hand on his cheek as he'd left her. *What the hell is wrong with me?*

He looked up to see confusion mixed with concern on the identical faces. It had always been his job to take care of them, so he tried to do so now, his gaze firmly on the table to disguise his own bewilderment.

"She's coming home in February."

Their exclamations of delight filled him with consternation. They loved Quinn, too, sometimes more than they loved him, he'd thought as they'd browbeaten him into admitting his own stupidity and forced him to give up his—what had they called it?—stiff-necked pride. Now they seemed to believe they had a vested interest in the outcome of his adventure. He tried to mask his own uncertainty as he raised his eyes to meet their matching gazes.

"She's coming to Reno as soon as her project is complete."

He started to explain what she'd been working on, but Vivian interrupted. "She told us, said it was done. Move on."

He was used to less complicated support. A hard swallow almost dislodged the lump in his throat as he struggled to concoct a tale they could believe. "I'm going to find a place for us." Like straw into gold, the words spun reality. Heart pounding, he barely noticed their excited murmurs.

"And?" Victoria finally prompted.

Another hard swallow. He didn't want to talk about Quinn's pregnancy, but he wasn't sure why. "And we'll live together while we finish deciding what to do."

Skeptical looks greeted that statement.

He wasn't surprised. Even to his own ears, it sounded shady. When they turned their identical brown eyes on him, he squirmed on the vinyl seat, feeling the way he had when Miss Haley, his second grade teacher, had wanted an answer he didn't have. "I mean, she still has all the things on her mind that she had when she left. You remember," he tried to refocus, "you're the ones who explained it to me—issues about her mother, about her daughter's death, about being rescued—you remember."

Not liking the desperate sound his voice had acquired, he blundered on, hoping he'd at least lulled suspicion. "So, if you'll be good enough to give me a ride, I'm off to give Karle my two-weeks' notice." He laughed at the thought that his friend would expect a formal notice. "Then I'll hook up with a rental agent. It's been a long time since I've gone house hunting. And how's Harold?" he asked, shifting the conversation, skillfully, he thought.

CHAPTER 58

THE PRETTY LITTLE HOUSE ON NIXON Avenue reverberated with Karle's wrath.

"What do you mean, you're moving out? You can't move out!"

She paced the living room, kicked at the foolhardy footstool in her path as she whipped herself into a frenzy. "I knew something was funny when your sisters wouldn't let me pick you up at the airport!"

Owen stood by the fireplace, transfixed, while Karle Moran methodically validated all his concerns.

"I know you think you love her. God knows, you've told me that enough times, and I can't tell you how much I've worried about you when you've rushed around at her beck and call. But this—"

She threw herself onto the chenille sofa, its deep green setting off the flaming red of her hair. Drama suited her beauty, and though he knew it well, Owen Johnson couldn't help but be moved by her passion.

"Owen, Owen darling," she begged, "use your head."

"Karle." He clamped down on his own emotions and stepped toward her, wanting to interrupt her tirade, dimly realizing that Karle had not relinquished her claim on him, that his own waffling had given her the right to these words. "Karle, I'm sorry, please stop."

"No, you can't make me stop. You've got to listen to me, Owen, before you make the biggest mistake of your life."

Shock: His words on her lips. Was this a mistake? Is that what he'd been picking at like something stuck in his teeth? What was Quinn hiding? What wasn't she telling him? He'd accepted that Quinn didn't love him as he loved her. He knew she was afraid that he'd run roughshod over her. He'd meant it when he'd promised not to fix and rescue and take over. He'd even accepted that the baby she carried might be McLean's, although she hadn't said as much and he'd been afraid to ask. His stomach clenched and his fists tightened. *What if she really doesn't love me?*

"Owen." Karle pounded the sofa, her delicate fist demanding his attention. "Owen, darling, you've got to listen to me. You've got to believe me. That woman doesn't love you. If she loved you, she'd never have left you, never have sent you away. You know that. Deep down inside, you know that, and it will eat at you every single day of your life."

His fears poured from her mouth.

Finally, her pause for a shuddering breath left room for rebuttal, but he could find nothing to staunch the flow of words that cut like knives into his heart. He stood silent, shaking his head.

Like a laser of righteous determination, Karle exploded from the sofa and stood quivering in front of the man she'd claimed as her own. Owen couldn't look away. The green eyes glittered, and he realized too late what she was doing.

"She's a tramp, Owen, she's a tramp, and now she's knocked up and wants you to fix it."

He cringed. How Karle had wheedled Quinn's pregnancy out of him, he wasn't sure, but he couldn't stand silent.

"She's a tramp and a slut and—" The titian-haired beauty wrapped her tiny hand around his bare wrist, and the touch roused him to action.

"Shut up. Shut up, Karle. Just stop it." He yanked his arm away, buried his fists in his pockets to keep from striking her. "I'm done listening, and I'm done with you."

Filled with shame, he turned away.

Miles away, guilt at her continued deception coloring her words, Quinn faced her doctor and friend in his little exam room. "So after we made up—again—I showed him the airline ticket and convinced him I meant to come home, and then we worked out the details. I'll go to Reno, we'll find some place to live together until the babies are born, and then we'll decide what to do next." That there might not be a *next* for her hovered in the air, unspoken.

Oakes frowned. "What to do next? I thought you wanted to make a life with him." Before she could respond, his expression cleared. "You didn't tell him, did you?"

He sounded so disappointed, Quinn realized he'd hoped she'd change her mind. "Sorry, Dusty, but nope, I didn't tell him there were two babies, and I'm not going to. I'm sure he thinks the baby is McLean's. He still didn't ask." She shrugged. "I still don't know why. He just called it a 'package deal,' and started making plans."

She patted her rapidly enlarging middle. "I could have told him, but I didn't, and I'm not telling him about the heart thing either, not yet. I love him too much to let him take this on." Grimacing, she raised her hand to forestall comment. "I don't want to die, Dusty, and maybe I'm afraid he'll be too persuasive."

I promised to trust, she thought, *and I really don't trust either one of us.*

Determination overrode guilt. "I'm going to give these babies life, Dusty Oakes, even if it means lying to Owen." Now the tears *did* spill, and her voice was thick with them as she repeated, "I'm going to give these babies life, or die trying."

CHAPTER 59

I N THE UNPREDICTABLE FEBRUARY WEATHER, CHRIS McLean and Quinn DeMello covered the miles to Dulles International Airport in silence. Everything that could be said had already been said. All the tears had been shed. Ignoring her protests, he parked, carried her bag inside, and waited while she got her boarding pass.

Now Chris watched as Quinn, awkward with her pregnancy, walked away.

He wanted to call her back, beg her to stay, but he did neither. He knew it would do no good—had known, really, from the beginning, when she'd come to him stinking of tequila and heartache and begging him to fill her. Because he knew, he'd worked with Dusty Oakes and Mason Orr to arrange the transfer of her care. Rich Bennett, a cardiologist located near the Sierra because his wife liked to ski, and Marion Apata, Hawaiian native and specialist in high-risk pregnancies, would take over as soon as Quinn arrived. He worried she'd left it too late, that even this flight placed her in jeopardy. Fear shot through him as he realized he might never see her again, and only the security barricades kept him from rushing after her as she disappeared into the airport's maw.

"You're waddling," he'd teased her earlier that morning. Anything to disguise his heartache.

"You'd waddle, too, if you were wearing two bowling balls," she giggled. "Whoops, you are."

The laughter died as she looked around the room he'd given her, picked up the scrunchie that had hidden itself under the bureau, wiped imaginary dust from the nightstand, and avoided his eyes.

"Enough, Quinn." He wrapped a shaky hand around her arm. "It's time."

He saw love and regret as she faced him. "McLean, I'm sorry."

"Shhh," he whispered over the lump in his throat, "it's not your fault. It just happened. I'll be fine, you know, and Gen and I needed to get on with things. You helped me see that. Besides," he attempted a grin, "there'll always be another disaster."

Now he just wanted her back.

Heartbreak Harry, she called me, and the joke's on me.

CHAPTER 60

QUINN UNPLUGGED HER EARPHONES AND HANDED them to the flight attendant. She'd watched two movies and listened through the entire *Fab Sixties* compilation—distraction. Soon she would leave this cocoon, thrust into a world different by dint of her own choices. What had seemed possible a month ago—making a home, delivering two healthy babies, maybe even surviving the heart thing—now seemed the ultimate in self-delusion. In her mind, Mary DeMello's voice rang clear: "Another stupid decision, Quinn. When will you ever learn?"

Tsunami-like despair crested, the landing gear clunked into place, and a baby, affectionately identified as T-one—short for Thing One, of Dr. Seuss fame—kicked her ribs, hard.

Dark thoughts vanished. *Wrong, Mama,* she thought, *this time you're wrong.* Her hand found the tiny foot. "It'll be okay," she murmured. "I failed your sister; I won't fail you."

As though in response, T-one kicked harder. On the other side, T-two's elbow jabbed agreement and a smile crawled across her face. *Damn right, kids, it's gonna be fine.*

She believed, but anxious palms still left wet spots on her new black jeans with the stretchy front panel as the plane nuzzled to its place like a piglet to its mother. In the dusk, the city's profile sparkled. *Home.*

Heart beating a little faster, she levered herself out of the seat, pulled the camel coat as far around as it would go, and reached up.

"Can I help you, ma'am?"

Before she could say, "I can do it myself," a scruffy-faced guy looking eighteen but probably closer to twenty-five reached over her head and hefted her swollen duffel to the aisle. When he nodded at her thanks and said, "No problem. My wife's pregnant, too," she remembered why she looked helpless. Laughing at herself, she headed for the exit.

Just past security, Quinn paused to catch her breath. To her left, the young man swept a toddler off her feet and into a giggling hug, then looped his arm around a very pregnant redhead, and the three disappeared around a corner. Earlier she'd seen two women—almost carbon copies except for the care worn into the face of the elder—greet stiffly but then join hands as they hurried away.

Families. Do they all have lives as messed up as mine?

As a therapist in what seemed another life, she knew they did. Hers was not unique, just ignored for too long. Remembering her resolutions, she straightened her shoulders, stepped forward, and saw him.

In the surge of humanity, Owen Johnson seemed to appear and disappear, a mirage. Then the crowd thinned, and he solidified into an Owen she hardly recognized—important in his dark gray suit and polished shoes, hair now businessman short. He was in conversation with an older man whose belly threatened to overflow an unzipped ski jacket. From her distance, Owen seemed impatient, hand movements abrupt and eyes drifting away from his companion to survey the passengers—handsome, cool, successful, a busy man in charge of a successful life.

Where was *her* Owen—the man of fire and ice, arrogance and desire, the man whose eyes held her soul, whose mouth promised the world—Owen, for whom she almost believed in miracles? Fingers of doubt probed the chinks in her determination. *Who is this stranger, and what does he want with me? What was I thinking? What the hell am I doing here?*

Breath short, heart pounding, palms slick again, she stood still.

She hadn't expected him. No one ever met her in an airport—if you didn't count McLean and the National Guard transport plane, that is. She turned around and bumped into the No Admittance sign: trapped. She turned back as Owen executed the briefest of handshakes and looked up. His eyes found her. Impatience faded, a smile transformed his face, and there he was—her Owen, gorgeous and arrogant and waiting for *her*. Happiness flared.

They had talked for hours, that day a month ago when she'd told him she loved him, when they'd agreed to create a life together.

She grimaced. *Battled is more like it,* she thought, remembering the many times she'd reminded Owen of his promise not to take over her life. He'd apologize, flash the smile of an impish boy, and minutes later be planning her life again. Sometimes they had been nose to nose, but she hadn't backed down. The stakes were too high.

Now, she stood in the Reno-Tahoe International Airport grinning like a baboon at the man who would change her life.

He reached her at a run, swept her up in a hug that lifted her from her feet, and planted a kiss on her mouth that left her gasping.

"Put me down, you idiot, put me down."

He set her gently on her feet, stood back, and raked her with his eyes. Black Levi's, red cowboy boots, and the camel coat that now barely met in the middle. His eyebrows rose, twisting the scar. "You're bigger."

"It's called pregnancy." She clutched the lapels with one hand, her other still locked in his. "It happens. Get used to it."

"Oh, I will, baby. You better believe I will." Before she could stop him, he leaned forward and kissed the bump. Then, ignoring her spluttering embarrassment, he slung her duffel over his shoulder and, grinning broadly, pulled Quinn toward the escalator. "Let's go home."

Home, she thought. *Now I know how E.T. felt.* Home was the only battle she'd lost.

IN THEIR HOURS OF DISCUSSING, FIGHTING, deciding, she'd been surprised at how little he argued. *Still being cautious,* she thought. *That'll change, and he'll try to boss me around like he does the twins.* Only once had he been adamant. She'd planned to return to her own place, the little duplex in old Reno, which was now occupied by Ben the Boarder and her own cat, Minnie the Mouser.

Fists on his hips, mouth set, he'd said, "This isn't another trial run, Quinn. This is us, building a life. That's what you said you want, remember?"

She hated it when he used her words against her.

He'd gone on, undeterred by her mutinous expression. "We can't build a home when I'm in Winnemucca and you're in Reno in a—"

Pause. She knew he wanted to say *dump,* but he didn't.

"When you're in a place that's too small. I want to live with you, and that's what I'm going to do, and that means we need a place big enough for two ... three," he amended in his only allusion to her pregnancy.

She'd argued but not wholeheartedly, relieved that she was not being relegated to some moldy basement where no one visited, surprised to find that worry still active in her mind. Nothing to do but capitulate with as much grace as she could muster and be ready to spend the next few days hunting for an apartment big enough for four. In the meantime, the Airport Inn had been happy to take her reservation.

She shivered as they stepped out into the February chill. *Almost as cold as DC.* She didn't share that thought.

Wrapping his arm around her, Owen headed toward a blue SUV, which beeped as they approached.

"New car?"

"Retired the Toyota beast. The Highlander ads were too good to ignore." He helped her into the vehicle, laughed as they struggled to get the seatbelt around her middle, and ignored her puzzled look.

A unilateral decision, she thought. He'd loved his ancient Toyota Land Cruiser. But this, this new vehicle obviously purchased to carry babies, was a decision that had clearly been made with so much hope that her heart twisted. *It's done, no more questions.* And it *was* pure pleasure to settle into the contoured seats. "Ahh, this is nice."

"You ain't seen nothing yet." He started the engine and adjusted something on the dash, and the leather warmed around her.

"Heated seats?"

"Nothing's too good for my honey." A strained laugh this time. "This kinda feels like a first date, doesn't it?"

She nodded, placed her hand on his arm, and quivered when he took it in his own and raised it to his lips. "A little weird," she agreed, "but nice." The familiar tingle started deep in her core. "Very, very nice."

He released her hand long enough to pay the parking fee, recaptured it as he maneuvered the vehicle toward Plumb Lane, and resumed car talk as though she had asked another question. "It's a Toyota Highlander, a midsize crossover, new to the U.S. this January. Great reviews. I special-ordered four-wheel drive; around here, we'll need it."

She relaxed into his recitation of antilock brakes, unit body construction, added-on side-impact airbags, and she was drifting toward sleep when she noticed their direction.

"Hey, you missed the turn."

"No, I didn't." Holding fast to the hand she tried to pull away, he continued toward the mountains.

"Yes, you did. My hotel's back there." Fighting to free herself from his now ruthless grip, she gestured with her free hand at the Airport Inn, fading into the dusk behind them. "I made reservations."

"I know. I cancelled them."

Stunned, she went still. "You did what?"

He released her hand and repeated, "I cancelled them."

OWEN FELT QUINN'S RISING FURY. *DON'T need those heated seats now, do we?*

When he'd recognized the depth of Karle's scheme, he'd stormed away and, knowing he risked Quinn's ire, searched for a home for his new family. He considered the facts: his work in Reno, Unionville too far from medical care, her sisters nearby, her place too small and already occupied—*thanks be*, he'd thought at the time as he remembered the moldering duplex. Reno it would be. Mara Nadimi, his Godsend of a Realtor, had patiently driven him from north to south and everywhere in between, mumbling "princess and the pea" under her breath as he turned down one lovely house after the other. Until this one.

The house was perfect. He'd known from the moment Mara had let him in the front door—light and airy, surrounded by trees and a sense of seclusion, beautiful woodwork and a deck with a view. In a nice part of town, it stood on a plateau, its position unique among its neighbors as the elevation left the back of the house private and the view wide and unobstructed. He'd pictured Quinn on the deck, a baby in her arms, the city laid out at her feet.

They needed a home; he'd found one. Asking her opinion had crossed his mind, but he'd decided against it. She might be a little miffed at first, but he'd deal with that and she'd come around. Quite sure that Quinn would appreciate his logic, he'd signed a lease, cancelled hotel reservations, and brought them to this moment.

Rubbing her wrist as though she could wipe away his touch, Quinn glared at him, speechless. With the ghost of a smile playing around his mouth, he waited for her wrath.

It didn't come.

She took a deep breath, and, as much as possible in the confines of the seatbelt, angled herself to see his face. He heard her suck in another deep breath.

Bring it on, he thought. *I'm ready.*

Instead, as though she'd made her own unilateral decision, Quinn settled back and said nothing.

Traffic noise and her silence filled the car as they sped west. By the time they crossed Virginia Street, she was humming a country song that sounded suspiciously like "Stand by Your Man." Braced for an explosion, he was unnerved by its absence.

"Quinn. Quinn, honey, say something."

"Why, Owen, honey," she mimicked, "whatever is there to say?"

His heart suddenly struggled to escape its cage. Praying the cars around him were nimble, he yanked the steering wheel toward the curb. Not funny any longer.

"I'm sorry. I just couldn't let you stay in a—"

"Sleazy hotel. Of course not, dear." In her sweetest *Father Knows Best* voice, Quinn continued, "And I'm sure you know best."

"Shit, I've done it again, haven't I?" Eyes straight ahead, he damned himself for his prideful silence.

"Yes, you have. Yes, you really fucking have. God, Owen, don't I get a voice in anything?" Her tone alerted him, and he turned to see her grinning. She giggled. "Oh, get a grip, Johnson, you obviously have a plan. What is it this time?"

The tight fist in his gut released. Shaking his head, he pulled carefully back into the stream of cars heading into the remnants of sunset. Just when he thought he knew her every move, she slid chameleon-like into a different self that left him bewildered, totally out of control, and acutely aware of the bumpy road he had chosen.

CHAPTER 61

WEN TURNED THE KEY AND THE lock released with a
respectably solid clunk. He paused, took a deep breath,
and turned the handle. Quinn heard and wondered. Nerves?
Why? He was getting his own way, wasn't he? The front door, a
deep forest green framed by twin sidelights, swung open. Owen
flicked the light switch, then stood aside for her to enter.

Time for new rules, she'd decided as her hotel had disappeared
behind them. *Change it up and see what happens.* Now, heart
fluttering like a baby bird's, she thought, *not as easy as it sounds.*

Sucking in her own deep breath, she stepped across the
threshold and looked around. Plain, none of the nooks and
crannies she was used to, but its banks of windows and new
paint gave it lightness, airiness, and the house wrapped around
her like a warm blanket in the February night.

Behind her, Owen ticked off its benefits in a real estate
agent's sing-song. "Living room here, formal dining not too big,
kitchen fully equipped."

Giddy with relief, she giggled and butted in. "And no spiders
to be seen and mold only in the crawlspace if special ordered."

Owen didn't laugh.

Okay, not joking. Quinn swiped away the grin.

He took her elbow, his grip a little tighter than necessary, and led her from room to room, his voice flat as he narrated the tour. "Basic furniture, comes with the house. We can change it if we want. Three bedrooms, one you could use for yoga, meditation—private stuff—and one for the baby."

His voice dropped to a whisper. She strained to hear his words as he opened double doors. "Our bedroom . . . that is, if you want to share one with me."

She felt another giggle rising—he sounded so like *Mission Impossible*: "Your assignment, should you choose to accept it . . ." But one glance over her shoulder at his set face and clenched jaw stifled it. He'd really left his sense of humor in the car.

A little nervous herself, she stepped into a room easily as large as her whole ancient duplex: one wall of floor-to-ceiling windows and French doors, the other walls creamy white; a king-sized bed fully dressed with sheets and pillows and a winter-plaid duvet on a fluffy down comforter; above the bed the painting of wild horses she'd admired at a gallery they'd visited the previous summer; two books she recognized as her own waiting on the nightstand.

"I love it," sprang to her lips.

Before she could utter the words, Owen spoke. "I wasn't sure. I mean, I know I forced this living together thing on you, and now I'm forcing this house on you." He coughed as though unclogging his throat. "Quinn, what I'm saying is, I want us here but . . . I mean . . . if you need your own space, I can understand that."

Like ashes, his quiet words settled over her, and she felt dirty and ashamed. *I said I loved him,* she thought, *and I didn't give one damn thought to how this would be for him. I've been so frigging busy*—she sucked in a deep breath to keep from bolting—*so busy getting my own way that I didn't pay attention to him at all. I didn't even think about it. I didn't really get how important this is to him. He had to make this right, his way, and now he's afraid.*

Remorse washed over her—remorse and love, an uneasy mix—and the fear she'd hoarded flowed away.

OWEN STOOD BEHIND QUINN, EYES DOWN and hands clenched to keep him from shaking her into submission. The house was right for them. He knew it. His heart thundered as he waited for her response. *Too fast. I should have taken her to the damn hotel and let her get used to the idea.*

He heard rustling and looked up to see Quinn perched in the middle of the bed, her finger crooked in his direction. "The house is lovely, Owen," she purred, "but I'm not sure about this bed. Maybe we should try it out?"

Released once again from his self-imposed torment, Owen jumped onto the bed beside her, tumbling her backward in a laughing heap. His mouth found hers, plundering, demanding, and she was liquid lightning under him, fighting his zipper as he yanked her jeans to her knees, and they came together in heat and passion and relief.

Later, Quinn pushed herself upright, then leaned forward, her breath coming in little gasps. "Wow, how did we manage that?" Her coat was still on, her pants were around her knees, and her belly was bare to Owen's exploring fingers.

He noticed her struggle for breath just before his attention caught on something else. His hand stilled.

"What?"

"This." No longer touching her, he pointed at the tiny sun rising on the point of her right hip.

"Tattoo, obviously." She sounded puzzled.

He slid off the bed and jerked up his trousers. "It's new." His stomach roiled. *Goddammit, it's for him.*

Her eyes met his, and he saw confusion give way to understanding. She knew he was jealous, and right now he didn't care. *Damn right I'm jealous. A stupid red rose on your butt for somebody you don't even remember, and now this!*

"It's for my sunshine girl," she whispered.

"Samantha?"

"Who else?"

He looked at the floor, embarrassed.

She patted the bed beside her and waited until he rejoined her. "It's to remember. I was afraid I'd forget her if I didn't keep the guilt, but now I don't have to worry. She's in my heart and," with a smile, she ran her fingers over the tiny new sun, "now she's inside *and* outside. It's all good."

He laid a tentative hand on her cheek. "Sorry, sorry, I didn't know."

She cocked her head, raised an eyebrow, and said nothing.

Feeling heat rise up his neck, suffusing his cheeks, he ducked his head. "Okay, you're right. I thought it was for him."

She grinned, obviously enjoying his discomfort. "Well, it's not. And just so you know, the next one's for you."

Relieved, he gathered her back into his arms. Quite sure there would never be an end to the Quinn roller coaster and certain he didn't want to get off, Owen held on tight and hoped he wasn't expected to get tattooed, too.

SOME TIME LATER, QUINN STOOD ON the deck, Owen's arms strong around her, and gazed out at the city lights—the Atlantis Casino with its fiery glow, John Ascuaga's Nugget to the east, the irregular cluster of casinos in the center, and the individual twinkles of family homes—and felt something settle inside. Home. The sweet odor of sage wafted in on the cold night air. In the distant hills, a coyote howled and, a heartbeat later, his mate answered. Owen nuzzled her neck, his breath warm on her skin. Tears choked her. They could be happy here. It was a good house, clean and compact and modern, a good place to bring the babies . . . until he could take them home. She wiped her eyes with the back of her hand and snuggled deeper into the arms that held her.

He tightened around her and whispered, "Thank you."

"For what?" she whispered back, as though even the wind eavesdropped.

"For being a good sport. For letting me do this for you." A shudder ran through him, and, as though sensing danger, he held her even closer. "There's room for the baby. And it's away so you won't feel too hemmed in, too cramped, too . . . trapped. I know you need time, that you have things to work out. I just hope you can do it here, do it with me."

The hope and fear in his voice undid her, and she turned in his arms. Trust. The time for subterfuge was over.

"Owen," she mumbled into his shirt, "there's something I need to tell you."

Chapter 62

Twins. *My babies.* Emotion threatened to choke Owen as he stood barefoot in the kitchen waiting for morning coffee to brew. It was almost too much to take in: two babies, a heart condition, appointments with two doctors this morning—and the relief that the babies were his. He had already loved the one, no matter, but still. His grin felt permanently carved into his face.

The night before, wrapped in his arms, face hidden against his neck, Quinn had disclosed her secrets.

Twins. Tears brimmed over, and he let them flow. *My babies.*

The coffee chuckled to completion. He reached for mugs, hand sliding over the honey-colored wood of the cabinets. *Nice, but not as nice as mine,* he thought, yearning for his own cottage in Winnemucca. *After the babies get here, maybe we can all go home.* Mentally crossing his fingers for luck, Owen poured the coffee and went to wake his woman.

Dr. Rich Bennett's office was all steel and glass and efficiency. Shivering as she perched on the end of an exam table,

Quinn twirled a strand of hair and listened to her new cardiologist. Owen stood beside her, one hand protectively on her thigh.

"I wish there was something else I could tell you, Mr. Johnson, but what Ms. DeMello says seems to be completely accurate. I reviewed the tests and Dr. Oakes's notes. I'll examine her, of course, but I don't expect to come up with anything new." Ensconced on the exam stool, the cardiologist turned to Quinn. "Did Dusty tell you we went to med school together?" At her nod, he continued. "Good man, Dusty Oakes. I suppose he tried to talk you out of this?"

Again, she nodded.

"Well, he was right. You should have listened."

Owen paled and his jaw clenched.

A look that might have been sympathy crossed the doctor's face. He stood, red hair and freckles giving a boyish look that belied his autocratic tone and the sophistication of his immaculately tailored suit. "Johnson," he gestured to Owen, "let's get out of here and leave Ms. DeMello to our lovely paper gowns." He draped his arm supportively around the other man's shoulders and escorted him from the room.

"I like Bennett," Quinn commented hours later as Owen negotiated the neighborhoods toward their new home. "He seems like a no-nonsense kind of guy. And her, Apata, I like her, too." After seeing the cardiologist, they'd gone directly to Dr. Marion Apata's office, where the high-risk obstetrician had interviewed them both and then examined Quinn. "Capable hands, but damn, by the time she was done, I was sure I'd been turned inside out."

Owen said nothing, and she went on. "I'm glad Dusty's office set up the appointments. If I'd done it, I wouldn't have gotten in for weeks. He said I needed to get under cover right away. Who knew it would be the day after I got here." A soft chuckle filled the car as Quinn mocked herself. "I think he was afraid I wouldn't get it done."

Owen's hands clenched the wheel. Bile rose in his throat. *Just get home*, he told himself. *Just keep it together a little longer.* He could hear her voice, but the words were gibberish in his ears.

His silence and her discomfort grew in tandem as they moved closer to the house.

"I'm so glad you were with me. It was good that you could talk to them. You'll have to tell me what Dr. Bennett had to tell you. He's not happy with me, I think."

Jabbering, Owen thought. *She's jabbering like she can't stop.*

He sensed her turn toward him. "Anyway, I'm glad you were there."

She offered her hand to his arm, but he couldn't capture it, bring her fingers to his lips. He was afraid to shift his gaze from the road, afraid that one look would undo him.

In silence, he steered the Highlander carefully through a school zone with its milling parents and turned up the hill.

After a moment, she moved her hand to rest in her lap, and kept talking. "If you want, we can call the twins as soon as we get to the house. Maybe we can go out there this weekend."

The muscle in the side of his jaw worked viciously.

"And I need to tell my sisters, too, and—"

He snapped. "Quinn, enough. Let's just get home."

She shrank against the passenger door, and ten minutes of unyielding silence claimed them before the garage door opened and the Highlander pulled in. Owen jerked the key from the ignition and fled, leaving Quinn to fend for herself. She caught up with him in the bathroom, where he leaned on the sink, his head resting against the mirror, his face flushed, and his breathing rapid.

"Owen?"

"Go away." He didn't look up, and his words staggered past the constriction in his throat. "Don't . . . want . . . to talk . . . to you . . . right now. Go."

He locked the door behind her, sank to the cold tile floor, and buried his face in his hands.

Sunset stained the clouds red and purple, but Owen didn't notice. His attention was riveted on the woman wrapped in the down comforter from their bed and huddled against the deck rail. Hard to remember that just this morning his only worry was how to get his two babies and this same woman home to Winnemucca.

Now his eyes were dry. His heart beat in regular time. His lungs once again allowed oxygen to influence his brain. *How could she*, he thought, ready for confrontation. *She lied.* But in the dusk, Quinn looked so like a little fat girl ready for snow play that the corners of his mouth turned upward, just for a moment, before the icy fear once again had its way with his gut.

She had lied by omission, it was true, in the hotel room when they had planned a life together. And last night, when she'd disclosed everything, all he'd heard was "twins." He'd missed the dying part. He drew a shuddering breath. Someone had to pay for his agony. Brows drawn together, he clenched his fists, set his jaw, and stoked his anger. Anything was better than the terror wedged inside by the cardiologist's words.

"I don't want to sound pessimistic," Bennett had said, "but the chances of all three surviving are slim."

The love in Owen's heart had mutated, become fear, and his knees had buckled. Only the physician's strong grip had kept him from hitting the floor. "Steady, man," the cardiologist had ordered. "She's taken a great risk for these babies, and she needs you to be strong."

Strong? How can I be strong when she's dying?

Now he pushed the thought aside and wrapped himself in hurt. He couldn't survive anything else. He opened the doors and stepped out onto the deck.

Quinn straightened as he approached and turned to face him, the comforter pulled around her like a shield. Her eyes were bright with tears, their tracks visible on her pale cheeks. Her hand escaped its cover and reached out. "Owen?"

"How could you do this?" Ice crunched around the words.

Her cheeks flushed and she dropped her hand, but her eyes remained steady on his and he couldn't look away.

"I'm sorry. I didn't tell you because I didn't want . . . I didn't want you to feel like this."

"Crap. That's just crap, Quinn, and you know it. You didn't tell me because you knew I'd try to stop you."

The comforter dropped away, and she thrust her belly out toward him.

Not fair—three against one. He held on to his anger with difficulty.

Her lower lip trembled. "Okay, that too. I knew you'd think I should have an abortion, and I didn't want—"

"Didn't want what, Quinn? Is it always about what you want? My God, do you think you have a monopoly on suffering? Do you ever think about anyone but yourself?"

Fresh tears spilled. Quinn averted her gaze, let his words cut into her as though she deserved the scourging.

Stricken, he reached for her.

She stepped back, arms akimbo, feet planted wide, eyes blazing. "Jesus, Owen, get a grip. I didn't want you to have to choose."

Like an anchor released to the sea, his anger dropped away, and he shook his head in disbelief. "Quinn, Quinn, Quinn." Words and the breath he'd been holding escaped together. Major annoyance remained. Chagrined, Owen could only laugh and shake his head in disbelief as he pulled her into his embrace. "And you worry about *me* controlling *you*."

CHAPTER 63

The hub of the Wildflower Inn B&B was its cavernous kitchen, redolent of tantalizing odors and the promise of melt-in-your-mouth deliciousness, and its heart was Vivian Johnson. A day without prepping, braising, boiling, or baking was rare as she experimented with the new and the different or whipped up comfort food for friends and family and, more recently, truly appreciative retreat guests. She just said, "Cooking makes me happy."

Not today. Today the Johnson twins prepared to welcome Quinn home. Owen had called on Tuesday, said, "Quinn's home. How about dinner Sunday?" and had since ignored them. Laced with frustration and worry, the days crawled by. Now it was Sunday.

At midday, Victoria stood on the wide front porch and waved as the last of their Valentine's Day Special guests drove away. Modeled after Quinn's extravaganza last V-Day, the special had featured gourmet meals and couples' massages courtesy of her massage-therapist friends Joe and Marci, followed by a long soak in the nearby hot springs. Effusive praises filled the pages of the inn's memory book.

In the kitchen, Vivian's signature dish, coq au vin, bubbled on the stove. Owen had dubbed it "coq au Viv," and Vicky always called her sister "happy as a clam" when she cooked it for him. Today, a vicious clanging against the side of the pot kept time with Vivian's humming—the Hitchcock theme, recognized by all who knew her as a big, yellow danger sign. If questioned, she'd just say "Hitchcock? No, it's Gounod's 'Funeral March of a Marionette.' Why do you ask?" Her family didn't ask; they just stayed out of her way.

A rare frown drew her black brows together, and a hard swish of the oversized wooden spoon sent sauce to sizzle on the hot burner. "Damnation fiddlesticks," she swore her mother's most ferocious oath just as Victoria stomped into the kitchen, the screen door slamming behind her.

"What's that sword," Victoria asked, ignoring her sister's ire, "the one hanging over people's heads?"

Vivian looked up from the mess she'd made. "Damocles, Vic. Why?"

"Well, it's hanging over our heads right now." Victoria lifted dishes from the shelf and deposited them none too gently on the trestle table.

Vivian shot a cautionary look. "We should be happy about Valentine's Day, not worried about some dumb sword." She didn't feel happy.

"This is nuts," Victoria grumbled as she arranged the heavy white plates, mismatched stemware, and their grandmother's gleaming silver cutlery that was saved for special occasions. She started to fold Valentine-themed napkins, but with a sudden "Happy fricking Valentine's Day," she tossed them willy-nilly onto the table and abandoned her task.

Vivian looked over her shoulder at the partially dressed table and said nothing as her sister grabbed a beer from the refrigerator, popped the top, and plopped herself into one of the high-backed chairs.

"This is nuts," Vic repeated and downed half the beer. She felt, to borrow her sister's phrase, "all aflutter," and she didn't like it one bit. She took another big swallow, emitted a loud burp, and ignored Vivian's admonishing, "Victoria!"

None of this made her feel one bit better.

"Is your boyfriend coming?" she asked. Maybe irritating her sister would help. Besides, Harold Anderson's tall, skinny presence might decrease the drama quotient.

The stingy afternoon light peeked through the window and matched her mood.

"Man friend," Vivian corrected with her first real smile of the day, but it faded quickly, to be replaced by a little pout. "No. He knows they're coming, said it was 'family business,' and he'd come by later to say hello." She poured a glass of wine, joined her sister at the table, and resisted the urge to correct the table setting.

"Coward." Vicky snorted and pulled at her beer.

Vivian sighed. "I guess."

Patience and Prudence rustled at their feet, as unsettled as their humans. Vivian got up and opened the back door, and the corgis scuttled out, their little legs churning. *Escape, you lucky girls.* She stirred the chicken and returned to her seat at the table. Right now, she wished she could be somewhere else, so maybe that made her a coward, too. Not that she didn't want to see her brother, and she loved Quinn almost as much as she loved her own twin, but there was something amiss. Even Victoria had felt it, and her sister was not attuned to nuance.

"Are you sure Wen didn't say anything else?"

"Nope, just that Quinn had gotten in and could they come for dinner today. He tried to sound like it was just another Sunday supper but..."

"But there's something going on? That's what you thought, Vicky, that there's something he's not saying?"

"Uh-huh. We know there's something. That stupid Karle told us Quinn was pregnant, and Owen doesn't know we know, so maybe it's just that. Maybe he's just worried about what we'll think. Maybe he's embarrassed because it's not his baby."

The sisters exchanged glances. Karle Moran had called to elicit their support, spewing her venom as she told them about the pregnancy, told them it was the other man's child. Mild-mannered Vivian had finally shouted, "Karle, shut up," and banged down the receiver, but the seeds of doubt had been planted.

"I didn't think Quinn would do that—try to fool him, I mean. I don't think she would. Not our Quinn."

"I agree, Vivvy, but what else could it be?"

When the door knob rattled, they jumped to their feet and stared at each other.

Stating the obvious, Vivian said, "They're here," and scurried back to the chipped enamel stove.

"Chicken," Victoria taunted her sister. "I'll go."

Owen and Quinn stood in the parlor, corgis cavorting at their feet. They were both laughing at something Quinn had just said, and Owen reached to help her with her coat when Victoria stepped into the room, mouth open in greeting. Quinn's coat swung open, and everything went still: corgis in midleap, yellow cat in unblinking repose, dust motes in the afternoon sunshine.

Victoria's greeting died unspoken, and her hand went to her mouth. *Uh-oh, she's too big.*

Removed from the still life, Vivian entered the room and bumped hard into her sister, tumbling them both into a heap at Quinn's feet.

Action resumed.

Laughing, Quinn surveyed the scene. "Wow, now I've got 'em falling at my feet."

Owen stepped around her and reached down to help his sisters disentangle. Laughing awkwardly, the four hugged, then Victoria, eyes anywhere but on Quinn's middle, mumbled, "Anybody want coffee?"

Silence lasted a beat too long.

Quinn tossed her coat on the stair rail and caught Owen's eye. "Owen, why don't you get everybody settled, and I'll get the coffee." She disappeared into the kitchen, leaving the siblings alone.

Vivian dropped onto the settee as though her legs would no longer support her. "She's pregnant," she stated, eyes on her big brother.

"Obviously," he replied, then recognition gleamed in his eyes. "You already knew."

Victoria, poking at the fire smoldering in the potbelly stove, nodded yes.

"But how . . .?" He paused. "Ahh . . . Karle?"

Over her shoulder, Victoria glared a silent order at her twin—*You're the sensitive one, you handle this*—and kept working the fire. Vivian's eyes were riveted on the scarred floor.

"What?" Owen's voice rose, anger edging over its restraints. Neither sister met his gaze.

The muscle in his jaw quivered. He shot a glance at the kitchen and lowered his voice. "What else did she say?"

Vivian stood and put her plump hand on her brother's arm, holding tight when he tried to pull away. "We didn't believe her,

Owen," she said, hoping he couldn't see the partial nature of that truth, "but she told us Quinn was pregnant with that other man's child and that she was using you to rescue her from her mistakes." She didn't add that Quinn's past had made it easier to accept Karle's story—that and worry that their brother would once again be hurt. "When you told us she was coming back to Reno, we thought there might be some truth—"

"To the story," Victoria supported her twin. "You can hardly blame us, Owen, what with you being so tight-lipped and all."

"So now it's my fault," he spat, then shut his mouth and ran his hand through his hair. Disheveled, he looked just like the boy his sisters sought to protect. "Ahh, girls, you should have asked."

In the kitchen, all the excitement of the past days dropped away as Quinn leaned against the door jamb paralyzed by her sense of loss. She, too, had felt time stand still and heard the muted conversation as she prepared the drinks. *I should have known this would end badly*, she thought, *and they don't know the half of it yet.* She straightened her shoulders, pasted a smile on her face, and stepped back into the parlor, the tray with its steaming mugs held out, a sacrificial offering. "Coffee, everyone?"

Conversation stopped midsentence, and the only sound was the crackle of burning pine in the little stove. *One of those you-could-hear-a-pin-drop moments*, Quinn thought. *My fault, but damn that Karle. I should have cut out her tongue when I had the chance.*

Now the sisters busied themselves with their coffee, and Owen stood facing the fire, his back to them all. She didn't blame the twins for doubting; after all, it was her own pattern of irresponsibility that had led to this mess. She just hadn't known how much it would hurt. More than anything, though, she didn't want them angry with Owen.

Shaken, she returned the empty tray to the kitchen. She'd had her share of hard truths recently. *Get a grip*, she ordered herself, *you can't hide in the kitchen all day.* She smoothed the new red sweater, long and bulky, over her rounded middle. Thus armored, she strode back into the parlor, perched on the edge of the ottoman, and waited.

Silence again, broken only by the crackling fire and the metallic clink of spoons against the china and the sighs of people who aren't sure what to say next.

Run, Quinn thought, relishing the picture of her red sweater flapping behind her as she sped down the lane, but she couldn't ignore her favorite AA slogan: Insanity is doing the same thing over and over and expecting a different outcome. She sucked in a deep breath. *I could run, or I could do something different.*

She stood. "Enough," she said. "Enough."

Three sets of identical brown eyes turned in her direction. *Well, that got their attention.* If everybody hadn't looked so miserable, she would have laughed.

"I could hear your conversation, of course. If you don't want eavesdropping, don't keep me around. And," she turned toward Vivian, who stared back, eyes now brimming, "you're partially right ... or, I should say, Karle was partially right."

She was proud of the lightness of her tone, the steadiness of her voice, and she hoped the hurt she felt at the other woman's meanness and her friends' lack of faith didn't show.

"As you can see, I am pregnant. I—"

Whatever she had been about to say was lost as Owen moved to her side, linked their fingers, and brought hers to his lips. "What Quinn's trying to tell you is, she's back, we're going to live in Reno for a while, and we're having a baby ... *babies*, as a matter of fact." Eyes hard, he glared at his sisters—Vivvy, the soft one, eyes gone round and smile spreading wide across her face, and Vicky, the doubter, whose quizzical look was slower to dissipate. "Questions?" The set of his jaw indicated questions would not be welcome.

With no time to sort out the feelings swarming through her, Quinn just wanted out. She tugged, trying to disengage her fingers. "Hey, why don't I go for a walk, and you can ...I mean, I haven't seen Girl George yet. You can explain—"

"What?" Owen shook away his anger but held tight to her hand. "In a minute, love, and I'll go with you." He looked back at his sisters, side by side and silent on the settee. "Nothing to explain. We'll go say hello to the horse, and you can let us know when it's time to eat."

He grabbed Quinn's coat and pushed her none too gently out the door.

COLD AIR SWIRLED INTO THE ROOM as they left, the door slamming hard behind them. Pine wood crackled in the little stove. The twins looked at each other.

Vivian spoke first. "Well, we really blew that one, didn't we?"

"Oh, Viv, he's really mad at us. We should never have listened to Karle."

"No, it's more than that. Our Quinn would just have laughed at that. Wennie's upset about something, and he took it out on us, and she's trying to smooth things over."

"God, Viv, I'll bet you're right. And if she's got twins, they're most likely Owen's. He seems to think so anyway. We should never have listened to a word that bitch said."

Victoria rose to look out the window. Across the lane, Quinn stood at the corral and fondled the little brown mare's nose. Owen, foot propped on the lower rail, his hand resting protectively on Quinn's back, leaned in to whisper. She pulled back, turned her gaze on him, and then lowered her head to his shoulder. Even at a distance, Victoria could sense something flow between them and, feeling like an uninvited guest, she turned away. "So what do we do now?"

Vivian stood and smoothed down the dress she wore for Sunday dinners. Owen was here. Quinn was here. There would be babies in the house again. Nothing else mattered. She smiled.

"Let's get dinner on the table."

CHAPTER 64

FEBRUARY GAVE WAY TO MARCH AS Owen and Quinn settled into uneasy domesticity. They slept wrapped in each other's arms, laughed themselves silly about babies' names—Pete and Repeat being the new favorites—and, over Owen's objections, she used trust fund dollars to furnish the nursery. "Two of everything," Quinn crowed. "Grandpa would be relieved that I'm finally putting his money to good use."

And hand in hand they endured the increasingly grim doctors' appointments. Dr. Apata suggested bed rest. Rich Bennett ordered it. Quinn refused, but the effort to walk across a room left her increasingly breathless and exhausted.

Sisters, his and hers, brought groceries and prepared food and scrubbed floors already clean.

"It's not that I'm not glad they're here," Quinn fretted to Cecily in Los Angeles. Of the sisters, only her youngest one knew the whole story. "I'm grateful, really I am, but I just wish they weren't here all the time."

After a moment of sympathetic silence, Cecily asked, "How's Owen handling things?"

Quinn snorted. "That lucky bugger orders me around and then escapes to work in the morning, and since I promised myself not to argue about everything, I just smile sweetly and waddle to my new recliner."

Cecily chuckled. "Must be hard to follow orders."

Quinn groaned. It seemed all the sisters, his and hers, knew and were amused by her new personal commandments—One: Thou shalt not argue until you've counted to ten; Two: Thou shalt not yell until you've counted to ten; Three: Thou shalt not assume that everyone wants to run your life. Owen was the worst, holding up fingers, usually three, to indicate the commandment she was about to break.

"Sorry, whining," she said. "Who knew how hard counting to ten would be? And I don't mean to dump it all on you. I know I need their help."

Hard to admit. A sip of herbal tea helped lighten her voice. "The chair *is* pretty cool, Cec. I just push a button and it stands me right up."

Cecily made a choking sound but didn't comment.

"I'm ordered not to leave the house. Huh, not likely. I can't even fit into Angelica the Auto." She smiled at the thought of her VW bug waiting patiently next to the Highlander in the garage. "I stagger to the mailbox, and Owen practically carries me back. And he hovers, Cec, like he's afraid." She paused a minute. "Of course, he's afraid. Me too. But thank the blessed stars *he* still has to go to work." A laugh caught in her throat, and she waited for breath before she continued. "So I sit here in my magic chair like a lump. I failed knitting. I failed crocheting. My hands are swollen, my feet are fat, and my legs look like sticks. I'm a mess. All I can do is gestate." This time, a full-throated laugh escaped without penalty.

Cecily's laughter was less robust.

Whoops, mood adjustment—not fair to mess up Cecily's day. "Sorry, sorry, sorry. It's really not a laughing matter that I can't see my feet, and I can't always make it to the bathroom, and I have to meditate standing up so I don't fall asleep."

This won a Cecily giggle.

"Besides, you're the only one I can bitch to."

"It's okay, sis," Cecily offered in a less-than-steady voice. "We all know a busy Quinn is a better Quinn. Just remember, you'll be busy enough pretty soon."

Wishful thinking was better medicine than melancholy. They laughed together and said their goodbyes.

In truth, Quinn's few hours of alone time overflowed. From her magic chair, with its view of new leaves unfurling and whiffs of spring wafting through open French doors, she meditated daily— the loving kindness meditations that had helped her forgive her mother, release the guilt of her daughter's death, and allow trust. Now they bolstered her for the future. May we be peaceful, happy, and light; may we be safe and free from injury; may we be free from anger, afflictions, fear, and anxiety. As she chanted for herself and Owen and the babies, she gathered her strength. Mostly, though, she thought about the babies, envisioning their development as though her intensity could get them ready faster.

Knowing that each day decreased her chances for survival, both physicians had demanded an early C-section. Quinn knew each day improved the odds for her rambunctious children, so she not-too-politely demurred. Marion Apata had grown used to her stubborn insistence on what was best for the babies and barely rolled her eyes any more. Rich Bennett was more likely to throw something and stalk from the room, but—so far, at least—he had returned.

In her journal, Quinn recorded daily thoughts, wishes, dreams—stories for the children who might never know her—the pages decorated with smiley faces and exclamation points and Rorschach blots of dried tears.

Chris McLean occupied his own niche in her meditation, in her thoughts, in her heart. She ached for him on days when fear and despair swept her, and could almost hear his bellow—"De-Mello, front and center!"—when she longed for just one tiny sip of tequila. Several times, she had dialed his number, wanting to erase the misery she'd brought him.

Who am I kidding? she thought as she felt the familiar punch in the gut, the whoosh as her breath sucked in and heat enveloped her. She wanted to hear his voice as it lapsed into the lilt that could coax her over the edge to just one last soul-shattering fall. *Selfish bitch, you just want to use him again.*

She sighed. *A hard lesson to learn—gotta live with the guilt.* Earlier this very morning she'd aborted a call, lamenting, *Fuck it, too bad I can't have my own man harem,* before a baby's kick dispelled the grin-inducing notion.

CHAPTER 65

On the last Saturday in April, the rain retreated, the clouds lifted, and blue sky hung as a backdrop for the wedding. High noon. Mismatched chairs stood on the spring green grass of the Wildflower Inn's west lawn, and purple lilacs, as though celebrating their survival, perfumed the midday air.

Owen and Quinn sat in the first row of the makeshift chapel. Quinn pursed her lips to keep her breathing slow and steady and hoped she wouldn't need the hated oxygen tank she'd left in the car. Eying the guests, she pretended to ignore the worried glances Owen darted her way. *Soon, soon, please God, just not today.*

She knew this morning's journal entry would be her last:

Hi kids,
Today's your last chance to get those toenails and fingernails in place. 10 and 10 for each of you—work hard. Tomorrow Mommy and Daddy will be kissing and counting each one, so you'd better be ready.

Love you forever,
Your mommy

She ran her hands over her silky new dress and the babies it covered. *Your turn tomorrow.*

Today was Vivian's day.

The opening bars of Wagner's "Wedding March" filled the air. Quinn's tears brimmed over, and her sister Camille tucked a well-ironed handkerchief into her hand. All the DeMello women were present. Somehow, since their mother's death, they had come together in a kind of solidarity that apparently included Owen's family as well. *Weird, but good,* Quinn thought as she dabbed her eyes and watched Vivian and Harold, flanked by Victoria, Scott, and two of Harold's cousins, walk across the lawn toward Father Chuck. She chuckled as Owen pulled out his handkerchief and wiped his own eyes. Then his hand found hers and their fingers linked. When he brought her fingertips to his lips, she thought her heart would burst.

After the rocky start in February, the siblings had quickly dispatched their differences. Quinn hadn't been sure how Owen would take it when Vivian announced her upcoming marriage, but nothing seemed to faze him these days; he just grinned and shook his head. "Hope you know what you're letting yourself in for," he'd quipped, and then, in a very un-Owen-like gesture, wrapped Harold in a man hug.

"He's just happy," Vivian had said, "that he doesn't have to take care of me anymore."

They had all laughed, but Quinn had known it wasn't a joke. Her man could no more give up his fixing ways than he could stop breathing. Their life together had smoothed out considerably when she'd accepted that simple truth.

Now the big willow cast flickering shade over the congregation as Harold and Vivian, bathed in sunlight, faced each other. The bride's vintage dress, a softly flowing deep-pink creation, dripped with handmade lace. Well-worn and well-pressed, the groom's dark suit hung from his broad shoulders.

The audience hushed as Father Chuck spoke about love and the sacrament of marriage. When it was time, Harold leaned down to hear his bride's voice. Years of railroad noise and moonlighting as a disc jockey had left his hearing impaired, but it was really the distance from his six-foot-two height to his bride's minute five feet that he bridged as he bent toward her.

As one, the guests chuckled.

"I, Vivian Johnson, take thee, Harold Anderson, as my lawful wedded husband."

Quinn smiled and let her puffy hand rest in Owen's lap. She no longer had a lap of her own.

Vivian continued, "I promise to honor you, and cherish you, and not put my beloved twin before you, at least not more than once or twice a week."

A loud guffaw erupted from the guests, and color rose up the back of Victoria's neck. The family and friends assembled on the lawn of the Wildflower Inn Bed and Breakfast knew how skillfully Harold walked the line. "And I promise to love you," she finished, "until the day I die." She slid the wide gold band onto Harold's finger.

Quinn squeezed Owen's hand, and his wet brown eyes met her own wet blue ones. "I love you," she mouthed. The babies churned inside her, and she both longed for and dreaded tomorrow when they would be free.

Harold spoke his vows in a voice easily heard, and laughter erupted again as he promised to honor, cherish and "never hold it against you, my darling, when the two of you double-team me." He slid a matching gold band on Vivian's finger, brought it to his lips, and then, without waiting for permission, heartily kissed his bride.

The music resumed. Clapping and laughing rang out as friends and relatives stood to congratulate the new couple. Quinn rose slowly—standing up was now an Olympic feat— and air refused to enter her lungs. Dizziness swept her and her vision tunneled. She grasped the chair for support, hoping Owen wouldn't notice, but his senses had become fine-tuned, and he slid a hand under her elbow.

"Love, can I help?"

"Nope, don't need it," she whispered, desperately hoping it was true. She was determined there would be no Quinn drama on Vivian's special day. With an effort, she shot him a grin. "All good. Go."

His eyebrow quirked.

Apparently the grin hadn't been convincing enough. Ignoring his frown and the protest that shaped his lips, she nodded toward the others. "Go. I'll just meander toward the shade and get my congratulations in later."

"If you're sure?" Owen dropped a kiss lightly on her mouth, but his brow didn't clear.

She nodded.

He stepped back and raked her with a glance that probably saw more than she wanted him to, but after a moment he kissed her harder and walked away.

Both hands pressed to the small of her back, Quinn watched him join the crowd just as she'd watched almost a year ago on the night he'd whirled her around the makeshift dance floor and then claimed her for his own. Now her heart thundered with the love she felt for this man and the babies he had given her.

So many changes since that snowstorm dumped me here with these women who saw something in me that I couldn't see. She thought about the retreats that had saved the B&B, about the man she had avoided until she couldn't anymore, about the mother who had died here with condemnation on her lips, and about her own flight into the mountains with Owen's gun, only to discover that death was not for her ... not then.

"They do look happy, don't they?"

Lost in memory, Quinn jumped as Cecily took her hand. "Sorry, didn't mean to scare you."

With a sigh, Quinn nodded agreement, then leaned into her little sister's support, and together they made their careful way across the uneven lawn and settled into white folding chairs near the house.

"Are you okay? You look a little ... peaked."

"I hate it when you say that. We all look peaked next to you." The youngest DeMello had come into her beauty and her first starring role in a popular made-for-television movie, and she glowed with health and happiness. "Next to you, I feel like the biggest slug in the world. Come to think of it, next to *anybody* I feel like a slug."

They both laughed. Cecily was one of the few people who didn't treat her as though she would break. Now the younger woman laid her hand over her sister's bulk. "Amazing. Are they swimming today, or dancing?" Her face lit with pleasure as the babies demonstrated their mobility.

Quinn placed her hand over her sister's. "They're quieter now. I think it's getting too crowded." She caught her breath, wondered if she should ask her sister to retrieve the oxygen canister.

At Quinn's words, Cecily's eyes held a question.

"Tomorrow. It's time, Cec, I can't hold out any longer, but it feels right. Apata says they're little but ready, and the surfactant test says their lungs can breathe real air."

Cecily DeMello turned her gaze toward the crowd, then brought her eyes back to her sister's face. "Owen?"

"He says he's ready, too. I didn't want to distract anyone from Vivian's day, but, sister mine, I'm a little tired." Quinn tried to laugh, frowned, and grimaced instead as the effort stole her breath. Cecily already knew her wishes (the if-then directions that Owen refused to hear); the babies would be in good hands, Winnemucca a good home. She patted her belly. "Anyway, if I stretch much further, I'll need a wheelbarrow to carry this around."

Metal clinked against glass, calling the unruly crowd to order, and Owen Johnson's voice rose in a toast to his sister and her new husband. "Love makes the world go 'round." His eyes searched the crowd until he found Quinn. "Love."

Only one more thing to take care of, Quinn knew, as her heart opened to her man's words.

CHAPTER 66

SHAFTS OF AFTERNOON SUN CAST AN intermittent glare across the windshield as Quinn and Owen left the wedding festivities, soon after the toasts had been drunk and the cake cut. Quinn had offered to stay home, miss the wedding, or find another ride so he could stay and celebrate, but Owen had refused all ideas, finally covering her mouth with his own to shut her up. "Let it be, Quinn, you're stuck with me."

Now, as he drove along Interstate 80 toward Reno, Owen hummed the wedding march, kept time with his finger on the steering wheel, and counted the road markers as they slid by.

Blocking thoughts of tomorrow, Quinn recognized in full sympathy. *Good time for my last surprise.*

"Am I too late to take you up on your offer?" She directed her question to his right ear, the despised oxygen canister at least allowing full sentences.

"What? Manny and Moe's? You're hungry?" They were approaching the country restaurant renowned for its gargantuan meals.

"No, the other offer." She watched his face.

Confusion and irritation raced across his spare features, highlighting the permanent lines that fear had carved around his mouth, across his forehead. His eyes left the road to look at her.

"What other offer?"

Teasing now, Quinn began, "Do you still want to . . ." intending to say "make an honest woman of me," but even the oxygen flowing wasn't enough, and the words stole her breath. She gasped for air.

In Owen's strangled "Quinn," she heard fear and indecision—speed up or dial nine-one-one? She sensed his heart thudding as his foot stomped on the gas pedal. More frustrated than scared, she pursed her lips and panted. Just when she thought it would never happen, air whooshed into her lungs and she could speak. "Oh, fuck, Owen Johnson . . ." Short little wheezes punctuated her words. "Will . . . you . . . marry . . . me?"

QUINN'S WORDS PENETRATED OWEN'S FEAR SLOWLY, as though they flowed over long-distance wires. Marry? He'd thought she wanted food, then panicked as her voice disappeared into a death rattle. When she finally wheezed out her Quinn-style marriage proposal, he wasn't sure whether to laugh or cry or strangle her.

Hands not quite steady, he guided the SUV to the shoulder, put the vehicle in park, and set the emergency brake before he faced her. Uncertainty flickered in her eyes. Her golden hair hung like parentheses around her pregnancy-rounded face, and she looked like a quizzical little girl. *My girl*, he thought. *I could kill her right now.*

"What . . . did . . . you . . . say?" His voice could cut glass.

He'd proposed daily. She had steadfastly said no. Two weeks ago, bruised by yet another refusal, he'd yelled, "That's all, Quinn! I won't ask again. You're afraid, I get it, but if you can't see that I'm proposing a partnership, not shackles, I can't do anything about it," and he'd stalked from the room. She'd come after him, but neither had uttered the M-word again.

"I said, will . . . you . . . marry . . . me?"

His heart did flip-flops. His mind roared, *Yes! Yes! Yes!* But he kept his hands on the steering wheel and his voice steady. She'd earned a few beats of discomfort.

"No, the first part, the 'oh, fuck' part. I want to be clear before I give my answer. Is 'oh, fuck' a protest or a promise?"

The lines on her face smoothed out. Her eyes twinkled as she giggled and flipped him the bird.

He wasn't done yet. "I take that to mean promise," he said, attempting to keep a straight face. "Does this mean you want to make an honest man of me?"

"Damn it, Owen Johnson, I know I deserve this, but," she wheezed one word at a time, "but just answer the damn question. Are you going to marry me or not?"

"Phrased so eloquently, how could any man refuse."

He eased toward her, ran his fingers gently down the side of her flushed cheek, and enjoyed the irritation that flashed in her eyes. Too much love and devotion from his woman made him nervous.

"I will marry you, Quinn DeMello, now and forever. And as soon as I can, I'll be honored to fuck your brains out."

CHAPTER 67

O n Sunday's early morning darkness, in the king-sized bed that took up half the bedroom—*our playpen*, Quinn had called it—Owen Johnson lay awake, listening to the labored breathing of the woman sleeping almost upright at his side. His lips played against the ring on his finger—a wide, smooth braid of her hair. "So I'll be with you," she'd said as she'd slid it on, and, if he didn't know better, he'd have called her shy. "I couldn't get out to buy anything, you know, but I will, soon." He imagined the makeshift ring still carried the kiss that had sealed it in place.

The babies would come today, he knew, as he listened to her struggle. It was nothing short of a miracle that the pregnancy had continued this long. Marion Apata had been adamant, at least as adamant as one could be with Quinn, when she'd demanded her presence in the hospital. "Quinn, I can no longer be responsible for these babies if you don't cooperate." She'd cast a desperate glance in his direction. "Owen, for God's sake, make her see reason," she'd demanded before stalking from the room.

"Sunday," Quinn had promised. "Sunday after Viv's wedding. Then I'll go." *She didn't want to spoil Vivian's day*, he'd thought, and, he realized now as the ring prickled his lips, *she wanted to make mine.*

Yesterday, his heart in overdrive, he'd gotten them back on the road to Reno. Once there, he'd pulled to the curb in front of the Chapel of Love. Quinn had been resting, eyes closed, but she'd roused then and clutched his arm. "Not inside, Owen, please not inside." He'd understood—her first marriage with its predestined sorrow had begun in a wedding chapel.

"We need help with this, love. I'll go in and make the arrangements." And that's what he did.

The owner, Gail Crump, a plump woman whose gray hair, wrinkled cheeks, and wide smile attested to many years of weddings, listened carefully and, as though she dealt with strange requests every working day, made the arrangements. She carried the papers to the car, didn't miss a beat as Owen introduced Quinn, and, with just a hint of sympathy in her eyes, handed her the license application. Quinn signed, mumbling something that sounded suspiciously like, "You were right, we should have done this sooner," but he acted as if he hadn't heard as he added his name to the paper. Gail patted Quinn's hand, said, "We all need someone, dear. Life isn't meant to be lived alone," and disappeared up the street to do her job.

As Quinn dozed in the car and he waited for Ms. Crump in the chapel, Owen called Pat, his friend and business partner, who suggested Dorokstar Park and Judge Arrigoni, a personal friend. Owen agreed, and it was done.

Thank you, Pat. Thank you, God.

LIGHTS WERE JUST APPEARING IN WINDOWS as Owen, license safely pocketed, turned the Highlander away from downtown.

Eyes closed, Quinn rasped, "Where's that woman, Owen? Aren't we getting married?"

"Just a minute, love, you'll see."

More of a romantic than he would have admitted, he'd wanted their wedding to be perfect—fancy dress, friends and family, music and party followed by mind-blowing sex. Now he was just thankful that the little park on the Truckee River would be quiet this time of day and its rustic bridge near enough to the parking area. He grimaced. He'd suggested a wheelchair in the past, had almost gotten his head bitten off, and wasn't about to revisit that issue.

A black Lincoln sat alone in the parking lot as Owen turned off Mayberry Drive and parked. Fatigue and emotion threatened, and he closed his eyes and rubbed the bridge of his nose. In a flash, memory claimed him—standing at the altar of St. Thomas Aquinas Cathedral, Mimi small and slim and radiant in her billows of white lace, himself so young and stiff and self-conscious in formal black. Both full of love, of themselves, of the future. *Ahh, Mimi,* he thought now, *we failed each other.*

He wiped his eyes and looked around. Sunset cast the sky in pinks and reds, and a breeze ruffled the willows that stood along the river bank. In the black robes of her office, the judge waited on the bridge. House lights seemed far away, traffic noise muted as though wrapped in cotton batting. In the silence, Owen gathered himself. *Be happy, Meems,* he whispered on a sigh and let his first love go, then turned to the woman who would now be his wife. Eyes closed, lids puffy and bruised, breathing ragged, her body swollen with a pregnancy that should never have been, she held his heart.

Now. Now and forever.

He brushed gentle fingers down Quinn's cheek.

She roused. "Are we there yet?"

"We're here, love. Last chance to back out."

"No way." Her sleepy gaze turned on him and he was forever lost. She squeezed his hand. "I've got a real yen to fuck a married man."

Awake beside Owen in the predawn darkness, Quinn smoothed her breathing, whispered her *Om*, and remembered.

Dorokstar Park had decorated itself for the occasion with the reds and pinks of sunset, the willows for music, and the lovely judge whose words wrapped them in magic and hope. Pat and Lia, Owen's partner and his wife—lovely people who acted as though this kind of thing happened every day—were their witnesses, and they all stood on the little bridge with the river flowing beneath them. Owen's arm supported her as they whispered their vows. The judge pronounced them man and wife, and when she nodded, he kissed her there—this man, this man who could have anyone and who had chosen her own impossible self—kissed her as though his life depended upon it.

Afterward, when they were finally alone, his arms strong around her, he helped her to the car, and they drove home in silence. In the big bed, flooded with feelings too deep for words, they undressed each other. His hands on her body made her beautiful, and she trembled now in the memory of his touch, his mouth, his body throbbing with desire and love. She loved him then, in the only ways they could, and when she shuddered and released herself to him, Quinn knew to the depths of her being that she had done the right thing.

Now she heard his breathing change and knew her husband was crying. She poked him not too gently in the ribs—healing touches came in many varieties. "Rise and shine, husband, you've been the boss too long. Let's go have these babies."

CHAPTER 68

Most of Reno's populace still slept as Owen pulled the SUV to the emergency entrance of Saint Mary's hospital. An attendant with a wheelchair arrived at the passenger door before the motor died. Everything was ready—tests done, forms signed—and the entire staff knew never to keep Dr. Apata waiting. Owen shouldered the orderly aside to assist Quinn from the vehicle to the chair.

"Go on and park, love." Quinn held up her face for his kiss. "I'm not going anywhere."

Reluctantly, he stood aside as she was whisked away, her panted words, "I'd have driven myself, but I couldn't fit behind the wheel," and the attendant's laughter floating on the air behind her. Doubled over as though sucker-punched, Owen collapsed against the car. *I can't bear this.* His thoughts seemed so loud he was sure the world could hear. *Help me.* When he could no longer see her, he straightened his shoulders, got back into the vehicle, and drove off to park.

INSIDE, QUINN TURNED HERSELF OVER TO helping hands. *No more pretending. I'm tired and I'm scared. I've done all I can. Let's get these babies born and see what happens next.*

Some time later, clad in a skimpy gown and tucked into a prewarmed blanket, she waited for her husband. *Husband*, she thought. *My husband*. Memory pushed doubt and worry and, yes, guilt to a dark corner: Owen on a gurney with a bandage over his eye as she proclaimed herself a runaway; Owen, gun in hand, staring at the rattlesnake he'd just killed—*my hero*, she'd thought then; Owen yelling in the barn, driving her away; Owen at her side, promising to be with her forever; and herself, always drowning in his dark eyes, rousing to his touch.

As she had this morning when he'd moved to her side and fumbled under the blanket for her hand. "Hello, husband," she'd whispered and smiled as he'd responded, "Hello, wife," and brought her fingers to his lips.

Now a plastic tube snaked around her nose and disappeared into the faded blue flowers of her hospital gown. A white blanket rose and fell over the rise of her abdomen, didn't hide the occasional ripple that proclaimed the unseen beings anxious to be born. They were quieter now, as though they had used up everything she had to give them and now just bided their time.

Pale hospital walls reflected the fluorescent light and hurt her eyes. With Cecily on one side and Owen on the other, Quinn laced her fingers through her husband's and squinted at the family who gathered around her gurney.

After their wedding celebration, Owen had tucked her into bed and called all the sisters. "We just got married, and we're having the babies tomorrow," he'd told them. She had heard his laughter and watched his shoulders heave as he cried.

Glad I didn't have to make those calls, she thought, woozy from the sedative and guilty that Owen's suffering was her doing.

Now they were all here, her sisters and his, and her face was damp from their kisses and tears. Vicky stood at Owen's side ready to support him should he falter, but he was steadfast. Dry-eyed, he inflicted none of his fears on her.

Brave man. Glad he's mine.

As though reading her mind, Owen tightened his grip, and his lips turned up just a fraction while he outlined the day's events.

"Two surgeries, Wennie?" whispered Vivian, her hands clutching Harold's.

"The cesarean section for the babies, Viv, and the other to repair Quinn's heart."

His voice broke on "heart," and Quinn squeezed his hand. She wasn't afraid, though it was ironic that now, when she no longer wished for death, it should be so ready for her. *Just gotta get these babies out, then somebody else can take over.*

Cecily squeezed her other hand gently. "You can do this," she whispered as though she, too, could read minds, but when Cecily laid her cheek against the cap that covered her sister's hair, Quinn could feel her sobs.

A nurse appeared, surgical mask hanging like a necklace. "Time."

Quinn turned big eyes toward her husband.

"I'm with you, baby." He kissed her long and hard before he pulled his own mask over his mouth and, still hand in hand, they entered the surgical suite.

"READY, QUINN?" DR. MARION APATA STOOD near the table where Quinn's eyes could find her. Anesthesiologist Pam Brown's competent fingers slipped the needle in place and began the saddle block. "I need you awake and breathing, girl, or I'll have to work too damn hard for a Sunday." She gave Owen an encouraging nod, but Quinn knew her eyes told a different story.

"And Rich has a dinner party tonight, you know." The obstetrician kept up a flow of chatter as she busied herself at the end of the table, now out of Quinn's sight. "We really should have held this event last week." Quinn heard irritation in the playful words and knew her doctor hadn't quite forgiven her.

When the anesthesiologist nodded, Apata spoke quietly to her team. "Ready now. We need to be in and out quickly." Heads nodded. The scalpel slapped against her waiting palm.

Owen paled and closed his eyes.

Surrounded by figures anonymous in their masks and caps, Quinn floated in her sedative haze and felt pressure but no pain as the doctor worked. *Surreal.* She tugged at Owen's hand. When he leaned down so he could hear, she giggled and whispered, "I feel like the Thanksgiving turkey."

He uttered a strangled sound that did not sound like a laugh.

"All right, if you're not going to laugh at my jokes, then tell me what they're doing." She forced a smile and ordered, "Husband, report."

With a ghost of his usual smile, Owen struggled to obey.

Dr. Apata kept up a light patter that seemed unintelligible, but the team moved to its rhythm. "Here," she cooed finally. Quinn tightened her hand on Owen's as a thin wail issued into the sudden stillness. "You've got a girl," she told them. "Let's see who else is in here."

"Go." Releasing Owen's hand, Quinn shoved him toward the sound and watched an idiotic grin spread across his face as he reached out for his daughter. She smiled. Her heart fluttered. Almost done.

"Another one," sang out Marion Apata as a louder cry emerged. "This sweetie's a little bigger."

"And louder," added a laughing voice. "Girl power."

The tension in the room eased, and chatter rose. People who worked OB loved babies, and these babies were alive.

I did it, Quinn thought as relief filled her. *I did it.*

"Show me."

Owen turned to her, love on his face and two babies in his arms. Marty Sequeira, the neonatal nurse specialist, lifted the smaller baby and nestled her into the crook of Quinn's arm.

"Here you go, Mom, but just for a minute and then we'll—"

Whatever she had been going to say was lost as Marion Apata's shriek stilled the room. "Goddamn it, what? No, wait."

Everyone froze.

Then Apata laughed, and they could breathe again. "Well, Quinn, you are full of surprises today."

Thrusting his armload at the hovering nurse, Owen grabbed Quinn's hand. "What? What's wrong?"

"I guess nothing's wrong, Owen. I just found another baby."

A mewly cry emerged, then grew as though the third baby just needed room to breathe. "A litter, for Christ's sake," the doctor griped as she worked, but the smile on her face was huge when she held up the squirming bundle, still attached to its mother by the thick and twisted cord. "Mr. and Mrs. Johnson, meet your son."

CHAPTER 69

Q UINN AND OWEN WAITED. A MAN in scrubs hovered, monitoring her tubes and wires. Quinn dozed, her lips curved upward even in sleep. Owen stood by the bed, his eyes flicking from her face to the monitors and back. The beeps were steady, the tracing on the screen regular. She still breathed and her heart still beat. Nothing else mattered.

Every so often, she would rouse. "Where are they?" she'd ask.

"NICU," he'd answer, knowing all three were safely ensconced in the neonatal intensive care unit, a usual first stop for preemies, and she would smile and drift away, only to wake moments later with the same question. Now, eyes still closed, she tugged at his hand. He leaned down and her labored breaths caressed him.

"Did I promise," she whispered, pausing for air between each word, "promise to ..." The pause was longer, and he thought she had fallen asleep again.

"Shh," he whispered in her ear. "It's okay. You can tell me later."

"Now." Even breathless, she sounded impatient. "Did I promise to forsake all others?"

He snorted. "You can have all the others you want, if you promise not to leave me."

She was so pale, her lips a blue he'd never seen, and her eyes were closed, but the grin she shot him said it all. Then her lids fluttered and she was still. Ice formed around his heart. *Don't die, Quinn. I need you. Please don't die.* He'd never have let this happen, had been so angry that she'd kept the truth from him until he could do nothing but watch her pregnancy continue, knowing her heart would fail.

Her hand, slack within his grasp, stirred again. Through the sedative mist, triumph lit her marvelous eyes, but he could barely make out her words. Once again, he moved his ear closer, felt her whisper against his cheek. "Aren't you glad now?"

Only an hour before, he'd have denied it, but the babies had changed him already, and, coward that he was, he was glad he hadn't had to choose. Her eyes closed, but the lids fluttered, and he knew she was still with him.

"Don't think you can escape so easily." Her lips curved around his whisper. "You can't just drop three of them and think you're getting away without diaper duty. Besides, they look just like you."

Tears fell, and he didn't try to stop them.

"Trouble with a capital T." He was jabbering and he knew it, but he couldn't stop. Somewhere behind him, another sob was stifled.

DR. CHRIS MCLEAN ENTERED THE ROOM unnoticed, his eyes fixed on Quinn's ashen face. His heart bumped and beat faster. He'd thought he'd never see her again.

Had it only been three months? It seemed an eternity since that February morning when she'd come to him in the kitchen where he'd stood, unseeing eyes on the city below, ears attuned to the sounds of her departure.

The heels of her red boots clicked on the hardwood floor as she approached. He didn't turn. She stood behind him, almost as tall as he, her pregnant belly pushing gently on his back and her breath a tickle on his neck, and he thought his heart would shatter.

"Ah, McLean," she said. "I'm sorry."

He ignored her words and repeated his earlier offer. "I can take you to the airport."

"No, I already called, and the cab should be here any minute."

He was sure she thought going to the airport would only prolong his agony. She was wrong. Only changing her mind could save him now.

She wrapped her arms around him, fingers just meeting in the front, and lay her head against his back. He folded his own hands over hers as they tightened on his chest. *Holding my heart,* he'd thought. "You're sure?"

He felt her nod, heard the tremor in her voice. "Sure as can be."

They stood in silence until the knock on the door.

She kissed his cheek and stepped away. He beat her to the door, opened it, and dismissed the cabby with a twenty for his trouble. "I'll take you," he said. "It's all I can do."

And he had taken her there, tortured himself further as he'd watched her stride away, then sat in the Jeep and cried.

Tears welled in his eyes now as he looked at her. Almost upright on the gurney, tubing snaking from her nose and her arm, a monitor blinking above her head, Quinn lay still. Only the tiny rise and fall of her chest let him know she still lived. *Dear God, let me be good enough.*

Owen Johnson and Rich Bennett had orchestrated his presence, Bennett happy for his experience and Johnson, it seemed, for moral support. He wasn't sure whether to praise or curse them, but it was Quinn's request that he honored.

Hers was the last voice he'd expected when his phone had rung a week ago. In her spaced-out words, he'd heard her struggle for air. "Hey, McLean," she'd said, "as usual, you'll think I'm nuts, but will you please come and help me?"

His heart had thundered in his throat. Before he'd been able to get a word out, she'd continued, "I know you invented this thing they want to do to me—the surgical procedure, I mean—and I think I just might make it if you're here."

There was only one answer. Now he was here.

He had missed Quinn with a pain he hadn't thought possible, but it had slowly subsided to a dull ache, and life had resumed its original shape.

Shite, what a load of bull, he thought now. She was a living presence in his heart, and there she would stay. Now it would be his job to fix *her* heart and help her remain on this earth.

As McLean watched, Owen, his own tears flowing unattended, tucked a strand of Quinn's golden hair under the paper cap, then leaned closer to brush a kiss over Quinn's slack blue lips.

Jealousy flared. For a moment, McLean yearned and wished himself in the other man's shoes; then, impatient, he dashed his tears away. *Get a grip, man, you've a job to do.* Resolute, he strode toward the gurney.

"DeMello. Goddamn it, DeMello, front and center."

Quinn's eyes flickered open. "McLean?"

"Goddamn right, it's me." He moved into her line of sight, a mountain in green scrubs, and reached out to shake Owen's hand as he dropped a kiss on Quinn's forehead. "Christ, woman, you're a sight. Let's get this show on the road. They tell me you've got babies to tend."

Her eyes gleamed and a wobbly grin appeared. His heart shattered.

He stepped back as the tech moved to the head of the bed and began guiding it toward the double doors. "Kiss your wife now, boy-o, and move out of the way. I'll be sending her back as soon as I'm done with her." The leer in McLean's voice had Owen smiling as the doors whooshed closed behind them.

Elbows on his knees, face in his hands, replete of tears, Owen waited alone. Adrenaline and coffee kept him upright— that and his prayers to a long-abandoned God. *Whatever works,* he thought as he promised everything he had for her deliverance. The DeMello sisters had gone in search of food. His were keeping watch on the babies in the NICU. Quinn moments flowed like old movies in his mind—eye to eye with the rattler, hands on her hips as she challenged him, body to body as she succumbed to him. *How can I live without her?*

Double doors swung open. Surgical cap askew, mask dangling from one hand, Dr. Chris McLean filled the room.

Cold as death, Owen struggled to his feet. "Quinn?"

"Touch and go, Owen, touch and go, but she's still with us."

McLean stepped forward to catch Owen as he sagged. "Stand tough, man. I whispered sweet nothings in her ear, but, God knows why, she says she's not done with you yet. What could I do but keep her here? Long days ahead, but our Quinn's a fighter."

Owen straightened. Relief bloomed. Maybe, just maybe … He grasped the other man's hand. "Thank you."

McLean laughed. "A blessing and a curse. She's not easily led." He shook his head. "Anyway, she said to tell you you're not rid of her yet." He draped his arm across Owen's shoulders and turned him away from the doors. "Come on, man, introduce me to those babes. I'm still not convinced they're not mine."

Epilogue

—Quinn DeMello Johnson—

MY HEART STILL BEATS.

In the soft glow of the NICU lights, Owen links his fingers with mine. I am surrounded by my family—baby Makena with Vivian and Victoria, her identical twin Megan with Claudia and Cecily, and tiny Will like a doll against McLean's broad chest. Christening complete, the new godparents will soon relinquish their precious burdens to the hovering nurses. My journey has been perilous—each step hard-won, bittersweet, seldom wise—and I will do anything, even consecrate my babies to a God I doubt, to keep us together on this earth.

Music has been flitting through my head, just now a Jimmy Buffett tune about not looking over my shoulder. I'm humming it—breathing is *not* overrated—as Owen brushes his lips against my hair. I look up and our eyes meet, and I see my future. He blinks and the moment is gone, but I know. As Jimmy says, "I know I can't go wrong."

Like an expert, my husband releases the lock on the wheelchair and, in defiance of hospital protocol, pushes me back toward ICU and rehab and, someday soon, home.

My life shines bright.

Acknowledgements

Writing a work of fiction is a solitary event. Getting a book ready for publication is not. Heartfelt thank yous to all my first readers and to my two High Sierra Writers critique groups, especially to Jackie, who worked her way through the manuscript twice. I owe debts of gratitude to my sister Linda, who read all the changes and said all the right things to keep me on task; to my friend Linda Fine Conaboy, who thinks I can be famous; and to my editor, Jessica Santina, who poked and prodded and annoyed me until I was compelled to make changes and, voilà, Quinn's story became deeper and richer and better. Thank you, Jessica.

Every day of my life, I am grateful to my parents, Mabel and Stan Doty, who encouraged me to read.

ABOUT THE AUTHOR

Patti Doty is a Nevada native. Although she won prizes for writing while she was a student, she chose a career in medicine as a physician assistant and marriage and family therapist. But she never abandoned her first love, and in 2013, she published her first Quinn DeMello novel, *Runaway*.

Retired now, Patti travels widely—most recently spending time in Washington, DC; Halifax, Nova Scotia; and Maui, Hawaii—always looking for new locations for her characters and their stories of love and change. When she's not circumnavigating the globe, Patti can be found at home in Northern Nevada, where she lives with her standard poodle, Izzy.